PRAISE FOR

A YOUNGER MAN

"…one of the best gay contemporary romances I have had the pleasure to read…love scenes are poetry…the author has such a gift with words…a truly wonderful read…I will read again and again."
—*Regina, Reviewer for Coffee Time Romance & More, a 5 cup review*

"…an intense and very emotional book. I couldn't put this book down once I picked it up…going on my keeper shelf for when I need to read a book with some emotional and angst-filled man love."
—*Tina, a 5 lips review from TwoLipsReviews.com*

"…incredibly talented Cameron Dane. I loved these two men and their families…brought all the Maitlands and Hallidays to life in such a way that I felt like I was one of the group…I'm not ready to let go of this fantastic series [CABIN FEVER] just yet."
—*Lily, Romance Junkies*

A
YOUNGER MAN

CAMERON DANE

ISBN (13) 978-1490919287
ISBN (10) 1490919287

A YOUNGER MAN

Originally released in e-book format in July 2012

Cover Art, Print Design, and Formatting by April Martinez
Edited by Maria Rogers

Manufactured in the USA

DEDICATION

This book is for everyone who fell in love with Noah in *Grey's Awakening* and asked if he would get a story of his own. Here it is. I hope you have fun spending time with Noah and Zane.

—*CD*

PROLOGUE

"**W**hy won't you at least go out with him?"

The female voice rang in Noah Maitland's ears, the question rubbing his last nerve raw. Noah sat across the dinner table from his oldest son, Seth, and Seth's girlfriend, Kim. After processing her comment -- no, her nerve -- Noah just barely held in the need to roar down the walls of his kitchen with a shout to get the hell out of his cabin. And Noah loved his son, loved the kid like hell. The boy had been his pride and joy from the moment his mother put the crying infant in his arms nineteen years ago on Thanksgiving morning. The only day that had matched his first son's birth had been the night his second child, Matthew, had come into the world fourteen years ago. In this moment, though, Noah could only be grateful his youngest son hadn't come to dinner with his eldest.

"Mr. Maitland, why won't you at least go out with him?" Kim, this young redhead Noah hardly knew, continued to drill a hole into his forehead with her stare. "Ken is a really nice guy, and I'd be more than happy to set you up."

Breathe. Noah silently listened to the clock tick on the wall, and

7

counted to ten. *She means well. Just breathe.* Only Noah's knowledge and respect for how much Seth liked this Kim girl kept Noah from telling her to back the fuck off and get out of his face. But shit, the girl clearly had no sense of boundaries. Had Seth cleared this line of conversation with Kim before arriving for dinner? One glance at his son -- the kid continually shifted in his chair and played with his glass -- told Noah everything he needed to know. *He's still uncomfortable with me being gay.*

Fuck. Noah sighed and ran a hand through his hair. His chest ached with the new distance between him and Seth. "I don't want you to set me up with this Ken person, Kim," Noah kept his voice nice and even, "because you just finished telling me about his birthday party you went to last week -- where he turned twenty." Christ, the guy wasn't even a full year older than Seth. "He's way too young for me. It wouldn't be appropriate."

Kim brushed his comment aside with her hand. "People don't care about stuff like age difference anymore when they're dating; you go out with whoever you want, and screw anybody who doesn't like it."

Noah parted his lips to disagree -- at least where his personal dating choices were concerned -- when Seth blurted, "How can you even say you're really gay anyway?" A hard edge filled Seth's tone, and a glint of cold steel iced his usually warm hazel eyes. "You told Mom, you got your divorce, and you're in your own place now. Matthew and I get to deal with shitty comments from people we thought liked us, but what for? You're always home. You never fucking go out."

"Hey." Noah raised his voice. "Language, Seth."

Seth snorted. "Matthew's not here to hear me."

"It doesn't matter," Noah replied. "You have a guest. Be respectful of that."

"Kim has heard me curse before. But you know what," Seth threw his arms up in the air, "fine. My point is still the same, and it's one you don't want to hear. You said you got divorced because you couldn't ignore the fact that you're gay anymore, but what has changed? You're still home every night, just like you were when you lived with us and Mom. And whenever I or Matthew calls you, you're never doing anything -- like being on a date -- that you can't interrupt, so why did you even bother? How do you really even know you want to be with another dude if you never even go out and talk to one, or kiss one? You might as well have just stayed married and kept everything a secret."

"And then your mom wouldn't be with Tom right now," Noah pointed out to his son.

"Oh." Seth's dark brows shot halfway up his forehead. "So this was about Mom then? Letting her go so she could be happy, not you."

Fucking Christ. Backed into a corner, Noah couldn't exactly tell his son -- particularly not with the kid's girlfriend sitting at the table -- about Sirus. About this beautiful man whom Noah had found himself wildly attracted to, to the point where he'd wanted the guy so much he couldn't hide his feelings anymore, only to discover Sirus was already passionately in love with someone else. By that point Noah had already separated from his wife -- ex-wife now -- only to find himself alone.

Haggard and weighed down all of a sudden, Noah could only say, "It's complicated." His gut twisted a little less now with thoughts of what might have been with Sirus, something that had in truth ended before it had even begun. "You'll have to trust me on that."

With pinpoint focus, Seth said back, "Or maybe you don't really want to go out on a date with another man. Maybe you're not as gay as you thought you were."

Noah's lip curled. "I know what I feel."

Seth sat back in his chair and crossed his arms. "So go out on a date with a guy and prove it."

Words, phrases, lectures, pummeled Noah's throat in their effort to get out. He slid a glance at Kim, someone not nearly close enough to Seth for Noah to consider her family, and pushed down the volume of frustration living inside him.

Through lips that barely moved, Noah looked at his son and said, "We'll talk about your tone and how you're behaving later."

Seth started to rise from his seat, but Kim put her hand on his arm. "Maybe we should just relax and eat."

Breathing, fighting the rise in his core temperature, Noah speared a roasted tomato with his fork. "I think that's a good idea."

Growling, using a rumbling noise Noah recognized as one he made himself when angry, Seth sat back down.

The rest of the meal was had in silence.

———

LATER THAT NIGHT NOAH STARED in the mirror, growling at himself in much the same manner his son had done during dinner. Noah took care of himself. His work, chiefly as a plumber but also as an overall handyman when needed by his clients, kept him in good shape. Great shape, even. And not just for a forty-two-year-old; just great shape in general. His eyes were a completely uninteresting, dull brown though; nobody would ever get lost in the depth of their blah color. But he still had a full head of hair, and only a very few grays were mixed in with the blond. He wasn't classically handsome or arrestingly, sexily attractive in any way, but Janice, his ex-wife, had once told him he had a strong, honest look about him that people didn't forget and that made a person feel safe.

Noah wouldn't get laughed out of bars or left at a dinner table when a date excused himself to use the restroom. *So why haven't you put yourself out there and gone on a date?* A year had passed since Noah had told Janice of his feelings for another man, and then had outed himself to Sirus, only to be sweetly rejected -- which might have been more humiliating than if Sirus had just laughed in his face and told him to go away.

The truth was, as much as Seth's accusations had pricked at Noah's pride, his kid was right. Noah did need to put himself out there in the world. Otherwise he'd broken up their family for nothing. He might as well have stayed married and away from men -- as he had done for over twenty years -- if, as a single man, he intended to carry on as he had up till now, dateless and celibate.

Noah growled again. *But you're not breaking that pattern with a twenty-year-old kid!* Noah would not humiliate himself or make himself the laughingstock of this town, or worse, become the newly gay, horny pervert chasing too-young men and turn himself into an even worse source for local gossip than he currently was. Noah's skin already crawled with the sensation of people staring at him when he went to the grocery store or a restaurant for a meal. He was determined not to make his homosexuality an even bigger source for fodder -- for himself, his children, and his ex-wife. By the same token, it was past time he got himself out into the world again.

It was time to go on a date. With a man.

Whoa. Noah stumbled and went a little light-headed. He had one episode in his life with another male to draw on as his entire repertoire of sexual experience and knowledge of the same sex. The moment had occurred in college, and had involved little more than frantic kissing and basic foreplay. *Not at all like what you'll be expected to do when you go out with another adult male.* A tremor rocked through Noah once more.

After taking a deep breath to steady himself, Noah treaded out of his room and picked up his phone to call Sirus and his partner Grey. If Noah was going to plunge into the dating world, he would need some advice about where to begin.

—

"You can take or leave the offer." Clint's final offer from a few hours ago rang in Zane Halliday's head. *"It isn't any skin off my ass either way."*

Tunneling his fingers through his hair, pulling at the roots, Zane didn't know what the fuck to do. The RENT OVERDUE notice loomed large on the fridge in front of his face. The letter from the bank that his paycheck had bounced, explaining Zane now owed them money they'd already given him when he'd cashed the check a week ago, was tacked right next to the rent notice -- both of which caused his stomach to burn with sickness. Good God, he would have an ulcer before he turned twenty-five.

You could call Aunt Patty. Zane's gut twisted even harder. *She might give you the money without a hassle.* Even though nobody could see him, Zane vehemently shook his head. *Not a chance.*

Suddenly the sound of the front door opening jerked Zane into action. He lunged forward, ripped the notices off the fridge and shoved them in the trash just as his younger brother called out, "We're home!"

His little sister added, "I won a candy bar at the youth center today!"

Psyching himself up, and putting on a happy face, Zane entered the living area of their small apartment. "That's awesome, Hailey." He took her backpack off her shoulders for her and hung it on a hook by the door. "What kind?"

After pushing her dark hair off her face, Hailey whipped a wrapped sweet out of her jacket pocket. "Hershey bar with almonds."

Zane unclipped the barrette that had slipped to the ends of his sister's hair, gathered a handful of the long strands, and reaffixed the clip behind her ear. "Yum. You can have half of it after dinner if you want." That done, Zane followed his brother to the tiny kitchen. "Duncan, did you remember to tell Mrs. Mangioni thank you for dropping you off?"

Duncan, in the way only a twelve-year-old can properly do, rolled his eyes at Zane. "Yes." He pulled milk out of the fridge and lugged the gallon container to the table. "Just like I do every day. Just like I tell you when you ask every day."

"Humor me." Zane tugged on Duncan's overlong auburn hair. "We'd be in a tough spot if she started to think we were ungrateful and you guys didn't have that transportation anymore." Zane had not had a car in close to a year. He took the bus or walked everywhere he needed to go. "Now tell me how school was today. Hailey, you start."

As part of a routine Zane had been performing for well longer than the time of his stepfather's death five years ago, Zane listened while he put the casserole he'd cooked on the table, then got the plates out of a high cabinet. Hailey chatted as she retrieved the utensils and set those in place, and Duncan got Zane a glass of water after pouring milk for Hailey and himself. By the time they finished eating, cleaning up, did homework with Zane's help, and had baths, Duncan and Hailey usually didn't have the energy to watch more than one TV show before they fell asleep on the couch. Tonight was no different. Zane had to rouse them one by one and help them into the room they shared. He knew he should set a bedtime so he didn't have to do this, but they didn't get to spend a whole lot of time relaxing together and just enjoying life as siblings, so he hadn't forced a nighttime bed routine.

Once Zane had gotten Duncan and Hailey settled, he walked to the window and sat on the ledge. Leaning the side of his head against the cold glass, he watched life happening on the street below. The cars driving by didn't much interest him, or even fill him with envy. He'd gotten used to going without a vehicle, and he managed all right. Every once in a while, though, headlights would shine over a man and woman making out in the shadows; the brief shock of light would display their passion, and Zane's chest ached at the sight. He'd never had a girlfriend. Shit, he'd barely even kissed a girl. Just two girls, a couple of times back when he was fourteen -- before his stepfather had become ill and Zane had begun taking care of him. Between caring for his stepfather, and his sister being only a baby back then, and his brother still young too, Zane had not had a free moment to even think about girls, let alone go out and kiss one again. Late at night, though, he sometimes pined for a connection to another human being. He wished he had someone to talk to, to trust ... to love.

Stop it. Zane had sole financial and legal responsibility for Duncan and Hailey. If he couldn't care for them and make ends meet every month then the courts -- via his aunt -- might come in and take them away.

Just then the couple on the street wound their arms around each other and walked away. As Zane stared, his heart hurt with what he couldn't have. More than that, though, his head pounded with fear at the thought of losing his siblings. He knew what he had to do.

Zane picked up the phone and dialed. When Clint picked up, Zane said, "I want the money. I'll take it."

Clint replied, "Come by the shop and get it in the morning."

I just took money from a loan shark. After Zane hung up the phone, he ran to the bathroom and threw up.

CHAPTER 1

With every ounce of willpower in him, Noah tried to gather his wandering thoughts and put his full focus on his date. It was his second with this man; Beau was his name. They weren't even through drinks at the bar while waiting for a table when Noah began to question why he'd agreed to a second date with this man in the first place.

Because you've been dating men for three months now, yet you haven't done anything more than eat, go to movies, and get a kiss on the cheek. It's time to give someone a chance.

Still … Noah just couldn't see himself having a genuine, deep conversation, let alone something more, with a guy who could spend forty-five minutes complaining about how his tailor had ruined his day by not fitting his suit jacket in the precise style he'd wanted it. And that's exactly what Beau had done since saying hello at the start of their date.

The buzz of a conversation happening at Noah's left -- one about new trees budding in the backyard of the couple speaking -- lured Noah away from the chestnut-haired, suited man sitting across from him. The conversation at the other table got Noah thinking about how he'd agreed to spend Sunday with Janice and Matthew, mowing the lawn and weeding the flowerbeds at his old house. He had to go over there early to make sure the blades on the mower were still sharp; while he was there, he might as well clean the gutters for her too.

Suddenly a voice that was not part of the couple chatting about trees jerked Noah back to his date, just in time to hear Beau say, "This isn't working for you, Noah, is it?"

As Noah lifted his gaze to his date, heat burned up his neck to his cheeks. "I'm sorry." *Damn it.* He didn't know how to behave on dates with men. Three months hadn't taught him much of anything. Sighing, he admitted, "I-I'm not getting a vibe. I don't know how else to say it."

Beau shrugged. "It's fine. It's not really working for me either. You're totally sexy, don't get me wrong, but you're not exactly the kind of guy I normally date."

"I --" Noah snapped his mouth shut, and took a moment to regroup. "I don't know what to say to that."

"You don't need to say anything. It wasn't a dig, just a fact. Look," his attention on Noah, Beau slipped a money clip out of his pocket, palmed a few bills, and slid them under the edge of his glass, "why don't we skip the meal, save ourselves a hundred bucks, and just go back to my place to fuck."

Noah whipped his head to the left, then the right, scanning the other patrons at the bar. *Good Christ.* They all went about their business, but Noah didn't understand how none of them had heard what Beau had suggested. To Noah it felt as if the man had shouted the word *"fuck"* at the top of his lungs.

Leaning across the small table, Noah whispered, "What?"

Beau grinned. "The night doesn't need to be a complete waste. Just because we don't want to run out and get commitment rings doesn't mean we can't have some fun." The guy put his mouth next to Noah's ear, and blessedly, this time, lowered his voice. "I've seen you adjust yourself twice, and I fuckin' know you must have a huge cock. I want that thing in my ass at least once before we part ways."

Jesus. Noah's dick twitched, and a wonderful pull stirred in his balls. He couldn't help it. He wanted sex with another man. Then he looked into Beau's eyes, at the gleam there, something that had nothing to do with Noah other than the perceived size of his penis, and his heart sank into his stomach.

Shit. Damn. Fuck.

As NOAH PULLED UP TO HIS cabin an hour later -- alone -- he cursed himself and his rigid ways for the hundredth time. Beau had been a very good-looking guy. And fuck, Noah needed someone to be his first, just to get the pressure off him and out of the way. He didn't want to goddamn fall in love with someone and have no real idea what to do or how to control himself during sex. Experience mattered. Not being a fucking forty-two-year-old virgin -- at least where men were concerned -- mattered. Beau would have fit the bill for all that criteria nicely. But what had Noah done? Paid for his drink, said *"Thank you, but no, good night"* and driven home.

Noah started up the steps to his wraparound porch, prepared to go inside, shower, and then jerk off to relieve the tension in him, when a beam of light flashed across the lake in his direction. Squinting, Noah looked toward the source, and located Sirus and Grey on their porch, beers lifted in Noah's direction.

A moment later, Noah's cell phone rang, and Sirus's name appeared on the screen. Noah answered with a "What's up?"

"Come have a beer with us," Sirus replied. "Tell us how things are going with you before we have to head back to Raleigh in the morning." Sirus and Grey split their time between Grey's apartment in the city, due to the venture capitalist's need to be in a metropolitan area for his business, and the cabin Sirus loved so much.

Noah groaned, and he almost squeezed the bridge of his nose. At the last second he remembered Sirus and Grey could see him and pushed his back up straight. "Sounds good." He put more enthusiasm into his agreement than burned inside him. These two men had helped him immensely these last few months -- Grey a bit grudgingly, but still -- and Noah owed them. "I'll be there in a few. Bye."

After pocketing his phone, Noah traipsed back down the steps and began the trek around the lake to Sirus and Grey's cabin. He used the vigorous walk and the sounds of nature filling the breezy evening air to get his head back on straight. By the time he climbed up the steps to Sirus's porch, shook hands with each guy, Noah breathed a whole lot easier.

"Take a seat." Sirus pulled out a chair at the small table and set a bottle of beer in front of Noah. "Tell us how the dating is going."

Noah grimaced. "Just got home from one." His gaze slid Grey's way; he met the man's hazel stare and fidgeted in his chair. This guy knew about Noah's former one-sided crush on Sirus, and Noah always felt as if Grey wanted to fuck Sirus in front of him whenever they were together in order to remind Noah that Sirus was his.

Giving Grey a good, hard stare in return, Noah then shifted back to Sirus. "You can tell how the date went by how early it is and the fact that I'm already home. Drove an hour away to meet him and everything, only to have us go our separate ways pretty damn fast."

Empathy filled Sirus's gaze. "Give yourself time. You've only been out for a little over a year, and during most of that time you've kept to yourself."

Using the end of the table, Noah pried the cap off his bottle of beer. "I've been dating for three months now." He took a swig of beer and let the bitter hops slide down his throat before adding, "It's just not working out."

"Don't give up," and "You're desperate and trying too hard," came out of Sirus and Grey respectively.

Noah snarled at Grey. "Thanks for the vote of confidence." He knew Sirus loved this man passionately, and therefore Grey must be a good person, but far too often Noah viewed Grey as an asshole constantly marking his territory. "I fucking know who to call the next time I need some salt rubbed into my wounds."

While shooting Noah an apologetic look, Sirus squeezed Grey's forearm. "What do you mean by that, babe?"

Grey lifted Sirus's hand and pressed a kiss to the back, but at the same time he put a penetrating focus on Noah, and spoke directly to him. "From the moment I met you, Maitland, I sized you up as a fierce competitor, as someone who puts his balls to the wall for everything he wants and cares about. In the beginning, I thought that meant I might have one hell of a fight on my hands if you decided to challenge me for Sirus." As Grey said that, Noah swore to God the man had hackles and that they rose in defense. But just as fast he settled and added, "My money says you're quietly forceful in dating in the same way you are at everything you do: you want to be good at it, you think you need to be good at it in order to meet someone special, and you are hungry as hell to have something meaningful in your life again. That's just the kind of guy you are. All of that, on a very subtle wavelength, is actually making guys step back from you, rather than wanting to get closer to see what you're about."

Falling back in his seat, Noah let his beer bottle fall to the table with a *thunk*. "Fuck."

"I might add," Grey flashed a one-sided grin, "I can see all of this in you because I know myself very well, and we're very similar in a lot of ways."

A sharp bark of laughter escaped Noah. "Not even close, man."

Grey raised a brow. "Yes we are; very. Only I used what I knew about myself as a way to pick a very particular type of man who would not challenge me, because I didn't want to love anyone, and I didn't want anyone to love me. I made sure I never let anyone in my life who would."

"Until you met Sirus," Noah said.

"Until I stumbled onto Sirus by accident," Grey corrected. "He was -- is -- unlike anyone I've ever known, yet I still foolishly thought I could control and manage what we would feel for each other."

With a chuckle, Sirus leaned over to Grey and pecked a kiss high on his cheek. "And you see how that worked out for him."

Crap. Noah rubbed at the tension growing behind his eyes. "So then you're saying I should stop dating entirely until I get my shit together."

"No," Grey corrected, again, but gently this time, "I'm saying become aware of the subconscious agenda you're projecting like a beacon when you go out on dates and adjust yourself accordingly to correct it."

Bad dates, his recently unleashed hunger for men, and the desire for a relationship all swirled in Noah's mind. Fear that whatever choices he made might hurt his family bore down on Noah and made him feel as if he constantly carried a boulder on his back. "It's something to think about," he murmured, not sure what else to say.

More sympathy filled Sirus's eyes. "You have more going on in your life than dating anyway." An upbeat tempo filled his tone. "How's business? How are Seth and Matthew?"

Noah breathed a sigh of relief. "The kids are great, and I just agreed to fix up the cabin on the west side of the lake. I'll work it between…"

As Noah circled part of the lake on his way back home, he reluctantly admitted Grey might have more going for him than a handsome face and killer body. Noah was beginning to see the layers in the man, and why Sirus found him so fascinating. The dude had fucking hit the nail on the head when assessing Noah and his demeanor -- not to mention his expectations -- when going out on these dates. Noah needed to find a way to relax, go with the flow, and stop hoping for an emotional connection before even saying hello.

For Noah, though, one thought kept filling his mind. *"Love and respect the woman you take to your bed, son; no advice I can ever give you will hold you in better stead than that."* Noah's father had spoken those very words to him when he was fifteen years old. Noah had such respect for his parents' marriage that the advice had been easy to take to heart. He couldn't help feeling the same advice should apply to being with a man. Upon that thought, an ache immediately filled Noah's chest and he stumbled at the foot of his steps, staying there while he regained his breath.

Since admitting to being gay, and sharing that he intended to pursue a relationship with another man, Noah had suffered a strained, stilted communication with his both of his parents, but mostly with his father. He'd always had such a good relationship with his mom and dad; he loved and admired them so much. It killed Noah not to be able to talk to his father about the turmoil living inside him daily. He was crushed by the loss, and --

Stop it! Stop being a pussy and feeling sorry for yourself. You made your bed, now quit complaining and lie in it.

Heeding the inner voice to buck up, Noah jerked to his feet and strode into his cabin, fired up to get his goddamn life back in order. Grey had given him good advice. Noah needed to just chill out and enjoy the time spent with a man on a date, and appreciate what that man had to offer him.

Stop trying so hard.

It was good advice. And something Noah needed to figure out how to heed.

A WEEK LATER, NOAH PULLED HIS truck to a stop in front of his next job -- a favor for his ex-wife's cousin -- when a heavyset man shoved a younger guy out of an apartment building and shouted, "I told you not to come back here! The owner ain't giving you any more chances. You don't pay, you don't stay!"

The dark-haired young man sprang right back into action and tried to push past the bigger dude. "At least let me get my stuff." His entire body strained visibly with his attempt to get back into the apartment building. "I have a right to our things!"

"Not when you've been evicted!"

The beefy guy shoved the smaller one away, sending the kid to the ground and skidding across the sidewalk. *No fucking way.* Noah growled and jumped into the fray. Pushing his way in between the pair, blocking the younger man on the sidewalk, Noah pulled up to his full height, opened his frame, and knew he presented one hell of an intimidating figure.

"I don't know what the fuck is going on here," Noah uttered in a lethal tone, "but you for goddamn sure don't have any right to put your hands on this person like you just did."

The burly guy clenched his fists and leaned into Noah's space. "Stay out of it."

Noah didn't back down an inch. "You put me right in the goddamn middle of it when you assaulted this kid."

"He's not a kid. He hasn't paid his rent and he's been evicted because of it." Movement on the ground behind Noah had the bigger guy glancing down at his victim. Quickly, the bigger man backed up to protect the apartment door again. "He has no right to be here. I'm just following the owner's orders."

With a grunt, the younger man got to his feet and stepped up to stand at Noah's side. As he brushed pieces of the sidewalk off his scraped-up arm, the *pings* and *dings* of pebbles hitting the concrete filled the air like the loudest rainstorm on a tin roof. "I just want the clothes, Terrell." A husky scratch textured the young man's voice, making Noah think he'd shed a lot of tears recently. In immediate response, beyond his control, Noah's gut twisted. "Let me get inside and bag up the clothes. You can keep everything else. Sell it to get the owner some of the money back -- whatever you want."

The burly guy -- Terrell, the kid had called him -- looked at the younger man and suddenly blanched. "I'm just doing what I was told." The rancor seeped from Terrell's tone, and the fight left his big frame. "I'm sorry I shoved you, Zane, I really am, but I gotta do my job."

Taking the forcefulness out of his voice too, Noah asked Terrell, "Why don't you give the owner a call to see if he or she will reconsider letting this guy get his clothes? I don't think that's too much to ask."

Zane's voice cracked again. "Please, Terrell." His eyes, the fucking purest blue Noah had ever seen, were awash with wetness. "Let me get our clothes."

Terrell mixed a curse with a sigh and then muttered, "I'll be right back."

Once Terrell entered the building, Noah exhaled and scratched his hands through his hair. He turned to the young man still standing on the street with him -- Zane. "I'm sure this Terrell guy will get permission for you to get your clothes; everything will work out okay."

As if a geyser had exploded, Zane suddenly burst with animated life. "No it won't!" Clear panic streaked through his voice. "You don't know the owner; he's a total asshole. We've been out for two days now and our stuff is probably already gone." The guy ranted, paced, and tunneled his dark hair into total disarray. "My brother and sister won't have any fresh clothes for school, and I'll run out of money for the motel by tomorrow." He swung his head to look up at Noah, and wildness ruled his gaze. "And if I don't have an address then nobody will hire me, and then I'll be homeless, and I won't be able to pay for food, or a place to live, or anything."

"Whoa. Whoa. Okay." Noah intercepted Zane on his trek and guided the young man to his truck. "Breathe, man. Take a couple of breaths or you're going to hyperventilate and pass out." After opening the passenger side door, Noah eased the guy onto the edge of the seat and pushed his head down between his legs. "There you go. Breathe." He squatted on the sidewalk in front of the kid and squeezed his shoulder in encouragement. "Give yourself a minute, and then start over."

In silence, Noah watched as this young man's frame lifted and fell with each breath he took, for a full minute, before things seemed to return to normal.

Zane finally lifted his gaze, and this time it was *almost* steady. "I'm sorry." He scrubbed his face, and the gesture exaggerated the paleness of his lips and the dark circles under his eyes. "I know I must look like one of those nut-jobs who rant and rave out in public, who people cross the street to avoid."

"No." Noah looked, stared, couldn't seem to break away. A vicious, yet somehow tender tightness clutched his chest. *Shit.* He took a breath himself. "You look like someone who's scared."

For a moment Zane's entire body went tense. Then the fight appeared to drain out of him and he slumped against the torn seat covering. "Yeah. I am."

"Okay." Silently, Noah ticked back through Zane's cacophony of rapid information and sorted out the basic information from the mania. "Correct me if didn't process everything, but I recall that you were kicked out of your apartment two days ago, you weren't given a chance to get any of your things, you have a brother and a sister, and that after tonight you won't be able to afford a place to stay." With that, Noah nodded and added, "Does that about cover it?"

Zane's lips thinned to an even paler line. "Yeah."

"Is there a relative you can call?"

Zane immediately went tauter than a drum. "That's not an option."

"All right." *There's a story living in that response.* Questions, dozens of questions that didn't make sense and Noah had no right to ask punched at his throat to get out. Instead, he measured his tone, and continued to tread carefully. "Do you have steady work?"

"Not full time," Zane replied. "I lost my job a few months back when the business I was working for finally went under." The more he spoke, the more color returned to his skin. "The last two checks they gave me before that wouldn't clear the bank. I have a part-time job now, but it doesn't pay enough, and it doesn't offer nearly enough hours or benefits to take care of my brother and sister."

Noah muttered, "Shit."

With a chuckle, something that sounded ridiculously sweet and genuine, Zane said, "Agreed."

Grinning a bit in return, Noah pushed to his feet and let the wheels start spinning in his mind. He churned and spit out ideas, certain that a solution sat right on the tip of his brain, if only he could grab it. While tossing out a few ideas that weren't realistic at all, or were far too presumptuous, Noah grabbed his tool kit and belt from the bed of his truck. Cans of paint -- and why he had them -- sent a rush of adrenaline through his system.

Yes. That could work.

"Okay," Noah turned to Zane and crouched down next to him again, suddenly full of adrenaline, "so here's what we're going to do. While you wait for Terrell to let you in to get your clothes, I'm going to go in and take a look at the leaky showerhead in one of these units, because apparently maintenance doesn't stay on top of their job in this place."

"They don't."

Noah flashed another smile. "Right. So I'll take care of that, and then I'm going to show you a cabin. It's just outside of town, up the mountain a bit, and right now it's empty. I live up there too, and in my spare time I'm fixing this other cabin for the owner. Once you see it, you can decide if you want to stay there with your brother and sister, at least until you can get back on your feet." Looking up at the guy from his kneeling position, Noah raised a brow. "How does that sound for a temporary solution?"

A long stretch of silence filled the air between them. During that time, Zane kept his head down, studying the series of scrapes and scratches on his forearm. He picked at a particularly nasty piece of peeled skin, but then suddenly lifted his gaze and blurted, "Why would you do that for me?"

Swirls of too many very readable emotions -- uncertainty, fear, suspicion, and good Christ, hints of what looked like desperate hope -- created layers and layers of unmatched color in Zane's stare, exposing a very human vulnerability he probably didn't understand showed so clearly in his eyes.

"Why --" Huskiness suddenly coated Noah's voice, a thickness of empathy he hadn't felt build in him so quickly in years. He cleared his throat and tried again. "Why wouldn't I?"

Furrow lines appeared between Zane's brows. "Won't you get in trouble for letting strangers stay at this cabin?"

An overwhelming desire to see this man laugh and feel free and full of ease washed over Noah in a powerful wave. "You let me worry about working out the details with the owner," he shared, his tone softer now -- at least, as much as someone with too much grit in his natural voice could achieve. "Seems like you have enough keeping you awake at night already."

Zane didn't reply, and the reality of this moment crash-landed straight into Noah's brain. *Fuck. He thinks I'm a pervert or some kind of murderer.*

"If you're not comfortable coming with me," Noah got to his feet and gave Zane plenty of space to call his own, "you can call someone to let them know where you're going. You can follow me up to the cabin in your own car."

Red crept up Zane's cheeks, turning them ruddy. "I don't have a car."

Noah bit back the urge to smile. "I'll give you the address and you can use the money you were going to spend at the motel tonight to pay for a cab instead."

Zane licked the edge of his lip and then started to worry it between his teeth. "I don't have anything to give you as payment or rent for the cabin. At least not today. Maybe in a few weeks I could come up with something."

Noah exhaled, and a hundred-pound weight flew off his shoulders. *He's not scared of me; it's just that his pride won't let him take charity.* Back on steady ground, Noah explained, "The cabin needs repairs done to it. Most of them are cosmetic, or only require a minimal knowledge of home repair. Painting, resurfacing the floors, some exterior beautification ... stuff like that. If you want to take a few of those tasks in hand, I think I can work out a deal with the owner for reduced rent for you. I know her. She's a good lady."

"Okay, it's a deal." Just as fast as Zane lifted his hand in offering, it fell to his side, and he slumped. "Living in town, I can walk my brother and sister to school in the morning, and they can get a ride home in the evening from someone who lives close by. If I'm halfway up a mountain, I won't be able to get them to and from school."

A solution flashed like a neon sign in front of Noah, but before it spilled out of him, he swallowed the offer back down inside him. *Good Christ. What am I doing? I don't know this kid.* Then Noah caught the way Zane rubbed his palms repeatedly against his jeans, and once again saw the cut-up forearm. On instinct, Noah let his gut take over from his head. "I pretty much drive my work truck everywhere," he shared. "As long as you can afford to put gas in it, you can use my car while you're staying at the cabin."

Zane's pupils dilated and took over the blue. "I don't know…"

Terrell emerged from the apartment building right then, with three overstuffed trash bags in hand. In a winded voice, he said, "Owner wouldn't let you back inside, but he let me get the clothes. I threw in a few other things from the kids' room I thought I could get away with."

In a rush, Zane flew to Terrell and shook his hand. "Thank you. I appreciate everything you were able to do for me for as long as you did."

With a nod, Terrell went back inside.

As Zane dragged the bags across the sidewalk, Noah settled his tool belt over his shoulder and lifted his kit from the ground. "I'm going to go take care of that leaky showerhead." He walked backward and jerked his thumb toward the building. "If you want to throw your bags in the back and wait for me, I should be out within an hour. I'll show you the cabin then. If you decide to move on, I'll understand that too. It's up to you."

With that, Noah gave Zane some space to breathe and think. As Noah rang the buzzer for the appropriate apartment, he got a glimpse of Zane, standing with his bags, still as a statue, a decision clearly not yet made. The young man hadn't moved by the time Noah went inside.

Noah knew what he wanted, though; what truth sat in his gut with a certainty he hadn't experienced in ages. It didn't make a damn bit of sense, but Christ, Noah really, really wanted Zane to be sitting in his truck when he came back outside.

CHAPTER 2

Twenty minutes into the tour of the cabin, listening to this Noah guy -- they'd finally properly introduced themselves on the ride up the mountain -- explain the repairs that still needed to be done to the cabin, and Zane's head spun. So much had changed in just a few hours, and his brain could not process it all as fact. He still felt as if he was walking in a dream, and that soon someone would blare loud music in the next room and he'd wake up to find himself back in the motel without a plan beyond the next twenty-four hours.

Except Zane had never dreamed about a tall, muscular, blond-haired man with a crazy-rough voice before, so why would he start conjuring one as his savior now? Repeatedly on their drive up to this place and while walking around the cabin, Zane had fought the urge to touch Noah, just to confirm he was real flesh and blood. Zane had shoved his hands into his pockets multiple times and instead had relied on a woodsy, natural scent Noah emanated -- something Zane had picked up on from the second they'd come into contact on the sidewalk outside his old apartment. And that was strange as hell in and of itself; Zane rarely noticed how people smelled, and definitely never another man.

"So what do you think?" The sound of Noah's deep voice yanked Zane out of his thoughts. "Will it work for you, your brother, and sister?"

At only five feet eleven, Zane had to look up to meet Noah's gaze. God, the man had to be at least six feet three. And no one who had such rough-looking hands -- Zane had noticed the calluses -- and who possessed shoulders like a quarterback should have eyes that invited a person to trust him. Yet Noah did.

That brown stare held Zane, and Zane murmured, "I still don't understand why you're being so kind to me like this."

With a shrug, Noah leaned his shoulder against an open door frame, but kept his focus fully on Zane. Finally, after what felt like minutes of scrutiny, Noah said, "Maybe it's because I have a son about your age. I'd like to think if he was ever in trouble, and I couldn't be there for him, someone else would."

In immediate response, Zane looked Noah up and down, and then barked with laughter. "I'm sorry, but there is no way you have a twenty-four-year-old son." The words "fit" and "healthy" filled Zane's mind in relation to this man, and any lines around his eyes had to come from happiness and being outdoors, not age.

Noah quirked a brow. "You're twenty-four?" As if he still couldn't believe it, Noah then shook his head. "I pegged you as younger than that."

Heat burned Zane's cheeks. "Yeah, well." He chuckled; he had to, or he would cry. "I guess I'm having a bad day like that."

New lines of crimson slashed Noah's harsh face. "Sorry. I'm sure you don't really look as young as I thought you were." Noah muttered a curse. "I'm bad at guessing that kind of stuff."

Zane smiled at the guy; he couldn't rein it in. "It's all right. How old is your son?" The question escaped him -- the desire to know so very real -- before he'd even consciously thought it.

"I actually have two," Noah replied. "Older one is nineteen -- that's Seth. My younger one is Matthew, and he's fourteen." Noah's eyes lit up as he shared, and it saturated the medium brown color with breathtaking depth. "They're my pride and joy." He looked to the heavens and shook his head. "And they pretty much hate when I say shit like that. It embarrasses them."

A lightness in the air buoyed Zane, and this man only lifted his spirits even more. "We'll keep your unabashed pride in them between us." No strain or tightness choked Zane's voice, and no tension ruled his body. He couldn't remember the last time he'd felt such ease. "My brother Duncan is twelve. And Hailey is nine, or as she brags, almost ten." God, Zane couldn't wait to tell them they would have a roof over their heads, at least for a little while. "I appreciate what you're doing more for their sakes than even mine."

With a shrug, Noah shoved his hands into his pockets and wandered outside. From over his shoulder, he said, "They'll both love the lake." He braced his arms on the porch railing. As Zane joined him, he noticed Noah fix his stare on the lake, where twinkles of sunlight made the water gleam as if its surface were covered in gems. "Matthew really loves the water," Noah said, his voice soft. "Seth does when he's home too. He's at college in Raleigh a lot of the time now."

Shifting, Zane leaned his lower back against the porch railing next to Noah and studied the beat-up cabin that to him looked like paradise. "I still can't help feeling like the work you want me to do here isn't enough to repay what you've done for me," he murmured, sliding his focus to Noah. Noah had shared the news that he'd spoken to the owner, and she was willing to accept a reduced monthly rent for a few months. After that they would have to talk again.

With only two feet of space between them, Noah adjusted to lean his hip against the railing, and he put his full attention on Zane. "I'm pretty damn busy with my business," strength and force rang in his tone, "and it's difficult to fit time in to come take care of this place. I'm doing it as a favor for the owner because she gave me such a great deal on my cabin. I felt I owed her, but working on the repairs have taken up pretty much all of my free time. You picking up some of the slack is more help than you think."

Translation in Zane' mind: *Stop badgering me about my offer. Take it or leave it.*

Nobody had ever called Zane an idiot. He stuck his hand out to Noah. "Then we have a deal."

Noah wrapped his bigger hand around Zane's. "Excellent." They shook on it -- quickly, Zane noticed. Noah separated the hold almost immediately and jammed his hand into his pocket. "Anyway," Noah started down the steps at a fast clip, "I'll drive you to the other side of the lake, and you can take my car."

Still standing on the porch, studying this man's back, Zane murmured, "I don't know where you came from, Noah Maitland, but I am grateful as hell you showed up when you did."

From the bottom of the steps, Noah looked at Zane sideways, and a positively wicked half grin emerged. "I'll remind you of that when I nitpick your paint job and sanding work."

Sudden warmth suffused Zane's flesh. He traipsed down the stairs, came to a stop directly in front of Noah, and found the man's gaze. "I think I can handle your scrutiny." Zane's words came out thicker -- sultrier -- *shit* --than he'd meant. He abruptly veered toward the side of the cabin. "Before we leave," he cleared his throat as silently as he could, "show me what kind of repairs you're going to need me to do with the exterior of the cabin. I want to start getting a sense of what to tackle first."

Noah quickly caught up and took the lead, and once again Zane fought the tingle in his hands that told him he wanted to touch this man, just to feel the solidness of his frame and know for sure he really existed. That handshake hadn't felt like nearly enough. Zane felt as if much more intimacy had passed between them with one look than should for two people who'd met only hours ago. *I'm grateful, and I don't know what to say or do to express it, that's all.*

Zane shook himself out of his strange thoughts just in time to veer his fingers away from the thick muscles roping Noah's shoulders. Instead he ran them along the outer wall of the cabin. *Damn.*

THE NEXT MORNING, NOAH LISTENED to excuse-filled words bombard his ear, and he wanted to slam the cell phone against the dashboard of his truck. *Fuck. Fuck. Fuck.*

"I'm sorry," Lois repeated. "I tried to tell Rick to ease up last night, that he had work in the morning, but he said he would be fine. Only now I can't get him up, and I didn't want you to drive to the house to get him when he obviously isn't going to be able to work for you today."

Noah rubbed at the headache already forming in his skull. "I can't keep having this happen, Lois. You know Janice and I have always had your back," Lois was a friend of both of theirs from their high school days, "but I can't keep giving your boyfriend chances if he won't keep himself sober enough for the days I need him to work." This was the fourth time in three months Rick had not come through for him on a job. "I'm going to have to let him go."

"Give him one more chance," Lois pleaded. "He told me putting in this new backyard for this client is a weeklong gig for you; give him a chance tomorrow. If he isn't ready to go when it's time for you to pick him up, you can fire him, and I'll only say thank you that you even gave him a chance."

Shit. "Fine." Noah practically bit off his agreement. He already knew he would regret this. "Tomorrow. But that's it. If he's not raring to go at seven a.m. then he's done."

"Thank you," Lois said. Noah could imagine her clutching the phone tightly on the other end. "I promise he'll be good tomorrow."

"He'd better be." Noah's patience had worn remarkably thin. "Bye."

After hanging up and tossing his phone on the passenger seat, Noah raced through his options, but quickly discarded one after the next. For a special job like this, Noah had often enlisted Seth's assistance. He worked gigs like these on the weekends and holidays in order to give his son a chance to earn some cash. But with Seth in Raleigh so often now, Noah hadn't had much choice but to break down and hire an assistant who could be available more often. Except now his employee was a no-show again, and Noah was screwed. He could not do this job solo. *Fucking last time I hire someone as a favor to a friend.*

Just then a flash of light glinted from across the lake. Noah looked up to see movement outside the west cabin -- Zane's temporary cabin. *Yes.* Without second-guessing, Noah honked his horn, knowing the other two cabins were empty and thus the sound wouldn't disturb anybody. After honking one more time for good measure, he hopped out of his truck, waved his arms, and then pumped his fist when Zane glanced up and waved.

Noah shouted, "Wait for me!" hoped like hell it carried the distance, then climbed in his truck as fast as he could. He made his way around the lake on the gravel road behind the cabins. Slowing as he got closer to Zane's car -- Noah's car -- Noah pulled to a stop and hopped out.

Before Noah could get to the porch, Zane met him halfway. Still on the steps a dozen feet behind Zane, an auburn-haired boy and dark-haired girl stood with backpacks hooked on their arms.

In front of Noah, Zane slipped off a pair of mirrored sunglasses, hooked them on his jeans, and grinned. "Good morning."

"Morning." *Jesus.* Noah swallowed, and his mind went blank. Over the course of the night, and a bit too much in his dreams, Noah had envisioned the depth of those pure blue eyes, and his stomach had flip-flopped and quivered in response. At some point, in order to get some sleep, Noah had convinced himself Zane's eyes weren't nearly as pretty as he remembered them being, but the light of day proved him a liar. *They are lovely.* On the heels of that thought, Noah jerked himself back into reality and put a clamp on the lid of any further inappropriate thoughts. *You're here about work; nothing more.*

With one more silent, stern warning to himself, Noah crossed his arms against his chest and put his mind back on business. "You mentioned a part-time job yesterday. I was wondering if you were working today."

"Nope." Zane crossed his arms too, and the action pulled his T-shirt against surprisingly toned biceps. "I'm going to drop the kids off at school and then see about getting out there and filling out more applications for work."

Yes. Perfect. "You feel like earning a day's pay?" Noah asked. "My guy called in on me today, and I need some help laying in some sod and sprinklers. It'll be a full day of work, and I'll pay you a good wage in cash."

Zane scratched his cheek, and he frowned. "I don't know anything about installing sprinklers."

With a chuckle, Noah replied, "That's okay. I do. All you have to do is be able to follow my orders."

"I can do that." A huge grin lit Zane's entire face, making the worry lines disappear. "Thank you." He suddenly shuffled a bit, and pink dotted his cheeks. "Again. I seem to be saying that to you a lot."

"I was in a bind just now." Noah hated being late, canceling, postponing, or out and out not coming through on a job. "You're really helping me out today."

Zane glanced over his shoulder before coming back to Noah. "Can I drop the kids off first and then meet you?"

Nodding, Noah backed up to his truck. "I'll follow you, and then you can follow me."

"Sounds good. Hold on for a second." Zane grabbed Noah's wrist with shocking strength, and the contact licked wonderful flames straight up Noah's arm. "Guys," he let go of Noah and gestured to his siblings, "come meet Mr. Maitland. He's the one who got us into this cabin."

Christ. He called me mister. Noah suddenly remembered his knees had cracked when he'd gotten out of bed this morning. The residual warmth from where Zane had touched him turned icy. Fuck, if Noah had bothered to look, he probably would have found another gray hair this morning too. *Shit.*

"Call me Noah," he said. That came out with a bit more of a growl than he'd intended. But damn, he fucking felt a hundred years old. Trying again, Noah added, "Please. All of you."

"This is Duncan." Zane put his arm around the auburn-haired kid. "And Hailey." He tugged the girl's hair.

Hailey held tight to Zane's arm. "Thank you for the cabin, Noah." She looked up at Noah with eyes almost as blue as her brother's.

"Yeah." Duncan shuffled his foot in the grass in the same manner his brother just had, but he maintained eye contact. "Thanks."

"No problem." Noah breathed easier. Kids ... now there was a group of people Noah had plenty of experience talking to and interacting with. He didn't kneel in front of them -- Matthew had once told Noah he'd found it patronizing when his mother's boyfriend had done that to him when they'd first met. Instead Noah leaned against the front of his truck and crossed his legs. "Are you guys gonna help Zane with the painting? There's a lot to do."

Both kids shook their heads, and Hailey said, "Zane says it has to be perfect or else we're not doing what we're supposed to and we'll have to leave."

Biting back a laugh, Noah shifted his gaze to meet Zane's. "Are you making me out to be some kind of slumlord or dictator, Mr. Halliday?"

The inky black of Zane's pupils crowded out the blue. "I didn't -- I'm not --" He abruptly snapped his mouth shut, sighed, and then muttered, "Fuck."

Hailey glared up at her brother. "Don't curse."

"Relax." Noah let Zane off the hook. "I'm just teasing. It's all in the technique, anyway." He shared with the kids, "As long as Zane teaches you how to guide the roller to get an even coat then it's just a matter of not letting your arms and shoulders get too sore. Age doesn't matter."

"Can you teach us?" Hailey asked. "Last night Zane said he's never painted nothing in his life, and that he was gonna go to the library today to look up on the Internet the right way to do it."

Did he now? Out of the mouths of babes. Noah found Zane's gaze again, and raised a brow.

"Busted." Red flamed up Zane's face once more. "I might have inflated my knowledge of home repair a bit yesterday."

Once again, as Noah stared at Zane, he had to bite back an indulgent smile. "It's fine. I'll give you a quick tutorial on the basics before you get started."

Obvious tension rolled out of Zane's shoulders. "That would be helpful and appreciated. Okay, guys," Zane corralled his siblings around the front of the Accord, "in the car or we're going to be late."

Noah lifted his hand as he moved to his door. "I'll follow you."

"Okay." Zane waved from over the hood of the car. "See you in a bit."

After climbing in behind the wheel, Noah waited for Duncan and Hailey to strap themselves in the backseat, and then for Zane to do the same in the front, and get them started toward town. All the way down the mountain, Noah couldn't stop smiling and occasionally chuckling as he replayed what had just transpired. He knew where this fizzy bubble of joy he could not control had come from too. *Zane.* Being in his presence. Around his light. Just goddamn admiring the younger man. And not just because of his pretty eyes either.

Fuck.

Noah didn't like this inappropriate interest. It wasn't healthy or good for him. Not one bit.

AT MIDDAY, ZANE SAT ON THE hood of Noah's truck and swallowed down the last bite of his sandwich -- part of Noah's lunch -- with a swig of orange soda. When it had come time for a break from work, Noah had driven them to a clearing on the outskirts of town. He'd explained that his job often entailed nonstop conversation with his customers while he did whatever repair they needed, and thus he preferred to bring his meal from home and pick a quiet spot to eat, rather than listen to the dull roar of a fast-food joint during lunchtime.

In the distance, Noah emerged from the line of trees surrounding the area and strode toward the truck. Assuming the man had gone to take a piss, Zane hopped to the ground to grab a package of cleaning wipes from inside the truck. When Noah reached the truck, Zane handed him the blue plastic box. Murmuring his thanks, Noah rubbed down his hands and arms, tossed the wipe into a paper bag, and then used another to clean his face. He did this all efficiently and in silence -- much as how Zane had observed he'd eaten his meal.

Noah had outright said he enjoyed his quiet, and Zane had respected that desire while eating. But as Zane watched Noah drink the rest of his water, he did battle with his desire to know what made this man tick. Who crossed paths with a stranger on the street and less than ten minutes later offered him a place to live, a car, and then the next morning a day's worth of work?

Zane found himself looking at Noah's hands again, for the hundredth time since their workday had begun. Seeing something beyond the rough, tanned skin he couldn't ignore, Zane suddenly blurted, "Can I ask you a question, Noah?"

Noah glanced up from grabbing a paper towel that had drifted to the grass. "Shoot."

After exhaling -- *you're allowed to ask, it's all right* -- Zane asked, "Are you divorced, or widowed?"

Noah's face blanched. "What?"

"You're not wearing a wedding band, but you have two kids." Zane darted his attention down to Noah's left hand. "And I can see a little bit of a line still on your ring finger where you once did."

Noah rubbed his ring-less finger, and his lips tightened. "I'm divorced. I probably kept the ring on for longer than I should have."

Visible pain filled the lines bracketing Noah's mouth, and Zane's chest tugged in kind. "I'm sorry."

All hard lines and angles from top to bottom, Noah busied himself, his movement jerky, as he cleaned up their small mess. "It was for the best."

Zane quickly started gathering debris too. "Still…"

Grabbing Zane's trash from him and putting it all in a cooler, Noah set everything in the backseat of his double-cab truck. "What about you?" Noah asked, busying himself so much with straightening his truck Zane would have thought he had to pass a boss's inspection after each lunch. "How did you end up raising your brother and sister?"

Understanding the man's actions, Zane stepped back to give Noah room, and leaned against the side of the truck. "My stepfather died five years ago," he shared, his heart constricting only a little bit as he thought about Burt's difficult final years of life. "There was no way I was breaking us up when he passed."

"Stepfather?" Noah gave Zane a sideways look. "What about your mother? And your biological father?"

"My mother died shortly after Hailey was born." The many losses in Zane's life occasionally kept him up at night in tears; they made him wonder who he might have been if his mom and stepdad had lived. Zane couldn't help feeling that if he gave Noah a bit of personal information about himself, then maybe Noah would open up more too. "My mom had an infection that wasn't detected or treated." He paused for a moment, thinking about his pretty, gentle mother. "It killed her."

Noah went still where he stood. "Oh, Zane." Such empathy warmed his stare it turned the medium brown shade rich with life. "I'm so sorry."

"Thank you." Zane nudged closer to Noah. The goose bumps on his arms, the flash of cold that had gone through him, immediately disappeared. "My stepfather -- Burt -- is the only father I've ever known. He's Duncan and Hailey's real father. I don't know where my father is. I've never met him; I have no interest in doing so."

Settling in, his attention fully on Zane now, Noah rested his shoulder against the truck. "Yesterday you said something about help from family not being an option."

Zane nodded; thoughts of Patty had him clenching his teeth. "I have my stepfather's sister. She lives a couple counties south of here. She never liked my mother, though, and didn't think Burt should have married her. She wants custody of Duncan and Hailey, and she doesn't want me to have a relationship with them if she gets them."

"Why the fuck not?" Shoving away from the truck, Noah stood up straight. In Zane's eyes he looked ten feet tall, shadowing the sun with his strength and size. "It's so obvious that you're a responsible, capable, caring person. Shit, I've known you one day and I can already see that."

More warmth filled Zane. He stood up straight too, closer to Noah. God, this guy made him want to spill all his secrets and fears. "Patty -- that's her name -- resents me. I don't know why. Maybe she doesn't think Burt should have cared for me as his own son. Maybe she thinks the money he spent on me would have been better saved or spent elsewhere. Maybe she thinks the little inheritance Burt did leave me should have gone to her and her two sons. Not that the money lasted long once I took care of the bills left over from Burt's illness." With a shrug, Zane added, "In any case, that's why I need an address, and why I need to find a full-time job. If she gets a whiff that I'm having financial trouble right now," *God if she only knew how much*; with the thought of the money he owed Clint, Zane shuddered, "she'll petition for Duncan and Hailey." Zane's heart dropped into his stomach with a nauseating thud, and he grimaced. "And I'm afraid that no matter what Burt wanted, she would get them."

Leaning closer, Noah squeezed Zane's shoulder. "Hey." The grittiness in his soft tone only made Zane listen even closer. "You have an address now -- at least until I'm told the owner wants to start showing the cabin again."

Going quiet, Noah took another step in, and he curled his hand around Zane's nape. As his stare caught Zane's, he moved his fingers, and the rough skin of his thumb scraped against Zane's Adam's apple. Zane's breath caught in response, and a little shiver rolled through him. Noah immediately narrowed his stare, muttered a curse, and backed away.

Whacking Zane's arm instead, almost hard enough to knock Zane over, Noah backed around the truck, pointing as he said, "If I hear anything about a job, I'll let you know."

Replaying what had just happened, Zane mumbled, "Thanks." As he watched Noah stride around the truck like a bat out of hell, Zane cocked his head, and his brow pulled. "Um, yeah. I appreciate it."

Noah climbed in behind the wheel. "No problem." Reaching across the seat, he jammed the heel of his hand into the handle on the passenger side and opened the door for Zane. "Let's go." Business ruled his tone and movement. "Time to get back to work."

Without further comment, Zane took his seat and buckled himself in. One glance at Noah showed the guy focused on backing his truck up to the paved road hidden by a line of trees, his hands strong on the wheel, his stare pinpoint on his rearview mirror. All appeared normal.

Still, Zane kept stealing looks at Noah and thinking, *What the hell?* He didn't know shit about anything that had to do with relationships and attraction and stuff like that, but he could still feel Noah's big hand curled around his nape. They'd been close enough for Zane to sense a subtle change in Noah's breathing too. For two heartbeats there, Zane had thought Noah wanted to kiss him. Zane thought he'd sensed interest, desire, in Noah. And more than that, just as Zane had thought Noah was going to lean in and press their lips together, Zane had gone a little breathless too. *Good God.* Zane's neck and jaw still burned with heat where Noah had touched him. *It can't be.*

Zane sneaked another peek at Noah, and the man looked all business and professional. *Nothing happened. It was my imagination.* Relief washed through Zane, and he slumped against the door of the truck. Noah exhibited such a natural kindness; clearly Zane was projecting his own gratitude onto Noah and making things weird. He needed to back the fuck up and stop seeing things that weren't there. He needed to stop acting strangely too, or Noah would do one thing to Zane for sure: he would kick Zane out of the cabin before he even had a chance to get himself and his siblings settled in the place.

Aside from that, Zane needed to be real with himself. He didn't know shit. He didn't have any firsthand experience, so he had no place thinking he knew how to read moves in another person. Especially another man. *Yeah,* Zane studied Noah one more time out of his peripheral vision, *everything is fine.*

Still, for the rest of the ride back to the job site, Zane kept rubbing his neck. He couldn't get the feel of Noah's hand on his skin out of his mind.

HOURS LATER NOAH SECURED THE last of his equipment to the flatbed of his truck, waited for Zane to climb down too, and then closed the tailgate.

Taking a step back, Zane raised his arms high above his head. With a little groan, he shifted to stretch his back. "That's it?"

"That's it. For today anyway," Noah qualified, amused as he watched Zane work the kinks out of his body from nine hours of physical labor. "You did a great job. Thank you."

"Thank you for the work," Zane replied, another little moan mixed in -- this one making Noah imagine the kinds of groans he should not be associating with this young man.

Heat burned Noah's flesh, and he scrambled to the front of his truck. "Speaking of which…" After letting himself in through the passenger door, Noah unlocked the glove box and removed his wallet. "Let me pay you." Noah counted out what he considered a fair price for Zane's work and then handed the cash to Zane. "There you go."

Zane folded the bills and stuffed them in his pocket. "I appreciate it."

Noah looked down at Zane's pocket, and raised a brow. "You're not going to count it?"

"After everything you've done for me," Zane raised his eyebrow right back at Noah, "I'm not worried you're going to shortchange me for a day's work."

"Fair enough." Jerking his head toward his truck, Noah then eyed Zane's car. "So I guess that's it." His brain told him to leave, but his feet stayed rooted in place. "We're done here."

Leaning in, Zane grabbed Noah's wrist, tilted it, and checked his watch. "I just have enough time to go to the grocery store before picking up Duncan and Hailey from the youth center."

Shit. Once again, Noah's belly fluttered with just that whisper-soft contact to his wrist. The sensation wandered dangerously south, toward his cock. As discreetly as he could, Noah rubbed his forearm against his shirt and tried to make the tingles go away. "I'll let you go then." This time, Noah did take a step to leave.

"Wait!" With a lunge, Zane grabbed Noah's arm. Again. "After everything you've done for me," a sweet blush filled Zane's cheeks, and the tell grabbed hard at places too close to Noah's heart, "I at least owe you a meal. If you want to give me an hour and a half to get myself and the kids back to the cabin, you could come over and eat with us." With a shrug, Zane shoved his hands into his pockets. "Maybe give us that painting lesson."

Pure light lifted Noah and flooded him with endorphins. "I would love --" *Goddamn motherfucking shit.* As fast as Noah soared, he crashed back down to earth hard enough to make his teeth rattle. "I can't come." *Don't say it.* He added, "I have a date tonight."

Zane's face fell. "Oh."

Staring at Zane, getting too lost too fast in pools of blue, fighting sexual and romantic things he shouldn't be feeling, Noah blurted, "It's with another man."

CHAPTER 3

The words of Noah's confession hung between Noah and Zane like wet clothes dripping on a line.

It's. With. Another. Man.

What in the fuck had made Noah share that his upcoming date was with a guy? Zane stood before him with his jaw practically on the ground, his eyes as big as Noah had ever seen them, and Noah wanted to slink under his truck and die.

"I'm sorry." Noah blabbed some more, his mouth apparently unable to stop spewing words. "I don't know why I said that."

Both of Zane's brows lifted. "So it's not true?"

"Shit," Noah muttered. He scrubbed his face, feeling more lines being added by the minute. "No, I didn't mean I was lying. It is true."

More lines pulled across Zane's forehead. "So you were married, but now you're gay."

"No." Catching himself, Noah bit off another curse, and corrected himself. "Yes, I was married, but I suspect I was always gay. I mean… Fuck." Snapping his mouth shut again, Noah clasped his hands behind his neck, looked toward the sky, exhaled, and then came back to blue eyes that scrutinized him much too closely for comfort. *Shit.*

With a silent command not to hide, Noah held his ground. "I don't merely now *suspect*" he made quotes with his fingers, "I was gay while I was married. I'm not on the fence about it. I know now I always was, but I pushed what I was feeling down. I didn't allow myself to focus on it. I never acted on it while I was with my wife, but I was always gay."

"What changed?"

How to explain the many wet dreams about Sirus, and the puppy-dog crush, without dragging him into this mess? Swallowing down specifics, Noah answered, "I found myself experiencing feelings for one particular person that were so strong I couldn't deny them, or what they meant about me, anymore."

Noah then -- finally -- closed his mouth. Only, Zane remained quiet too, studying Noah like a carnival sideshow curiosity. The air turned oppressive. Noah wiped at sweat pouring down the sides of his face.

"Anyway," Noah spilled, driven to fill the awkward silence, "I'm divorced, those feelings for that guy didn't ever become anything, and so now I'm trying to figure out how the hell I'm supposed to live the rest of my life."

"So you're going out with a man." Zane appeared as if he were still trying to process Noah's confession into information he could understand. "Tonight."

"Yes." Feeling put under a microscope, Noah wiped his face with his drenched T-shirt. "Jesus Christ. I don't know why I told you any of this. Or why I said I was even going out with a man in the first place. It's not relevant to you or your life in any way, shape, or form." With a start, Noah jerked up straight. *Crap.* "I wasn't trying to use it as a come-on or anything. I swear."

As if coming out of a trance, Zane stood up straight too. His stare cleared and he zeroed in on Noah. "No, it's fine. I didn't think that. I'm not gay or anything, but shit, you've been so nice to me, it's not like I'm all of a sudden not gonna want to live in your cabin or talk to you anymore just because you are."

"It's not my cabin, but thank you." Noah hadn't even realized he'd been strung so damn tight, waiting for something resembling acceptance from Zane, until his muscles released upon Zane's *"It's fine."*

Noah breathed a thousand times easier. "Hell, maybe I just didn't want things to be weird between us down the line, since you're bound to find out. It was hard for me to start telling people why Janice and I got divorced. Once I did, there were a lot of guy friends who didn't shun me or anything, but I could see in their eyes that they thought I'd been picturing them naked for the twenty years I'd known them, thinking I'd been fantasizing about fucking them when I was having sex with my wife -- when in fact I never fantasized about any of them. They acted different around me once they knew." Noah's chest ached for the friendships that had slipped to acquaintances upon the news of his homosexuality. "Maybe I didn't want to start out one way with you and then have it change when you found out." He shrugged, out of steam. "I don't know."

"It's fine." Zane brushed Noah's worries aside.

"It is fine," Noah promised. "Don't worry about me saying inappropriate things to you, or putting moves on you, or anything like that." *No more accidental, innocent touches either.* Noah made that vow to himself. "That's why I'm going out on all these dates." He nodded, needing to back up his words with action. "I'm trying to meet someone who is also gay, and who is appropriate for me." Characteristics that matched his were exactly what Noah needed in a mate; then maybe his life would return to order.

With a shrug, Zane said, "Maybe you'll meet him tonight."

"Maybe." Noah shrugged too.

"Okay, so…" Zane pointed behind him and started backing up to the Accord. "I have to get going if I want to get food before picking up Duncan and Hailey."

Noah put his ass in gear too. "Right. Go." As he opened his driver's side door, he called, "I'll come by this weekend to give you some of those home improvement basics you requested."

Rather than shouting back, Zane got in the car and pulled up alongside Noah. He rolled down the passenger window and leaned across the seat. "Make it Sunday. I have to work on Saturday."

Noah stooped down so he could see Zane. "Sounds good. See you then."

With a smile, one of those genuine ones that lit up his pretty eyes, Zane waved and drove away. Noah got behind the wheel and drove himself home to shower for his date, with one passage repeating on a nonstop cycle in his head: *No matter how sweet and cute he is, Zane Halliday is not gay. And just as important, he is not age appropriate for you. Stop thinking about him and find someone who is.*

Later that night, long after Zane had settled his brother and sister in bed, he sat outside under a star-filled sky and let the breeze from the water drift across his skin. In just his underwear, he'd dragged a chair from the porch down to the dock, sat in the glow of a lantern he'd found in the kitchen, and nursed a can of soda that for one of the few times in his life he wished were a beer. He didn't drink, though; he couldn't afford to be incoherent or passed out if something happened to his siblings and they needed him.

Zane hadn't been able to sit still or focus all night. Not even a shower and crawling into bed had settled him down enough to relax and sleep. Too much filled his mind and he could not turn off his brain. The money he'd earned today was already gone. He'd taken just a small portion to use for food and had given the rest of it to Clint with a promise that he would pay again as soon as he could. The piddly amount he'd given would not satisfy Clint for long, if at all, but Zane had nothing more to give.

When Zane had originally borrowed money from Clint, the first of three times total, he'd made the disastrous mistake of believing that his old job -- working at a T-shirt factory -- would still be there. His bosses of three years had assured him they had a plan to keep their heads above water until business picked up again. Then the dozen employees had gone into work one day to find the doors locked and the owners long gone. When the first paycheck had bounced a few weeks prior to the plant closing, a coworker had said to get the hell out right then and find something new. But Zane and a handful of others had stuck with the small business, believing that if they just filled the orders in the next few weeks, everything would be fine.

Now I'm royally fucked. Zane could not sustain himself and his siblings on the income generated working part-time as a line prep/server in a local home-style eatery. Two perks kept him working there, rather than moving on to another part-time job that might give him a few more hours. First, the owner was a nice lady, whose family happened to have a hundred-year history with the restaurant; thus Zane didn't worry about the business collapsing around her. More important, on the days he worked, the owner always sent him home with food, while allowing Zane his dignity by saying it was time to make a new batch of this or that, whatever, and if Zane didn't take the leftovers, then they would be thrown away.

Groaning, Zane scrubbed his face and scratched through his hair. Job security and a pleasant work environment weighed heavily against his need to at least find another part-time job, one that would be compatible with the one he had, or better, one good full-time job. Patty would come and check on Duncan and Hailey in person soon. Zane's sleepless night revolved around what she would do when she discovered that as of right now he only had a roof over his head for himself and his siblings due to the charity of a stranger.

A charitable stranger who happens to be gay. Patty would have a field day with the information. Her idea of gay people consisted of guys who dressed in leather or guys who wore drag. And to her mind anyone gay who didn't dress that way openly just did so in private. Zane could only imagine what she would think of Noah, and what terrible things she would be certain he was hiding behind that gruff, incredibly masculine exterior. Not to mention how much she would freak out if she knew Zane had invited Noah to eat dinner with him and Duncan and Hailey.

With that thought, Zane couldn't help wondering how Noah's dinner with another man had gone. Zane was rather proud of the fact that he was becoming one heck of a good cook. Without a doubt he knew Noah would have enjoyed the pork chops, apple salad, and red potatoes he'd made for dinner tonight. He grinned as he recalled Duncan and Hailey gobbling up every bite. *Except it wouldn't have been a date if Noah had come here,* Zane's smile fell abruptly, *and Noah probably doesn't care about the food so much on these evenings as he does the company.*

Whoever had gone out on that date with Noah surely had to be ecstatic that he'd lucked out with such a nice guy. Zane might not have ever gone on a date, but surely sincerity and kindness in a mate mattered more than anything else. Sure, a person would want the guy to be handsome, but if he was a jerk who couldn't be trusted, what good did attractiveness matter? Not that Noah had to worry about other men thinking he was ugly; he had a ruggedly attractive thing going for him; he had a big, muscular frame that looked tighter than most guys half his age. If a person bothered to look twice they would see Noah had such fine character that it made his eyes a deep, rich brown a person could easily find more intense and inviting than the purest emerald green or sapphire blue.

Wait. Zane jerked up in his chair. *What the fuck is wrong with me?* He didn't have any reason to sit here and assess Noah's attributes, and he didn't have any business caring if other men saw Noah as attractive. Zane wasn't gay; the few times he hadn't been so exhausted or caught up in his family issues that he'd given himself five minutes to think about dating, kissing, or even sex, he had always imagined a girl as the other half in any of those scenarios. *Or woman, now,* he corrected.

Which just went to show how long it had been since Zane had even given himself time to seriously dream about romance and love. Last time, he'd been a teen thinking about high school and girls. He was almost twenty-five now, and in every way except romantic and sexual experience, he was a man.

And now, the first time you give yourself a minute to think about dating, it's on the heels of a very attractive person, who has been very kind, admitting that he's gay. Noah's confession had to be why Zane's thoughts had drifted to thinking about men on dates, and to what other men viewed as sexy and desirable. It wasn't Noah specifically lingering in Zane's mind, but rather just same-sex dating.

Not that Zane would be anyone's dream -- be they woman or man. First, he only had a part-time job and a high school education. And second, when he wasn't at work, he spent all of his time taking care of his brother and sister. Not exactly exciting and alluring to a potential partner. Then there was the fact that while he had decently nice arms and shoulders, and his chest wasn't bad, he otherwise leaned toward being a bit too slim for his liking, and probably anyone else's. He didn't have much of a tan or healthy glow to his skin either; paleness gave credence to his working indoors. Although after working with Noah today, Zane might get some color to his face and arms. His skin was a bit pink and warm; with luck it would turn into some healthy color over the next few days.

Just as Zane started to feel a bit better about himself, the crunch of tires on gravel broke the stillness and silence of the night. *It's him. He's home.* It didn't take more than another minute for Noah to pull his truck to a stop alongside his cabin across the lake. *Shit.* At the same time Noah doused his headlights, Zane blew out the lantern and cast the area into almost full darkness. Only the full moon and the lights from the stars offered a glow to the night sky.

Zane didn't have to look at a watch to know the lateness of the hour. It had already been well past midnight when he'd come outside, and that must have been over an hour ago. *Noah's date must have gone well.* Where he sat, Zane stared across the lake at the shadowed image crossing the front of his cabin at such a late hour. As Zane observed, he squeezed the wood arms of the chair under his fingertips. His breathing became more labored too.

Interior and exterior lights suddenly flooded Noah's cabin. For just a moment, Noah stood in his open doorway, light surrounding his commanding frame. *God, he is magnificent.* Zane's cock thickened with blood and pushed hard against his belly right where he sat. *Oh hell.* Zane couldn't deny his very real, physical response to Noah Maitland -- and Zane wasn't even gay.

That meant whoever Noah had gone out on a date with was probably already completely in love with the man.

Zane crushed the wood under his hands even more. He didn't like the thought of that one bit.

Fuck.

As soon as Noah flicked on the lights and closed his front door, he made a beeline for his couch. With a groan, he threw himself onto the plush taupe suede. He should probably get up to take a shower, or at least change his dirty clothes, but right now he could not make his body move.

In the middle of his date -- which had been going decently well -- Janice had called with an emergency situation. Her boyfriend had volunteered to fix a leak in the kitchen sink, but instead had caused a geyser to erupt that they couldn't stop. Noah had apologized to his date -- his second with a guy named Ramsay, Ram for short -- and had driven home to fix the pipe and help clean the mess, all with Tom drilling Noah with his glare. They'd only just finished sweeping water out of the kitchen a half hour ago. Noah would go back over there tomorrow to assess the kitchen overall and decide if anything had taken on water damage and needed further repairs.

Need to make a call tomorrow to see if I can do damage control with Ram too. The look in the redhead's eyes as Noah had explained the situation with his ex hadn't exactly said Ram believed Noah's excuse for ending their date early. Noah had experienced a few similar situations, where a date had gotten a very convenient call during dinner, one that had pulled them away from the date, so he could understand Ram's skepticism. *If he could see me now,* Noah grimaced as he pulled off his damp, dirty shirt and tossed it to the floor, *he'd be a believer.*

Ram had lots of characteristics Noah wanted in a potential partner: roughly the same age, he was thirty-nine; came from a similar background of a tight-knit family, although Ram had come out to his family in his early twenties. The man had a white-collar job, opposed to Noah's blue, but Noah suspected they had a similar annual income. Most important, though, Ram had said he was looking for someone to build a life with too. And hell, Ram was even very handsome, so bonus points that he wouldn't be hard to look at across a table or in bed every night. Yet with everything Ram had going for him, Noah couldn't deny the sense of relief that had overcome him the moment Janice had asked him to come fix her sink.

While having a drink before dinner and during their conversation while eating, Noah had checked item after item off his list of things he wanted in a mate in regard to Ram. And with everything positive about Ram, Noah had felt certain that with this second date Ram would probably want something more than the brief kiss they'd shared at the end of their first date. Hell, Noah had even spent a lot of time thinking about those next steps, and even looking forward to them a bit.

Noah's one experience with a guy in college, something he'd allowed himself during a brief breakup with Janice, had involved him kissing another boy like there was no tomorrow. Then they'd sucked each other's dicks, fallen into bed, and ground their cocks together until they'd both come. But then the boy had immediately wanted to get some condoms and have sex, and had very aggressively talked about everything they could do together and with other guys. Noah had instantly gone cold and withdrawn from the situation. A few days later, Noah had missed everything he'd had with Janice so much he'd pleaded with her to take him back. Shortly thereafter, they'd gotten engaged and married.

Now Noah was looking to pursue those sexual feelings he'd briefly unleashed more than twenty years ago -- only this time paired with a deep meaningful relationship. Ram could fill both of those needs in Noah. Noah knew it, yet he continued to hesitate. Ram had been in a handful of same-sex relationships; he'd talked of them a bit during their two dates. The man clearly had already had sex with other men; he knew what to do and already knew what he liked, while Noah had done nothing but force down thoughts of sex with other men for the entirety of his life. Noah didn't know what the hell to do, or the right ways to do it, or if he had any kind of natural inclinations or qualifications that would make him good at having sex with another man.

Cringing inside, knowing it didn't make a damn bit of rational sense, Noah reached for the remote, turned on the TV, and searched through the adult pay-per-view options. He selected a gay film he hadn't seen before, clicked on the icon that said he agreed to pay the fee, and the movie began. Moments into the flick two buff, beautiful men filled the screen, already naked and in bed, kissing and rubbing against one another, with pleas from the man on the bottom for the other to suck his cock.

It was stupid as hell but Noah tried to watch the movie, as he'd done many others, with an eye toward learning some technique -- or at the very least to find a pattern of things most men did when going down on a guy, or penetrating a guy, or even where and how to touch another male body to give the most pleasure. Before long, though, as was always the case, Noah's dick stirred and his skin started to heat.

For once Noah wanted to prolong the inevitable release that would rush through him in a firestorm. Quick orgasms left him satiated and weak afterward but still pining for more. He watched the more compact, dark-haired man swipe his tongue all the way around the other guy's shaft, and Noah groaned where he sat. He rubbed his length through his jeans, allowing the fabric to mute the sharp sensation of contact against his cock. With each lick or suck from the guy in the movie, Noah stroked his shaft in time, attempting to mimic what that man's tongue would feel like on his prick.

Soon the man went to town swallowing half his partner's length, to his partner's shouts of delight, and Noah could not hold back touching himself fully any longer. After fumbling to get his belt and zipper open, Noah shoved his jeans to his thighs and his erection quickly pushed toward his belly. *Good Christ.* He was so fucking hard already.

Noah told himself to go slowly, but the guy on the TV already had his face in his partner's crack, licking his asshole as if it were a sweet piece of candy. And good God, Noah craved intimacy with someone like that so much he couldn't control his responses. Noah's balls rolled in his sac; early beads of creamy cum pearled across his fat slit, as if his body begged him to increase the level of sensation and make him come.

Unable to ignore his needs, Noah smeared the pre-ejaculate over his length, spit in his palm to lube himself up some more, and began jerking himself off in unison with the dark-haired porn star now sucking his partner's dick in earnest. The more Noah stared at the TV, the more he could envision the very man on the screen kneeling between his thighs, his lush lips wrapped around Noah's shaft, sucking him with every ounce of power in his body.

The image became so real Noah broke his stare from the TV and glanced down at his lap. He swore the three-dimensional likeness of that dark-haired guy bobbed up and down on his shaft for real, his sweet mouth taking as much of Noah's length as he could. Moaning, Noah spread his legs even wider and tentatively touched this incredible man's hair. Silken tresses threaded through his fingers, so very real. Noah ran his fingertips over the slightly wavy stuff. The man made a needful little noise in response, then looked up at Noah with the most innocent, yet sultry, pure blue stare he'd ever seen.

Noah gasped, but with just a light hold the young man, already much too familiar, held him in place. The guy dug one hand into Noah's hip and slid the other between his thighs to fondle his ultrasensitive balls. Noah instantly jerked again, but this time a hoarse shout followed. He punched his hips upward, hungry for more of this man's suddenly seductive mouth. *Jesus God.* Noah slipped further into this wonderful yet terrible fantasy, and he silently willed this innocent person to understand his recently unearthed desires. *Please help me come.*

More insane, powerful suction surrounded Noah's cock, and gentle pressure kept his balls on the edge of exploding. The man seemed to have no gag reflex, and his pretty eyes encouraged Noah to let go of his inhibitions. *Please. No.* Slipping under the tide, Noah buried his fingers in that luscious dark hair, held the guy in place, and began to drive his cock up into that welcoming mouth again and again and again, fucking the man well past his throat. The sight of those full lips wrapped around his dick pushed at Noah's sanity equally as much as the feel of that tongue and mouth licking and sucking every nerve ending in Noah's shaft did. Then that ocean gaze locked on Noah, held him prisoner, and invited Noah inside his world as well as his mouth. Noah cried out as he flew headfirst into an unknown abyss at rocket speed.

Noah arced his entire body, shoved his cock straight down the throat of the first honest home he'd ever known, and whispered gutturally, "Zane … Oh Christ, Zane … Zane…" and rode the wave of the sharpest orgasm he'd ever experienced, spewing seed with a vengeance. "Zane, please…" Noah lost himself completely in the younger man's sincere eyes and sexy mouth, and he cried, "Zane, Zane," repeatedly, with every spurt of semen he had to give.

For long minutes afterward, Noah stared down between his legs and just grinned at the guy smiling back at him, sharing in the glow of an experience more real and honest than any in his life. *Zane.* Noah could have run his fingers through the younger man's hair forever, but just then two other shared cries of delight filled the room and slammed Noah back into reality. In a flash, the image of Zane kneeling between Noah's legs disappeared. Noah looked up just in time to see the dark-haired man in the adult film, his legs parted and up against his chest, spray cum all over his stomach as the other guy pounded away in his ass, clearly in the throes of his orgasm too. Noah grimaced. When the two men lovingly kissed before the scene ended, Noah wanted to throw up.

You can't have Zane. Stop pretending like you can. Those two guys in the movie might only be fucking each other because they were being paid to, but what they'd done together in that scene was more real than what Noah had experienced on his living room couch. And it was for damn sure more a reality than anything Noah could ever share with the real, flesh and blood Zane Halliday.

Disgusted with himself, Noah turned off the TV. He couldn't bear to watch another scene with two men fucking as if they loved every second of the encounter. Deep down Noah feared that no matter how much he ached for a man, he would never find someone he could equally love, desire, and respect, who would feel the same about him. Especially when he kept thinking about a young man who was not gay and could never be his.

Noah went to take a shower, determined to imagine a certain redhead with a very nice body -- a man who seemed to find Noah interesting. In a way Noah hadn't been able to do in years, he stroked his shaft a half dozen times, immediately grew hard again, and coated his shower wall with ejaculate as he came a second time in minutes.

It was not Ram consuming Noah's thoughts and heart as he lost it, though. Once again, it was Zane.

Fuck. Noah punched the shower wall. The impact didn't batter his knuckles enough to make him understand the unhealthy ramifications of his desires, so he did it again. And again.

Only when his hand was bleeding did Noah relent.

CHAPTER 4

Four days later, as Noah pulled his truck to a stop in front of his old house he tried to keep his thoughts from wandering forward a few hours to what seeing Zane again would do to him. He hadn't seen the younger man since the night he'd jerked off to the fantasy of a lust-filled Zane giving him a blowjob. And then, while in the shower shortly thereafter, losing his shit again to the even rawer vision of Zane crying out with pleasure as Noah pounded his cock into the man's ass.

Stop it! Noah reminded himself that even though he would see Zane in a few hours, he would have his son with him and Zane would have his brother and sister too. It was inappropriate to have such full-bodied sexual fantasies about Zane at all; to allow them to fester in his consciousness while in the presence of three children was unacceptable. *Beyond that,* Noah reminded himself, *you have another date with Ram next week. You need to start thinking of ways to make that evening a success, not ways to sabotage it before it starts.*

Noah had given Ram such a detailed description of his evening fixing a sink and cleaning a kitchen that at a certain point the man had barked with laughter through the phone and said, *"Okay, all right, enough. I believe you. You weren't trying to ditch me on our date."* After Noah had promised, *"No, I wasn't,"* Ram had murmured, *"So, would you like to try again?"* Noah had said he would, and they'd agreed to a night and time to get together. Noah just had to keep his focus on next Friday evening and steer clear of daydreams and porn featuring young, dark-haired men. He needed no more reminders of Zane Halliday than necessary, if for no other reason than that Noah craved a return to his usual relaxed state of living. He'd had such while married and living with his family, but it was something he feared he would never get back in this new life.

Just then the best possible cure for Noah's mood swings burst out of the front door and ran toward him at the speed of light, shouting, "Dad! You're here!" and then barreled into Noah and wrapped his arms around his waist.

Joy and light instantly filled Noah, practically lifting him off the ground. "Hey, Matthew." He squeezed his kid and pressed a kiss to the top of his blond locks. "How's my boy?"

After drawing back, Matthew said, "It's Matt now, Dad. I don't like Matthew anymore."

Noah crossed his arms and studied his son with a deadly serious eye. "Matt it is," he replied. "I like it. It makes you sound at least seventeen."

Mimicking Noah, Matt crossed his arms against his chest too. "Daaaadddd."

"Okay," with a critical stare, Noah pretended to reconsider, "at least fifteen and a half."

Matt rolled his eyes. "Whatever." He gave Noah one more quick hug. "I'll go wait in the car."

"In the truck, kiddo," Noah corrected, watching his son as the boy -- still all arms and legs -- ran toward the sidewalk. "It's unlocked. Strap yourself in the front seat."

As Noah watched Matt climb in the passenger side, a slender, familiar presence appeared at his right.

"Where's the Accord?" Janice asked.

"Hey, honey." Biting his tongue as soon as the endearment left his lips, Noah muttered, "Sorry. Hard habit to break."

"It's all right." With a nudge against Noah's arm, Janice then jerked her shoulder toward the street. "What's with the truck? Did something happen to the car?"

The image of a very distressed Zane on the sidewalk outside his former apartment filled Noah's mind. "Someone was in a tight spot and needed transportation for a while." An uptick in Noah's heartbeat and somersaults in his stomach increased the grit already in his voice. "I lent him the Accord."

"Him?" Janice's eyebrows shot up so fast they almost looked like they'd changed zip codes. "Someone new?"

"New, yes," Noah conceded, but then added, "But not like that. Just someone who needed help." The crazy idea that Zane might hear Noah's explanation of him, and think Noah viewed him as a charity case, poisoned the jitters in Noah's belly and propelled him forward recklessly. "He's a young man with responsibility for his younger brother and sister. I came across him when he was in a tough spot, and did what I could. But he's clearly resourceful and will be on his feet and thriving again soon."

Janice continued to study Noah closely. In her green eyes, Noah could see the thirty years of friendship and knowledge they shared. *Shit.* He'd known the woman since they were both eleven-year-old kids.

"What's his name?" Janice pressed.

"Za --" Activity at the open door to the house had Noah twisting to look over his shoulder. *Oh wow.*

"Dad. Hi." As Noah looked upon his father, the man still more blond than gray, his throat grew tight. Visible discomfort shaded his father's face. Shaking the heartache, Noah turned to his silver-haired mother. "Mom." He rushed to the stoop to give her a hug and kiss. "I didn't know you were here."

Standing a pace behind Noah, Janice gently squeezed his arm. "It wasn't planned." The way she rubbed his arm, still so familiar, told Noah she would have called him to keep him in the loop if she'd had the time. "But I was happy to see Cathy and Hoyt when I opened the door a bit ago."

Noah's mom hugged him in return but then pulled to stand next to Noah's dad. "We were having brunch after church with Norman and Hilary," Cathy shared, mentioning Noah's old neighbors. "We decided to walk over to say hi to Matthew."

From the truck, Noah's son shouted, "It's Matt now!"

Hoyt sent a thumbs-up Matt's way. "Gotcha, kiddo."

Noah stared at his dad, who kept his focus on his grandson, and he silently told himself not to dwell on the stabbing sensation digging repeatedly into his gut. Instead, Noah put on a happy face and turned to his mother. "I know you said you just ate, but you're welcome to join us anyway." His gazed darted to his dad; he couldn't help it. "You could have coffee, and we could all catch up."

Cathy gave Noah another fast hug and then moved toward the drive. "We've already been rude to leave our hosts for as long as we have. We should really get back."

Hardly making contact, Hoyt grabbed Noah's hand and shook it. "Son." His lips barely moved, and in fast strides he was at his wife's side.

"Bye, dear." Cathy waved and then linked her hand in her husband's elbow. "We'll call you soon."

As Noah watched his parents walk away, it felt as if huge chunks of his very being fell off his body and crumbled into the grass at his feet. Their rejection, but particularly that of his father, scraped away a little more every day at the choice Noah had made to face his sexuality. More than that, with every frustrating, lonely day that went by, greater doubt crept in, and made Noah question if what he'd gained in his life could match the many things he'd lost, and if in the end he'd made the right choice.

Janice rubbed Noah's arm again. "Try not to let it hurt you. They'll come around."

"I don't know if they will." Rust coated Noah's words, and it hurt his throat to talk. "I think I just lucked out with you. Most everybody is more like them. Polite but," he struggled to explain the volatile emotions roiling inside him right now, "they act as though they don't know me anymore, like if they touch me for more than a second they're going to catch the gayness I'm apparently carrying around like a disease. It's like I'm a different species now or something."

Stepping in front of Noah, Janice gave him the eye contact his parents no longer would. "In their minds you were their straight son for forty-one years. Married and with kids too; everything they expected in their only child. Certainly they always were and are very proud of you, but you also never once threw them any real surprises in that time." Her vocation as a counselor at their local high school shone through every part of her. "Now you've been their openly gay son for fifteen months. Intellectually you have to understand it will take time for them to adjust."

"You didn't need time," Noah shot back, knowing he could still say anything to her. Christ, he missed this closeness with another adult. "If you hadn't been so fantastic we would still be gearing up for a battle in divorce court, rather than already settled and moving on."

A shot of laughter escaped Janice, and she quirked a dark brow. "Maybe you've conveniently forgotten how I tore up our bedroom when you told me. I threw some very nice things at your head, more than once."

"I know," Noah conceded. "But you never stopped talking to me, even when it was yelling and crying. You never treated me like a stranger, or as if it might burn your fingertips off if you touched me."

"I also knew you'd had that one experience with a guy; your parents didn't." Janice went quiet then. Her gaze changed to cloudy, as if she'd drifted away. "Maybe buried deep in some secret part of me," she said, her voice gone soft, "I was always waiting for that shoe to drop, for you to tell me that you needed the freedom to try something with a man. I think some part of me always knew you would have to leave me one day."

Guilt flooded Noah, and he second-guessed the decision he'd made more than two decades ago to tell Janice of his one-time slip with another guy. "Were you worried the need might get so great in me that I would cheat on you?"

Her focus sharpening once more, Janice shook her head. "It's not in your DNA to cheat on a person you're committed to, man or woman. Beyond that, we were both so busy with work, the kids, and making sure we were saving money, you never would have had the time to stray." She chuckled again, this time in commiseration. "Me either, for that matter."

Noah suddenly put a laser focus on his ex. "Did you ever think about cheating on me?"

"Nothing more than the occasional fantasy every couple has but never admits to feeling." She raised a brow. "You?"

With a shrug, Noah admitted, "The same."

"Daaaddddd!" Matt leaned out the window and wailed loud enough for the entire town to hear him. "Come on!"

Noah rolled his eyes at Janice. "He must be hungry again." The kid burned so much energy he sometimes consumed more in a meal than Noah did. "Let me get him to the diner before he threatens to pass out on me."

"Have him home by nine." Janice waved as she walked backward to the open front door. "He has school tomorrow."

"Will do."

With that, Noah jogged to his truck and strapped himself in, along with a promise to Matt that he would get the kid to some food as fast as he could. As Noah drove past his parents' car parked in a drive a few houses away, his heart once again squeezed with unbearable tightness. He had a glimmer of hope he might get his mother back in time, but with each tense moment that passed between him and his father, Noah feared the strong bond he'd shared with his dad for so many years was gone for good. Another crushing wave of loss bore down on Noah, suffocating him.

He'd never experienced such pain in his life.

PAUSING TO WIPE SWEAT FROM his forehead, Zane eyed Noah from across the spare bedroom. The man painted the disgusting wall -- Zane didn't want to know what the previous renters had done to create such stains -- with such efficiency he might as well have been a robot.

More than once in the last two hours Zane had found his gaze straying Noah's way. When he found himself fixating on Noah's strong back and shoulders, staring at the man's muscles moving with such precision as he rolled a brush across the wall, he would avert his attention. The guy might as well have been naked from the waist up for all the good his thin T-shirt did to conceal his muscular frame. *Good God.*

Zane's knee-jerk reaction to rip his stare away once more kicked in, but this time, before he did, a band suddenly constricted his chest. Instinct pulled him closer to Noah. Zane couldn't stop himself from drinking in Noah's incredible hardness and physique, or keep his throat from going a bit dry as he closed the distance between them. This time, though, he ignored the strange confusion he experienced when around this man, and instead zeroed in on the way Noah repeatedly clenched his jaw. Zane reassessed the tension in Noah's shoulders, as well as his silence. As he did, his heart inexplicably tugged again.

After putting down his roller, Zane curled his hand around Noah's arm. *God, his muscles are so fucking tight and hard.* Noah jerked away, muttering a curse.

Zane immediately lifted both hands in the air. "Sorry. I didn't mean to startle you."

"No," Noah rubbed his arm where Zane had touched him, as if hurt by the contact, "it's me who should apologize. It's fine."

Studying Noah more closely, Zane took note of the tightness still coiling in Noah's hands and arms. "I notice you didn't say *you* are fine." Tingles in Zane's palms pushed him to touch Noah, to try to ease the tension in the man. Only having known Noah for a short while, Zane squashed such a presumption. Still, the urge to help overwhelmed Zane; he kept his tone soft, and said, "I don't think you are fine, Noah. I don't think you're okay at all."

Noah's pupils flared, and he abruptly stepped back. "It was just a poor word choice. I am." After a terse second, he added, "Fine, I mean. I am fine."

The kids had abandoned painting after completing one wall together. Matt had shown Hailey and Duncan his portable gaming device, and he'd taken them outside to teach them a few games. Their loud chatter drifted through the open windows of the cabin, so Zane had no fear they would wander inside and overhear any exchange between himself and Noah. He could speak freely.

"I know you said you enjoy the quiet, but you've been even quieter than the day we worked together. And maybe I don't know you very well yet, but I feel like there's something … I don't know…" Zane soaked in every rigid, firm line in Noah today, much more pronounced than before, and he struggled to explain that whatever Noah had festering inside him right now had leaked through his pores and infected Zane too. "Something is *off* with you today. Like you're agitated, or angry, or upset, or something like that, and that you're biting your teeth together hard enough to wear down the enamel so that you don't vomit what you're thinking all over the nice walls you're painting."

"You're painting too." With those words, Noah's frame only locked up even tighter.

Zane sighed. "All right, that *we're* painting. That's not the point. What I'm feeling vibrating out of you is still the same." Compelled beyond what might be considered good manners, Zane stepped closer and put his hands on Noah's forearms. Warmth immediately licked against Zane's palms, but he ignored the buzz shimmering through his hands and went deeper to the rigidity coiling the muscle beneath. "It's like you're trying to keep something inside you from snapping or exploding." Caressing down to Noah's wrists, and then lower, Zane ran his fingertips along the tendons cording the back of Noah's hands. Each sliver of contact filled him with accompanying tension. "Whatever you're feeling, it's pretty powerful."

Noah yanked his hands away from Zane. He whispered a string of curses as he paced across the room. Glancing over his shoulder, he said, "I apologize." Gruffness ruled his tone. "I should be able to hide my crap better."

"Why?"

Stalking around the room, Noah shot Zane another sideways glance. "Because it's not professional to bring private stuff into a work environment."

"You're not officially on the job today, so don't worry about it." Some friendly taunting about gaming skills from young voices outside prompted Zane to add, "Your son isn't within hearing distance, so you don't have to worry about him hearing or seeing you upset. If you want to tell me what's wrong, you can."

A small hitch broke Noah's stride. Then he began circling the room again, his stare laser sharp in front of him at all times. "Talking won't change things."

"It might make you stop strangling that roller handle," Zane pointed out. "You're acting like it did you wrong or something. Come on, Noah." When Noah passed by, Zane grabbed the paint roller out of his hand. "It's not exactly like you met me on my most stellar day. I think I was near to hyperventilating at one point. You can spill." This time, when Noah made to move past him, Zane stepped in and blocked his path. Noah locked his gaze on Zane, his stare intimidating in its focus. Zane held his ground, even though his heart suddenly pounded like a motherfucker. "I promise that whatever you say will go to the grave with me."

"Shit," Noah released a rough chuckle, "it's not that dire."

"Then it shouldn't be a big deal to get it off your chest."

Silence reigned between them, and a battle of wills ensued. Or, at least, Noah glared. He took a step closer, in a way that felt as if he were trying to use his extra height and size to get Zane to break and back away. And, fuck, Zane did find it harder to swallow, and drops of sweat trickled from his neck down his spine. At the same time, though, he didn't think a roar in his face would make him tuck tail and slink away. Something inexplicable, forming in his gut and solidifying in every limb, nerve, and vein in him wouldn't let him pull his stare from the intensity burning in Noah. He wouldn't shrink back from the powerful waves of heat emanating from Noah. Something elemental in Zane's being, beyond his ability to control with conscious thought, would not let him walk away. *Fuck.* Breathing became a tangible thing, and Zane swore Noah had trouble too.

Accompanying the muttering of a few more expletives -- God could only know how long later -- Noah finally muttered, "Fine."

Zane exhaled. *Thank you, God.*

After scratching through his hair one more time, his fingers leaving the blond tresses in sweaty tufts, Noah launched into a fast-paced explosion of sentences. He explained the difficulty his parents were having being around him, with being affectionate with him, with being natural in his presence, since his telling them he was gay. Noah paced as he spoke, and with each sentence, his throat seemed to fill with more gravel than usual, making Zane think the man swallowed down tears -- ones he'd likely been fighting for a very long time.

On the heels of the battle of wills that had just occurred between them, Noah's words and cadence were surprisingly very matter-of-fact, but Zane catalogued the pain etched into each line on Noah's face and in the tension filling his body. He added the information to the struggle Noah had overcome just to share, and Zane knew the truth. *His parents' response has crushed him, and he doesn't know how to process such a monstrous loss.*

Matching pain swelled in Zane, and he barely kept from pulling Noah into his arms each time the man crossed his path. He didn't understand the urge, or why such emotions had all of a sudden come alive in him -- particularly for another man -- but such empathy erupted in him, squeezing his insides so terribly, Zane could not pretend they didn't exist. They did. For Noah. Another man. An older, gay man. *Shit.*

Just then Noah came to a stop at the window. As if he no longer had any strength, he dropped to sit on the sill, leaned his elbows on his knees, and clasped his hands together. "So when I ran into my parents this morning," he looked up at Zane, his face now shadowed by the light at his back, "and they seemed even less comfortable with me, I forced myself to start accepting in a way I hadn't before that I've lost the parents I'd always known, for good."

Losing the connection of Noah's stare prompted Zane forward. He didn't stop until only inches separated them. He then kneeled in front of Noah, making eye contact with that haunted brown gaze once more. "It's the loss of your father that's killing you, isn't it?" Losing Burt five years ago, the distinct knowledge that the one person who'd had his back emotionally was no longer there, remained fresh in Zane's mind and heart. The eye color might be different, and the loss might not be to death, but looking into Noah's eyes right now felt like looking in a mirror for Zane all those years ago. "There's such love in your voice and eyes when you speak of your father, it's hard to miss."

Blinking repeatedly, Noah looked briefly toward the ceiling. "I made my bed," his jaw ticking once more, he looked to Zane, "now I have to lie in it."

Zane took hold of the sill on either side of Noah and caged him in. "That's not a real answer, and you know it."

"Yes." The rasp in Noah's voice, the need in that one word, punched a hole straight through Zane where he kneeled, leaving him gutted. "Yes, okay? I want my father back in my life. He was a lawyer before he retired, and he was a hell of a good one. I respected and idolized him in a way I can't explain. I've never lived in a world without his level-headed guidance and ear when I needed it." Noah's voice hitched, and his entire body heaved. "Right now I need him more than I ever have, and he's not there."

Oh damn it. In an instant, overcome, Zane surged up and took Noah in his arms. "I'm sorry." He clutched the bigger man with all of his might, desperate in his need to make Noah understand he wasn't alone. "I'm so sorry." He dug his fingers into the man's back and pressed his cheek to his shoulder. "So fucking sorry."

His tone rough, Noah sank into Zane and clutched him too. Raspy as hell, he whispered, "It's not your fault."

Zane only squeezed Noah even tighter. "I'm still sorry."

"Okay." Still as gruff as Zane had ever heard him, his mouth against Zane's nape, Noah muttered a few more curses. Each foul word brushed warm air against Zane's neck and sparked new awareness under his skin. *Oh my goodness.*

A sudden new consciousness of their bodies touching so intimately made Zane shiver. His balls pulled in his sac too. *Holy God.* So very quickly, hot need sprouted to life from a place deep inside Zane. He scraped his fingers across Noah's shoulders, absorbing the man's heat beneath that thin layer of fabric. *Yes.* He brushed his fingertips against the edges of Noah's hair and the brief contact tingled all the way through his being. *I want more.*

Right then, though, Noah abruptly stiffened and pulled away.

Crap. Zane went still as a statue and prayed for a miracle.

With a gritty chuckle, Noah let his head fall back to rest against the window. He exhaled, and Zane started breathing again.

"Fucking hell." Noah averted his gaze. "I apologize. I don't usually lose my shit like that."

Still fearful of what Noah might have read into the contact between them, Zane took a few steps backward, giving them both some breathing room. "It's all right. Everyone is entitled to let off some steam once in a while."

Noah rolled his head and found Zane halfway across the room. "You went above and beyond." As he held eye contact, some of the brackets around his mouth began to diminish. "Thank you for listening."

A new ease visibly worked its way through Noah. And that soft *"Thank you for listening"* seemed to release a bubble in him and let all the tension out of the room. Zane let his stupid anxiety about what had, or hadn't, happened drift away.

"You know what you need?" As an idea hit Zane, he suddenly bounced with excitement. "A little levity and fun."

Crossing his arms, Noah quirked a blond brow. "If you're calling me Pot, I'm calling you Kettle."

Warmth crept up Zane's neck, but he grinned too. "Fair enough. I could use some mindless fun too." Murmurs outside from the kids prompted Zane to add, "So could Hailey and Duncan, for that matter. Everything has been a bit heavy lately."

Noah got up and walked backward toward the door. "What do you have in mind?"

"I found some water darts, a volleyball net, and a few other things in the shed yesterday. Everyone in the lake for a swim and some games? What do you say?"

Now in the hall, Noah jerked his thumb toward the front room and open cabin door. "I have to run to my cabin to gets trunks for me and Matt."

"No, no, no." Rushing to Noah, Zane grabbed his arm and dragged him to the porch. "This is fun because it's spontaneous. Take off your shirt, go in your cargo shorts, and we'll all do the same." His sister's high-pitched giggles twinkled from the grassy slope up to Zane. "Hailey can stay in her T-shirt too."

A wicked grin -- something Zane remembered Noah briefly flashing the first day they'd met -- appeared. "Yeah?"

Somersaulting acrobats went crazy in Zane's stomach -- the good kind. Without looking away, he huskily said back, "Yeah."

In a holding pattern on the porch, Noah looked like a rugged carpenter who was somehow also meant to be in the ocean. A heartbeat later, he beckoned Zane with his hands. "Race you to the water? Do cannonballs off the dock?"

Grinning back, Zane let a challenge ignite in his stare. "Start running."

With a glint of competition sparking in the bigger man's dark eyes, Noah took off at a dead sprint, surprisingly fast and nimble for such a muscular body. He yelled at the kids, "Come on! Get ready to get wet!" as he ran past them on his way to the water.

Laughter bubbled in Zane, and watching Noah made his insides flutter in the sweetest, most wonderful way. Zane grabbed Hailey and Duncan on his way past them, pulling his brother and sister out of their stunned stupor.

Just then Noah ripped off his shirt. The garment cleared his head and the fabric drifted across the warm air to settle behind him on the grassy slope of front lawn. *Good God Almighty.* In response to the spectacular sight of Noah's sculpted, bare back, Zane stumbled. Forget Zane's thought that the T-shirt had been too thin to conceal anything. This, this bare skin, the visible definition of spectacular muscles, had not been on display before. Zane gulped, and he stared. No one man should be so beautiful that he rendered straight guys -- albeit this one inexperienced and a virgin -- speechless.

"Zane?" Hailey tugged his hand. "Are you okay?"

Ripping his gaze from the perfection that was Noah, Zane looked down at his sister's puzzled expression. *Holy hell, I was staring like he was a model or something.* Shaking himself, Zane promised, "I'm fine."

As Zane got his head back on straight and ran for the lake, getting closer to Noah and his shirtless chest with every step he took, Zane deep down feared he wasn't fine. At least not in relation to his growing, perplexing attraction to Noah Maitland. He didn't understand his responses to the man, or how to handle them, at all.

Then Zane's brother and sister, happier and more exuberant than he'd seen them in ages, hit the water, shrieking with delight, and nothing else mattered.

———

HOURS LATER, AS THE SUN began to fade over the lake, creating shimmers of soft light across the surface of the water, Noah held his hand extended to Zane, waiting for the guy to take it so Noah could hoist him to the dock.

Even with sun block eventually having been applied, Zane still had a rosy hue to his skin, and Noah suspected he might have a sunburn by the time he hit the sheets tonight. *Good Christ.* Noah glanced at the kids trudging up the slope to the cabin, and he silently reminded himself not to put Zane in any scenarios that involved a bed or his body stripped of clothing. Not even in his imagination.

"If you don't get out of the water soon," Noah wiggled his fingers, but deliberately kept half his focus on the brood headed toward the cabin, "the kids are going to take that as a sign to raid the kitchen for food on their own."

His eyes still half-closed, Zane floated near the dock on his back. "I don't have enough food in the fridge to make that a compelling threat."

Smiling for a moment, feeling fucking indulgent, Noah forced himself to rein in the ridiculous giddiness coursing through him -- all as a result of the last two hours in the water spent in Zane's company. "Doesn't mean they can't still make a huge mess."

With a groan, Zane forced himself upright. "Good point. Okay." He swam backstroke a dozen feet away, grabbed a few stray water darts, and handed them up to Noah. "Grab this stuff."

After tossing the plastic toys into a pile with the others, Noah wrapped his hand around Zane's forearm and hauled him out of the water. They both broke contact quickly; Zane rushed toward the cabin, and Noah was thankful for the reprieve. He quietly followed.

The temptation to touch Zane had simmered within Noah for much of the time they'd spent in the water. He could only attribute the presence of the kids for keeping their play light and innocent. Christ knew Noah had fought an insanely powerful urge to take Zane into his arms more than once. The hug they'd shared in the spare bedroom earlier remained front and center in Noah's mind. Jesus God, the feel of Zane's arms wrapped around him, the always surprising strength in his hold, the way his lips had brushed Noah's nape when he'd spoken… Hell, that little accidental graze of lips against skin had given Noah far too much of a vision of what a kiss would feel like from that soft, sexy mouth. Fuck, even the way Zane had pressed his fingers to Noah's lower back had pushed Noah's thoughts toward reciprocating -- but without a shirt between Noah's fingertips and Zane's skin.

Just then, in front of Noah, an "Oh fuck," slipped from Zane's lips. The man's arms spun like propellers and he lost his footing on the damp grass covering the slope to the cabin. Zane toppled back into Noah, and together they *oomphed* as they lost control of their tangled limbs. Gravity forced them both backward, and Noah grabbed Zane just as they hit the ground. Noah slammed into the soft earth, with Zane on top of him. As they started to roll, Noah wrapped his arms around Zane, and Zane did the same to Noah. Their teeth and bones clattered and rang together in their rolling descent back to the dock.

Noah's side made impact with the wood, and he grunted as a slice of pain ripped through his shoulder and hip. Zane thudded to a stop in a sprawl across Noah, making the air whoosh out of Noah's lungs. A minute went by, and then two, where Zane lay pressed against Noah, and both men struggled to regain their breathing. Then Zane made a grunting noise and shifted to straddle Noah's stomach. He braced himself on Noah's chest with one hand, and, with a groan, he rubbed the back of his head. The sunset, full of pinks and oranges, set a beautiful backdrop for Zane, and Noah didn't know where to land his gaze first. Then Zane's palm slipped; his fingers grazed across Noah's nipple, and everything around them ceased to exist.

Zane's fingertips, brushing in innocence across Noah's nipple, made the flesh twist; wonderful, powerful sensations shot straight through Noah's body. In immediate response, Noah's cock reared, suddenly full of delicious rigidity, and pushed toward his belly. Right near Zane's ass.

Fuck.

Noah froze.

CHAPTER 5

On top of Noah, Zane shifted again, and a second rush of unbearably wonderful sensations zinged through Noah's cock and pushed his shaft harder against his belly. *Good Christ.* If Noah were to shift his lower body just a hair, the fat head of his dick would push out from the waistband of his cargo shorts, visible for anyone to see. Noah gritted his teeth. Then again, much worse, if Zane moved his ass just one inch lower, his buttocks would brush against Noah's cock, and Noah would lose control and spill himself faster than he had in twenty years. Noah looked up at Zane, into blue eyes he'd let himself get lost in too many times already, and his nuts pulled dangerously against his body. *What in the hell am I supposed to do?*

Zane's stare suddenly narrowed. "Noah, are you all right?" He rose up to his knees and started feeling all over Noah's chest, stomach, and arms, sending Noah's flesh into a fiery inferno. "Where are you hurt?"

Just as Zane pushed his hand toward Noah's lower belly, Noah groaned and shoved the man off him. Rolling to his side, Noah grunted, "You were on my bladder," shot to his feet, half hunched, and started to run. "I have to take a piss."

Without looking back or apologizing for his rudeness, knowing he didn't have a spare second, Noah stumbled for the cabin as fast as his state of arousal would let him. Once inside, he tore down the short hall, straight for the bathroom, and pushed his way inside. Sparing the quickest second to lock the door, Noah then shoved his damp cargo shorts and underwear down to his thighs while moving to the toilet. With his cock practically plastered to his stomach, Noah began jerking his length, and didn't even let the sharp sting of pulling his shaft dry slow him down. His balls rolled in his sac. The veins shaping his cock quickly filled with even more blood, and Noah parted his lips to release a silent moan.

Feeling the endgame already upon him, Noah went to brace himself against the edge of the sink and instead his fingers twisted in a lump of fabric. As if he could feel Zane with him -- his heat, his presence, in the room -- Noah opened his eyes and zeroed in on the black T-shirt with the toaster design on it. *Zane's T-shirt.* Noah remembered the guy wearing it the other day. Noah crushed the T-shirt in his hand, brought it up to his face, and buried his nose in the material. Zane's musky yet sweet scent filled Noah's being. His essence mainlined straight to Noah's cock, feeding his ever-growing fantasies. Suddenly Noah no longer jerked on his own cock. In his mind, Noah now felt Zane standing behind him. Zane now held Noah around the waist, keeping them close. He stroked Noah's cock for him, and whispered dirty words about Noah's big dick and needing to see him come.

Yes. Noah pumped his shaft with an even harder drag, yet the hand wrapped around his cock somehow felt smaller, with a different kind of strength. The words *"Let go for me, Noah,"* in a smooth, sweet voice filled Noah's ear, as if Zane whispered the order against Noah's shoulder -- much in the way he'd done when he'd hugged Noah so tightly earlier today. In the bathroom, Noah nodded. His entire frame jolted, and he smothered his cry of Zane's name into the T-shirt as he lost it and shot his release into the toilet. Jet after jet of seed splashed into the water, and endless streams of pleasure rushed through to every corner of Noah's being. And all the way through, Noah swore Zane milked his cock and whispered how pleased he was to see Noah come so hard for him.

His legs temporarily weak, Noah crushed his fist with the T-shirt into the sink ledge, supported his weight, and breathed heavily while working to recover from such a powerful orgasm. He caught a glimpse of himself in the edge of the mirror, and the sight filled his gut and psyche with humiliation and shame. Lust-filled, desperate eyes stared back at Noah. Release had not doused his desire one bit; all that hunger still lived within, visibly, all for an innocent guy nearly young enough to be his son. *Fuck.* Noah dug his knuckles into the marble counter surface harder, grinding until spikes of shooting pain filled his hand. He needed something, anything, to shove him back to reality; anything to help sober him and make him see and understand that Zane was not standing behind him encouraging him to come. Noah stood in a bathroom by himself, and he had pathetically jerked off to inappropriate fantasies about a young man who appreciated Noah's generosity but not his sexuality and body.

A soft knock sounded at the door, and Noah jerked as if someone had shot a bullet into the bathroom.

"Noah?" Zane's voice carried through the thick wood. "Are you sure you're all right?"

Jesus motherfucking goddamn Christ. Noah yanked up his shorts and underwear, wincing when the damp fabric pulled at his flesh. "Just a sec." In quick succession, he flushed the toilet, washed his hands, and barely took a second to dry them on a towel before opening the door. Zane stood a few steps back in the hall, donning a fresh T-shirt, dry and dressed once more.

Noah blurted, "I apologize." He tore his stare off the sliver of flat stomach still visible as Zane adjusted his shirt. *Damn it. Stop looking.* "I didn't mean to hog the bathroom. I've gotten used to having one to myself most days."

After pulling down his T-shirt, Zane stepped forward, almost over the bathroom's threshold. "If I had to pee I could use the toilet in the master bathroom. I don't care about that." He let his focus slide down the left side of Noah's body. "You jammed your shoulder and hip into the dock pretty hard, though, so I just wanted to make sure you hadn't done any permanent damage."

Noah growled; he couldn't control it. "I might not be twenty anymore," he glared as he moved past Zane, "but I can still recover from a hit. Somehow, I think I'll live."

"Shit, no." Zane scrambled to get side by side with Noah, stopping him before they reached the living room. "I didn't mean it like that. You look good for," red forged its way up Zane's neck to his face, "for … for…" he gestured with his hands, "for…"

"My age?" Shit, it wasn't as if Noah could get around being almost two decades older than this man.

Zane reared and narrowed his stare. "For a guy, I mean. For any age. For a person. Shit." Zane dug his hands into his dark mess of hair. "I don't know how to explain stuff like this, except I'm not blind, so I can see when someone is in way better shape than I am. And you are that, so I wasn't trying to make some kind of dig about your age, whatever it even is."

"I'm forty-two," Noah supplied.

"It doesn't matter," Zane shot back, a snap in his tone. "I just came to see if you were okay, that's all. Not because of your age, but just because I already bandaged up some scrapes on myself. You took the harder hit, so I wanted to see if you needed anything. You were in the bathroom for longer than it takes to piss," pure reason sounded in Zane's tone, "so I got worried something might be wrong. Period. End of story."

In the face of such logic, Noah dropped back and leaned against the wall. "Christ," he banged his head against the plaster, "I am such an ass sometimes."

Empathy filled Zane's smile. "You've had a shitty day. You're allowed."

Shaking his head, Noah dug his fists into his forehead, muttering, "And you've already gone above and beyond by listening to me bitch and moan…"

"Hey." Zane pulled Noah's hands away from his face and looked into his eyes. His voice softened as he said, "I didn't see it as complaining."

"I appreciate that. Point being, though, you didn't deserve to take the brunt of any mood still hanging on to me." *Or any defensiveness I might have because of my own stupid attraction*, Noah added silently to himself.

"I'll survive." Zane turned Noah's words back around on him, arching a brow. Then added, "Been doing it for a while already."

"I guess you have at that." Noah's heart rate started to slow to normal, but he still couldn't tear his gaze away from Zane. "Better than most," he murmured, his admiration growing leaps and bounds for this young man.

"Thank you." Pushing away from the wall opposite Noah, Zane jerked his thumb toward his bedroom door. "Do you want some dry clothes? I have some sweats that might be a bit snug, but will probably work."

"You're okay sparing them?" Noah asked. Damn, he knew the guy had been pushed out of his apartment with hardly any of his possessions. "I don't want you cursing me tonight when the weather dips and you don't have them."

Zane chuckled, and the joyous sound reflected in his eyes too. "I promise I won't." He cheeks pinked a bit. "Duncan already gave Matt some dry clothes too."

"I'll take you up on the sweats then." Noah became very aware of how his wet shorts clung to his legs, and he cringed. "Thank you."

Pointing into his room one more time, Zane said, "They're on the bed. Join us in the kitchen after you've changed." With another fast grin, Zane trekked backward to the living area. "I already have supper going. It's a good one too. Don't be late."

Smiling in return, Noah replied, "Looking forward to it," unable to help his response. He always wanted to smile and laugh around Zane. The urge to touch him, even in innocence, constantly crackled in his fingers, pushing him to make contact.

Crap. As Noah entered Zane's bedroom, he cursed himself ten ways from Tuesday. How in the hell was he supposed to steel himself against Zane when the man was so fucking sweet and sincere at every turn? Not to mention goddamn sexy without even trying. He was ... wonderful. *You have to stay away from him.* Noah groaned, even as he accepted the truth. *Get through dinner tonight, tell him where to find information online to help him with the repairs, and then keep your relationship restricted to the occasional phone call.* Noah didn't have to like it, but that was what he had to do. With a grimace, he accepted his course.

After changing, Noah got up and dragged himself down the hallway, his body feeling heavy. The setting sun sparkling against the windows didn't seem quite so warm or bright anymore. The sound of Zane's laughter twisted a deep pain in Noah's gut this time, rather than making him grin in return.

Fuck. As Noah entered the kitchen, he plastered a fake smile on his face. He might as well start getting used to the loss.

———

AN HOUR LATER, ON THEIR WALK around the lake to return home, Noah slung his arm around his son's shoulder. "Did you have fun today?"

"Yeah." Matt shoved his hands into his pockets -- well, Duncan's pockets. They were the boy's shorts, just as Noah still wore Zane's sweats. "Duncan is nice. And I never met Hailey before, but she's cool too. Even for just a little girl."

With a chuckle, Noah squeezed his son's shoulder and then gave him a noogie. "I'm sure Hailey will be happy to hear she's all right -- even if she is just a little girl."

Slipping out of Noah's hold, Matt gave Noah one of his familiar eye rolls. "Whatever. I didn't mean it like that."

"I know." Noah tugged his kid back to his side and gave him a squeeze. "I'm just teasing you."

After shuffling along in silence for a moment, Matt pulled his stare up from the grass and met his father's gaze. "They're poor." His voice was nearly silent. "You know that. Right?"

His chest constricting, Noah came to a stop and zeroed in on his son. "What would make you say that?"

"Nothing." Matt shrugged. "They just are. I go to school with Duncan, even though we're not in the same grade. Everybody knows he doesn't have a mom or dad and that he doesn't have any money."

Sighing, Noah pulled Matt to his side and got them strolling again. *Christ. How much or little to say, without violating a family's right to privacy?* "I suspect they struggle as a family," Noah shared, "but I hope you don't make fun of Duncan at school for what he doesn't have, compared to what you and your friends do have."

"I don't, but I know some kids do."

"I would hope you don't associate with people who would bully him, and I'd hope if you were a witness to a situation like that developing, you would defend him."

"I've never been around when it happened or anything," Matt explained. "I'm just saying what I've heard."

"It's not cool to hurt someone's feelings or try to make them cry just because they don't have everything you do, or if they're different."

Matt rolled his eyes at Noah again, with even more petulance than before, if possible. "I know that, Dad. God." The kid sounded downright offended by Noah's little lecture.

Noah raised his hands in surrender. "Okay. Point taken. It was just a reminder."

"Besides," Matt glanced up, for the smallest split second, before he plastered his stare to the ground again, "I would defend him anyway, if I heard someone making fun of him, because I know what it's like too."

The unspoken *it*, Noah knew *it* all too well. *My son takes shit at school for my being gay.* "I know, kid." Noah's voice roughened, thickened terribly. "I'm so sorry for that. You have no idea."

"Mostly I ignore it. I know it's dumb." With his hands shoved in his pockets, and his shoulders hunched, Matt looked up at Noah, his brown stare surprisingly steady. "Seth says people are stupid about things they don't know, and we can't take it personally if they don't want to know the truth about how you still take care of us, and how you still love Mom, even if we don't all live together anymore."

Noah skidded to a halt. *Fuck.* "Your brother said that?" His voice rose ridiculously.

Matt nodded, and his shaggy hair dipped across his eyes. "Yeah. He's right too. I know it." Matt began his shuffling walk again, and Noah moved slowly to stay at his side. "Sometimes it's hard not to get in a fight to make the dickweeds shut up, though. But so far my friends have always been with me, and it helps to have them, just so I can stand up and call the other guys jerks, and then walk away."

Shit. His throat unbearably tight, Noah yanked Matt against him and hugged the breath out of the boy. "I'm real proud of you both." He pressed his lips to the top of his son's head. "Do you know that?"

"Daaaddd." Matt squirmed and wiggled his way out of Noah's arms, his cheeks burning red. "Cut it out."

Noah hauled him back in and smacked a loud kiss on his cheek. "I can't help it. I love you," he kissed Matt on the head while tickling him, "love you," he pecked another wet one on the other cheek, "love you."

Matt twisted his way free again and shot Noah an exasperated glare. "You're such a dork."

Noah grinned back at his son. "Then I'm a dork who loves my kid."

"Whatever." Impatience rang in Matt's words, but he couldn't completely hide the smile pushing at the edges of his mouth. "You're worse than Mom."

Yeah, Noah could admit, with his kids, he did devote himself to them fully, and he never shied away from affection. His father had been wonderful and loving too. *Yet another thing I patterned after my dad.*

Noah looked at Matt, and he couldn't imagine a world where he and Janice weren't the two loudest cheerleaders and biggest support for their child. For both of their kids. Seth too. That dull, too-familiar ache started to creep up in Noah, but this time he yanked himself back into the present. *Stop moping about what happened this morning.* He had to get over his father and the distance between them.

Hell, no matter how kind Zane had been, Noah knew he had whined enough about his problems already today. So much so the guy probably thought Noah was a wimpy little bitch. After all, Noah only suffered a strained relationship with his parents. *Boohoo.* Yet there Zane was, having lost his mother and stepfather, and his full-time job, and his apartment, and he had to take care of his brother and sister -- and he did it all without bemoaning his situation. It was no wonder Noah couldn't stop thinking about the guy. Forget the sexiness, sweetness, and beautiful eyes; Zane was a fucking survivor in the truest sense of the word, and nothing was more attractive than someone capable of coping with every hardball life threw in his direction.

Shit. Shit. Shit. Stop it. Noah could no more let himself drown in thoughts of Zane than he could sink into the loss of his relationship with his parents. Wishes for success with both were futile desires; he could have neither one in his life on any more than a superficial level from now on.

Right then, the sound of clomping footsteps on wood pulled Noah back to reality. They'd reached the cabin and Matt had employed his usual heavy foot up to the porch.

Just as Noah made to take the first step, Matt said, "Can I ask you a question, Dad?"

Noah leaned his hip against the stair railing. "Shoot."

In a similar stance, Matt crossed his arms and leaned on the top porch railing. His focus laser sharp on Noah, he blurted, "Is Zane, like, your boyfriend or something?"

Shit. "No." The denial burst forth from Noah as fast as Matt's question had. "Not all of my new friends are going to be…" *Christ.* Noah zipped his lips. He and Janice had openly explained to their children why they'd gotten divorced, and that Noah wanted to fall in love and have a relationship with a man, but they'd felt deeper conversations needed to come naturally and in their own time. *I guess this is one of those times.* His adrenaline rushing much too fast, Noah forced himself to face his son head-on. "Not everyone is going to be like me, Matt." *Shoot.* "What I mean is, not every man I introduce you to is going to be someone who wants a boyfriend instead of a girlfriend."

"Sirus and Grey are."

"I know. That's different. They're a couple."

"Do you like Zane, though?" Matt pressed. "Like, do you want to kiss him and make out with him and stuff?"

"Jesus, Matt." Wild heat rode up the back of Noah's neck, and he suddenly wanted a drink. "This is not an appropriate conversation for someone your age."

"Why not? I asked Mom the same thing about Tom when he came to our house for dinner the first time. She didn't think it was wrong." From the porch, Matt fixed a pointed stare down on Noah. "You didn't either when I told you about it."

"Fair point." Damn, this was what Noah got for praying for smart kids.

"Thanks." Matt beamed. "I'm doing really well on the debate team. Coach says I might go right to the first chair in my second year. That has never happened in our school before."

"That's great, Matt. Congratulations."

Matt came back down the steps, stopping in front of Noah. "So what's your answer?"

With another sigh, Noah dropped to sit on the steps and tugged his son down with him. "My answer is that finding someone interesting and attractive isn't always enough." He crossed his arms against his knees and rested his head against his forearms, his focus on Matt. "Other factors have to come into play too, mainly how the other person feels, and who they are able to like in a romantic way."

"In my debate class, Coach would have told you to simply state what you mean. Which is, you kinda like Zane, but he isn't gay."

Fuck. Noah muttered, "Another point to you."

"Sorry, Dad." Shock of all shocks, Matt scooted closer and rubbed shoulders with Noah, instigating closeness in a way teenage boys rarely did. "I like this girl at school, but she only wants to hang out with this boy who is already practicing with the high school basketball team, so I know how you feel."

Noah nudged Matt's shoulder in return. "That's her loss. You're a great guy."

"You are too, Dad." Matt even smiled without looking away.

"Thanks." Glancing up at the rapidly rising moon, Noah cursed and checked his watch. *Still have some time.* He hauled Matt to his feet. "You want to drown our losses in a couple of beers before I have to take you home?"

"Can mine be a float?" The kid knew their ages-old code, and that Noah meant a root beer, not an alcoholic beverage.

"Why not?" Noah replied. "I could use one too."

"Awesome." Matt booked it to the truck. His speed and enthusiasm reminded Noah of times when simpler things had made everyone around him happy. Matt rolled down the window and shouted, "Let's go!"

Noah climbed in behind the wheel and started them to town. As they passed the west cabin, Noah noticed soft light twinkling from within. The sight twisted a sweet pain in Noah's chest, but this time he managed to put a clamp on his imagination before he could paint a picture of Zane inside. Noah reminded himself that he could never have the younger man.

Hell, the truth was, Noah might never have any guy -- at least not with a depth of closeness and trust he'd achieved in his marriage with Janice. Noah refused to dwell in a pity party anymore, though. He'd lost an element of his relationship with his parents, but he had one hell of a fantastic son in Matt. And with what Matt had said about Seth, maybe his eldest supported Noah too. Along with still having a friend in Janice, Noah knew he had a heck of a lot more than most men who came out of the closet at this stage in their lives did. Anything else that came along with the good fortune of still having a family was just gravy.

And what Noah had learned through being married to someone he loved with all his heart, but wasn't insanely attracted to sexually, was that mashed potatoes all on their own were still very filling. If he had to, Noah would learn to live and thrive without ever tasting a drop of gravy.

Truth was, he didn't have any choice.

———

HUGGING HIS PILLOW, ZANE ROLLED onto his back, unable to sleep. He seemed to be having the problem a lot lately. Even more than when he'd first started having money troubles, and that was shocking. He hadn't thought he'd ever have more insomnia than the first few weeks after taking Clint's loans. *Or then the first time I couldn't make a payment.* Zane groaned, but not even the thought of finding a way to get Clint a few more dollars quickly, within the next week, could fully pull him from what kept him awake tonight.

Noah. And how it felt to straddle his lap outside tonight.

God, Zane hadn't ever sat on somebody in quite that way; everywhere his body had touched Noah's still buzzed with awareness of the contact. Right where he lay in bed, Zane's thigh muscles contracted; he remembered doing that very thing while sitting on Noah; he could still feel the man's hard waist rub against his legs. Then when he'd touched Noah's nipple -- purely by accident -- the man had sucked in a sharp breath and his entire frame had tensed. *He liked it.* In that moment, though, in his naïveté, Zane had thought Noah's response had happened due to an injury, not a sexual response. But having spent pretty much the whole night reliving those few moments of physical closeness since they'd happened, Zane now thought Noah had reacted in such a way because Zane had excited him, had made the rigid man's body stir with life.

Oh God. In the darkness, Zane moaned. Just in thinking he'd aroused Noah in some way, Zane swelled with growing hardness, and his shaft began to tent the sheet covering his nakedness. He'd never slept completely nude before, yet tonight he'd forgone the only other pair of sweats he owned. He'd consciously decided to slip off his underwear before crawling into bed too.

Immediately, Zane's thoughts had drifted across the lake, and he wondered if Noah still wore the sweats he'd borrowed. *Noah. In my clothes. His skin touching up against sweatpants I've worn a thousand times.* At one point during dinner, Zane had excused himself to use the restroom, and at the foot of his bed he's seen Noah's underwear folded on top of his damp cargo shorts. That meant Noah did not have an extra layer between himself and Zane's sweats, and that knowledge made Zane's nuts tingle with awareness and his dick get even stiffer.

What is the matter with me? Zane didn't understand his body's responses, yet he couldn't kill this waking dream or keep his thoughts from shifting back to outside, by the dock, to straddling Noah while the last vestiges of daylight twinkled all around them.

As if Zane could see Noah right now, he stared into the man's eyes, the brown color like the richest blend of coffee. Zane's heart fluttered in response. His prick twitched, but the rest of his body didn't feel right; his legs weren't tense and his fingers couldn't feel warm skin either, and the loss of those things put a damper on his memory. *Damn it.*

Panic seized through Zane's entire being. Certain he would lose Noah's image entirely if he didn't act quickly, Zane shifted to his knees in bed. He shoved the three king-size pillows between his thighs, giving him something to straddle. *Oh yes.* Zane spread his thighs, bore his weight down on the pillows, and he swore Noah's hardness and body heat rubbed against his inner thighs, nuts, and ass.

Better now, Zane began rocking his hips back and forth, feeling only Noah's rock-hard stomach scraping against his flesh. Zane rubbed his own chest, across his nipples, and the tactile sensation vividly brought back the moments when he'd run his hands over Noah's skin. Noah materialized completely in Zane's thoughts, in his bedroom, and in response Zane whipped his lower half faster and faster on top of Noah, needing the feel of that hot, solid male flesh between his thighs.

Zane stared down at Noah, at the fire in his eyes, at the hard lines mapping his roughly beautiful face, and wanted to do anything that would make him happy. Noah deserved only good things in his life, and Zane wanted to be the one to give him everything.

Zane whispered, his voice choked, "Tell me," and brushed his fingers over Noah's hard lips, feeling the man's breathless desire. "I want to make you come."

The words *"Touch yourself for me,"* filled Zane's head. He nodded, eager to please, desperate to assuage this hunger consuming his being whole. As Zane ran his hand down his belly, he trembled. When he wrapped his cock in a smothering-tight hold, a shudder rocked through his frame. Early ejaculate beaded down Zane's shaft, giving him all the slickness he needed for the task. Zane dragged his fist up and down his pole with full strokes, and he kept up a steady rocking of his weight down onto the man beneath him, loving every swish of contact between his balls and ass and Noah's hard flesh. Line after line of crazy-excited nerve endings zapped against the surface of Zane's cock, making more blood rush to his shaft and harden his member, but Zane did not slow down.

Please. Jerking off his cock with ever-increasing pulls, Zane writhed on top of Noah, trapped in the man's heated gaze. Noah looked up at him with a dark stare full of raw need, and the sight filled Zane with desires equally base and desperate. With every whip of Zane's hips, Noah's thick penis -- so fucking hard and hot -- pushed against Zane's ass, into his crease. *Shit. Oh shit.* Zane's heart thudded so fast he could hear it roaring in his ears. He knew he only had to shift a little bit and Noah's cock would slip right into his hole. Zane's channel contracted tightly, and his prick spit out another fat pearl of precum.

Beneath him, Noah tensed, and with eyes full of passion, he said, *"Give it to me. I want your ass."*

Biting his lip, fighting his accompanying desire, Zane whispered, "Me too," and impaled himself on Noah's shaft, taking him to the root. White-hot fire shot through Zane's asshole, but he didn't care. He froze in place, suspended on Noah's wonderful cock, as the most unfathomable pleasure raced through his ass channel and up his spine, ripped through his balls, and shot through his dick. A split second later electricity jolted through Zane. "Oh God, Noah, Noah…" Zane moaned from somewhere deep in his gut as seed spewed from his dick, line after line after line, and washed his belly in sticky, hot cum. Zane rode the wave of release, his passage clenching Noah's cock with each spurt. He held the man deep inside his ass, each moment confusing pleasure with the pain.

A long minute later Zane blinked, letting wisps of light from the shadowed room back into his consciousness. A white wall filled his vision. He regained his faculties enough to process that he had his forehead plastered to the wall above the headboard, one hand gripping the headboard, the pillows still clutched between his thighs -- and that he rode his hand, with his middle finger tucked halfway in his virgin ass.

Oh my God. Zane's rectum squeezed around his partially embedded digit. Freaked out, he yanked his hand from between his legs, and bit back a shout as a wickedly strange sensation consumed his now empty hole. Semen streaked down his belly. Sudden cold swept through Zane; he wiped the milky stuff away with the sheet and then tossed the material onto the floor.

As Zane shifted to his back to lie down -- his head still full of Noah, and his body still extremely aware of that new invasion in his ass -- confusion put his thoughts to racing a million miles a second. *Am I gay?* Zane had never wondered if he was before. He'd never even really thought about his sexuality, period, but he could not deny he'd also never had such an explicit fantasy about a girl or woman as he'd just had about Noah. Then again, he'd also never had a fantasy or dream of that nature about a boy or man before. Not until Noah. Now, every time Zane found himself in Noah's presence -- or even just thought about him after spending time together -- he found himself imagining what it would feel like to run his fingers through Noah's short blond hair; or he would recall the powerful heat the man's body emanated, and a longing to touch would pang in him. Zane would now surely think about sitting on Noah's lap purposefully too, and not because they'd gotten tangled up together in a fall.

Now that Zane had experienced this crazy waking dream, something that had felt so real he'd stuck his finger in his own ass as a way to get closer to the sensation of Noah fucking him, he had to rethink everything. Zane had never played with his pucker as a way to arouse himself. Hell, he'd never even thought about playing in that area -- at least not until today, when he'd sat on Noah's stomach and had become very aware of his cock, balls, and ass.

Maybe Zane was just dealing with a late-blooming libido. *Could just be that I'm horny, and Noah is right there, being kind, generous, and attractive.* Zane chuckled, and then pushed his face into his pillow and groaned. He could not play a game of indulging in a curiosity, not with a guy like Noah. It wouldn't be right. As a result of coming out, Noah had uprooted many elements of his life and had put a lot of relationships in jeopardy. Zane would not fuck with that upheaval as part of an experiment, as some way to figure out his emerging sexuality. Noah had been far too wonderful with him, and Zane would not muddy the waters and ruin Noah's chances with a man who knew what he wanted. That being another gay man. An adult. Someone who had his life in order.

Zane's chest banded with awful tightness. At the thought of denying himself a chance to learn more about himself with Noah, Zane wanted to cry. Then he reminded himself he had other priorities in his life anyway. He had his brother and sister to consider, and he would not do anything to put his custody of them on the line. If Zane so much as kissed Noah and Patty found out about it, she would say he wasn't fit and would petition the court to take Duncan and Hailey away from him. Zane didn't exactly live in a liberal state, and he could not predict what a judge would do if he or she were to find out Zane had an interest or was pursuing a relationship with another man.

At the thought of how Patty would eviscerate him until she got what she wanted, Zane shivered. Strange dreams and fantasies about Noah or not -- shocking, newfound awareness of his ass because of those dreams or not -- Zane had to put a damper on his confusing attraction to Noah before it got out of control.

Zane had to make every effort to avoid Noah whenever possible. A dull pain filled Zane's gut, leaving him with a sick emptiness inside. It didn't matter, though. Zane knew what he had to do.

Truth was, he didn't have any choice.

CHAPTER 6

Noah glanced at his watch again, and cursed under his breath. Where in the hell was Rick? The guy should have been back from lunch fifteen minutes ago. Noah was on one hell of a tight schedule with this job. He had something to prove. This salon had its pipes explode on a level that had done so much damage they'd been forced to temporarily shut down the business. Significant water damage had ensued, and the result was a hellacious mess. Today was Tuesday, and the woman needed her business back open by Friday or she would have to cancel every appointment she had with *"pretty much every teenage girl in town"* -- her panicked words -- due to the end-of-year school dances at the junior high and high schools. If Noah could make this miracle happen the owner said she would contract him for all of the salon's future plumbing, electrical, and labor needs.

As the owner of a small business specializing in plumbing but also offering all types of repair, Noah rarely got opportunities to contract long-term, steady work from a business owner such as this. Usually, two or three times a year, a homeowner would need a shower or toilet fixed, or need him to look at an air conditioner, or maybe install a sprinkler system or water feature outside. Noah maintained a successful business due to having cultivated a loyal clientele over almost twenty years of providing honest, affordable work. But since word had slowly gotten around that he was gay, he'd lost a few of those regulars. Not enough to keep him up at night with worry about how to pay the bills, but more than he liked to admit. Getting a contract in writing with this salon for future work would be great for Noah's business. If Noah could prove he was a guy a business wanted on the other end of that phone in emergencies, it might even open the door for a few other small business owners to offer him the same.

But not if his employee took extra-long lunches and threw off Noah's schedule.

Goddamn fucker. Noah hauled in piles of new piping from his truck on his own, breaking his back, when he should have an assistant to help distribute the weight. He laid down his third load of copper piping, turned to go back for the next, and stopped dead in his tracks. *Great.* The salon owner, Dana Culpeper, popped her sleekly-styled, dark-haired head in through the open front door.

Carefully stepping over the mess, Dana found Noah. "I just came to take a look at everything, and to grab a few things from my office."

"Work is still in the early stages, Ms. Culpeper," Noah shared, "but don't let the mess make you nervous. It'll get done on time."

The more Dana looked around at her partially gutted salon, the wider her eyes became. "I'll take you at your word." With a tight smile, she gingerly moved to the back of her store. "Let me get what I need and get out of your hair."

Cursing up a shitstorm worth of foul words under his breath, Noah strode back outside to finish unloading his truck. Just as he grabbed another three lines of piping, Rick stumbled against the side of the truck and then crashed into Noah. Reacting on instinct, Noah let the pipes fall and grabbed Rick around the waist before they both hit the sidewalk.

With a lumbering twist, Rick spit at Noah and shoved him away. "Get your hands off me, you fucking faggot."

Noah crinkled his nose. "Are you shitting me right now?" Wiping spit off his shirt, Noah snarled, but forced himself to ignore the personal slight. Grabbing Rick's hair, Noah yanked the man's head back and sniffed his skin, getting a strong whiff of piss and beer. "You're drunk."

Disgust rippled through Noah, and he pushed Rick away. "You spent your lunch hour drinking."

"I don't need to tell you anything about what I did." After wiping sweat from his face, Rick lifted his arms out to his sides, as if to strengthen his physical presence. "That's my time, not yours."

"Considering the fact your lunch ended twenty minutes ago, you're on my time now," Noah hissed. "That makes it my business."

"What did you want instead? For me to stay and suck your cock on my break?" Rick pounded on his chest and leaned into Noah's space. "I ain't doing that for some shit job like this. Fuck you."

"That's it." The last thread of Noah's patience snapped, uncoiling all of his good will. "You're done. Get the hell out of here. I'll send your last check in the mail."

"You can't fire me!"

"I just did!"

"Fine." The useless bastard circled around Noah, as if he were some kind of gangbanger punk. "I don't want to work for some ass licker anyway. You fucking cunt." Rick spit again, and the wet projectile hit Noah's cheek with force.

Noah grabbed the prick by his T-shirt and slammed him into the side of the truck. "Spit on me again. Go ahead." As Noah presented his other cheek, he promised with a vicious softness, "I will break every fucking bone in your body for it, one at a time, and put you in a goddamn coma for life." He made eye contact with less than a half dozen inches between them. "You take one look at me and decide if I can't do it."

With a struggle, Rick managed to get Noah's fingers out of his shirt. As he ran, he shouted, "Fucker!" and shot Noah the finger.

Once the guy turned the corner, Noah exhaled, and adrenaline rushed from his body, leaving him weak. He'd never had to fire anyone before. And for all the discomfort with friends and family about his newly exposed sexuality, he'd never had to deal with someone getting right in his face with name-calling, nor had anyone ever spit on him. Grimacing, Noah used his T-shirt to wipe his cheek.

From behind, a voice reached him with, "At least he didn't get in a car."

"He doesn't have one," Noah replied on automatic. "Thank God." He turned and went stiff as a board. Again. Dana stood in the entrance to her salon. Clearly she'd witnessed the entire fiasco with Rick. Noah held up his head and made himself meet her stare. "I apologize, Ms. Culpeper. You should not have witnessed something like that from someone you hired to do a job."

"It was ugly, I'll grant you that," she replied, "but warranted on your part."

Noah clenched his teeth so hard he made his jaw ache. "Still, I should have stayed above his tirade."

Studying him, the woman's tough-girl vibe softened. "Sometimes it's not possible; I get that. Look, I hate to rain on what is clearly already a downpour on your day, but what is the status of my repairs now that you've fired your employee?" Gentle camaraderie gone, she pinpointed him with an unblinking stare. "If I have to bring someone else in, I need to know now."

Noah fucking hated when anyone, but particularly a client, saw him in a vulnerable state. "I promised you I would have everything done by Friday," he repeated in a low tone, "and I will."

Dana crossed her arms and stood her ground. "I need a guarantee, or I have to let you go and find someone else."

"I don't walk away from jobs; that's not who I am." His mind racing, searching ten steps ahead, Noah said, "If for some reason I don't complete this work for you by the deadline, I won't charge you a penny for my labor. My work will be free. Think of that as my driving incentive to finish the work. How is that for a deal?" He extended his hand in her direction, and held his breath.

With a grin, Dana clasped her hand in Noah's. "It's one I can shake on." After sealing the deal with a handshake, she added, "I still prefer you get the job done by Friday, though. I'd rather pay you *and* be open for business."

Noah locked his hands behind his back in a military stance. "And that is what will happen."

"I'll leave you to it then." Dana dipped her head and walked to her car, her crazy-high stiletto heels clicking on the brick sidewalk the whole way.

Shit. Fuck. Damn. Once Dana was out of sight, Noah banged his fist into the side of his truck. He should have known that not only would Rick turn out to be a pain in the ass, he'd also become a liability.

Now Noah had zero time to find someone to take Rick's place, or else give away a shitload of his time for free. One person immediately came to Noah's mind -- someone who'd never been far from his thoughts even though Noah hadn't seen him in over a week. *Zane.*

Hellfire and damnation. Noah had just gone on a decently successful date with Ram this past weekend. By the time dessert had come to the table, Noah had actually managed to stop comparing their dinner together to the one he'd shared with Zane and the kids. Did he really want to tempt a good thing by yanking Zane full force into his life again? The few phone calls he and Zane had shared in the last nine days were hard enough for Noah to get through without melting into the floor whenever Zane inevitably chuckled in a way that made Noah's stomach flip-flop. Or worse, made Noah get hard the few times Zane had said his name.

Noah knew the guy still needed work. One of the things they'd discussed was Zane zipping through the repair work on the cabin due to the huge amount of free time he still had on his hands. Zane would certainly appreciate the money. But could Noah handle a renewal of their growing friendship if he gave Zane the job?

The nearly barren fridge in Zane's cabin suddenly filled Noah's mind, and he muttered a curse, aimed squarely at himself. *I am so fucking selfish.* Zane didn't have a whole lot for himself and his siblings, yet he'd openly shared what he did have with Noah and Matt over dinner last week. Was Noah so goddamn unsure of his ability to control his emotions and actions that he would deny a good person some honest work and a decent wage? Noah glanced at the torn-apart salon, and he whispered another curse. More than that, it wasn't as if Noah could afford to give away his labor for free. And that was exactly what would happen if he didn't have another person assisting him in this job.

With his options limited, and a heart already ticking much too fast with his decision made, Noah grabbed his phone out of his pocket to make a call.

ZANE PICKED UP A SPOON, dipped it into a humongous pot of boiling liquid, and brought the Bolognese sauce to his mouth for a taste.

Mmnn. His taste buds tingled with the near-perfect mix of wine, a handful of seasonings, the perfect mixture of ground beef and veal, and a hint of tomato paste for zing. Mickey, the restaurant's chef, had said Zane had a good tongue for flavors and food, and had offered to show him how to prepare some of the signature dishes on the restaurant's eclectic menu. Mickey was a mountain of a dude, who had to be at least sixty-five, and he'd been running the restaurant's kitchen for nearly thirty years. Many of the most popular dishes on the menu were his personal creations, and Zane was ridiculously touched and honored the guy had chosen to pass along this knowledge and wisdom to him.

"How's it taste going down?" Mickey asked, his thick Southern accent seemingly out of place for a guy who created such complex, global food. "Damn great. Right?"

Zane bit his lip, but then blurted, "I'd maybe add a little bit more celery salt." *God, please don't go off and roar me right out of the kitchen.* "Just a touch."

"What?" Mickey thundered over to Zane and grabbed a spoon off the counter. Dipping it in, he took a taste of the sauce too. And then he snarled, which made him look like a gray grizzly bear. "Damn it. Who laid out my ingredients after lunch?" As he spun, he glared at the few people working and cleaning in the kitchen. "Who?"

"Pipe down, Mick." Violet, the widowed matriarch of the family-owned business, breezed into the kitchen through the swinging doors. "I did. I guess I got distracted." With her diminutive size, Violet's pink-tinted, gray-haired head barely reached Mickey's shoulders. "You always taste everything, so it's not like I ever worry about something bad going out to a table."

Mickey leaned down in Violet's face and growled, "Woman..." He looked as if he wanted to pick her up by the shoulders and remove her not only from his kitchen but his life. "You are not in charge in here. Your daughter and son-in-law know I only trust them, myself, and now Zane to lay out my ingredients. You are not precise. You never have been, and you never will be!"

Violet, all five-feet-four of her, poked Mickey in the chest hard enough to make him step back. "Don't get all high and mighty with me. I don't have to tell you that I ran this place single-handedly for ten years after Walton died. If I was that bad you would have walked out on me straight after he passed away. I know what the gosh-darn-heck I'm doing," she smacked the metal worktable in the center of the kitchen, "and I'll fire you before you can get that pork roast in the oven if you keep up with your mouth. I swear I will."

Mickey bared his teeth, and a rumble erupted out of him. "One day I'm gonna take you up on that threat, woman!"

With a smile that had surely laid men out in her day, Violet pulled on Mickey's chef jacket, straightened it for him, and replied, "But it ain't today, so get on with it before I get tired of your pretty face and order you to move on from employment in my restaurant." Violet then strolled across the kitchen, as if perusing items in a store.

Behind Violet, Mickey flexed his hands as if he were going to strangle the woman. But then he just cursed, turned to Zane, and grumbled, "Fix it."

Zane blanched, and his throat fell into his stomach. "Me?"

"Yes you." The man's whiskers twitched with as much impatience as his tone. "Or don't you trust my judgment that you're ready yet?"

"No. I mean, yes." Flummoxed, Zane bowed stupidly. "Thank you."

Right then Violet came up next to Zane and squeezed his shoulder. "After you do that, I'd like you to start resetting the empty tables for the dinner crowd, honey. All right?"

"Yes." Zane stood up straight. "Absolutely."

Violet's eyes twinkled. "Relax, sweetheart. It's just food. Besides," she lowered her voice to a whisper, "that grouchy bastard likes having you around." She shot Mickey a quick glare. "As much as he might not think so, I don't take his opinions lightly. You're doing a fantastic job."

"I appreciate your kindness, ma'am." Zane dipped his head, but he knew nothing could conceal the red consuming his face. "Very much."

"And I appreciate the sweet smile and hard work you bring to my establishment." Giving him another quick squeeze, Violet then turned the gesture into a fast hug. "Keep it up. I have to run out for a bit now." She wiggled her fingers at the handful of employees in the kitchen. "Ta," she added, and breezed out as theatrically as she'd come in.

Zane shook his head and chuckled, but he'd also never stood prouder in a workplace. God, it was nice to have people who genuinely seemed to care. With this restaurant's long family history, Zane could only hope their kindness was more sincere than his previous employer's had been. He couldn't see himself showing up to work here one day to find the doors locked and the bosses gone with whatever money remained in the business's coffers.

Just after Zane added the necessary celery salt to the Bolognese sauce, his cell phone buzzed in his pocket. *What the heck?* Zane's heart instantly shot up into his throat. Duncan and Hailey knew that with their prepaid service this phone was only to be used in emergencies. Zane could not afford a big monthly contract or cell phone bill.

He put the phone to his ear, his voice tight, and said, "What is it? Is everything okay?"

"Hi, Zane." A familiar gritty voice filled Zane's ear. "It's Noah."

"Oh, thank God." Zane wiped perspiration from his face. "I didn't think to look at the screen. I thought something had happened to my brother or sister."

"Shit." More curses, softer, came through the phone. "I'm sorry. I didn't mean to scare you."

"I should have looked at who was calling." Now that Zane's initial panic had passed, the sound of Noah's voice rushed a little tingle up his spine. *Shoot.* Zane tried to ignore the sensation, but couldn't keep from rubbing the back of his neck. "What's up?"

"I know you asked the phone be used at a minimum," Noah said, "but I'm in a jam. Again. I need someone ASAP. I fired my employee, and I can't complete this project on my own. I know you're still looking for work, and I need someone right now."

"I'm at the restaurant now." Zane glanced over his shoulder to the clock on the wall. Just after one in the afternoon. "I don't finish until four."

"That's fine. I'll take you whenever I can get you." A rushed quality filled Noah's voice. "I'm working in a business, not a customer's home, so I can extend my hours into the evening if I have to -- whatever it takes. You're helping me out, so that means I'll accommodate your schedule. I'll help you line up someone to watch Duncan and Hailey for the night work, if you need it..." Another expletive, and then, "Whatever you want."

Oh God, this is perfect. Zane opened his mouth to automatically say yes. Something about Noah brought out this need in Zane to say yes, and help, and soothe as much as he could. Over the last week and a half, when Zane had been alone, he'd done precious little more than daydream about Noah -- and about the sexual fantasy that had frightened him in its intensity. Then Zane would inevitably imagine letting go and going to Noah, confessing the turn of his thoughts, to then have Patty find out about his feelings. His fear of the courts taking Duncan and Hailey away from him would halt Zane before he made a move. *Oh God. Oh God.* Zane didn't know what to do.

He rubbed at the knots forming in his neck, and looked up to find one of the servers beckoning him from the swinging doors. With the phone still attached to his ear, Zane walked to the older woman and mouthed, *"Yes?"*

She pointed into the body of the restaurant and mouthed back, *"For you."*

Zane followed the line of her finger, and his legs nearly buckled. *Clint.* The white cowboy hat and white snap-front shirt gleamed like two bright orbs across the restaurant. *He wants more money. I know it.* Zane did not have more than five bucks in his wallet right now.

"Zane?" Noah's gritty voice broke into Zane's silent heart attack. "Are you still there?"

"Yeah, I'm sorry. Someone --" Zane abruptly snapped his mouth shut. Just in time too. He could not tell Noah about Clint and the stupid, idiotic loans he'd taken from the man. "Can I call you back in a few minutes?"

"Yeah, uh, sure," Noah replied. "Take a few minutes to think about the job. But I'll need to know within an hour, tops."

"No ... I just..." Right then Clint began crossing the restaurant toward Zane, and Zane slipped his features to a cooler facade. "I have something I have to take care of first and then I'll get back with you. Bye." He hung up just as Clint came upon him. With one glance over his shoulder, Zane pulled the guy to a table on the empty, quiet side of the restaurant. "What are you doing here again?" he whispered heatedly as soon as they sat down. "I can't have you visiting my work all the time. I'll get fired, and what good will that do?"

Clint leaned across the table and replied in an equally low tone, "Don't be a little bitch with me. You owe me money. Maybe that first warning wasn't enough?" As he leaned back in his chair, he looked Zane over with a nasty glint in his dark eyes. "Do I have to beat you down again to make you understand?"

"No." Zane automatically grabbed his gut. Almost two months ago he'd taken a beating that had left his face intact but his middle bruised and sore. "I get paid next week, and I promise I'll give you as much as I can."

"I want more than that shit amount you dropped off last time. If you don't start giving me more, fast, you're gonna have to accept a few of those jobs we talked about to pay it back."

"No way." Zane darted his focus around the restaurant, fearful the walls could somehow hear Clint's threat and know what he meant by it.

The guy shrugged. He looked way too down-home, good old boy for anyone to ever think such a thug lived behind the amiable cowboy shell. "You have a cute brother and sister," Clint said. "I took a chance on you because I figured with them you'd hustle for work in order to pay me back. That ain't happening so far. Do what you need to do, or decide you're gonna do what I need you to do. Otherwise, those cute kids might not be so cute anymore."

"You wouldn't." Zane's heart lodged up in his throat, making it a challenge to breathe, let alone speak. "Please."

"Bring me some money soon," Clint stood up, got close to Zane, and whispered in his ear, "or you're gonna find out." Then he tipped his Stetson, as if they were best friends, and ambled to the exit.

Once Clint left, Zane slid down into the seat, his entire body turning to jelly. His hands shook. Sickness churned in his gut, and he thought he might throw up. Duncan and Hailey. *How could I have put them in danger?* Zane couldn't process how he'd gotten in so deep with Clint so fast. The loan had seemed manageable at first. Zane had understood how these kinds of private loans worked, but when he'd originally taken the first loan, he'd stupidly thought he would still have his job at the textile factory. Then he'd lost his job, couldn't find another right away, and a second and third loan had been the only way to stay above water. Except, Zane hadn't kept them floating, even with the money. Before he knew it, with outrageous interest added in, he owed more than he could possibly repay.

Clint had already hinted at some of the things Zane could do to take care of the loan. Like help him set up an inside job to rob the restaurant at the closing of their busiest night of business. Or move some of Clint's "product" at Duncan's school when he dropped his brother off every morning.

God. Tears pushed behind Zane's eyes. He was such an idiot. When he'd agreed to take the money from Clint, he hadn't even realized Clint also ran a small-time drug operation. What the hell other kind of nasty stuff might the guy be trying to nose his way into? And by then would Zane have any choice but to participate?

No way.

Once again, the savior came to Zane in the form of a blond-haired, rough-looking angel. Zane dialed Noah's number, but nausea still held him in its grip. Noah had been so wonderful, and in return Zane's feelings were so confused. Now he only felt put in a more awkward position by asking for another favor.

Still, when Noah answered his phone with a gritty, *"Hello?"* Zane swallowed down the nasty taste in his mouth and said, "I'm in to help you out with this job, but I could really use whatever you intend to pay me, in full, upfront. Are you okay with that?"

"I'm not worried that you'll bolt on me midproject." Noah sounded as if Zane's request were the easiest in the world to grant, and Zane felt like an even bigger jerk and liar for keeping secret why he needed the cash. "If you need the money upfront," Noah said, "then it's yours."

Zane exhaled, but his insides didn't get any less queasy. "Great. Tell me where the job is and I'll head over to the site as soon as I leave here."

After Noah gave Zane the address, and thanked him for stepping in, they said their good-byes and hung up. No matter how generous Noah intended to be with his wage, though, Zane already knew whatever remained after paying rent and a few other bills wouldn't come close to covering what he owed Clint.

Zane could only hope it would be enough to appease Clint for a while and buy himself some more time.

CHAPTER 7

The first twinkles of daylight broke through the darkness outside, ushering in Friday morning, just as Noah and Zane swept away the last of the debris in the salon. Grit filled Noah's eyes, and he wondered how in the hell he was still standing upright. With a glance across the salon to the dark-haired man who'd saved his ass, Noah had to wonder the same about Zane. Zane surely wasn't used to this kind of relentless physical labor, but he'd come through and given Noah every free hour of his life for the last three days, and never once complained. *Yet another reason I want to pull him into my arms every time I get too close.* Work and a deadline had taken 99 percent of Noah's focus these last few days, but that one percent left over was filled with his work partner. That one tiny percent still drove Noah to look at Zane much more than he should. Noah ached to sink into a long, deep kiss with the man to see if it would feel as amazing in reality as his dreams made him think it would be.

"Oh my word." Dana entered the salon from the back, her voice hushed, drawing Noah's and Zane's attention. "It looks beautiful." Circling the area, she let her fingers flit over every surface she passed. "Better than I could have imagined."

"With a few hours to spare," Noah shared, "so you can get your stations set back up to how you like them before you open the door."

Drawing to a stop in front of Noah, Dana crossed her arms and looked up at him from her petite position. "I have to admit, Mr. Maitland, I wasn't sure you could do it. But I am so happy to be proven wrong."

With a chuckle, Noah replied, "I'll be honest. Without Zane," he couldn't help his attention sliding the younger man's way, "it wouldn't have happened."

Doing an about-face, Dana reached out to shake Zane's hand. "Thank you for your hard work."

As Zane exchanged a handshake with Dana, red burned the tips of his ears. "It was my pleasure."

Back to Noah now, Dana shook his hand too. "Send me the bill. Until we can get a paper contract together, our verbal agreement stands. Anytime I need work done on the salon, you are my guy."

Yes. On the inside, Noah pumped his fists, but for Dana, he just dipped his head and said, "Excellent. Oh," he jerked his thumb over his shoulder, "the key you gave me is in the lock on the front door."

"I'll be in back," Dana replied. "Give a shout when you're ready to leave so I can come lock up behind you."

"We're good now." Noah gathered the last toolbox left in the salon and gestured for Zane to grab the remaining cleaning supplies. "We'll get out of your hair so you can start setting up for your day."

Once Dana let Noah and Zane out, locked up, and disappeared to the back of the salon, Noah made eye contact with Zane. He absorbed the spark in that blue stare, thought about the miracle they'd just pulled off, and he let out a huge *whoop* that echoed down the empty street. Zane threw his head back and laughed, filling the breezy morning air with even more joyous noise, and made Noah feel as if he could leap mountains and swim oceans without ever taking a breath.

"So? What do you say?" Happiness pushed words out of Noah's mouth without examination or second-guessing. "I have a part-time job to fill, and you need one. How about you accept this gig as your other permanent part-time job?" Zane's pupils flared, and Noah added, "I'd be happy to sit down with your other employer to see if we can hash out a compatible schedule. I want something that will work for all of us, but you most of all." He lowered the tailgate to the back of his truck and then stepped aside so Zane could put his clunkier stuff away first. "What do you think?"

After climbing onto the flatbed, Zane quickly secured his items and then reached back for Noah's toolbox. From over his shoulder he said, "I think I have to give Violet preference on when she feels she needs me the most, but if she's open to working something out, and what is left of my days is acceptable to you," Zane came to the edge of the flatbed, right in front of Noah, and squatted so they were at eye level, "then I say yes." Light from within brightened his gaze to something spectacular. "I would be honored to work for you."

His arms raised in victory, Noah shouted his pleasure once more. "Excellent. Fucking A, Zane." Noah laughed, filled to the brim with bubbling, good feelings. "You have no idea how it feels to know you've just hired someone reliable, who is going to work hard on every job. I am suddenly wide awake." Noah's mind, his body -- everything -- was racing much too fast, and he knew it would be hours before his adrenaline would crash enough to let him rest. "How about we have breakfast at the diner to celebrate? My treat. What do you say?"

"Okay." Zane stood, giving Noah a quick grin. "But then I have to go drop dead in my bed for about seven hours before I have to go pick up Duncan and Hailey from school." Zane had shared that a woman who sometimes kept watch over his siblings when he had to work -- a Mrs. Mangioni -- had kindly agreed to let the kids spend these last three nights with her.

"Sounds good." His heart skittering ridiculously, Noah lifted his hand to Zane. "I'll even give you a call to make sure you wake up. Let's go."

Zane took Noah's hand, and the fleeting brush of their skin rushed through every nerve in his body. Still so fucking high from his job right now, though, Noah didn't let his response to this young man freak him out. He'd just completed a tough as hell renovation, gotten a long-term contract out of it, and had acquired one insanely great employee too, all without losing his mind over his attraction to Zane. Feeling attraction and acting on those feelings were two completely different things. This job had taught Noah that. He could work with Zane and keep everything professional and under control.

As for the sense of loss that swept through Noah when Zane hit the ground and severed their brief handhold … well, Noah would keep the touching between them to a minimum. When that couldn't be avoided, he would ignore the insanely perfect sensation that rolled through him whenever their skin had reason to come into contact.

FIFTEEN MINUTES LATER, AS BOTH men entered the bustling diner, Zane looked over his shoulder to Noah, laughing at a recounting of one of their hairier moments during the salon renovation. "You should have seen yourself," warmth infused Zane's voice, heck, his entire being, "whoa, whoa, whoa!" Zane physically mimicked Noah's windmill arms and fall from grace off the sink station at the salon. "Once I realized you weren't going to break your neck it was one of the funniest things I've ever seen."

"I thought I completely nailed the landing." Noah straightened his legs, put his hands on his hips, and struck an Olympic athlete pose. "I think the U.S. judge would've given me a ten for sure."

Zane opened his mouth to disagree, but just then a petite blonde woman in a grocery store cashier uniform barreled across the diner and shoved Noah into the cash register station, knocking boxes of gum and candy bars to the floor.

"You fire Rick without any reason and then you just go about your business, laughing and whooping it up like you didn't just ruin a man's life? Got your new employee here already," she sneered at Zane but then got right back in Noah's face, "making up stories and laughing about good times like you've been best friends forever."

In a flash, the woman slapped Noah, and the sound of her hand cracking across his cheek filled the room. Everyone around them gasped.

"You should be ashamed of yourself," the woman went on. "What will this boy do that Rick wouldn't? Does he let you pay him in blowjobs?" Noah blanched whiter and whiter with each word this woman shrieked, but he didn't so much as twitch a muscle. "Or maybe for every full day of work he lets you fuck him up the ass and --"

Right then the loud *crack* of metal banging together ricocheted through the diner, and everyone's attention swung in the other direction, like a grandstand full of people watching a tennis match.

Ruthie Costa, the diner's owner, rushed across the room, a frying pan and pot in hand. "There will be none of that kind of talk in my diner, little missy." With vibrating force, the stout woman pointed her frying pan toward the door. "You get out of here and get yourself straight before you set foot in this place again."

The blonde woman -- Zane guessed she was this Rick guy's wife or girlfriend or sister or something -- snorted, her focus still trained on a pale Noah. "Guess that means you and your little boyfriend have to go too. You sure as hell aren't ever gonna be *straight* again."

Noah appeared as if someone had shot him. "Lois, I-I --"

"Don't even try," she uttered in a low tone. "I thought you were my friend. But I should have known when you fucked Janice over to be with a man that you'd screw Rick too."

"I-I-I gave Rick multiple chances," Noah stated, finally finding his voice. "He failed every time. I told you I couldn't keep propping him up. You said you understood."

"That was when I thought you cared about me more than you cared about having a pretty boy to stare at while you work." Looking Noah up and down, she added, "Cocksucker," and lifted her hand to swing at Noah once more.

No way. Moving fast, Zane intercepted the woman's wrist. He burned inside, and he refused to let her slap Noah again.

"Go!" Ruthie waved her frying pan at Lois again. "Now."

The blonde wrested her arm from Zane's hold, glared at Ruthie, and stormed out of the diner. The diner remained stock-still for a handful of heartbeats, the air thick with silence, almost as if every single person was afraid to speak or move.

Abruptly, Noah dropped to his knees and started gathering gum and candy. "I'm sorry," he murmured. He dumped chocolate bars back into boxes and replaced them on narrow shelves with frantic, jerky movements; the sight of him so uncomfortable and disoriented cut Zane up inside. "I'll pay for anything that was damaged."

Within seconds Ruthie put her hand under Noah's arm and brought the much bigger man to his feet. "Don't you go apologizing to me, honey. There ain't no need. Y'all go get yourself a booth. We'll clean this up."

Noah still seemed to be in a partial stupor, so Zane said, "Thank you," for him and walked to an open booth, hoping Noah would follow. Noah did. Many minutes passed, wherein Noah did nothing more than look at his menu long enough to surely memorize it, then quietly order an orange juice and egg plate special when the waitress arrived. He then stared at the colorful paper placemat in front of him as if he would soon be quizzed on the lovely North Carolina scene. Zane watched as every hard line seemed to dig itself deeper into Noah's rough face, and his gut twisted with the need to slip to the other side of the booth and pull this strong yet achingly vulnerable man into his arms.

Instead, Zane clasped his hands under the table, tightly, in order to keep from touching Noah. He had to keep this new, potentially damaging part of his feelings for this man under control. Unable to rein his empathy in, though, he softly asked, "Are you all right?"

Noah jerked his focus up from the table; rich dark chocolate saturated his stare. "I hate feeling like people are staring at me." Too much rust coated each word uttered. "And like I can never get away from the sideshow curious looks."

On automatic, Zane almost said, *"Nobody is looking at you,"* but stopped himself. He didn't want to placate the man with a lie. Taking a moment, he discreetly checked out the other diners, and in doing so clashed stares with more than one person who tore their gazes away the moment they met Zane's. "Some are watching," he finally admitted. "But more than half are back to their own business, not looking at us at all."

What little color had returned to Noah's face fled in a heartbeat. "Fuck." The curse came out with the fierce precision of an arrow. "*Us* is right. I'm sorry I dragged you into this, Zane." With a glance around the diner, Noah lowered his voice. "If you want to rethink being here -- working with me -- I understand."

Their waitress came to drop off their juices, so Zane held his tongue until she walked away. A fierce pain grabbed his chest. "Do you want me to rethink working for you? Did you change your mind?" His voice squeaked just a bit.

Noah bit off another curse, but he looked Zane in the eyes as he answered. "I'll admit I'm damned self-conscious being with you, only because I know a lot of people are going to think what Lois just did."

Ruddiness tinted his cheeks. "They are going to think I hired you as some kind of young, pretty boy-toy to stare at and flirt with. That's my problem, though," he amended, "not yours. You shouldn't have to worry about what people might say about you because of me."

In this moment Zane's fears and concerns about his Aunt Patty were edged out by Noah's painful discomfort. "Twenty minutes ago I was happy because I had a second job, and you were happy because you said you had someone you could rely on. Has that changed?"

"No," Noah answered whip-fast. "I'm damned happy to have you on board."

"And I'm damned happy to have a second job." To Zane's way of thinking, bringing in a second wage had to be more important to a judge than the fact that Zane's employer was gay. Or that Zane had even begun to have strong feelings for the man. It had to. His Aunt Patty couldn't stir trouble. Particularly since Noah was such a fine person and upstanding member of this community. "The other stuff … people looking, maybe whispering too," sitting with Noah right now, thinking over the last few days with him, Zane couldn't imagine never being near him again just because of gossip, "that's their bullshit, not yours. Or even mine."

Noah's shoulders, his whole body, visibly loosened, and he trained a narrow stare on Zane. "You sure you're only twenty-four, Halliday?"

Zane beamed. "I'll be twenty-five very soon."

"Ahh, almost twenty-five." Returning light finally -- *finally* -- brightened Noah's gaze and made it twinkle. "That must be why you're so wise."

Zane could feel his blush. He grabbed his glass, and into the rim said, "Shut up and drink your juice."

"Yes, sir, Oh-Wise-One." Laughter busted from deep in Noah's gut before he took his first sip.

Zane wondered if Noah had noticed that more people looked at him when he laughed and smiled than when he'd been so self-conscious during the aftermath of Lois's verbal attack. *He probably doesn't realize how handsome he is when he smiles and laughs.*

The observation, and how very inappropriate it was, hit Zane, seized through him, and took his thoughts briefly back to Patty. But right now he couldn't hold onto those concerns and nerves. Noah had been humiliated and sad, but now he was upbeat again, and Zane had played a part in making him feel better. The knowledge that he could affect Noah's spirits in a positive way rushed warmth through Zane in a way he couldn't deny.

I like him. I can't help that I do. Zane could spend time with Noah, admire him, and even let himself fantasize about the handsome man all he wanted. As long as he never acted on anything then Patty had no ammunition in her vendetta to take Duncan and Hailey away from him.

Making eye contact with Noah, feeling his heart skip a beat, Zane let go of any fear and attacked his meal.

WITH A PLUCKED BLADE OF grass in his hand, Noah walked with careful steps to the open passenger side door of his truck. Zane lay across the seat, fast asleep, his sneakered feet sticking out through the open driver's side door on the other side. Darker smudges under his eyes conveyed this newer, heavier work schedule, and Noah wished there was something he could do to take that exhaustion away. The young man had pride, though, and knowing that kept Noah from offering him a loan or even just some more financial assistance. Still … Christ, how Noah wanted to do just that.

Even tired, he's so fucking beautiful. Noah's fingers tingled with his need to touch, as if just by putting his hands on the man, and letting himself feel everything so very alive inside him -- a new spark that existed because of Zane -- he could draw the tiredness out of Zane. *But you can't; so stop wanting it already.*

A few days ago, when Noah had asked Zane about the darkness under his eyes, Zane had reluctantly admitted he could use a few more hours of sleep every night. Noah couldn't give Zane more hours in the evening, and so instead had suggested Zane take a nap during his lunch hour, and that Noah would wake him up with enough time to eat something on the drive back to the job. It was a damn paltry offering, but was the best Noah could do.

Hating that he had to do it, Noah brushed the blade of grass against Zane's nose and softly said, "Time to get up. You need to eat something before we get back to work."

His nose twitching, Zane brushed at the area, and with a grumble rolled onto his side. "A few more minutes." He snuggled his hands under his cheek. "I don't need to eat."

"You do, hon --" *Crap.* Noah snapped his lips tightly together. The more time he spent with this man, the harder it became to keep endearments in check. These terms had been completely natural in Noah's relationship with Janice, and in his head they were becoming more and more so with Zane every day they spent working together.

Dropping the stalk of grass, Noah cleared his throat and tried again. "You can't go all day on just breakfast. You'll pass out, and it'll take a lot longer to recover from that than just taking five minutes to eat a sandwich." He nudged Zane's shoulder, but was careful to keep the contact arbitrary and to a minimum. "Come on."

Zane pushed himself to sit upright, his eyes still mostly closed. Mumbling, "Sorry," he scrubbed his face and then pushed his hands through his hair. "I'll eat fast. You don't have to worry about being late."

After grabbing Zane's food from the cooler, Noah handed him the bagged lunch. "I'm more worried about how tired you are." Noah's comment carried as he walked around to the driver's side and climbed in. "Are you sure everything else is okay?"

Fear and self-consciousness still gripped Noah. Lois's taunts at the diner nearly two weeks ago -- and how so many people had overheard them -- still sat like a giant ball of undigested food in his throat, going rancid, and eating at him. With Zane at his side for work so much since that morning, Noah couldn't help wondering if something beyond a lack of hours to sleep was stressing Zane. Maybe Zane was facing some blowback for working with Noah; maybe he was concealing it to protect Noah's feelings. Keeping secrets could exhaust a person. Noah knew that better than anyone. *Shit.*

As Noah backed the truck out of his usual, secret lunch spot, Zane slumped into the passenger door. Hitting the brakes, Noah grabbed the guy before he slid to the floor. "Zane?"

Zane snapped upright, his back suddenly straight as an arrow. "Sorry. Yes, I'm awake."

"But are you all right?" With his hands back around the steering wheel, gripping it hard enough to make his palms sweat, Noah couldn't stop himself from assessing Zane from top to bottom. As he looked, he absorbed every nuance within Zane that screamed of discomfort, as well as exhaustion. Noah couldn't ignore what he saw. His voice scratchy, he asked, "Are you really okay?"

"Just tired," Zane replied, but tension held the lines of his mouth captive.

"You swear?"

Zane nodded. "I'll be good to go by the time we get back to the Cornish house. I got the sleep I needed," he dug into his brown paper bag and produced a sandwich, "and now I just need the food." He took a big bite, but the moan of pleasure as he swallowed sounded forced.

Awareness of each day, where Zane worked himself to the bone just to keep himself and his siblings afloat, cut through Noah's heart. "If you need me to work your schedule so that you have some more time free --"

"I'm fine." More than his words, Zane's tone and a flash in his eyes made Noah snap his mouth shut. "I can do the job you hired me to do. End of story."

Noah heard Zane loud and clear. *Don't treat me like a child.* Christ knew Noah only saw a fully-grown man -- albeit a young one -- since about the second day he'd known Zane. He could give Zane no less than the full respect and equal treatment the guy demanded with his every word and action. Just because Noah did, though, didn't mean an equal part of him still didn't want to help.

With all of the empathy and misplaced lust twisting Noah up inside, he simply said, "All right, Zane," and got them back on the road to work. He would keep his fears and concerns to himself, just as Zane clearly wanted it.

THAT EVENING ZANE SAT ON his porch -- a place he had courtesy of Noah's generosity -- and cursed his behavior. He'd been short with Noah repeatedly today. Noah had clearly picked up on Zane's mood shift, had shown concern, and Zane had practically ripped his head off for it.

Damn it. He deserves better. Zane only had one excuse. Well, he had two. But neither justified being ultra-quiet or snippy with Noah all day.

Just before Zane had dropped the kids off at school that morning, Aunt Patty had called to speak with them. Duncan had shared that she had a short visit planned to see them soon. Zane did not need an impending visit with Patty as another stress in his life. Beyond Aunt Patty, though, Zane owed Clint another payment, and he wasn't sure he could spare as much as Clint now demanded. He didn't know what in the hell to do.

How about not alienating the guy who gave you a second job and a place to live, for a start? Once again, Zane groaned at the memory of his childish behavior. He'd done exactly what he didn't want to do; he'd acted like a kid around the undeniably masculine, adult Noah. Zane's growing friendship with Noah, and absolute respect for him, made Zane want to spill all of his fears about Patty and Clint to him, with a hope that Noah could help him find a solution to his problems. At the same time, if he exposed his problems to Noah, and pleaded for an answer, then Zane would come across to Noah as a kid, and not a man capable of solving his own issues. *I don't want him to look at me like a boy. I want him to see me as an equal. As another adult man.*

Another noise, full of distress, escaped Zane. He slid down in his chair and covered his face with his hand. Memories of sticking his finger in his ass, and losing himself to orgasm with the vision that it was Noah taking him in such a raw, sexual way, assaulted Zane anew. He hadn't touched himself in such a way again -- in fact, he hadn't even let himself jerk off since -- but he knew those sexual feelings were why he wanted Noah to view him as an equal and notice him as another male. *I must be gay. I have to be.* Just as fast *'I can't be'* rushed through Zane's thoughts. At least, not if he wanted to keep his brother and sister. Zane might have to walk away from Noah, and everything wonderful the man had brought into his life, in order to keep Patty from launching a bid to take Duncan and Hailey away from him.

Just then, Zane's brother and sister trudged up the steps to the cabin, both of them sweaty and smiling and laughing from running and playing -- carefree like the kids they should be -- and Zane couldn't help grinning too. The pleasure and joy bursting forth from his siblings brought instant bright light to the shadowed porch where Zane sat.

Unbidden, Zane's stare lifted to the cabin across the lake, and the man he could see sitting on the porch as well. *Noah.* Zane's chest squeezed with exquisite tightness. Through Noah's generosity, he offered security and comfort to Zane's family, the results of which manifested in Duncan and Hailey in dozens of ways. In this moment, seeing his siblings so at ease, knowing they all had warm beds to sleep in tonight, Zane couldn't feel anything but gratitude that fate had brought Noah Maitland into their lives. Zane would not let the idea of quitting his job with Noah enter his thoughts again.

As to his increasing attraction and sexual thoughts about the man... Well, Noah had let slip something about seeing a guy named Ramsay. So, even if Zane wanted to, it wasn't like he'd have a shot at Noah anyway. And Zane didn't have dreams or fantasies about anyone else -- man or woman -- so his cherry wasn't in any danger of being popped any time soon.

Zane ignored the way his feet dragged as he followed his siblings into the cabin to make them dinner.

CHAPTER 8

Zane pulled his car -- Noah's car, he really had to stop thinking of it as his -- to a stop in front of Noah's cabin. After getting out, he followed the shouts and shrieks of laughter down to the dock. His throat turned dry at the sight of Noah, his bare back turned to Zane, standing next to another guy, also only wearing swim trunks. Both men cheered Duncan on as he did a cannonball off the dock. *Who is this guy?* A hot wave of fire rolled through Zane; he didn't like it one bit when the dark-haired dude nudged his shoulder against Noah's and pointed out to the water. *Is this the infamous Ram that Noah is so reluctant to talk about?* For a date that wasn't supposed to start until nine, the man had shown up awfully early, to Zane's way of thinking. *I guess he couldn't stay away.* Zane had yet to meet Ram, but a bad taste already filled his mouth.

Maybe Zane shouldn't have asked Noah to watch the kids while he went to work at the restaurant. But damn it, he'd been in a bind. Late last night Mrs. Mangioni had called to share that an emergency had come up with one of her sisters and she wouldn't be able to watch Duncan and Hailey. That left Zane either calling in sick or asking

Noah for help. It wasn't as if Zane could afford to lose a day of pay, so for him, it hadn't been a choice at all.

"Zane! Zane!" His name filled the air in his little sister's high-pitched voice. "You're here." Hailey spotted him from the dock and started waving her arms. "Look!" After he waved to acknowledge her, she executed a perfect dive off the side of the dock -- and Zane's heart screeched to a stop. The water didn't ripple at all when she went under, but Zane still stumbled.

Immediately, Noah turned and shouted, "Don't worry!" He beckoned Zane to him and the other dude. "The water is a lot deeper off my side of the dock." Hailey popped up right then, breaking the surface with a smile, and Noah added, "See? She's fine."

Zane started breathing again, but his legs still felt like molasses as he made his way to Noah. "Sorry. I know you wouldn't let her do anything dangerous, but when she jumped, I could only imagine my feet touching the gravel under the water in front of our cabin, and I had a flash of her breaking her neck against the bottom of the lake." His face heating, Zane slid his attention to Ram and he murmured, "Hi." The guy was a lot younger than Zane had imagined, based on the few things Noah had said about him.

"I'm sorry. I didn't even think." Noah slid his arm around the dude's shoulders, and Zane's stomach plummeted straight down to the ground. "You've met Matt already. This is Seth, my oldest son. His classes ended early, so he's back in town for a few months."

A monstrous flood of relief rushed through Zane with enough speed to make him dizzy. "Seth. Oh. You're Seth." *Seth. Not Ramsay. Thank God.* Shaking his head to recover his equilibrium, Zane extended his hand. "It's nice to meet you. I'm Zane."

"I figured you must be the big brother." After shaking Zane's hand, Seth said, "I'm the one who taught your sister how to dive. I hope that was okay."

"Seth is very qualified," Noah interjected, before Zane could respond. "He has a ton of medals from his days on both the swimming and diving teams at school. In fact," beautiful, spark-filled life filled Noah's eyes as he looked at Seth, "he's on a partial scholarship because of his talent. And --"

Seth snapped his hand out and covered Noah's mouth. "Dad. Stop. This guy met me two seconds ago. He doesn't want to hear a list of my extracurricular achievements. You're being all over-the-top proud and embarrassing again."

The sight of Noah, with his son -- with either of them -- made the air around him appear as if it sparkled with extra bright light. Watching them, Zane chuckled and then said, "Believe me, Seth, this is not the first I've heard about how wonderful you and Matt are. Noah brags about you both a lot."

Seth covered his face with his hands. "Oh Jesus. Let me just go die now." After putting his arms back at his side, Seth shot Noah a sideways glare. "I swear you'll have people thinking we piss liquid gold next."

"No." Zane looked from Noah to Seth, and kept his face and voice deadpan. "He told me platinum."

"I said titanium," Noah replied, wearing a big grin.

"Riiiiight." Dragging the word out, Zane smiled in return. "Sorry, I forgot."

"You're forgiven."

Putting his hands out in front of him, Seth took a cautious, exaggerated step backward. "I'm going to walk away now, Dad, before I get even more embarrassed for you." He then turned, jogged to the end of the dock, and jumped in the water with Duncan and Hailey.

His arms crossed against his chest, Noah looked out toward the lake, light still capturing his features. "That's my kid. What can I say? He obviously loves me so much and thinks I'm insanely awesome."

Zane looked too, and his chest swelled over what he'd just witnessed. "Actually, he clearly does. Seth wouldn't be like that with you if he didn't have confidence and comfort in your relationship. Matt's the same way. You joke about it a lot, but such love and camaraderie like that is a rare thing." With every new thing learned about this man, Zane's esteem for him grew. "You and your ex should both be very proud of them, and yourselves."

"The kids are everything to us." Noah's focus remained trained on the water and his son. "I wasn't sure with Seth there for a while after … after I…" Noah's mouth opened and closed a few times without words, and his cheeks flooded with pink, "after … you know. Sometimes I'm still not sure how he really feels. He says I'm all talk, and that I might as well not have left Janice if I'm not going to take advantage and be gay gay gay, all the time, in every way. Whatever that means."

"But you do have a date tonight." *Good God.* Zane couldn't believe how much those words stuck in his craw on the way out. He cleared his throat and forced himself to add, "He has to know about it. Right?"

"He does." Noah nodded, but the movement seemed jerky. "I'll go out to meet Ram, though. Seth will stay here and keep an eye on Matt, once Matt gets here. They haven't seen or met anyone I've dated. I don't think … I don't know…" Once again, words were pulled from Noah with obvious difficulty. "I don't know if I'm ready for something like them meeting men yet."

Oh God. Please stop. Suddenly Zane didn't want to know anything more about the mysterious Ramsay or Noah's readiness to deepen their bond. Hearing about Noah with another man, about his fears and plans, or that guy possibly being important enough to one day meet Seth and Matt, ignited a powerful mix of panic and sickness in Zane's gut. Pictures of Noah with this faceless person, kissing or making out or having sex, automatically filled in those blanks Noah had left open to interpretation. Zane couldn't bear to see this man's passion for another person. Noah was his.

No! Zane couldn't think of Noah with such possessiveness. He had no right. No place. Yet, if he continued to stand here, so close to Noah, he might blurt out something detrimental to the future custody of his siblings. "We'll get out of your hair." Zane tore his gaze away before Noah could see something needful in his eyes. "I shouldn't have taken up so much of your day with babysitting. You should have time with Seth and Matt before your date." Zane turned and started striding down the dock.

Footsteps immediately thudded behind him. "Zane. Wait." Noah grabbed his arm and spun him around before he'd taken five steps. Confusion mapped Noah's face. Still holding onto Zane, Noah tugged him closer. "What's the matter?"

Zane looked up and got trapped in the light burning Noah's eyes to the color of rich espresso. "I don't want…" He snapped his lips shut before the rest of that sentence *"…you to go out with Ram"* left his mouth. Scrambling, he said instead, "I don't want to take up any more of your time."

Noah's entire face softened and his grip on Zane's forearm loosened to a gentle hold. "You never have to worry about that." Sincerity layered every softly spoken word Noah gave Zane. "My time is yours, whenever you need it."

Caught up in this unique man, Zane took a step closer, into Noah's airspace. "I'm sorry I was snappy and withdrawn with you yesterday." His voice was nearly a whisper too. "It wasn't about you, and I didn't mean to be rude."

"You don't have to worry about that either." Noah slid his fingers down and curled his hand around Zane's. His voice slipped to a whiskey-drenched tone. "As long as you're okay, then we're fine."

Heat radiated from Noah in powerful waves, surrounding Zane in a drugging, wonderful cloud. With Zane's hand tingling where Noah touched him, and the sight of Noah's bare, glorious chest only inches away, Zane could barely process what Noah said, let alone form the words needed to hide his many problems. "I-I'm working it out."

"You can talk to me whenever you want. About anything." Without moving a muscle, Noah seemed to envelop Zane and cover him in warmth. "I hope you know that."

"Yeah." The word, the emotion behind the truth -- that Zane could trust this man more than any other -- scraped Zane up inside. "I…" Zane moved even closer, their chests nearly touching, and both his and Noah's breath caught. The balmy, late spring air suddenly seemed to crackle with crispness, bringing new vitality to the early evening. Noah trembled too. *Oh my. So beautiful.* Zane lifted up on his toes, so close he could see every line fanning from the corners of Noah's amazing eyes. He leaned in…

Right then the crunch of tires on gravel, and Matt shouting, "Seth! Seth! You're here!" ripped through the silence like a sonic boom, and Zane and Noah jumped a mile apart.

His heart still racing like crazy, Zane became acutely aware of what he'd almost let happen. *I almost kissed Noah.* A car, with Matt hanging out the passenger window -- the kid waving at a now approaching Seth -- came to a stop in front of Noah's cabin. Zane had never been so grateful for an interruption in his life. A half dozen feet away, Noah stood, red-faced, his body rigid as hell, and Zane could only think the same burning discomfort had a tight grip on him too.

Matt tore out of the car and hugged Seth. An older man emerged from the driver's side, moving at a much slower pace, and kept very close to the vehicle. The guy had to be at least twenty feet away but Zane categorized the graying blond hair, square jaw, tall frame, and strong shoulders as if he stood right next to him. *Noah's father.* The man did not look at Noah for more than a heartbeat -- obvious tightness throughout his body, and ruddiness filling his face when he did -- before averting his stare to his grandsons.

This was the man who'd been at the heart of so much pain in Noah's life recently. Zane took an automatic step to Noah's side. Nothing in him would allow Noah to think he was alone in this moment. "Are you going to be okay?" His fingers itched to take Noah's hand and hold it tight.

Still stiff as hell, Noah seemed to force an upward tilt to his lips. "I thought that was my line to you."

"It works both ways," Zane murmured. "I'm here for you too. You know?"

Noah's nod was barely perceptible. "I'll be right back."

As Noah made his way to his father, Zane knew he should walk to the edge of the dock and immerse himself in conversation with Duncan and Hailey, where they still played in the water. But as Matt ran toward the cabin with his bag, and Seth held back at the car as Hoyt approached Noah, Zane could not command his legs to take the first step. He managed to shift so that he wasn't outright staring, but he could do no more than that. Silently asking to be forgiven for snooping, Zane strained to hear every word exchanged between father and son.

"Dad." Noah's voice held none of the ease he exhibited with his children. "Thanks for taking Matt with you today. I'm sure he enjoyed seeing all the vintage cars." A pause, and then, "I know I always did," slipped from Noah in a much softer tone.

Hoyt, his voice also deep, like Noah's, but less gritty, said, "I should go."

"You should stay." A plea suddenly filled Noah's reply. "You can eat with us before I go --" Noah jerked to a stop, and Zane looked up to see Noah's entire body flush red from top to bottom. "Before ... before..."

"Say it, Dad." That was Seth. He rounded the car to his father and grandfather, storming his way into their conversation. "If you can't tell Grandpa, how are you ever going to have a life? This is what I'm talking about. You're going out on a date tonight. With a guy you've gone out with a couple of times. Tell him."

Noah glared at his son. "Seth. Stop."

Taking a step away, Hoyt rubbed his hand over his face. "I can't do this."

"Dad." Noah reached for his father, but the man sidestepped out of his touch.

"No." Hoyt lifted his arms in front of him, creating a physical barrier. "I know I'm supposed to be able to accept you, and this, just because, but I can't. I can't *just get used to*," he threw his fingers up in quotation marks, "driving up to your home and seeing you holding hands with another man, and almost kissing him --"

"No, Dad," Noah interrupted, surging forward. "It wasn't like that." Noah's explanation -- the fact that he needed to make one -- burned heat through Zane too. "Those kids are Zane's little brother and sister." Just as Noah said that, Hailey and Duncan came up on each side of Zane, taking his hands. Zane squeezed, reassuring them, as Noah went on. "Zane has custody of those kids because they don't have their parents anymore, and he doesn't want them to be apart. I was keeping an eye on them while he went to work. Zane works his ass off for --"

"Why are you explaining yourself?" Seth broke into the conversation once more, shaking his head and throwing his hands in the air. "This is the problem with --"

Hoyt, talking over Seth now, loudly, said to Noah, "I don't want to know what your boyfriend's name is, and how you're carrying on with all these kids like you're some big family now. I don't care about him, or --"

"*No. Goddamn. Way.*" Noah's denial cut across the evening sky. His tone, something filled with rust and ice, overpowered the other two trying to speak. "You have your issues with me, Dad, and that is fine. But you do not get to come to my home and disrespect someone I consider a friend. You don't get to trash him or his siblings. You do not get to tell me what my kids can and cannot see with me, in relation to any man. That is between me and Janice and whoever I happen to be dating. That is something I have and will continue to talk to my children about, and I will always gauge their level of comfort before I make a move. If you can't look at me and still see the boy you raised, and the man you have said many times you respected, then maybe you aren't the man I idolized and wanted to be like from the moment I was born. And if that is the case," visibly running out of steam, Noah's voice cracked, "then I'm more heartbroken over losing who I thought you were than you could ever be over learning that I'm gay."

Hoyt, his face burning, said, "You were married. You have two kids. You already had a family. You can't all of a sudden be gay." Shaking his head, Hoyt held eye contact with Noah, almost looking dejected, and hissed in a low tone, "Something must be malfunctioning in your brain."

Like a cobra defending its territory, Noah drew up straight. "That's enough. You need to leave." He drew Seth away from Hoyt, and kept hold of Seth's arm. "I want to spend some time with my kids tonight before I leave for my date."

In silence, something it hurt Zane's heart to watch, Hoyt got into his car. Without looking at his son, he backed out and drove away. Noah stood in place, as if in a state of shock.

Seth, staring as the car disappeared from sight, said, "It's about time that happened, Dad."

Noah looked up at the sky, and Zane swore he blinked away tears. "I didn't want it to go down that way, kid." His voice was rough enough to crack glass.

Shrinking back, regret filled Seth features. "I'm sorry."

With a softly uttered curse, Noah yanked his son into a clutching hug. "No. Thank you for the push." Pressing a kiss to the side of Seth's head, he said, "Love you," and squeezed him again.

Seth muttered something back to his father; Zane couldn't make out the words. Then Seth pulled away and jogged to the cabin, where he met his brother at the front door. As they slipped inside, Noah made his way to Zane, and Zane whispered to his siblings to go gather their things.

Visible tension still held Noah's body hostage; where he'd been flushed moments ago, his lips were now pale and narrowed to a thin line.

Before Noah could speak, Zane said, "You don't have to say a word. You don't owe me a single explanation, and you certainly don't have to apologize for your father." Zane quirked a brow when Noah made to open his mouth. "Which, yes, I could tell you were about to do."

"You shouldn't be in the middle of anything with my father." A thousand apologies -- humiliation -- lived in Noah's tone and gaze. "You didn't sign up for that."

No. That right belongs to Ramsay. With that truth, Zane's heart sank into his stomach. *Buck up.* Zane forced a steel rod into his spine before he slumped. *Noah deserves your loyal friendship.* "You should do exactly what you told your father you were going to do. Go spend some time with Matt and Seth," taking a breath, Zane refused to let his voice waver, "and then go have a blast on your date."

Commotion behind Noah had him glancing over his shoulder toward the cabin. At the sight of Duncan and Hailey traipsing down the steps, on their way to the car, Noah went even more rigid. He looked to Zane again, his eyes now bleak. "I am so sorry your brother and sister heard and saw some of that."

Every ounce of visible discomfort and apology in Noah spurred Zane's need to soothe the man. "Don't worry about it." His palms burned once more, and he just managed to hold back from pulling Noah into his arms. "I'll take care of any questions they have. First and foremost, they clearly had a great day with you and Seth; that's what they'll remember." Switching places with Noah, Zane started backing up to the car. "Thank you for stepping up to help me out. Again. And please thank Seth for Hailey. She's obviously thrilled to know how to dive."

"Any time." Noah held Zane's stare; his was darkly intense. "I mean that."

Zane felt stroked by strong, sure hands all over. *Oh God.* Tearing his gaze away, before his cock could twitch visibly, Zane scrambled into the car. "I'll see you Tuesday." He waved and then put his full attention on driving, but he could still feel Noah, as if the big man sat next to him in the passenger seat.

On the drive to the other side of the lake, Zane wondered which cabin repair he could tackle tomorrow, which one would be strenuous enough to keep his mind from wandering to Noah -- and what that man would do with his time spent in the company of Ramsay.

ON THE COUCH, IN RAM'S ARMS, Noah rose up on his knees as Ram pushed his hands under Noah's shirt, going for skin. Noah pressed his mouth to Ram's, and he even moaned as Ram slid his tongue past Noah's lips for another deeper taste. His body tingled where Ram touched him. He liked the strength in Ram's kisses, but when Ram popped the snap on Noah's jeans and started to push his hand under the waistband of his underwear Noah found himself shaking for all the wrong reasons.

Breathing heavily against Noah's lips, Ram scraped his mouth against Noah's cheek and said, "Let's go to my room." So close, the blur of desire filled his green eyes. "I have everything we need there."

Ram stroked his hand deep along Noah's shaft, and Noah instantly jerked to the other side of the couch. "Wait." Wiping the sweat beading on his upper lip, Noah wanted to slink away into the night, but he forced himself to look Ram in the eyes. "I'm sorry." *Christ.* He hated that he couldn't make his body relax. "I'm not ready to go to your bedroom with you."

With a push off the couch, Ram grimaced as he adjusted his cock in his khakis. "I can be a patient guy," his tone held remarkable calm, "but we've been moving very slowly for a long time already."

"I know." With every reasonable word Ram spoke, Noah wanted to dig himself an even deeper hole where he could go to die. "I like you, and I thought I could do this tonight. But I'm not ready yet."

Sighing, clearly full of frustration, Ram sat back down next to Noah and looked him dead-on in the eyes. "Maybe you're just not ready with me."

"What?" Icy fingers suddenly danced down Noah's spine.

Another sigh, softer this time, escaped Ram. "God knows you're sexy, and I sure as hell wanted this to go somewhere. I like you, Noah. I like the way your mind works, and I like the way you look at relationships. We've talked a lot, and I get you -- I think I do anyway -- so I think I'm correctly reading a vibe in you that this hesitation isn't about not being ready for sex." Nodding, almost seemingly to himself, Ram added, "It's more specifically about not being ready or comfortable having sex with *me.*"

"What are you talking about?" Noah's voice rose to a ridiculously high level, but he could not control the tightness in his throat making it happen. "You're a fantastic person. I like you, and I even trust you."

"Which are great things to have in a new friend." Ram leaned against the couch cushions and rolled his head to meet Noah's stare. "But you're not cool having sex with a friend just because you're both horny. That's not who you are. You need someone you click with in a different way, and he's clearly not me."

Noah opened his mouth to protest, but one look at Ram made him snap his lips shut. Instead, he sank even deeper into the couch. "Fuck."

"Nope." The freckled redhead flashed a fast smile that made him truly handsome. "At least not with me."

"I am so sorry." If Noah burned with a degree more humiliation he would combust right on Ram's couch. Shooting to his feet, he said, "I need to get out of your life right away," and then frantically eyeballed the various surfaces in Ram's apartment for where he'd tossed his keys.

As Ram stood too, he grabbed Noah's arm. With a tug, he made Noah face him. "You don't have to feel like shit about this, you know. I can see that you do."

"Because you're probably certain now that I was using you," Noah implored with passion, "but I swear I wasn't. You are everything that should be right for me. And you're kind, and you're attractive, and --"

Ram slapped his hand over Noah's mouth. "But I'm not what you want. I'm not in your heart. And for a man like you," Ram softened his hold, and with a little smile, brushed his fingers against Noah's cheek, "that's everything."

Christ. Noah ached inside. He needed. So terribly. Now. "Forget it," he suddenly said. "I changed my mind. I'm ready." He took Ram's hand and started to pull. "Let's go fuck."

Ram held Noah in place. "Go home, Noah. We'll go out again one day." Kissing Noah's cheek, he added, "As friends."

"Thank you." His chest banding, Noah squeezed Ram's hand. "You've been so much cooler with me than I deserve."

"Go after the guy you really want," Ram advised. "I can feel that someone already owns that part of you. Tell him. That's the only way it's gonna work for someone like you."

Zane. The mere thought of the man rushed sweet fire through

Noah's blood. Right on top of that, though, came the awareness of how inappropriate and wrong his attraction was. Noah dropped back to the couch. Elbows on his knees, face in his hands, he admitted, "It's not that simple. He's so much younger than me." Piercing need he could not assuage stabbed Noah in the gut. Looking to Ram, sandpaper coated his confession. "But worse than that, he's not gay."

"Well, fuck." With a stilted nod, Ram squeezed Noah's shoulder. "Let me get you a drink."

Grimacing, Noah responded, "Bring the bottle."

Noah rarely drank, and he couldn't even remember the last time he'd gotten himself pissed-off-his-ass drunk. But at this point in his life, probably already half in love, and definitely in full lust for a man he couldn't have, while his relationship with his parents had completely hit the skids, Noah figured he deserved one night of inebriation that would briefly let him forget his pain.

God knew it would be soon enough he would again have to work alongside the only man he wanted. As Noah downed his first shot of vodka, he began to question aloud his sanity in ever beginning a friendship with Zane in the first place.

Not to mention if there was any possible way he could sever the relationship without ripping away the only solid foundation Zane and his siblings had.

CHAPTER 9

From across the stretch of an opulent shower stall in a luxurious home -- their newest worksite -- Zane eyed Noah, and his heart grew sicker at the tiredness still dogging the man's actions. *Stop thinking about it, damn it.* Zane couldn't help it, though. His mind replayed the events of Sunday morning, as it had been doing on a loop for the last fifty-three hours straight...

...Zane hustled his brother and sister into the kitchen, and for one of the few times, didn't make them something hot for breakfast. They were all running late, and with Aunt Patty already on her way for a visit, Zane needed Duncan and Hailey fed and presentable by the time she arrived. He had one goal and one goal only for today: send Aunt Patty on her way with no more information about their current circumstances than when she arrived. Zane hated to ask his siblings to tell an outright lie, but he'd had to tell them that if Aunt Patty asked, Zane had moved them here by choice rather than necessity. The kids didn't know anything about Clint and the money Zane still owed him -- thank God -- so he figured he was safe on that front. At least for now.

The doorbell gonged pleasantly through the cabin right then; Zane was very proud of the fact that he'd fixed it himself; he needed to remember to brag about that to Noah soon.

He said to his brother and sister, "That'll be Aunt Patty. Rinse out your dishes and put them in the sink before you come to say hello."

Zane then rushed to the door. Before opening it, he took a breath, made a silent vow not to rise to any of Aunt Patty's baits, and adjusted his clothing until he was certain he was as presentable as possible. Then swinging open the door, Zane plastered on a vibrant smile. "Aunt Patty." The sight of such a plump, diminutive woman shouldn't fill Zane with anxiety, but he couldn't ignore the way his hands immediately started to perspire. "I hope your drive was smooth. It's great to see you."

"That bottom step is not secure." Patty's short, frost-tipped brown hair surrounded her face in a hair-sprayed halo. "I shouldn't need to be the one to tell you that a child could step wrong and easily get hurt."

The bottom step maybe, *maybe* creaked a bit, and was in no way, shape or form a hazard, but Zane replied with a smile, "I'll be sure to fix it today while you're out with Duncan and Hailey."

Her lips compressing into a tight frown, Patty looked up at him with a cool glare. "You said you would have them ready for me at nine."

Before Zane could open his mouth to reply, Duncan and Hailey emerged from the kitchen, practically spit-polished enough to make their cheeks shine. Patty lit up when she saw the kids. They ran past him to give her hugs too, which was only one of the reasons Zane never tried to fight against Patty's desire to spend time with Duncan and Hailey. They loved her. And even though Zane hated that she wanted complete control -- more than he would ever allow -- she did love her niece and nephew very much.

"Have a nice day." Pulling in his siblings, Zane gave them both a quick, abbreviated hug, and then lifted his focus to Patty. "If you can get them back by seven, I'll have a great dinner ready." Even she couldn't dispute a wonderful, light vegetable lasagna, with homemade bread on the side. Making a point to hold eye contact, Zane added, "One I hope you'll stay and enjoy with us."

With a murmured, "We'll see," Patty hustled Duncan and Hailey to her car, along with an over-the-top excited explanation about her plans with them for the day. From what Zane could hear of them, much would involve poor Duncan having to grin and bear a day of activities that were a little too young for him. With her two sons already adults, Patty had forgotten what twelve-year-old boys liked versus what they merely tolerated.

Duncan would survive the day, though. Zane even chuckled, his step light as he traipsed down the stairs to double-check that bottom step. He wanted Patty to see he had not ignored her claim. As Zane waved them off, Noah pulled his truck to a stop on the opposite side of the lake, and Zane automatically lifted his arm to wave. When Noah took forever to emerge from the driver's side, and then he didn't even glance toward Zane's cabin as he staggered to his front door -- holding onto the rail as he pulled himself to the porch -- Zane's arm fell to his side, numb dead weight.

His date last night. He's only now getting home. Bullet-fast images of the hot, raw things Noah must have done last evening, things Zane remembered and wanted from that fantasy he'd created of riding the man to completion weeks ago, filled Zane's mind and crushed tight pain in his chest. *He spent the night with another man.* If Noah had stayed away from his cabin all night, when Seth and Matt were there, Noah had to really like this Ramsay guy a lot. *As he should.* Zane forced himself to stand up straight and lean into the metaphorical blow. *It's entirely his right.*

His feet now dragging as if he wore bricks for sneakers, Zane went into the cabin to grab the toolbox, determined to be a supportive friend to Noah when next they worked together, even though he suspected this wicked pain inside him was what it must feel like to have a broken heart…

———

…And all this morning, and even through lunch, Zane had done his best to act naturally around Noah. He'd even asked how the man's date had gone, with a smile on his face and everything, as what he already knew of it made his insides burn with new feelings of jealousy. Noah had stiffened tighter than a plank of wood upon the question;

with his response, Zane had found himself barely able to push words past the clog in his throat. Obviously Noah wasn't comfortable talking about having sex with another man with Zane. He'd already openly stated that he never wanted to make Zane uncomfortable. He clearly didn't want to say anything Zane might consider inappropriate, so Zane had let the subject drop.

Once again, though, Zane found himself looking to Noah. He studied the way the man's thick muscles moved under his shirt as he grouted a wall of freshly laid tiles. This shower stall had to be as big as a small bedroom; for more reasons than that, though, Noah felt very far away.

Zane couldn't even bring himself to share that Aunt Patty had stayed for dinner on Sunday. From the moment Zane had said hello to Noah this morning, he'd wanted to spill that everything had been so pleasant and had gone so well with his aunt that he'd wanted to climb onto his roof and whoop to the heavens. As Aunt Patty had driven away, Zane's first thought had been to run to Noah's place to blurt out his good news. But then a vision of Noah stumbling into his cabin in his clothes from his date clouded Zane's vision, and he'd gone inside to quietly watch TV with his siblings instead.

Zane's chest hurt, still, two days later, and he couldn't stop his brain from creating pictures of this Ram person removing Noah's shirt, of his hands running over Noah's flesh, of his lips parting around Noah's cock … *No!* Zane jerked and knocked his hand against a pile of pre-counted tiles stacked on a small workbench. The marble pieces toppled and two of them clattered to the floor and cracked into dozens of pieces.

"Shit." Zane dropped to his knees and frantically started gathering the broken tiles. "I'm sorry."

Stooping down too, Noah used a little broom to brush sharp pieces of the tiles from the plastic tarp. "It's all right." He dumped the shards into a bucket they used for trash. "That's why we get extras."

So close to Noah like this, Zane dropped his focus to the tarp. Heat reddened his face. "I'm such a klutzy spaz."

"No you're not." Sympathy filled Noah's words. When Zane lifted his gaze from the floor, the same soft emotions filled Noah's dark eyes too. "Are you okay, though? You haven't seemed like yourself today."

Every second Zane kneeled so close to Noah like this, and every moment he couldn't make himself look away, he found himself sinking

deeper and deeper into the feelings this man had awakened in him --
ones that at a certain point in his life he'd given up on ever experiencing
with anyone. Yet today Zane had spent the day feeling as if Noah was
building a wall between them, something Zane found he couldn't bear.
The distance pushed Zane to raw places he'd never gone before.

"Why won't you talk to me about your date?" Zane blurted, his
voice huskier than he'd ever heard it.

Pulling away, to his feet, Noah paled. "Zane..."

"I'm serious, Noah." Zane got up and rounded the workbench,
closing the distance Noah had created. "I know you didn't come
home until the morning. I saw it." Words spilled from Zane's mouth
unchecked; he didn't understand what place inside him provoked this
perverse need to press at Noah about his date; he wouldn't like hearing
the details. His entire body felt as if it wanted to snap, but he couldn't
stop. "Maybe you don't think I'm mature enough to handle what you
did with Ram, but I am. I can take more than you think I can. Treat me
like an adult you trust and respect, not a little kid."

"Christ, Zane." Noah went from ghost-white to ruddy-red, and his
jaw started to clench with visible rigidity. "You're way out of line with this."

Desperation and newly found desires shoved their way through
everything practical and sane inside Zane. "Just because I've never had
sex doesn't mean I can't listen or talk to you about what you've done
with another man."

"Zane," Noah cut in, his stare now flashing with nearly black fire.
"Stop pushing me."

"Why?" Blood rushed with ridiculous speed through Zane's veins,
and he'd never felt more alive than he did in this moment with Noah. "I
was there for you with your father, and we've talked about your kids, and
even your ex. I know so much about you, and I swear you know more
about me than any other human being on this earth, yet you won't even
tell me a single thing about your dates with Ramsay." Zane's breath came
heavily, making his chest heave, but he couldn't lift a leg to move or walk
away. "You won't even tell me something as simple as whether or not you
like Ram. But I already know that you must," Zane's throat burned with
that knowledge, "because I saw you coming home Sunday morning, and
you wouldn't have spent the night with someone if you didn't care about
him very much. Or maybe --" Zane suddenly snapped his lips closed.

The mere thought, what he'd almost spoken, ripped out Zane's gut, and he had to stop. *But I have to know.* Forcing his head up, and sound into his voice, he said, "Or maybe you're already in love with him, and that's why you were with him all night."

"Jesus, Zane." Fiery as hell now, Noah bit off a bevy of colorful curses. Looking at Zane through a narrowed stare, he added in a clipped tone, "I didn't fuck Ramsay. He didn't fuck me. We didn't fucking do anything! All right?"

Zane's mouth gaped. He snapped it shut, but then parted his lips twice more before he could respond. "But…"

Noah's nostrils flared, and he spat out, "But, nothing. We didn't screw each other. We talked." A grating chuckle escaped Noah. "Or rather, I drank and talked, and he listened."

The air whooshed out of Zane's lungs. "Oh." *What?* Somehow this confession -- Noah admitting that he'd opened up to someone else -- stabbed through Zane worse than imagining him and Ram having sex. "If something was bothering you so much," Zane hated the betrayal of his voice cracking, but God, he didn't like this turn of events at all, "why wouldn't you talk to me about it?"

Noah's pupils shrank to pinpoints, and he reared. Spinning away, he grabbed one of his tools with jerky movements. "We have to get back to work." More rust than normal coated his order.

More than Noah's voice, the stiff lines of his back and the agitated way he tried to spread grout on the wall snaked into Zane's system and guided him on pure instinct. "No, Noah." This time, Zane didn't fight the beckoning need to touch this man. He put his hand on Noah's beautiful back, and it felt as if the man's very essence sank into him through the firm, warm skin beneath the shirt. Zane moved his palm across the broad line of Noah's shoulders, knowing from the way his skin came alive with first contact, he could never go back. With every confusing feeling for this man simmering at the surface, Zane waded even deeper into the heat. "I want to know why."

Zane ran his hand down the line of Noah's spine, and Noah couldn't control the shudder that racked through him. *Jesus. Another minute and I'm going to be rock hard.*

His voice so fucking strained, Noah confessed, "You're killing me here, man."

"Look at me." Zane's voice, the feel of his breath caressing Noah's nape, and his palm branding Noah through his T-shirt, all pushed at the needs Noah had been fighting from the moment he'd met this man. Zane then slipped his hand to Noah's hip, where Noah could picture Zane holding him as they fucked, and the avalanche of wanting came crashing down on Noah in a maelstrom. Zane pushed once more. "Tell me why you didn't come and talk to me."

With a fast turn, Noah found himself right in Zane's face. Too close to ignore. He said in a viciously soft tone, "Because I was goddamn talking about you! Okay?" Noah twisted his hand in Zane's shirt and pushed him away. "You. We were talking about you."

Rather than take the hint, Zane curled his hand around the fist Noah had bunched in his shirt and kept them connected in another way. "About what?" The way he squeezed his fingers around Noah's hand implored in a way that hammered straight through the hard shell protecting Noah's deepest desires. Leaning his weight against the connection, his eyes so fucking beautiful, Zane said, "Tell me."

Noah snaked his hand around Zane's neck and yanked him in close. There was hardly enough room for a sliver of paper to fit between their bodies. "We talked about how fucking much I want you, Zane." Noah could barely breathe through the pounding in his heart. "God help me," he searched every inch of Zane's face, memorizing, worshipping, "but I fucking ache to be with you more and more every day we're together." Noah then dipped down, the pull too strong to ignore. Just as he got dangerously close to Zane's lips, so goddamn eager to take a taste, their location, and whose mouth he was about to take, rocketed him back into reality. Hard. "Shit." Noah scrambled away, angry at himself and afraid of the need coursing through him like the highest grade alcohol. "I knew seeing you every day would be a bad idea." He looked at Zane, the guy still as a statue, and everything he'd almost done made Noah stumble back against the shower wall. "I said I would never cross a line with you, and I meant it. I --"

Zane rushed forward and slammed his hand over Noah's mouth. His stare, so very steady, bore a hole through Noah, straight to his heart. As Zane let go, he curled his hand around Noah's nape and drew him down. "Cross the line, Noah. I want you to." He lifted to his toes, pressed their foreheads together, and whispered against Noah's lips, "Please."

No. Noah's heart leaped into his throat, and his cock reared to full staff faster than it ever had before. Terror raced through him, and his hands shook like hell. *This can't be real.* He looked into Zane's eyes; he parted his lips to speak, needing something more, but nothing came out. The question must have vibrated through every element of his being, though, because Zane nodded, his forehead still attached to Noah's, and softly said, "Yes."

Drowning too fast to get out of the water, too needful of a drink to feed his thirsty soul, Noah groaned and slipped completely under the tide. He slashed his lips across Zane's and kissed him with a voraciousness that had no equal in his life. *Oh Christ. Too fucking good.* Losing himself, Noah crushed and bit and licked at Zane's mouth, too hungry, too rough, but unable to retreat. Just as Noah licked deep, tasting the honey-sweetness that was Zane's flavor, Zane moaned in response, sank every bit of his weight against Noah, and tentatively began kissing Noah back. On the inside, Noah cried out with joy. Zane pushed in closer, making them both stumble into the shower wall, and Zane took his first lick into Noah's mouth.

Oh fuck, yes. Zane flicked his tongue against Noah's again, and Noah went up in flames. He wrapped his arms around Zane and jerked them flush together, desperate for crushing, full body contact. As Noah took Zane's mouth, trembling every time Zane stole a taste of him too, he ran his hands all up and down Zane's sleek back, reveling in the hot flesh warming his palms through the thin T-shirt Zane wore. Noah wanted skin against skin, though, and cursed the layer of fabric that kept his hands off Zane's tight body. Pushing his hands under Zane's shirt, Noah shoved at the material, hating that getting the T-shirt off meant breaking their kiss, but too desperate for Zane's skin to let him keep his shirt on. While he was at it, in a frantic tear, Noah ripped his shirt off too and tossed it to the floor.

Breathing heavily, his sight foggy with desire, Noah stared at Zane, glorying in his bare chest and flat, hard stomach. While intellectually Noah knew he'd seen Zane shirtless before, in his gut, this time it was different. The sight of all that firm male flesh -- with a bit of a tan now -- rushed blood to Noah's cock and balls, but this time he didn't have to hide it. Zane studied Noah in return, with equal brightness illuminating his blue eyes, and that open perusal only made Noah's dick stiffer. Noah ran his hand along his rigid-as-hell shaft, trying to adjust himself in his jeans. As Zane's focus dropped, following Noah's hand, Zane sucked in an audible breath. Zane pushed at the waist of his shorts, and the very tip of his erection emerged from the waistband. *Shit.* Noah's nostrils flared; he was certain he could smell Zane's arousal.

Both men jerked back up to eye contact, and the heat arcing between them had each flying at the other again. Their lips met with searing contact, and Noah grabbed hold of Zane's hair to tilt the angle of his head for deeper access. He ate his way into Zane's mouth, and the man's taste mainlined sugar straight into Noah's bloodstream. The need to dominate coursed through Noah unchecked, and he muttered an apology against Zane's lips for his roughness. His total possession of Zane's mouth limited Zane's ability to reciprocate and taste in return, but Noah did not know how to stop.

With a tight, high moan, Zane pushed at the thin levels of Noah's control in another way. He put his hands on Noah's stomach, causing the flesh there to quiver, and then worked his way up Noah's chest, down his arms, to around his back. Zane instigated the lightest glide of fingertips against the small of Noah's back, and Noah felt the soft contact as if Zane had done the same to his cock. Zane edged those fingers into the seam of Noah's jeans, touched the cleft of his ass, and Noah closed his eyes and quaked where he stood.

Oh fuck. As Noah went statue-still, Zane rubbed against Noah and took his chance to lick his way past Noah's lips. He pecked small kisses everywhere, and then went deeper with sweet, tentative darts of his tongue, learning Noah's mouth in a way Noah had never imagined Zane ever would. *Shit.* Noah scraped his lips across Zane's in return, then did it again, and again, until he needed with such desperation he pushed his way inside for another full taste. With a throaty little noise, Zane grabbed hold of Noah's hips, holding him, and rocked their cocks together, creating the most excruciatingly wonderful sensation Noah had ever experienced.

So fucking hard. Noah needed to fuck Zane. Now. In a flash, he assessed the layout of the bathroom. Noah saw himself bending Zane over the sink and jamming into the man's wonderful ass from behind, rutting so deeply into Zane's body that he took them right up onto the counter, where he would trap Zane against the mirror for the full brunt of his thrusts. Then, Noah would take Zane to the floor, onto his back, and spread him wide open for the full pounding of Noah's cock. Noah's roar of pleasure at completion would be so great he'd send every goddamn neighbor on the block running to see what was going on.

Still attached to Zane, Noah shoved, frantically guiding them both out of the shower stall. So out of control, Noah pushed Zane over a box of tiles and sent the man careening toward the glass. Yanking on Zane's arm, Noah pulled him back mere inches before he would have crashed into the glass wall of the stall. Noah's heart lurched into his throat. At the same time, a thousand other pieces of reality rushed at him like oncoming race cars: where he was, what he'd been doing, and who he'd been about to do it with. Everything penetrated Noah's brain at once. The fog cleared. As Noah looked at Zane, other truths bore down on Noah too, weighing him down with shame, embarrassment … and debilitating hurt.

Lava still rushed through Noah's veins, and his prick still raged hard enough to snap off like glass, but with his face burning for an entirely different reason now, he grabbed Zane's shirt off the floor and thrust it at the younger man. "Here." Noah grabbed his own too. "Put your shirt on," he ordered, as he did the same.

Open confusion mapped Zane's handsome face. "What?" He struggled into a T-shirt that clung to every sleek line roping his torso. "Why did you stop?"

Every suppressed need in Noah's body pushed at him, tried to move him a step closer to Zane and drag the man back into his arms. But beyond the fact that they were in a workplace, and that Noah had violated professional boundaries -- not to mention that the homeowner could have come home and walked in on them -- one other fact seared itself into Noah's brain and heart now more than any other. "We can't do this. You're straight, Zane." Exposed vulnerability roughened Noah's voice. "When I told you I was gay, you said you were straight."

Pushing his hands through his hair, Zane then clasped his fingers behind his neck. "I know. I thought I was. But I've never done anything, with anyone, so maybe I'm not. Maybe I was just asleep inside until you came along. God, Noah." Zane closed the gap between them and tugged on Noah's shirt, right against his belly. "You've woken me up big-time. Forget that I've never felt this way about another man; I've never felt it for a girl or a woman either."

Noah dropped his weight back against the shower wall, uncaring that he'd have to repair all the work he'd just spent an hour doing. His gaze on Zane, the heels of his hands digging into his forehead, Noah waged an internal battle. "Christ, you just admitted again that you don't have any experience." Bleak sadness filled Noah's chest, making the muscles there squeeze. "You're so young, and you're grateful to me for helping you."

"No," Zane responded, lightning fast. The second he did, Noah raised both his brows, and Zane flushed with color. "Okay, fine. When I first starting thinking about you in this way -- thinking about kissing you, and thinking about your body so much -- I wondered if maybe it was only because you'd been so nice to me. But now, with the things I've been feeling for you, and the stuff I've been picturing us doing together, I don't believe it's happening because of gratitude anymore."

I don't believe... Three little words that each poked a tiny knife into Noah's heart. "But you're not sure," he said, his throat tightening. "And in the short time since I've rediscovered my sexuality, I've been crushed once already. I don't think I could bear it if you woke up one day in six months, with your feet under you and everything going right, and you decided you're straight after all."

Zane parted his lips, but just then the distinct sound of the front door squeaking as it opened made him close his mouth. The homeowner shouted, "I'm back! I have some sodas for you guys, if you're thirsty," and killed what little remained of Noah's erection. Zane's cock no longer peeked out of his shorts either.

With a sigh, and a scrub to his face, Noah said, "Let's just get as much work done as we can in the hour more I have you," Zane would leave then to take his siblings to their sitter and then head to his other job, "and shelve this conversation for another day, when we've both had some time to think."

Zane looked like he wanted to protest, but the homeowner entered the bathroom then, sodas in her hands, and took care of the debate for Noah. As most homeowners do, she stayed to chat after that, supervising while Zane and Noah worked, until well after Zane had to leave. Forget the chance for a private conversation; with the homeowner, neither got much of a word in edgewise, period. Noah didn't know whether to kiss her or strangle her.

Noah knew one thing: that he didn't know what the hell was the right thing to say or do when he and Zane met next. Noah had never been more confused.

Fuck.

CHAPTER 10

At four a.m. Noah gave up his battle to fall asleep. As he got up to take a piss, he wondered who in the hell he was trying to kid? Darkness saved him from having to face himself in the mirror when he washed his hands, but it didn't matter; he knew what he would see if he looked himself in the eyes: smoldering hunger for a much younger man.

Goddamnit, though. Noah's mind had not turned off for more than two minutes since kissing Zane fourteen hours ago. He still didn't know how to accept or believe that Zane really wanted him. But Christ, he'd repeatedly relived the feel of the man's mouth under his, and the euphoria of sliding his tongue against Zane's, to the wickedly insane sensation of their chests, stomachs, and cocks rubbing up against one another in a feverish desire to mate since the incident had happened.

Noah's balls pulled and his dick twitched in his flannel pajama bottoms -- his body reminding him once again that it hated Noah's brain for the decision it had made to put a halt to the natural progression of the make-out session with Zane. With a private little snarl at himself, Noah shuffled to the kitchen, the hardwood floor chilly beneath his bare feet.

Once he flipped on the lights and got the water for his coffee warming, Noah moved to plop down on the couch but bounced back up just as fast as his ass hit the cushion. He'd been sitting and lying in bed for five hours now, and a restlessness shimmering inside him wouldn't let him stay still. *You probably could have slept for eight hours straight if you'd dragged Zane home and spent the afternoon fucking him.*

With a groan, and another swell of need in his shaft, Noah softly cursed himself while tapping his forehead against the wall, frustration filling his entire being. He wanted Zane with a power that defied any fantasy he'd experienced about other men from the time he'd understood his attraction to the same sex. At the same time, Noah not only knew next to nothing about having sex with another male, he now had to throw in the fact that Zane apparently didn't have any experience at all, period. Noah didn't have any idea how to move forward with that information, other than to feel wildly inadequate and intimidated. *Not that it matters, because you're not going to do anything with him anyway.*

But fuck, how Noah wanted to do everything with Zane. The guy already filled up every space in Noah's thoughts that wasn't occupied by his children and family. He wanted to do more than just have sex with Zane, though -- although getting him on his back in a bed and sliding his cock into that perfect ass did invade most of Noah's daydreams these days. Noah fantasized about doing a thousand other things with Zane too. Like, he wanted to get up early, eat breakfast, and then spend the day hiking in these mountains with the guy. He wanted to slowly take Zane against a tree with the sounds of birds and bugs chirping all around them as they shouted at completion. He wanted to come back to the cabin, lie on the couch together, and figure out what kind of movies they liked, and if they could agree on the perfect one to watch to cap off the day. Every part of Noah's dream looked and sounded perfect, but the further he let those thoughts take him, fear would then creep in, and his heart would start to race as he wondered where in that scenario Zane might tell him that he'd changed his mind and wanted to get some experience with women too.

Noah hated the hypocrisy bubbling in him over such a fear. Here he'd been married for twenty years and had two kids -- certainly less than perfect in owning his feelings and taking a stand on them -- but he didn't want the guy he fell for to have any doubts about being with him. He didn't want Zane wondering what it might be like to be intimate with a woman. When they went to bed Noah didn't want to see curiosity about another gender living in Zane's eyes. *I want him all for myself, and I want him to be sure about me.*

Beneath that feeling, though, what made Noah quake in his boots and break out in a sweat was the fear that he would risk his heart, let go with Zane, to learn down the line that Zane not only wondered about being with a woman, but such a curiosity would burn in him so greatly that he had to act on it. Right where he stood, Noah's legs turned to marshmallow and he had to grab a support beam in the center of his cabin so that he didn't fall to his knees. *I don't know if I can keep upright through another loss.*

Noah's father's rejection still cut him to the quick. Once again, Noah was hit with an avalanche of pain, making his chest band with nearly unbearable hurt. The confusion in Noah, having to face a decision of this magnitude about acting on his feelings for Zane, was exactly the kind of problem he would have taken to his father, trusting that the man's linear, lawyer's mind would help him sort out the facts from the fear. *He always used to help me see the truth.*

A fisting tightness clutched Noah's heart, and a terrible lump clogged his throat. Right then, footsteps thudded against his steps. A moment later, a knock reverberated through his home.

"Noah." Zane's muffled, yet sexy voice reached through the wood and made Noah tremble. "I need to talk to you."

In three steps, Noah was at the door. He ripped it open, and the sight of Zane, so disheveled in a T-shirt, zip-up sweater, rumpled jeans, and flip-flops, worked more potently on Noah than a cover model in a three-piece suit.

An amber-colored porch light barely cut the darkness outside. "What are you doing here?" Noah glanced over his shoulder to a clock on his cabin wall. "It's four-twenty-two in the morning."

With a shrug, Zane shoved his hands into his pockets. "I wasn't asleep. When I saw your lights go on, I decided to come see you. I've been stuck thinking over and over what happened today -- yesterday, I guess now -- and I had a few things I needed to say." Zane's breath came unsteadily, and he switched to rubbing his palms against his jeans, but he kept his head up and looked Noah in the eyes. "I might not have any practical experience with other people, with romance or sex, but that doesn't mean what I'm feeling or how much I wanted to kiss you is any less real for me than it is for you. I like you, Noah." A smile came from Zane then; a tremulous, sweet as hell one. "I like you in a way I've never liked another soul on this earth. And God," Zane brushed his fingertips up Noah's belly to his chest, "I am so attracted to you."

Sucking in a gasp of air, Noah covered Zane's hand, bringing it to a stop. "Zane…"

"Let me just say this one other thing, because it's important." Zane's fist, curled and trapped under Noah's palm, scraped a slow pattern against Noah's chest, right over his heart. He looked up at Noah, and nothing but pure, unfettered light showed in his blue, blue eyes. "You said you'd already been crushed once since you came out, and you didn't think you could handle it happening again. I want something to happen between us, Noah." Once again a nervous, sweet-as-all-get-out smile lifted Zane's lips for the briefest second. "But even if you say no, and nothing ever does, I need you to know I would never do anything to hurt you." Zane sucked in an unsteady breath, and his voice trembled as he added, "I think if I did, and I knew it, it would break me. I just need you to understand exactly how much I already care about you. I would never do anything to bring you harm.

"Okay." Zane finally exhaled, and that smile, so fucking full of clear nervousness, appeared once more. "You can say whatever you wanted to now."

Every light touch of Zane's hand against Noah's bare chest, and every second he remained locked on Noah without wavering -- while Noah could see fear coursing through him -- pushed against Noah's own trepidation and ideas for what he needed in a relationship with another man. Noah already respected Zane more than he'd imagined possible. And God knew he desired the man more than he'd ever thought he could crave another human being.

Zane slid his other hand up Noah's stomach and chest, over his shoulder, as if he'd been fantasizing about touching another man his whole life, and Noah slipped a little deeper under the spell that was Zane Halliday.

As Zane stepped closer, he curled his hand around Noah's neck. "Noah?"

Christ. The man's fingers brushed against Noah's nape, and blood rushed straight to Noah's cock. Zane then rubbed his palm down Noah's chest and grazed his nipple.

With a shudder, on pure emotion, Noah said roughly, "I don't really want to talk right now."

Zane lifted up on his tiptoes and whispered against Noah's mouth, "Then don't."

Shit. He's intoxicating. Wise or not, impulsive or not, Noah let himself slip under the tide. His body raged to mate, and it only wanted this one young man. For the first time, not knowing where the hell this move would take him in his life, Noah grabbed Zane, crushed his mouth down on the other man's, and lost himself in his feelings for another man.

The moment Noah slammed his mouth against Zane's, Zane cried out and flung himself against Noah, making them both stumble a few steps into the cabin. Zane had spent every minute working at the restaurant last night thinking about Noah's kiss and imagining where it could have gone if they hadn't been at work. Then after he'd gotten his brother and sister organized for the morning, and then into bed, he'd paced the cabin with a picture of Noah in his head. The sensation of the bigger man's mouth seared against his remained on Zane's lips too, and Zane knew for certain that was how a kiss should taste between two people who were meant to be together. That kind of power and passion ... Zane didn't have to kiss a dozen other people to know it wouldn't be like that with anyone else. *Not even close.*

When Zane had seen the lights go on in Noah's cabin, he hadn't even thought twice. After throwing on clothes and grabbing a handful of things he needed, he'd run straight to Noah. If nothing else, Zane couldn't bear for this kind, sexy man to ever believe Zane would hurt him. *Not for the world.*

Right then Noah shoved Zane against the wall, next to the open door, and plastered his body to Zane's, sandwiching Zane in the most amazing way. Zane forgot about anything but living in this moment, right now, with Noah. Pressure surged against Zane's jaw, and Zane reveled in the force Noah used to push his way inside for a deeper kiss.

Zane might even have a thumb-shaped bruise on his face later today, but he didn't care. Zane tangled his tongue with Noah's the moment the man thrust his inside, clumsily on his part for sure, but full of sincere eagerness. Noah groaned and rubbed himself harder against Zane, clearly pleased, and Zane suddenly didn't care about his inexperience anymore.

"Please." Zane pecked kisses all over Noah's face and struggled with the zipper to his sweater. "Help me get my clothes off." He cursed the damn zipper and his frantic fingers. "I want to be naked with you."

Noah's pupils flared. Rather than help Zane get the stubborn clasp, he tore the sweater and T-shirt over Zane's head and threw them aside. They went at each other again in a shot, lips clinging, tongues flicking. Zane kicked off his flip-flops and Noah shoved his hands down to get at Zane's jeans.

Instead of tearing at the snap and zipper, Noah chuckled and brought their foreheads to rest against one another. "What the heck is all of this?" He came up with a walkie-talkie and gum in one hand and a mini-flashlight and cell phone in the other.

Heat burned through Zane's cheeks. "I needed the flashlight to see in the dark, and the cell phone and walkie-talkie are in case Hailey or Duncan needs me. I left a note on their nightstand, my pillow, and the bathroom door in case one of them wakes up. We started using walkies when I needed to work in the cabin and they wanted to explore around outside."

Noah put those three things on a catchall table, then, stealing another kiss from Zane, he whispered, "The walkies are a good idea."

Zane blushed an even deeper red. "Thank you."

"And what about the gum?" Noah held up the green packet.

Oh God. If he'd been red before, now Zane went up in flames. *Shoot.* Wishing like hell he was just a bit smoother at all of this, Zane stubbornly kept his chin high. "I was hoping you would want to kiss me, so I wanted to have nice, minty breath." Nerves and honesty had Zane blurting, "I spit out what I chewed and stuck it under your porch railing before I knocked."

Noah barked with laughter, and the sound, and the mirth in his eyes, lit up the whole room. "Just this once," Noah murmured as he descended again, "I'll forgive you for littering on my property."

"Thank y --" Noah claimed Zane's mouth right then, deep and hard and full of aggression, and with a moan Zane shut up.

Zane clung to Noah, sinking into the man's hot flesh as Noah invaded his mouth. Eagerly parting his lips, Zane accepted the thrust of Noah's tongue, still shocked, but loving the voraciousness with which Noah kissed. In every movie or TV show Zane had ever watched, or even every real couple he'd observed with envy, Zane never could have dreamed that kissing could feel like this. One part of Zane wanted to let Noah ravage his mouth, leaving Zane raw and swollen from Noah's passion. Yet with an equally powerful need, Zane flung himself even harder against Noah, desperate to kiss him back and get so close their bodies would meld into one entity.

Breathing heavily, Zane let Noah own his mouth, for the moment, and instead obeyed the tingling firing in his palms. *I need to touch him everywhere.* Zane ran his hands all over Noah's stomach and chest, loving the feel of the man's hot, firm flesh. When that wasn't enough, Zane pushed his hands around to learn every hard, sinewy line of Noah's strong back. Good God, Noah's skin was burning hot and rock solid, not an ounce of give anywhere. Every square inch of Noah that Zane touched spurred the fiery need already lit inside him and sparked a full-fledged wildfire. Zane had never understood the raging need to touch another person everywhere, but he suddenly knew that if he didn't get his hands on Noah's ass and cock he would expire on the spot.

Just then, just as Zane slipped the very tips of his fingers into the waistband of Noah's flannel pajama bottoms, Noah bit Zane's lips and then pulled a few inches away. He visibly struggled to regain his breath, and his eyes burned the deepest, hottest espresso Zane had ever seen. "You're so beautiful." Noah brushed his fingers against Zane's cheek and mouth, and the sight of such big, rough hands trembling with the slight contact speared straight to Zane's heart. His gaze too bright, Noah pulled his hand away and hid it behind his back. "I've never desired someone so much that it makes me shake the way I do with you."

Zane took Noah's forearm and pulled his hand out of hiding. "I've never had such wet dreams and daydreams about being with a person all the time as I have since I met you." More huskiness than Zane had ever heard filled his voice. "I want you, Noah." Zane's heart had never raced so fast. He'd also never been so goddamn hard either. Reaching out, he put his hand on the tie holding up Noah's flannel bottoms, dangerously close to the visible line of the man's erection. "I'm not so naive that I don't understand what that means." Zane let the edge of his pinkie graze the head of Noah's cock, and they both gasped. Still, his throat tight, Zane looked Noah in the eyes and admitted, "I've come more than once on the fantasy of taking you inside me." Zane pulled on the string and let Noah's pajama bottoms fall to the floor. "I'm not afraid of your cock."

Noah's shaft reared, and the head reached well past his belly button. Just as a pearl of seed pumped out from the slit, Noah muttered, "Fuck," and stole a fast, hard kiss, sensitizing Zane's lips even more. "You have no idea what your sweet sexiness does to me." Noah's stare seared through Zane. He yanked at the snap and zipper holding Zane's jeans in place. "But you will." With that, Noah shoved Zane's jeans down to his knees and fused their bodies together once more.

Oh God. Oh shit. Zane shouted, right into Noah's mouth, as his bare cock touched Noah's for the first time. *Fucking shit.* Nearly crawling straight out of his skin with first contact, Zane wrapped his arms around Noah, holding on for dear life, and he rubbed and rubbed and rubbed his dick against Noah's. Nothing had ever felt as perfect or right as his rigid flesh touching Noah's hot body.

"Christ, Zane…" Forehead to forehead, Noah pinned Zane to the wall, his stare a hazy blur of need. He curled his big hands around Zane's hips, then slid down to cup his ass, and he used the strength in his hold to grind their dicks together even more. His lips parted, Noah looked almost frightened. "Feels so fucking good…" His fingers flexed deep into Zane's ass cheeks, surely bruising the flesh.

Uncaring of marks left on his body, Zane, on his tiptoes, bit Noah's lower lip, desperate for a way to contain the havoc Noah wreaked in his body. Zane churned his hips repeatedly, unable to stop, and moaned with each slide of hard cock against hard cock, something he'd never understood could feel this good. "Noah…" Hardly able to breathe, Zane squeaked high with his need. "Oh God…" With another rough grind of their pricks, a fast coiling pull twisted from Zane's nuts up to his spine and belly. Frightened by the intensity of the pleasure coursing through him, Zane jerked his gaze up to Noah's as the feelings coalesced into a tight ball of pure joy low in his belly. "It's too much."

Noah's entire frame jolted, and he crushed his fingers into Zane's buttocks. "Let me see it." His breathing was ragged, and the brown in his eyes had turned nearly black. "Let me see you come." He slid one hand around and stroked the length of Zane's cock.

Zane cried out, the unfathomable pleasure of someone else's hand wrapped around his shaft too much to bear. As orgasm raced through him with too much speed, he grabbed hold of Noah's cock too and squeezed. With Noah's hoarse shout in response, Zane jerked up to eye contact with the handsomest person he'd ever laid eyes on. Zane lost himself a split second before Noah did; he shot a milky line of cum high between their bodies, like a fire hydrant blowing its safety cap. Before Zane's first load sprayed ejaculate on their chests, Noah came too, spurting thick white seed right onto Zane's bare stomach. With each seizing of Noah's frame, he continued to shower Zane with his hot release. *Oh my.* Zane shivered as proof of Noah's desire coated his stomach. *He is amazing.*

Rather than his sexual need waning upon coming, Zane only wanted more. Seeing Noah lose it, touching his penis, and feeling the man's cum on his flesh, made Zane rock hard again in an instant, no dwindling to his cock at all. Zane slid his hand along Noah's length, this newfound attraction making him bold, and Noah clenched his jaw and went stiff as a spike again too.

Noah exhaled and braced himself against the wall in a push-up stance, with Zane trapped between his arms. "I want you so much," Noah said. He scraped his mouth against Zane's, and coal embers burned in his eyes. "I've never craved another body the way I do yours. But I --"

Zane pressed his lips to Noah's, smashing their mouths together for a moment, and effectively shut him up. God, Zane already loved the hardness of Noah's strong lips, but he forced himself to put a sliver of space between them once more. "I want you too. I think you should be able to tell that by now." Zane took Noah's strong hands and ran them all over his body, desperate for this man's rough hands on him. When Noah took over, his coarse fingertips abraded Zane's flesh with a hunger Zane could feel, and Zane hummed and vibrated. "Kiss me, Noah,"

Zane begged. Noah dug his fingers into Zane's hips in response, and Zane's breath caught. As Zane's need grew, he added, "Do everything you've wanted to; things I don't have to have done before to know I want too." Zane's ass passage clenched as he said that, proving his body was already all-in for this new ride.

Noah pressed his head to Zane's. Fused together, his stare glued to Zane's, Noah said in a raw tone, "You can't possibly understand even half of what I want with you."

"Then show me." Full of newly unleashed emotions, Zane ran his hands up Noah's thickly muscled arms and held onto his shoulders to keep them close. "You've only ever made me feel safe with you. Nothing you desire is going to make that change for me." The trajectory of their fast friendship, to the lovers they were now about to become, sped through Zane's mind and made his voice tight. "I don't think it's even possible with an honorable man like you."

"Fuck." Pure exposed life flared in Noah's eyes. He plastered himself to Zane and said, "I don't deserve what you think of me, but I'm not going to fight you anymore." With that, he captured Zane's mouth with his and sank into a deep, luscious kiss.

Zane had one thought before he succumbed to pure emotion: *Yes.*

Fucking shit. Noah didn't know how to stop shaking -- visible proof of how much he wanted Zane in every way. For the moment, he stopped trying to hide his desires. Zane was kissing him back, without a lot of finesse, but Christ, with a ton of enthusiasm, and nothing had ever turned Noah on more. *I have to know everything about him. Right now.*

Noah started with a fast taste of Zane's flesh. He bit Zane's lips and nipped at his tongue, starving to keep kissing him, but even more eager to learn about the rest of his body. Reluctantly, after one more quick lick into the minty heat of Zane's mouth, Noah broke the kiss. Breathing too heavily, but unable to rein himself in, Noah locked onto Zane's true-blue wild stare. "I want your cock."

Between them, Zane's penis jumped and jammed into Noah's stomach. Zane bit his lip and replied, "Yes, please."

Noah couldn't believe it, but he actually chuckled. He stole another kiss; he couldn't help himself. "Glad you and your dick approve." Zane's shaft pushed between their bellies again, leaving new pre-ejaculate on Noah's flesh. Hunger returned to Noah in full force.

Forgoing his plan to kiss every inch of Zane's shoulders, chest, and stomach on his journey to the man's cock -- at least for this round of mating -- Noah instead groaned against Zane's throat and licked a line straight down the center of his torso. Hot firm flesh singed Noah's tongue, and he loved the quiver that ran through Zane's body when he licked down to the man's soft thatch of fur. On another day Noah might have savored the taste of his release on Zane's belly but right now the need coursing through him was too great to ignore. It had been more than twenty years since he'd had another man's cock in his mouth. Yet to Noah, because this was Zane, and because he already cared so damned much, this was like the first time all over again.

Zane's long slender shaft, so fucking red and hard with his arousal, called to Noah in a siren's voice he could not ignore. Not even bothering to touch Zane first, with a low, needful moan, Noah parted his lips and went down on half of Zane's prick in one shot. *Oh Christ. Yes.* Velvety smooth, firm, scorching penis filled Noah's mouth; a slightly salty essence sparked on his taste buds, and Noah moaned around the invasion like a starving man getting his first meal in years. Zane bucked and cried out above him. He buried his hand in Noah's hair, holding on tight, and Noah knew he'd pleased Zane as much as he had himself. Grabbing onto Zane's hips, Noah went to town suctioning his cheeks, moving up and down Zane's shaft with deep pulls, and made a feast out of Zane's cock.

It's so fucking good. Saliva filled Noah's mouth easily, the moisture helping him in his endeavor to give Zane enough pleasure to make the man's head blow off his neck. With one hard drag up Zane's shaft, Noah then teased the tip of his tongue around the sensitive head and across the leaking slit. Zane shouted and shuddered so deeply in response that he lost his legs and slid down the wall. Noah stayed with him, right to the floor. After quickly shucking Zane's jeans the rest of the way off, Noah filled the space between Zane's legs; the man spread his thighs wide for more of what Noah had to offer.

Noah went down on Zane as far as he could. Zane shoved his hands above his head, bracing himself on a large wooden sculpture in the corner of the entryway. "Oh God ... Noah..." As Noah captured Zane's balls and gave the high, tight orbs a good tug, Zane bit his lip and shot his hips off the floor. "Noah, shit, that's so good." Pearl after pearl of seed beaded in Zane's slit, only for Noah to lap them up as fast as Zane's body created the natural lubricant. "You're gonna make me come again."

Zane's entire body was flushed red with his desire. The man couldn't remain still, and nothing pleased Noah more. Each suck on Zane's cock -- feeling that hard, swollen shaft take ownership of his mouth -- only made Noah's own dick stiffer. Zane's verbal and physical response only added tinder to the fire already blazing within Noah, pushing him to do more.

Quickly Noah spit Zane's cock from his mouth, pushed down, and flicked his tongue over his taint. He licked and pressed against that thin triangle of skin, knowing what lay on the other side, and Zane cried out with sheer delight.

Spurred to do more, faster, wanting a complete loss of Zane's control, Noah moved up to lick the man's lightly furred sac. Zane jerked and churned his hips, as if he couldn't decide if he wanted more or to get away. Noah stayed with every stilted move; he sucked Zane's balls past his lips, moaning around each orb as it filled his mouth. Noah's dick pushed with full rigidity against his stomach, and he knew he'd never loved doing anything sexual more in his life than what he did to Zane right now.

Voracious as hell, Noah went to shove Zane's thighs high and wide, eager for his ass, but right then Zane yanked on Noah's hair and groaned, "Oh God ... I'm coming, I'm coming..." and changed Noah's course in a flash. Noah shifted to stuff Zane's cock back into his mouth; he managed to part his lips around the tip just in time to feel Zane's shaft thicken and swell. Then, just like that, Zane came again. As Zane's shout of completion bounced off every wall in Noah's cabin, he spurted deep inside Noah's mouth. Jet after jet of acrid, salty, wonderful seed spilled onto Noah's tongue, filling his mouth. With every taste, with every drop of Zane's cum Noah eagerly swallowed down, Noah slipped to an even rawer, needier place for this man.

Christ almighty. Noah was so fucking hard, and his blood raced so goddamn fast he knew if he didn't fuck Zane he would explode all over his cabin. *I need to make him mine. Now.* In one shot, Noah spit Zane's dick from his mouth and flipped the man over onto his stomach. *Holy hell.* Noah feasted his eyes upon the sweetly rounded, perfect hills of Zane's ass. *That is a thing of rare beauty.* Noah had never seen such a thing of pert perfection that was somehow masculine as hell, as well as seductively, innocently alluring, but Zane's amazing ass was all of that and more.

Unable to keep his hands off, Noah smacked each firm globe of flesh, pinking the pale skin, and then quickly pressed his thumb into the crack to finger Zane's hidden bud. Zane whimpered softly in response, and his ass cheeks clenched. *Fuck.* Swallowing thickly, Noah nudged at Zane's hole again. The tight, striated muscle contracted and quivered against Noah's touch, as if shying away, and Noah had to know more. Using the heels of his hands, Noah parted Zane's cheeks and revealed the tiniest, goddamn pinkest, prettiest asshole he'd ever seen. With another utterance of the Lord's name in vain, because Christ, this man's body seemed to call for it, Noah dipped down and licked the starry bud. He immediately groaned with need and tasted Zane's pucker again.

Zane instantly expelled a high, breathy "Noah," in response and pushed his buttocks higher in the air. He pressed his cheek against the wooden sculpture in front of him, wrapped his arms around its considerable width, and looked over his shoulder, right into Noah's eyes. His eyes beyond sparkling bright, Zane whispered, "Please, Noah. Fuck me."

Holy mother. Noah dived in again, taking a moment to lick and suck at Zane's pucker, getting the area nice and wet with saliva. With every dart of Noah's tongue, Zane made a little keening noise and pushed his ass back into Noah's face. Each small grinding move made Noah think he could spend all day eating this man's ass enough to make him come just from that. But Noah's cock raged much too hard to ignore, and he had a guy he liked more than a little bit bent over, begging for a fucking.

After one more lick to Zane's hole, Noah slapped the man's buttocks a few more times, and then quickly lined up his middle finger with Zane's bud. Just as Noah rubbed at the star pattern, loving the jump in the muscle and gasp of breath from Zane, the walkie-talkie on the side table crackled to life, the sound so jarring it was like a machine gun going off and blowing up the room.

Faster than he'd ever moved in his life, Noah scrambled in a crabwalk all the way across the floor, to the wall by the door, and slammed the door closed, ridiculously fearful the entire town might have been able to see through the wall to what he and Zane had been doing. *Fuck. Fuck. Fuck. Fuck. Fuck.* Noah leaned against the wall, his heart racing even faster than when he'd been making out with Zane a minute ago. What had he been thinking? If one of Zane's siblings -- that's who it had to be on the walkie-talkie -- had checked in even five minutes later, Noah might have already had his dick in Zane's ass, fucking him, only to get the harsh reality of that interruption.

Zane pushed to his feet, a little unsteadily, still as naked and perfect as anything Noah had ever seen. He grabbed the walkie-talkie as Duncan's cracking adolescent voice came through the device with, "Zane? Are you there?"

"I'm close by, Dunc," Zane answered. "I'm across the lake at Noah's. Is everything okay?"

Duncan replied, "Hailey woke up. She was calling for you like she does sometimes, but I told her everything was okay and to go back to sleep 'cause it's summer vacation now. She was okay and went back to sleep quick. Everything's cool now."

Before speaking again, Zane put the walkie-talkie down to scramble into his underwear and jeans. "Thanks for taking care of her, bud. I'll be home in a few minutes." Zane found Noah, still on the floor, and apologized with his eyes in a way that put a clamp on Noah's heart. "Okay?"

"I'm not a baby," Duncan said with impatience, and Noah recognized the tone as a petulant preteen who wanted to be eighteen already and treated like an adult. Noah had already been through that stage with both of his kids. "You don't have to come running back," Duncan added. "I just wanted you to know about Hailey."

Scratching through his mussed hair, Zane shook his head and looked toward the high, beamed ceiling. "I won't rush then. But I'll still be home within the hour." Moving across the floor, Zane opened the door Noah had just closed. "You can step outside and see me on Noah's porch if you need to. Okay?" He took one step outside.

"I don't need to," Duncan drawled out. "I keep telling you I'm not a little kid anymore."

His voice soft, Zane answered, "I'll be there anyway."

With Duncan's soft, "Okay. Bye," Noah suspected the boy wasn't quite the grown-up he wished he was in his young warrior's heart, and that he would peek out the window or door at least once to look for Zane.

"Bye," Zane said into the walkie-talkie, and then turned to find Noah in the cabin.

First, because he was still bare-ass naked, Noah got out of the line of the open doorway. He grabbed his pajama bottoms with one hand and Zane's tangled shirt and zipper sweater with the other. With a quick toss, he sent Zane his clothing. Zane caught his stuff, but as Noah went to put on his bottoms, Zane said, "Wait."

Noah jerked his stare up. "What?" His cock still raged against his belly, and it hurt like a motherfucker. Still, Noah ate up Zane with his eyes, even as he pointed toward the interior of his cabin. There was no way Duncan would be able to see him in this position, but Noah still said, "I really can't keep standing here like this, honey."

Zane suddenly beamed from within, as if someone had just gifted him with a new house, car, and a million dollars. "I like that. *Honey* feels nice to hear."

Holy mother. Pretty much every day, this guy made Noah feel like a Nordic god. "I like it too," Noah admitted, his tone way too gruff. "Been thinking of you with those kinds of words in my head for a while now."

Pink dotted Zane's cheeks, making him look younger and somehow even sexier. He glanced down to Noah's crotch, and the most innocent yet somehow sinful grin appeared. "Take care of that right here," he said, making eye contact again, "where I can see you."

Shit. Noah stumbled. "I can't." Fucking A, his voice croaked. With a fast glance at the open door, and then to Zane, Noah whispered, "Not now."

Zane leaned against the door frame, half in and half out of the cabin. "I'm the only one who can see and hear you. Come on." He openly looked at Noah's hard-on again. "You have to be more than a little uncomfortable."

"It doesn't matter." Even as Noah said that, he couldn't hold back a grin. When had this young man become so bold? It was heady to witness and have directed at him. Noah let the wadded-up pajama bottoms fall to the floor. He stroked just into the crease of his thigh to under his swollen sac. With a hiss, he said, "I've been unbearably hard for you before without getting the final result I wanted, and I managed to take care of it in private, on my own."

Zane's pupils flared. "Think about if we could have kept going. God, Noah." As Zane bit his lip, he briefly shifted his focus to the wooden sculpture and now cleared space. "I was on the floor there begging for you." He rested his shoulder and head against the door, but his bare toes curled against the treated porch flooring over and over again. Softly, he said, "I've never pushed my ass at somebody before and pleaded for them to fuck me."

As Noah stared back, he slowly dragged his hand up and down his shaft. "You have the sweetest ass in the world." With that admission, Noah recalled the small taste of that sweet hole he'd already had. He pulled harder on his dick, unable to hold back. "It's perfect in every way."

"You have the fucking biggest cock in the world," Zane replied, flicking between eye contact and Noah pulling on his dick.

"Not true," Noah said, surprise shocking a bark of laughter from him. His hand stilled. "You own the fact that you've never even seen any others."

Zane quirked a brow. "And how many asses have you seen to know mine is the best?"

Heating, Noah answered, "I've seen enough in porn over the last year to know yours is something special."

Once again, Zane flashed that sunbeam of a smile. "Flatterer."

Stone-cold sober, Noah shook his head. "Fact." *Christ.* Using an overhanded grip, Noah started working his dick from root to tip, driving every nerve ending in his penis into a frenzy. "You are something incredible to witness, Zane, and it's hard to keep my eyes off you."

Zane's hips jerked. "You're going to make me hard again." A visible twitch pushed against his jeans.

With the taste of Zane still on his tongue, Noah's mouth watered. "Your cock is something spectacular too." Needy now, Noah pulled on his balls while stroking his cock, his muscles tensing with renewed desire.

A pretty blue fog started to glaze Zane's stare. "That was my first blowjob, what you did to me just now. I never knew being in your mouth could feel like that. More than that, though," a soft huskiness took over Zane's voice, "every time you moaned you made me more excited."

"I liked what I was doing a hell of a lot." His attention fully on Zane, getting lost in every piece of the man, Noah produced bead upon bead upon bead of early seed; the early cum slicked his dick up all that was needed. He increased to rougher pulls under Zane's watchful stare. "I want to touch you and taste you everywhere." The slow burn in Noah's core intensified, and he slipped back to that place of unquenchable desire for this person. "I want into your ass, and I want your cock all the way down my throat, and I don't want to stop licking your body until I've memorized every little freckle or birthmark dotting your skin."

"Oh God, Noah." Now facing fully inside, Zane rubbed his cock through his jeans, and it felt as if he ate up Noah's naked body with his eyes. "Every time I see you without your shirt on I spend half the time we're together thinking about running my hands and lips all over your back and chest and arms."

"Go for it next time." Rubbing across his chest, wishing his hand was smoother so it felt more like Zane's, Noah tweaked his nipples and scraped at his flesh, his body tight with its need. His balls rolled in his sac, so fucking good it hurt; with each drag on his cock, Noah picked up speed, his world full of everything Zane now. "Tell me more," he ordered, his voice harsh.

"I want to do what you did to me too." Still fully clothed, Zane might as well been stripped bare, for Noah only saw the nakedness they'd shared a short while ago. "I want to get on my knees and smell you up close," Zane admitted, and Noah jerked, working his cock even harder.

Staring at Noah, Zane went on, "I've already felt those two veins that run up the underside of your cock with my fingers. Next time I want to lick along that line, and then I want to learn to get as much of you in my mouth as I can. I want to go up and down, sucking and sucking and sucking you, until you're so hard it feels like you might shatter. Then I want to get on my hands and knees, my ass in the air, begging, like we were before, and then I want you to take over. I want you to put your cockhead against my hole," Zane gasped and bit his lip, as if he could feel Noah doing that very thing right now, "and I want you to push and push and push, until" -- *Oh Jesus Christ, yes* -- Noah's prick burned with the speed with which he jerked himself off -- "your cock is inside me so deep and fully, digging and digging inside me, I don't know where you stop and I begin.

"Noah…" Zane's voice cracked, and his frame tensed from stem to stern. "Oh God, Noah…" Gazes locked, Zane's so glazed with desire that he reached back, as if he could feel Noah behind him, inside him. "You're fucking me…"

With a roar, Noah punched his hips forward, and release exploded through him. His cock, so fucking rigid, pointed straight north, and Noah shot a load that rained ejaculate high into the air, each jet coming so fast it was like one consecutive stream of milky white seed. Fat drops hit the floor while Noah continued to come, his focus entirely on Zane, and he swore the younger man shuddered and came right along with him.

Noah came hard and fast and long, with far more intensity than he had in forever; the fact that he could maintain his legs in the aftermath amazed him. Fuck, he could hardly breathe.

"Wow, Noah." Zane practically breathed Noah's name. "You don't even know what perfect is because you didn't see yourself just now." Sparks of blue diamonds lit his eyes. "You were beautiful."

Heat of a different kind burned Noah's cheeks and the tips of his ears. Still, he didn't dip his head or look away. "You entice me and tempt me and inspire me like nobody else." Cum dotted the floor all around Noah, and he blushed even more furiously.

Zane grinned. "Now you're back to flattery again."

"Just back to the facts, Mr. Halliday."

"God." Zane rolled his back against the door frame and looked toward the lake; a groan filled his tone. "I don't want to leave you yet."

"Will you stay for coffee?" The request, the need for more time with Zane, spilled from Noah unchecked. Quickly, though, he understood Zane's dilemma and rushed to add, "I know you have to head back soon, but we can sit on the porch for a little while, just in case Duncan or Hailey looks for you, and we can watch the sun rise together first."

That smile of Zane's grew bigger, and it brightened his whole damned demeanor. "There's nothing else I'd rather do."

"Go get comfortable." Zane's jeans remained stain free, so Noah figured that even if he had come again, he hadn't spilled enough seed to make him uncomfortable in his clothes. Noah, however, took one look at himself, remembered how goddamn stark naked he still was, and took a step deeper into his cabin. "I'll throw on some jeans, get us a couple cups of coffee, and meet you out there in a few."

Motherfucking Christ. Zane blew Noah a kiss before disappearing in the direction of the deck chairs. So hell, if Noah moved with record speed, and the coffee sloshed onto the counter in his effort to pour as fast as he could, then so be it. He would clean it, along with the ejaculate all over his floors, after Zane left.

Noah needed as much time with Zane, sitting on his porch at the man's side, just talking and spending time together, for as long as he could get before life intruded and separated them again.

CHAPTER 11

Oh my God, Noah. Yes. As Noah slid his fingers into the back of Zane's jeans to get at Zane's ass, Zane lifted up on his tiptoes and sank even deeper into Noah's kiss. A cool early morning breeze drifted from the lake and caressed Zane's heated flesh -- just not nearly enough to cool his desire for Noah Maitland. Five days' worth of stolen kisses and touches fueled Zane's need, and from the feel of titanium-hard cock pushing against his equally hard dick, Zane knew Noah felt the same.

With a low moan, Zane slashed his mouth across Noah's and swept his tongue inside, taking control in a way Noah usually maintained whenever they came together. Just as fast as Zane licked deeply, tasting orange juice and toothpaste, Noah shuddered, and he picked Zane up, right off the ground. Turning him, Noah shoved Zane against one of the cabin's support beams, bit and kissed at Zane's sensitized mouth, and regained complete control.

Oh please. Zane wrapped his legs around Noah's waist, squeezing his thighs and grinding his cock into Noah's bare belly, clumsily doing anything he could to get closer to this man's delicious heat. In response,

Noah groaned and ground his cock back at Zane just as hard. His fingers slipped into Zane's crack and moved on a shiver-worthy slide toward Zane's clenching pucker. Zane raged hard enough to spurt, but God, even though he knew it might hurt, he desperately wanted to come this time with Noah's cock in his ass. Even though Zane had yet to feel Noah inside him in even the smallest way, he knew this time not even Noah's finger would do.

Breathing heavily, Zane pressed kisses all over Noah's face and then put them nose to nose. "Noah…" He looked into bright, espresso-colored eyes and trembled at the depth of passion clouding Noah's stare. "Help me." His own snap and zipper already undone, Zane fumbled with Noah's jeans fastenings, sliding his legs from around Noah's waist as he did. "I need you." The second Zane got Noah's jeans and underwear down past his hips, the man's thick, steely pole rose and plastered itself to his flat belly. *Good God, that is insane.* Zane took Noah in hand -- *oh yes* -- and stroked his searing length. "I feel like I've been waiting for you forever."

Noah hissed with first contact, and Zane eagerly tugged on the man's cock again. Until Noah, Zane had never understood how much pleasure he could receive in watching someone he liked become aroused and needy. But over these last days, every time Noah moaned, twitched, shook, or grew ridiculously big and hard as a result of something Zane did, Zane became excited to touch Noah even more. With another firm tug on Noah's cock from Zane, Noah barked a hoarse noise. A fat bead of early cum appeared at his tip, and Zane suddenly knew what he wanted to try more than anything else.

Before that pearl could drop to the ground, Zane fell to his knees, in line with Noah's glorious penis. Locking in on Noah's heated stare from above, Zane darted out his tongue and licked across Noah's wide, weeping slit. Warm salty essence flooded Zane's taste buds, filling his system with base desires. Without thinking he leaned forward and licked all around the thick mushroom head of Noah's prick.

Noah bucked in front of Zane, and his haunches and stomach tightened visibly. "Shit, Zane." He grazed his fingers through Zane's hair, down his cheek, and Zane rubbed against that rough skin he'd so quickly come to love. "You have no fucking idea how much you stir me up."

With his lips pressed against the tip of this big man's cock, amazed at how perfect and right it felt to taste another man, Zane said, "Nobody has ever said such sweet things to me." Zane licked in a whorl again, loving the smell, feel, and taste of every hot inch of Noah's dick. "Nobody makes me feel special the way you do." Parting his lips, Zane then sucked Noah's cockhead fully into his mouth.

Noah swelled and reared against Zane's lips. "Jesus Christ, honey." It seemed a blender had cut Noah's words up into all jagged edges. "Suck me harder." Noah wrapped his hand around the thick base of his shaft and pushed forward hard. "Fucking take it all."

Just as Zane felt Noah slide deeper into his mouth, the sight of Noah's wrist, and the metal watch wrapped around the strong bone, penetrated Zane's brain. Real life came rushing back to Zane. *Shoot.* Before Zane could get a good taste of Noah, he spit Noah's cock out and shot to his feet. "Shoot. Shoot. Shoot." He fell backward, against the cabin's support beam, and struggled back into his pants.

"What?" His visage falling, Noah shoved his cock against his belly, covering it with his hand and forearm. "I'm sorry. I didn't mean to push."

At the sight of Noah, Zane's heart constricted terribly. "No." He rushed forward, planted a fast kiss on Noah's wonderfully firm lips, and then went back to doing up his clothes. "It's okay; it's not that." As always, they ran out of alone time far too fast. "I saw your watch and the time. I'm already fifteen minutes behind schedule." Zane had only meant to come over this morning for a few minutes to share a kiss and say good morning.

Circling the bush on the side of Noah's house -- something they'd used for cover from the gravel road -- Zane walked backward, toward the lake. "I have to go get the kids up, dressed, fed, and to the youth center in record time or I'm going to be late for work." Thank God Zane had put on his sneakers this morning instead of his flip-flops. He would have to sprint along the edge of the water back to his place. "I'm so sorry, Noah." Zane couldn't help his stare slipping to Noah's hand and what he knew was an incredible erection still pumping full of blood, hidden from his sight. "I shouldn't have started something without the time to finish it."

Ruddy faced, Noah winced, but he also shook his head. "Forget it. It's on us both. I should have been aware of the time too."

Stalling in place, memorizing the stunning picture that was Noah, with no shirt and his jeans and underwear holding midthigh, Zane felt his heart kick back into high gear all over again. "It's hard to remember anything when you start kissing me," he admitted, finding Noah's fine brown gaze and holding it with his own.

Noah offered a lopsided smile, one that caused somersaults in Zane's belly. "I'm familiar with that concept in relation to you." Noah's voice was too grittily sexy for words.

Good Lord. Zane swallowed thickly, and his legs went a little weak. If he stood here a second longer, he would run straight back to Noah and throw all his responsibilities out the window. "Sweet talker." Zane spun away, unable to stand looking at Noah, all his gorgeous muscles, and his warm eyes a second longer. "I'll meet you at the job site tomorrow, bright and early!" he shouted as he started his run around the lake. "Bye!"

Zane had a whole day working with Noah tomorrow. He might need this day and night alone in between to get his libido back in check. He'd gone twenty-four years without any kind of sex or romantic intimacy. Yet now, he was no longer sure he could stand to be in Noah's presence for twenty-four minutes without opening for the man and making their bodies one.

Noah had awakened Zane's dormant desires. Lately Zane did nothing but think about how Noah would help him quench every last one.

His feet bare, his jeans and underwear held up by his hand, Noah watched Zane get smaller and smaller in his trek back to his cabin; a growl of unresolved need slipped free. His cock had not dwindled in the slightest and he knew this time not even jerking off -- at least not without Zane as an audience to help him along -- would satisfy, even temporarily, the urge to mate. Noah needed Zane's ass or nothing at all.

If I don't get the chance to pound away at him soon -- Noah sucked in air as he painfully worked his full erection back into his jeans -- *these blue balls are gonna kill me.*

Problem was, when the blood eventually moved back to his brain and he had time to think with something other than his cock, Noah knew that having sex with Zane scared the shit out of him as much as not taking him left him frustrated. Noah loved every kiss and touch Zane offered; each soft peck or deep taking left him light-headed. But within that contact, Noah was constantly bombarded with signs of Zane's inexperience. Worse than even Zane's lack of sexual knowledge, though, was that when Noah slipped deep into the throes of his need for Zane, no matter the younger man's virginity, Noah pushed aggressively without thinking, as when he'd just tried to shove his cock down Zane's throat for a deep, full blowjob. In that moment, Noah should have realized Zane had never seen any cock up that close before, let alone ever tried taking one in his mouth. Yet just then, when seeing Zane's full red lips parted around his dick, one thought had taken over Noah's mind: *I need to feel him swallow my cock. Right now.*

"Fuck." As that shameful realization flooded Noah, his erection finally started to soften.

As if cruel fate thought Noah might need more help, a shrieking catcall whistle filled the air. Noah jerked into a spin, searching for the source of the sound. *Double fuck.* Noah's attention stopped at Sirus's cabin, and his heart sank with a thud into his stomach. On the porch, Grey whistled again, and lifted a cup of coffee in Noah's direction. *Son of a bitch.*

One thought on his mind, Noah stormed around the side of the lake, his hard-on no longer even remotely an issue. Noah's big hyacinth bush had well covered him and Zane from someone coming up Noah's gravel drive, but it allowed a clear view to one cabin. *This one.*

Taking the handful of porch steps two at a time, Noah stalked to the table where Grey sat. He slammed his hand against the surface, and with his voice scratchy from emotions boiling inside him, Noah pointed at the grinning hazel-eyed tycoon and growled, "I don't know how much or what you thought you saw --"

"Oh," Grey's grin above the rim of his coffee cup was truly devilish, "I saw all of it."

Noah got down into Grey's face, and his lips barely moved as he spoke. "If you turn what you saw into so much as a whisper of gossip I swear to God I will beat you down so hard Sirus won't recognize you when I'm finished."

"Relax, Maitland." Without blinking or pulling back, Grey kicked out the chair next to him, offering Noah a seat. "Why would I tell anyone? Other than Sirus when he wakes up, of course." Then Grey finally leaned back, and when he did he let his attention drift down Noah's body, pausing at his derriere. "Nice ass, by the way. Looked good from this distance."

"Holy Christ." Heat filled Noah's face, but he eased into the chair anyway, still glaring at Grey. "I swear I'm itching to beat the shit out of you anyway. Every time I see you, you give me a dozen reasons to do it."

"I'd say you're just pissed I got Sirus," Grey murmured, "but from what I saw just now you're doing a damn fine job of working your way past that."

Sitting up straight, Noah snapped, "What I feel for Zane has nothing to do with Sirus."

Like a man who knew his place in the world and was damned comfortable and happy in it, Grey smiled, a real one this time, not one full of cockiness. "That's good to hear," he said, his voice now gentle and warm.

"And I'm not ashamed or anything." Noah felt compelled to explain himself. He shoved his hands through his hair and tipped his head over the back of the chair, looking toward the morning sky, searching for words that would allow for private things to remain so, while also releasing some of his worries. "It's just that this is so fucking new," his gaze slid to Grey, holding on that hazel interest, "and I don't know how Zane feels about sharing what we're doing yet -- not that we've done anything."

"I don't know about that." Grey's dark brow shot up, and that annoying grin reappeared. "It looked like you were doing some fun shit just now."

"I don't ... I mean..." A rumble Noah could not contain escaped, bruising the morning air. He absorbed the easy confidence emanating from Grey and bit off a clipped, "Fuck."

The know-it-all glint slipped away from Grey's eyes; a depth of clarity and focus took over, showing the man Noah figured Sirus must see in Grey all the time. "You mean you haven't had full-on sexual intercourse yet." Antagonism no longer colored Grey's tone.

Noah nodded, but it felt jerky and stiff. "Right," he said with an unsteady exhale.

With a small nod in return, Grey then pulled his mouth in a hard line before he spoke. "You just said a million things by only saying that one word and looking like you are right now, my friend."

Crap. Suddenly the keen intelligence and shrewd nature of this man shone too brightly in his knowing stare. "I should go." Noah pushed to stand.

Grey whipped his hand out and held Noah in place. "You're scared, Noah," Grey told him, as if he could see into Noah's mind. "You want him. You're scared of how much you do, and that fear is holding you back from pursuing anything more than what you've done so far. You're hesitating because you want to top him so goddamn hard you think it could make your dick blow clean off if you don't get him soon. The need is raging so damn deep inside you that you're sure you're going to hurt him when you finally do take him. Am I right?"

"He has no experience, Grey." Christ, Noah hated himself for spilling Zane's personal information, but he didn't know how to explain his fears without sharing that pertinent part of the facts. This time, Noah didn't try to hide from Grey's scrutinizing stare. "I mean *none.*"

Grey paled a bit, and he wiped at his mouth and jaw. "Shit."

"I know." Jesus, if this man could see the magnitude of that information, then Noah felt certain he had reason to worry. "When I get close to Zane, the need starts to fuel everything I do. I'm so fucking scared that the aggression inside me is going to take over when I'm with him, and it will rule what happens. Zane's not tiny or slight or thin by any means, but he is smaller than me. And what if my control slips, even for just a moment, and things go bad? That's a thousand times more pressure than I ever thought I'd have going into sex when I made the choice to come out, and you already know how fucking nervous I was before I even met Zane."

Half an hour ago Noah had been full of testosterone and hard as a rock, more than willing to fuck Zane right against the support beam of his cabin. But his senses had returned now, and Zane's innocence and sweet naïveté -- conveyed in almost every shyly eager move he made -- flooded Noah with uncertainty. Lifting his gaze to Grey's, Noah whispered in a sandpaper-scraped voice, "I'm terrified I could tear him open or hurt him in ways I don't even know to imagine yet."

"You're going way too far to the extremes now, Noah," Grey replied, his tone much too rational for Noah's peace of mind. "You have added pressure, for sure, but you're not going to scar this guy for life."

Noah surged to his feet, his emotions ruling everything inside him. "You can't say that! You have no fucking idea what could happen."

Grey shot to stand too, and he got right in Noah's face. "Of course nobody can say for sure," he hissed at Noah, his voice dangerously low but clear, his eyes flashing. "But I've been that scarred, damaged young man you are so afraid your lack of control and raging desires are going to turn Zane into, so I can fucking say with some expertise that I know what the eyes of an insensitive, irresponsible jerk look like. You do not have those eyes, Maitland. More than that, you don't think the way a guy like that thinks. You have a heart that is ridiculously big, and an unflappable honor that goddamn terrified me when I thought Sirus might have an interest in you." Quiet authority filled every word shooting past Grey's lips like bullets. "If there was one man who might have had a shot at taking Sirus from me, it would have been you, and I know it. I've spent too goddamn much time thinking about you, Noah, much to my irritation, so I've observed your character and the man you are. That is how I know you would never hurt this person you care about and want so much. I had to trust Sirus with my hang-ups about sex, and when I did, being with him, in every way, trusting him, cleared up a whole lot of the screwy views I had about sex and love. But if you're not willing to give Zane a chance to open himself up and show his trust in you, then when you're alone yanking your dick in the dark and wishing it were him, you only have yourself to blame.

"Now," Grey straightened and patted down his bare chest and stomach, as if smoothing an expensively tailored shirt, "I've admitted way more to you than I ever planned to do with any man other than Sirus in this lifetime, so it's fucking time you showed me some gratitude for pointing you in the right direction, yet again, and get the fuck off my porch so I can go get back in bed with my husband."

From behind them, a clearing of a throat sounded. Both men whipped their heads toward the front door. Sirus stood there, clad only in low-slung jeans, his eyes suspiciously moist.

His stare locked on Grey, Sirus said in a raspy voice, "You've never called me your husband before."

Defiant, almost angry sounding, Grey spat, "I don't care what this state says, or if it'll ever give us a paper that legally allows me to call you so." He stalked Sirus, adding, "You are the person I trust and believe in most in this world; you are my partner for life; you own my heart, and that makes you my husband. Don't ever forget it or think you're getting away."

Sirus touched Grey's face, head, and shoulders over and over again, everywhere, as if he couldn't believe this handsome man stood before him. "I love you more than I can ever say." Sirus spoke the vow softly, but his adoration for Grey filled the air as if he'd shouted it.

Grey swooped in and claimed Sirus's mouth with a hard, fast kiss. He locked his arms around the bigger man's waist and guided him over the threshold, in complete control. "Take me to bed and show me how much." Grey moved in for another kiss.

From the porch, Noah grinned as he watched, amused by, but also now in complete understanding of Grey's possessive nature in relation to Sirus.

"Grey…" Noah called; something fitting filled his thoughts in just that exact second, and he had to share.

"I gave you good advice, asshole," Grey muttered without turning around, his mouth pressed against Sirus's chiseled cheek. "Now go away."

Although still so uncertain of the power of his attraction to Zane, Noah warmed inexplicably inside as he thought about the first night Zane had come to his cabin and admitted to his feelings. "I know it bugged the hell out of you when Sirus designed that sculpture for me as a housewarming gift when I finally moved into the cabin." Noah's mind's eye, full of Zane with his arms wrapped around that enormous slab of carved wood, holding on tight while he pushed his stunning ass into Noah's face, begging for a fucking, would be something Noah would never forget. Noah moaned softly where he stood, his cock stirring anew just with the small memory of their too-brief coming together. "I want to share a little something about that sculpture now."

Grey let his forehead fall to rest against Sirus's shoulder, and he muttered, "You're losing what goodwill I have for you, Maitland."

Noah grinned, even though Grey couldn't see it. "I just thought you might like to know that Sirus's face isn't the first thing I see now when I look at that beautiful, massive piece of carved wood in my entryway."

That got Grey to look over his shoulder, his eyes widening. "No?"

Noah raised a brow right back. "No."

"Well, hell." A shot of laughter burst forth from Grey. "This Zane guy might finally make me start liking you, Maitland." Dark steam filled Grey's stare once more. "Now leave." He slammed the door in Noah's face, ending the conversation whether Noah wanted it or not.

Sirus shouted "Bye!" to Noah through the door. But just as quickly as he did, a deep needful moan took over, and Noah knew both men had already forgotten about Noah entirely.

As they should. Noah traipsed down the steps and back toward his cabin, envy filling his being with a painful tug. Only now, unlike before, Noah wished for the trust and closeness the two men shared, whereas a year ago he'd often pined and thought about himself in Grey's place, wishing Grey would go away. Noah understood now why, so seemingly inexplicably, Sirus had so passionately desired and wanted the contrary, hard-ass Greyson Cole, and so had not been able to give Noah a chance to compete for his heart. Sirus had already known he belonged to Grey. Noah felt the same way about Zane. Noah grinned again, laughing at how much he actually appreciated Grey these days. *Zane is mine, the way Sirus is Grey's. Zane's is the body and heart and soul that fit in every way perfectly against mine.*

Noah now just needed to find the right way to keep a rein on his control while still staking a claim on the man he so desperately wanted in every way.

CHAPTER 12

At noon the next day Noah slid a glance -- for probably the thousandth time -- at Zane. Noah pulled the truck onto the shoulder of the road and then through the split in the trees that led to their usual lunch spot. Once again Zane wore a little grin, something so sweet and private the sight of it made Noah smile too. The guy had radiated a light happiness about him all morning while putting in a new sink and toilet at a customer's home. Any time Noah had teased him about it or asked him what the hell was going on, Zane would shrug and say, "It's nothing."

When Noah pulled the truck to a stop, he looked again, and he goddamn swore the little smile had traveled and now twinkled in Zane's eyes.

Noah openly stared, his brow cocked, and in response pink spread across Zane's cheeks. As Zane opened the door, he grinned bigger. "What?" he said, blushing even harder under Noah's scrutiny.

"There is something up with you today." While still watching Zane, Noah grabbed the cooler out of the back of the double cab seats. "I don't know what it is, but I swear to everything holy it is beaming straight through you."

"I just like being with you," Zane said as he lowered the tail door of the truck. "That's all."

Letting the cooler fall to the thick grass, Noah grabbed Zane and wrapped him up tight. He loved like hell that Zane automatically closed his arms around Noah too. Noah grazed his lips against Zane's cheek, always craving the smooth warm skin, and then murmured against his lush mouth, "You make my cock hard and my stomach flutter when you say shit like that, but that is not what has you smiling so much today."

Looking up at Noah, hands linked at the small of Noah's back, Zane grinned. "A big part of it *is* just getting to be near you." Then Zane's nose wrinkled. "But maybe not all of it today."

Noah lifted his hands and looked toward the heavens. "Finally, he admits something is up. Tell me." Noah stepped back, but not before pressing kisses to the backs of Zane's hands. "If you're happy, I want to be happy with you and for you."

A catch in his voice and his eyes watering, Zane curled his hands against his heart. "You really mean that, don't you?" It wasn't a question, though; Zane seemed to understand how important he was to Noah already.

Even though he didn't need to, Noah replied, "Yeah, baby, I do." Then he licked near the corner of Zane's eye before a tear could fall.

As if that exchange had lit a firecracker under him, Zane suddenly grabbed the cooler off the ground and thrust it at Noah's stomach. "Check the cooler." When Noah *oomphed* at the hard jab to his gut, Zane added, "Sorry." He still bounced like he had cherry bombs going off under his feet though. "But still check it anyway."

As Noah put the cooler on the back of the truck, he quirked a brow Zane's way. "What is going on?"

"Look in the cooler," Zane insisted, pointing at the blue insulated box. "When I got to the job site this morning I put something special in there for us today before going inside to find you."

With no clue where to begin to send his thoughts, Noah popped the cooler top. He spotted an enormous square wrapped in wax paper positioned at the top. *That ain't the cheap-ass bologna and cheese sandwiches I made for us to eat today.*

"Try it." Zane nudged Noah with his elbow, everything about him animated and full of joyous spirit. "It's for you."

Good Christ, if Noah's heart hadn't already pooled itself in a soppy mess around his feet, Zane would have made it happen in that moment. *He made me a special lunch.* Ridiculously choked up, hoping he'd be able to get the food past the thickness lodged in his throat, Noah unfolded the protective paper to reveal thick slices of white bread with mounds and mounds of dark meat nestled between. A tangy scent filled the air and tickled his nostrils, which had to have come from the sauce he could see dripping over the edges of the bread.

After getting a grip on the thick sandwich, Noah leaned in and bit off a huge hunk. *Oh dear Lord.* He chewed, and it seemed like the beef melted in his mouth; it was so tender. The meat was heavenly. But deeper than that, the rub cooked into the edges of each slice of beef sparked spicy warmth on his tongue; the tangy sauce drizzled over the beef had a bite at first taste but chased the heat and tang with a hint of sweetness at the end. Even the bread had the right texture. It wasn't so soft that it would become soggy, yet the crust wasn't so hard that it would cut his mouth with each bite taken.

Once Noah swallowed, he murmured, "That is so fucking good, Zane." Moaning, unable to stop the pleasure from escaping, Noah took another bite and savored every layer of flavor anchored in the beef and basting sauce. He met Zane's stare over the sandwich and got trapped in the vulnerable excitement lighting the man's too-blue eyes. Hell, if Zane couldn't see that Noah was near to having a food orgasm then the man's sight would have to be professionally examined. "I swear if God himself ate this brisket," Noah shared, "he would swear on his own name that he'd never had any better."

Zane grabbed Noah's forearm and squeezed. "I made it. I don't mean I put the sandwich together -- although I did that too. I mean I made the brisket and the sauce and the bread myself. I changed the ingredients of Mickey's rub and sauce a little bit. After he stopped roaring in my face for fucking with the brisket for last night's dinner at the restaurant, he tried it, and he said it was the best flavor on a piece of beef he'd ever eaten." Pulling on Noah's arm, Zane looked as if his skin couldn't contain the buzz hammering inside him. "Do you get what that means? Do you know how good Mickey is and how nobody does anything better with beef than he does?" Zane pressed his hands against his chest and spun in a tight circle. When he came back to

Noah, he let out a little squeal and added excitedly, "But he said *mine* was good."

"No, honey," Noah corrected gently, his heart nearly exploding in response to just watching the happiness busting out of Zane. "He said yours was *better*."

A blush filled Zane's cheeks again, but it couldn't compete with the light turning his eyes the color of the sky. "I can't believe it, but yeah," Zane's voice dropped to an awed whisper, "he really did."

"And yes," Noah took another bite of the delicious sandwich, chewing before saying, "I do know what that means. I've eaten at that restaurant plenty of times. I've had Mickey's damn good food the whole time. The flavor infused in this thing," Noah lifted the piece of sandwich, as if raising a glass in salute, "is better."

Zane sucked his lower lip between his teeth. "You really think so too?"

With a nod, Noah said, "I do. Congratulations."

As if he'd been standing on a springboard, Zane launched himself at Noah and flung his arms around his neck. The force swayed Noah back against the lip of the truck, where the sandwich fell back into the cooler. "Thank you." Grinning, Zane planted a kiss right on Noah's mouth. "Thank you, thank you, thank you." Zane pressed kisses over Noah's face with each thanks he gave. "Thank you, thank you." Pulling back, he met Noah's gaze, and his voice went very quiet. "Thank you for understanding my excitement and for being so happy for me."

"Honey," Noah grazed a kiss high on Zane's cheek, "it is the easiest thing in the world for me to be happy for you."

His frame jolting against Noah's, Zane clenched his arms around Noah's neck. A high, needy sound escaped him, and he scraped his lips across Noah's face on a fast trek back to Noah's mouth. Once there he crushed his lips down on Noah's, instigating a hard, hungry kiss. Instantly Noah moaned and parted his lips, eager to take the soft thrust of Zane's tongue. Every time they came together Zane got a little braver and found his own way to match Noah's ardor with another level of innocence laced with carnal intentions. Zane dug his fingers into Noah's upper arms, holding on tight, and slanted his mouth against Noah's to deepen the kiss. He swept his tongue inside, surely as far as he could go, tasting Noah's throat, and Noah lost his head a little bit more to Zane's steady climb toward mastering Noah in every way.

With every lick Zane took against Noah's teeth, tongue, and even the roof of his mouth, Noah felt the flick of contact as if Zane were on his knees servicing Noah's cock. Noah grabbed Zane around the waist, jerked their fronts fully together, and ground his swelling penis against Zane's crotch. He tangled his tongue with Zane's, desperate for a full taste and to retake control.

Slashing his parted lips against Zane's, Noah kissed the smaller man so deeply and with such aggression it was as if he thought he'd never get the chance to touch Zane again. Only this time, rather than succumbing to Noah's dominance, Zane clutched at Noah harder, and he bit and thrust past Noah's lips in return. Zane strained his whole body against Noah's, rubbing as if he needed the full contact in order to scratch a deep-seated itch. Zane forced his hands between their bodies to yank at Noah's belt. With quick-learning, deft fingers, Zane had Noah's jeans open, his zipper down, and his hand closed around Noah's shaft.

One gentle squeeze around his painfully sensitive prick, and Noah hissed through gritted teeth. *Shit.* Zane rubbed him again. In accompaniment he flicked his tongue softly against Noah's. Noah wanted this so badly, but what little element of sanity remaining inside him shouted so loud within his head the sound rattled his brain.

"Wait … wait." Noah grabbed Zane's wrist, and he tried to clear the lust from his vision and mind. He rested his forehead against Zane's and did his damnedest not to think about the man's hand wrapped around his dick. Exhaling roughly, Noah said, "We should keep this light before we get to a point where all I can think about is tearing off your clothes and shoving you facedown onto the grass." *Holy hell.* Noah's cock wept against Zane's hand, proving just how much he wanted that very thing to happen. His jaw involuntarily clenched, and he admitted, "I don't have a whole lot of control when it comes to you."

"I don't want anything to interrupt us anymore." Zane kept locked on Noah; he didn't waver in any way. He kept his hand on Noah's rapidly thickening erection, stroking him with every word he spoke. "And I can't think of anything better than feeling you inside me for the first time outside," Zane did tremble then, "under the sun, in the place where you let me know a little bit more about you every day we spend talking and eating lunch together."

Noah gripped the edge of the cooler. "Your lunch…"

"Will be even better after you fuck me," Zane finished for Noah, his voice shockingly strong. "Give yourself what we both want, Noah. I'm nervous but I'm not scared of you." Zane did let go of Noah's dick then, but only to slide his arms around Noah's waist and lean fully against him, mashing their bodies together from top to bottom. "I'm excited to know even more of you." He looked up at Noah, studying him, as if in wonderment, and Christ, the sweet admiration pumped rocket fuel straight into Noah's bloodstream. "Give me a chance to learn."

"Fuck, honey." Noah slipped fully into his need and lowered his mouth to Zane's. "I think you're already a master of me." With that he took Zane with a voracious kiss, one of claiming, one full of every desirous thought and sex-laden dream he'd had about this man from the moment they'd met.

Zane released another of his goddamn needy noises, while clutching and leaning into Noah to receive every lick and thrust of Noah's tongue. Noah felt Zane's passion sink into his flesh and shimmer over every nerve ending in his body.

Once upon a time Noah had reconciled himself to never having a man the way he'd always so secretly, desperately wanted. The knowledge that not only could he now mate with another male, but he could with a young, sexy, sweet man who seemed to like and care about him, made pretty much every drop of blood pool in Noah's cock, pushing his shaft harder against his stomach than he'd ever imagined possible.

With a low groan, Noah muttered, "This way." Lips still attached, hands still gripping Zane's hips, Noah started pulling Zane around the side of the truck. He couldn't bear to part from Zane for even thirty seconds. "I have stuff in the glove box." He'd thrown condoms and lube in the truck back when he'd first forced himself to go out on dates, telling himself he would do something pretty fast and want to be ready. None of the seals had ever been broken.

On their shuffle toward the passenger side door, Zane pushed his hands under Noah's T-shirt, lifting the fabric as he brushed his palms up Noah's belly and chest. Each caress of Zane's fingers, soft at first, and then rougher when he scraped his chewed-down nails across Noah's nipples, made every nerve ending in Noah's body clamor toward the surface of his flesh, eager to get just a little touch from Zane's wonderful hands.

Zane managed to get Noah's T-shirt off; the second he did he rubbed his face all over Noah's shoulders and collarbone and chest, making the most shiver-inducing humming noise as he did. "Your skin is always so hot." Zane dragged his fingers down Noah's back and then shoved them into his jeans, clutching at his ass, helping to keep them close. Kissing his way back to Noah's mouth, Zane looked up, his eyes drugged with honest need. "At night I dream about burrowing into you and crawling all over you to keep warm."

Shuddering from top to bottom, Noah pushed Zane a measure away. "Shit, baby." Noah yanked the door open nearly hard enough to rip it off its hinges. "Get those clothes off," he ordered as he dug into the glove compartment, searching for where he'd hidden the condoms and lube. "Right now."

Zane instantly shrugged off his shirt, revealing firm skin, now a light golden color from being outdoors more often. Noah moaned in response. Looking into Zane's pretty eyes twisted the sweetest sensations in Noah's heart and gut, but staring at Zane's body did an even harsher number on other particular parts of his body -- parts beyond painful right now. Precum coated Noah's cockhead completely and drizzled down his shaft, and his balls pulled with exquisite discomfort. *Shit.* Noah forced himself to turn away and put his full attention on finding the box where he'd stored the necessary items, needing a moment to regroup.

Turning away barely cleared the need coursing through Noah enough to focus, but at least by actually looking into the glove compartment, rather than feeling around, he could see the double-size box of staples he wanted. Noah had known if either of his kids had need to get into the glove compartment they wouldn't have any reason to open a box they thought held industrial-strength staples. As Noah grabbed the cardboard case he caught sight of a blue plaid bundle from the corner of his eye. *Yes.* Before backing out of the truck, he leaned over the seat to grab the faded flannel blanket.

With his treasures in hand, Noah spun, and his heart staggered to a stop at the sight before him. *Sweet merciful God.* Zane stood a half dozen feet away, gloriously nude, his cock lifting high from a soft patch of dark fur. Noah's knees got a bit shaky. "Holy fuck, honey."

Zane rubbed one bare foot against the other, studying Noah with dreamy eyes. "I'm okay then?'"

"Baby," Noah rushed forward and grabbed Zane around the back of his neck, letting the items in his hands fall to the ground, "okay doesn't begin to describe what I feel when I look at you." Tunneling up into Zane's hair, Noah held the man's head in place and descended, taking his mouth once again.

Zane rubbed his tongue against Noah's, kissing Noah back while writhing against him, and Noah quickly lost himself to lust again. When Zane stood on his tiptoes, his cock lined right up with Noah's, and the shock of contact again had Noah groaning and tripping Zane down to the grass. The blanket had opened partway on its own when it had fallen to the ground, and that would have to be good enough. Noah had no intention of stopping to spread the material out as if they were having a Sunday picnic. The lube, condoms, and open staples box were nestled in the grass next to the fabric.

Panting heavily, Zane whispered, "Please," and clung to Noah, kissing Noah with a desperation that pumped a flood of endorphins into Noah's blood. Noah locked an arm around the small of Zane's back and shoved them both a foot to the side, onto the partially open blanket, and then came down on top of Zane with all of his weight. Zane immediately wrapped his legs high around Noah's waist, almost at his armpits. The hot, guileless move put the younger man's cock against Noah's stomach and his sweet ass right against Noah's rigid erection. *Holy mother.* Noah shuddered on top of Zane. He barely had his jeans down to his thighs, but his cock was free, and he had mobility, and right now he didn't need any more than that.

Zane nipped and licked at Noah's parted lips. He clutched Noah's upper arms with digging fingers too, and Noah felt the white-hot flame of his long suppressed need ignite straight through his limbs to combust in his core.

Gotta have him now. As Noah grabbed the lube, he bit at Zane's mouth, but then pulled back to look into his eyes. "Tell me if you've done anything with your ass." His voice was rough with his desire and fear, but he would find some way to stay attuned to every cue from his partner. "I don't want to hurt you."

Red burned through the pink already darkening Zane's cheeks, but his dick surged, pressing hard against Noah's belly. "I only stuck a finger in once when I was thinking about you." Flaming crimson traveled down Zane's neck to his chest, and he added, "It made me come."

In response Noah dumped a lake's worth of early ejaculate onto Zane's balls. "Fucking A, honey." Noah tore the wrapper off the lube with his teeth, dumped a dollop onto two fingers, and pushed them between their bodies to Zane's pucker. "I swear if you keep saying such sweetly hot stuff to me, one day it's gonna kill me."

Right then, Zane's striated bud quivered and pulsed against Noah's finger, and Noah lost a little bit more of his mind. *Oh Christ.* He leaned down to capture Zane's mouth, clinging to his soft lips, and at the same time pushed his pointer finger all the way into Zane's ass.

Zane's channel instantly squeezed in a vise-tight hold. He exhaled sharply against Noah's mouth, moaning, "Oh God … God … Noah, please," against Noah's lips, and crushed his fingertips even deeper into Noah's arm muscles.

Fuck. Fuck. Fuck. It's not working. His heart cracking, Noah shifted to ease up his weight and withdraw his digit, but Zane held tightly to Noah with his thighs around his back.

Too much brightness lingered in Zane's eyes, and the sight of it killed Noah. Still Zane said, "Don't leave."

"Babe…" Noah's voice was strangled, and he couldn't get another word out.

"Give me a minute." His face still pinched with too much pain for Noah's peace of mind, Zane bit his lip. He gasped as he shifted his tail end, the move making Noah's finger move within his hot, tight passage. "Your finger is bigger than mine. Let me get used to feeling you there."

Noah couldn't bear to see the twist marring Zane's beautiful mouth, but at the same time he wanted to give the man the time he needed to acclimate. Whispering, "I'm sorry it hurts," Noah dipped down and brushed a kiss to Zane's mouth, then did it again, desperate for this man's kiss as much as his body. Zane parted his lips for Noah, and Noah licked just inside at first, then deeper, softly though, just grateful for the gift of Zane's taste, always dipped in honey, and always seemingly with warm welcome.

Grazing brushes of lips meeting time and again; gentle forays into each other's mouths were the only movements either man made. Soft moans from each of them mingled into one joyously masculine sound. Noah had no idea how long they kissed, just those touches of their mouths and flicks of their tongues, when Zane slid his fingers up from Noah's arms to around his neck and then into his hair. He grabbed at Noah's locks, holding him close, and then rocked his lower body onto Noah's finger, once, then twice, and experimented with guiding his fluttering passage up and down Noah's stationary penetration.

On the third bump up of his hips, Zane gasped, shivered, and then bit Noah's lip. He wiggled his ass on Noah's buried digit again, and with another moan switched to biting his own lip. "Oh God, Noah … right there, right there." With each tiny nudge of his buttocks, Zane worked himself off on Noah's invasion. He pinned Noah with a wide-eyed, wondrous look. "It feels so good."

Feeling a grin kick up his lips, Noah licked the tip of Zane's nose. "I got your sweet spot." He worked the pad of his finger over that little bump in Zane's ass once more.

"Goddamnit." With a small buck of his hips -- as much as he could surely move in his folded position -- Zane pulled Noah's hair harder. "Whatever it is, get at it more."

Noah parted his lips against Zane's to kiss him, but then he chuckled and whispered, "My pleasure."

Slipping into kissing Zane again, this time Noah added working his finger in the man's ass at the same time. This time around Zane not only accepted Noah's penetration, but with the full slide of Noah's finger in his hole, he exhaled an eager little breath against Noah's lips -- and Noah went rock hard again in victory.

His blood now humming at top speed, Noah pushed his finger in and out of Zane's channel in a steady pattern time and again. Every glide of his digit inside Zane's steamy tunnel drove his imagination wild with thoughts of that snug, hot passage surrounding his cock instead. *Fuck yes.* Back to full speed, not sure how much longer he could wait, Noah held against Zane, looking into the blur of his bright stare, and warned, "I'm giving you two now." He locked on the man's open gaze as he forced another finger into Zane's ass, doubling the thickness of the invasion.

Zane's lips parted, his breathing still choppy. His chute throbbed fast and powerfully around the thicker taking. Zane groaned with each deep pulsing in his ass, though, and his cock reared hard against Noah's belly. *Amazing.* His two fingers still fully embedded inside Zane, Noah twisted his digits, lubing and stretching Zane's passage as deep as his fingers could go. In response Zane moaned. He fluttered inside too, and he smeared more early cum on Noah's abdomen. *Damn.* Noah marveled, studying Zane as he turned his two fingers within Zane's passage again. *He loves it.*

The knowledge went straight through Noah like the purest North Carolina moonshine. All of the adrenaline and arousal Noah had been trying so hard to control flooded straight into his cock -- his long-denied, hungry cock. *I can't wait.* In a flash, Noah withdrew his fingers and moved his cock into place, telling Zane, "You are so ready for a fucking."

The word "Yeah," started to leave Zane's lips. But right then, Noah's tip kissed the pulsing entrance to Zane's body, and Noah couldn't wait a second longer to take what he'd coveted for so long. Noah pumped his hips, drove his cock straight into Zane's ass, and Zane's agreement morphed into a sharp, strangled cry.

Oh fuck. Zane's ass channel suffocated Noah's cock in the sweetest, hottest way, and Noah couldn't control the second and third thrust of his hips, or the groan that filled his being as he experienced the sensation of his cock in another man's ass for the first time. He wasn't even in to the base yet, but Christ, each lick of Zane's passage around the portion of Noah's shaft that was buried sent frissons of awareness up the rest of his dick, making the neglected nerve endings cry for part of the action.

Noah rocked into Zane repeatedly, losing himself in the act of fucking. Simultaneously, Zane grunted with each push in of Noah's cock, and the sound assaulted Noah like shrieks in the dead of night. *Shit. Damn. Fuck.*

Using supreme willpower, Noah forced himself to stop. He wrapped his arms around Zane's head, put them forehead to forehead, and tried to penetrate into Zane's soul via his glistening gaze. His voice gritty with too much emotion, Noah's voice barely held sound. "Tell me you're okay."

Still clutching Noah's hair, Zane held him close and scraped their lips together. "I'm okay." He winced though. "It hurts," Zane admitted, his skin ruddy. His breath caught as Noah slid inside him once more. "But sometimes it feels good too."

Instinct had Noah clinging to Zane in a kiss. He whispered roughly, "Hold on to me." Reaching back, Noah unlocked Zane's legs from around his back, but didn't move them far. "Clutch your thighs against my sides." As soon Zane complied, Noah held tightly to Zane and rolled them until Noah was on his back and Zane was on top. Noah pushed his fingers through Zane's thick, glossy hair and looked into his eyes. "Now ride me, baby. Set whatever pace you need to make it feel good all the time."

Zane parted his lips, but nothing came out. Finally, his pupils widening, he said, "I-I don't know what to do."

This man's uncertainty melted Noah's fears right into the grass. "Honey," Noah brushed his rough knuckles against Zane's smooth cheek, "I won't know any better than you will if we're doing it right or wrong." Noah's cock felt mighty happy buried partway in Zane's hot, tight ass, though, so he figured they were at least a good way down the right track. "Do whatever you want."

Sucking the edge of his lip between his teeth, Zane lifted upright and slowly rocked himself on Noah's embedded cock. Both men shivered, and Zane did it again. Undulating his hips, Zane found a gentle rhythm that Noah had to figure the sexy young man liked because his lip slipped from between his teeth and a small smile appeared. *So pretty.* Noah gritted his teeth against the urge to slam his full length all the way up into Zane's ass, repeatedly, ferociously, and instead let the burn of sinful pleasure coursing through his cock drive him slowly insane.

With Zane now steadily fucking himself on Noah's cock, Zane's own shaft rose, stiffening to a thing of true beauty, into something Noah could not ignore. Noah took the long, slender length in his hand, stroked the full, velvety-firm shaft from the base to the perfectly shaped mushroom head. In response Zane gasped and jammed himself a little harder onto Noah's penis. Groaning, loving every little and big response this man gave him, Noah spit in his hand and pulled on Zane's prick again, working the reddening shaft repeatedly, wishing he was dexterous enough to fold over to take the burning hot, throbbing pole into his mouth.

Just thinking about sucking Zane's cock made Noah's prick swell and throb ridiculously in the man's rectum. *Fuck. It feels too good.* Noah pumped his hips automatically, unable to pull the action back, and forced a rougher shafting of Zane's ass.

Noah opened his mouth to apologize, but at the same time Zane dug his fingers into Noah's forearm, his eyes alight with new knowledge. "Do that again."

Noah took another stab into Zane's ass. Zane moaned, his ass clenching in the snuggest damned hold around Noah's penis. *Goddamnit.* Noah took hold of Zane's hand, tangled their fingers to let Zane brace himself against the connection, and thrust himself past the man's hole and into his tight, slick passage again.

A low, needy groan, something from deeper inside Zane than Noah had ever heard before, escaped the younger man. At the same time, the softness in his stare slipped to raw, open desire. "Oh God, Noah…" Zane grasped Noah's other arm, clearly wanting Noah to give him balanced support on both sides. "Fuck me … Fuck me." Zane gripped Noah's hands with ridiculous strength. He quickly forced a downward push, one that met Noah's upward thrust, and merged their bodies with increasing speed and force. With another ragged moan, Zane whispered, "You feel so good."

Noah lost himself equally in Zane's eyes and the hot clutch of his body. "Zane … Christ…" Noah punched his hips up, shoving as far as he could go into Zane's amazing ass. "You're so fucking beautiful."

"Don't stop." Zane locked his stare on Noah and held onto his hands with a death grip. He slammed his ass down onto Noah's impaling cock again and again, making needy little noises with each coming together of their flesh. "Oh God…" His skin was flush with color and a fine sheen of growing perspiration made him glisten in the sunlight. "Noah…" Zane jerked himself back and forward and side to side, riding Noah without any style or finesse. "I need you… Don't let me go."

"Never." Noah growled and jammed his dick up into Zane's ass, as if he needed to stake a claim and prove his worth to Zane as a mate. His dick exploded with sensation, almost too much to bear, and with

a grunt he knifed his way into Zane's flaming passage again. "Fuck..."
Line after line of joy coursed through Noah's veins, and the heightened
pleasure pulled deep in his balls and up into his belly. Noah couldn't
break away from the display of emotion and pleasure mapping Zane's
face and lighting his eyes. The connection snaked deep inside Noah
and coiled itself all the way around his heart. A flood of feelings cut up
his throat, but Noah managed to say, "You're amazing, Zane."

Zane came down on Noah, almost impaling himself to the hilt.
He whimpered and said, "Play with my cock, Noah." He even shoved
Noah's hand over his straining shaft. "I think I'm gonna come."

Noah gave Zane one full stroke, and Zane trembled.

Whispering, "Please," almost as if to himself, Zane rocked his
buttocks against Noah's buried cock, working himself off in fast
circles on the rigid member owning his ass. A soft, groaning "Noah,"
left Zane's lips, just as he pinpointed on Noah's eyes. He bore down
once more -- *oh Jesus, yes* -- and a deeper barrier inside Zane collapsed.
Noah's cock slipped into the farthest reaches of Zane's body, all the way
to the hilt, and a hoarse shout filled Zane's being.

In immediate reaction to the complete taking, Noah roared with
deep-seated pleasure, unable to hold back, and drowned out Zane's cry.
Unfathomable deliciousness surrounded Noah's penis completely and
consumed his entire being. With no warning whatsoever, Noah arced off
the blanket and grass, lifting Zane a measure off the ground, and spurted
his release deep inside the man's perfect ass. Almost instantly, Zane went
statue-still too. His lips parted, but he produced no sound. Then he
jerked. A second jolt went through Noah, leaving more seed inside Zane,
and with that Zane swelled in Noah's hand, and he shot all over Noah's
stomach and chest. With Zane's release, his passage clamped tightly
around Noah's dick, pulling another shudder and wave of cum through
Noah's body. Somehow Noah kept his hand locked around Zane's cock;
he stroked the man's shaft repeatedly, making Zane jerk on top of him
and shoot more milky hot ejaculate all over Noah's flesh.

Fucking shit, yes.

Once the final tremors left their bodies, Zane collapsed on top of
Noah and buried his face in Noah's neck. The move made Noah's cock
slip out of Zane's ass, but other than another shared shiver, neither man
acknowledged the separation.

Although Zane's breathing didn't slow much, his body relaxed completely, making Noah think Zane had fallen asleep. Then, as if coming out of a fog, Zane kissed his way up Noah's jaw to his mouth. His eyes full of sunlight, he murmured, "Wow."

Shit. Pure warmth enveloped Noah both inside and out; he threw back his head and laughed. "That's a good word for it." He wrapped Zane in his arms, loving the feel of the man's weight on top of him. "Insanely wow."

As if he was settling in, Zane bent his arm, planted his elbow against Noah's shoulder, and put his chin in his hand. "I had no idea." The most endearing half grin tilted Zane's lips, and the ocean glittered in his gaze. "Nothing I could have done would have prepared me for that." He teased his fingers over Noah's lips, nose, and forehead, and his voice softened to nearly a whisper. "Nothing ever could have prepared me for you, Noah." Zane pecked a kiss to Noah's jaw and then rubbed his nose against the stubbly skin. "I can't believe I just got to do that with you."

"How do you feel?" Tension suddenly thrummed inside Noah. He cupped Zane's cheek, studying closely what Zane conveyed with his eyes. "Are you in pain?"

Taking a moment, Zane shifted on top of Noah, wiggling a bit, his brow furrowing. "There's some soreness, but nothing too crazy." Zane didn't glance away or look down, and he didn't wince. In fact, a twinkle filled his stare, and a lopsided smile appeared. "We're not the first people to do this," he blushed as he said that, "so I have to imagine I will be fine."

Noah went to cross his legs at the ankle but got tangled in his jeans bunched around his knees. Grimacing, he raised a brow at Zane. "Next time I'll get the rest of my clothes off for you." The quickness with which he'd shoved a finger into Zane's ass flashed through his memory and made him flinch. "And I'll try to work in some better foreplay too."

Zane arched a dark brow down at Noah. "We've had six days of foreplay, Noah. And that doesn't even count the time we've been attracted to each other but were pretending we weren't." Back to rubbing Noah's lips, Zane had a faraway look in his eyes. "I look forward to slow and easy one day, where we get to spend all day in bed, and I get to kiss every inch of your hard body," he tickled Noah's waist, and then laughed and planted a fast kiss to Noah's mouth, "but I loved what you just did to me here too."

"Did you now?" With lightness streaking through his being, Noah nipped at Zane and rolled them to their sides, but kept Zane wrapped up in his arms. While rubbing playfully against the sleek, strong man attached to him, Noah slid his hand down Zane's waist to cup his ass. "You say you loved it," a wolf's smile slipped free, "did you?"

Zane pulled back. Taking a moment, he looked Noah over with an exaggerated eye. "Ummm," he put his finger to his chin, "I'd say it wasn't bad to have as a memory of my first time."

"Not bad?" Noah's voice rose to a high, comical pitch. "Not bad?" he said again, giving Zane the stink eye. Still grinning wickedly, Noah took Zane's hand and rubbed it all over his sticky torso. "Feel that? That's your cum, baby, all over my chest and stomach." His tone went all grittily husky as he felt the seed drying on his skin, and his cock twitched against Zane's thigh. "You shot hard, honey, and you looked gloriously stunning as you did."

As Zane fingered the ejaculate on Noah's skin, sapphire suddenly enriched his stare. "Man, when you got deeper at the end there, and then I felt you come inside me," Zane trembled, "I lost it."

Growling, Noah went in for another fast, biting kiss. "It was insane -- shit." Zane's words suddenly fully penetrated Noah's brain. *Fuck.* Noah rolled onto his back, and his stomach fell into his feet. "I came inside you," he told Zane, answering the clear question in the other man's eyes. "I didn't put on a condom. I got them out of the truck, but I didn't even think. It never even hit me. It didn't feel strange to enter you without protection. I've been with my wife -- ex-wife -- since I was fifteen. We trusted each other, and we never used them. And with you, I was so excited … fuck. Protection isn't something that's part of my sexual routine, but I shou --"

Zane slapped his hand over Noah's runaway mouth. "Noah." He leaned across Noah's chest, perpendicular, and put his chin back in his hand, his focus fully on Noah. "You are my entire sexual history -- unless you count two girls I kissed a few times when I was a teenager, before I got so busy taking care of Burt. After that he and my brother and sister became my whole life."

His chest swelling with sweet emotion, Noah brushed Zane's cheek and jaw, needing to touch him. "Janice is my whole history -- except one time in college where I kissed another boy and we sucked each other's cocks a little bit before rubbing our dicks together until we came. I wasn't ready for more with a guy," Noah admitted, weirdly not ashamed with this man. "I wanted the safety of the trust and friendship I had with Janice, and we got back together shortly after."

Zane covered Noah's hand and trapped it against his cheek. "So I think we're okay. Right?"

"Yeah. I guess I just feel like I should have thought to give you the option."

"I don't know." Zane shrugged, making his elbow dig into Noah's armpit. "I like that we know and trust each other and we went with the moment."

Christ. "But you shouldn't ... I mean, you should be prepared... Other men... Shit." Noah took his hand back and dug the heels of both into his forehead. He felt so goddamn inadequate, and like he was supposed to have memorized some handbook about being gay that he'd never even been given. "I feel like I should be telling you something about safe sex and being responsible for your protection."

Zane removed Noah's hand from his face, and his brow pulled as he met Noah's gaze. "You're the only one I want to be with, Noah." Color suddenly fled from Zane's cheeks, and he sat up straight. "Is it different for you?"

"Christ, no." Black humor pushed a bark of fatalistic laughter out of Noah. Still on his back, he looked up at Zane, the man so beguilingly sexy, yet at the same time innocent. Attraction Noah had never believed he could feel for one special man thickened his words. "You have no idea. I have been so fucking hungry to have sex with a man, but with every date I went on, and every man I got to know, for some reason I held myself back." Taking Zane's hand from the ground, Noah lifted it and pressed a kiss to each finger. "Then you came into my life, and I knew what I wanted." Old heartache slipped in, and he admitted, "I liked you instantly, but I thought you were another guy I couldn't have."

Zane slid his hand down Noah's arm and twined their fingers together. "There's been something about you, right from the start. You intrigued me." The sweetest pink burned the tips of Zane's ears and dotted his cheeks. He bit his lip, but suddenly blurted, "I could not stop thinking about you, and a lot of the times when I did it would give me an erection. I'd never had that with anyone before. I wanted to touch you all the time. And then when you mentioned Ramsay … I was so envious and jealous." Leaning down, Zane pressed a kiss right under Noah's belly button, and then laid his cheek against the cum-crusted skin, looking deep into Noah's eyes. "I knew I wanted you for myself."

"Don't, baby." Noah's heart squeezed exquisitely. His penis did too. "You're gonna make me hard again, and we eventually have to get dressed and back to work."

"Not yet." Shooting to his feet, Zane then ran to the back of the truck, fully animated. "I didn't even show you the rest of the lunch I made for you." He hauled the entire cooler back, adding, "There's potato salad and green beans, and I even have strawberries and cream for dessert."

Noah shifted to sit up. As much as he didn't want to, he accepted there was one thing he couldn't ignore. "Let me get the wipes from the truck." His skin was not only covered with cum, but Zane had to feel the need to freshen himself too. Pulling his underwear and jeans back up to his waist, Noah trekked back to his vehicle. "We'll clean up, get dressed, and sit down to eat."

As Noah came back with the packet of wipes, and as Zane snapped the blanket and spread it across the grass, Zane said, "Can I tell you something?"

After taking out a few wipes for himself, Noah handed the box to Zane. "Absolutely." Zane fidgeted with the wipes, and Noah frowned and covered his hands. "What is it, honey?"

Zane straightened, and his attention jumped to Noah's face. "Oh, nothing bad. It's just, when I was making this food, and I knew I was going to bring some of it for you, it made me really excited. That's what I wanted to tell you." With a shrug, Zane started fidgeting again, this time using the wipes to enthusiastically clean his newly used body. "It's silly, huh?"

Noah fucking melted into the grass all over again. "Not even a little bit." Moving closer, he pulled Zane's hand away and took over freshening the man's body himself. Using clean wipes, Noah took away all evidence of lube and ejaculate from between Zane's ass cheeks, between his legs, and down his thighs, all the while keeping his stare fully fixed on Zane. "Whenever I'm around you," Noah moved to clean Zane's hands next, getting into the webbing of his fingers as if he were somehow making love to him all over again, "I feel happy and alive. You do that to me. You make me excited to wake up every morning. Have I ever told you that?"

Trembling again, Zane started to lean into Noah. Just before their mouths touched, Zane jerked back and shook himself. "We should probably stop talking now," he eyed Noah as he dropped to his knees on the blanket and dug into the cooler, "or I'm going to jump you again, and we'll never get back to the food."

"Good idea." Before sitting down, Noah wiped cum off his chest and belly. He openly stared at Zane's naked perfection. Sitting with his legs folded under him, Zane still looked like a most satisfying eight-course meal. "Put on your clothes, though," Noah ordered as he took a seat on the blanket, "because your cock is so fucking tempting I might start with it as an appetizer and end with your ass as the meal."

"Same with your shirt," Zane countered, looking Noah over with equal frankness as he grabbed his clothes. "Your chest and those wide shoulders and thick arms are just as distracting to me."

While digging out the rest of his sandwich, Noah shook his head and rolled his eyes. "You're such a good cook I'm not gonna call you out as a liar on that."

Zane shot back, "You liked my brisket so much I'm not going to tell you that your false modesty is complete bullshit." He stuck his tongue out too.

Glaring, Noah raised an exaggerated brow as Zane wiggled his sweet body into his shorts. "I swear I'll throw you over my lap and smack your ass."

"I thought we were going to hold the foreplay till next time."

Hungry again, Noah tackled Zane and rolled the half dressed man under him. "What a wonderfully dirty mind you have, Mr. Halliday." He dipped down to steal a kiss.

Instead, Zane shoved the strawberry he'd been holding into Noah's mouth and said, "Shut up and eat."

Zane bit off the other half of the piece of fruit, though, and Noah moaned as he got one more taste of the most delectable entrée on the menu before they went back to sharing actual food.

CHAPTER 13

Zane glanced at the clock in the restaurant's kitchen. As the time ticked closer to two p.m. his insides started to do an Olympic gymnastics routine, leaving him jittery in the best possible way. *He'll be here soon.* Noah would pick Zane up for work soon, and Zane couldn't wait. Noah's car was at the mechanic's for an oil change -- just regularly scheduled maintenance, Zane hadn't hurt the car in any way. The vehicle wouldn't be ready for a few more hours though, so Noah had agreed to pick Zane up between jobs.

Two days had passed since they'd had sex, and during that time they hadn't gotten much time alone to dive into each other again. In fact, with their normally packed schedules and Noah having Matt and Seth at his cabin, those additional constraints took away their few minutes alone together in the mornings. With a groan last night that Zane had been able to hear through the phone, Noah had said it was for the best anyway, because he wouldn't be able to keep his hands off Zane, and that Zane's ass was probably still tender and needed a few days to recover from what they'd done.

Right where Zane stood at the center prep table, straining tomatoes to make a smooth, cold summer soup, he blushed as his buttocks automatically clenched, making him very aware of his channel. After they'd gone back to work that afternoon those few days ago, after what they'd done together under the sun, Zane had been sore and extremely aware of his ass, enough that he'd almost been concerned enough to say something to Noah. But he'd held his tongue, and the soreness had lessened steadily after that initial discomfort, enough to where Zane had spent much of last night and this morning picturing nothing but spreading himself open for Noah's cock again.

Zane took another look up at the clock. At the same time, a big, meaty hand yanked the bowl from in front of him and grabbed the strainer out of Zane's grasp. *Oh crap.* Mickey glared at him. The burly old man dropped his focus to the table, and Zane followed to see tomato juice all over the surface rather than in the bowl where it should have gone. Mickey came back to Zane and growled, "You are completely useless to me today, kid. Get the hell out of my kitchen right now."

Before Zane could grab a towel and apologize, Violet piped up from her corner of the kitchen. "You leave that boy alone." She waved her mayonnaise-covered butter knife in Mickey's direction. "He is nothing short of wonderful, and I will not have you saying anything that runs him out of my employ."

"Woman," Mickey shook the dripping strainer, "nothing I have taught him today has penetrated his skull and gone into his brain." After glaring at Zane again, Mickey added to Violet, "Hell, you could have done that peach cobbler better than he did this morning."

Her sandwich clearly forgotten, Violet strode across the kitchen, her hair tinted blue this week, and slipped her arm around Zane. With her diminutive height, her head tucked itself in right near Zane's armpit. "Don't you pay him any mind, honey. We all have our off days. Why don't you go on out and check the stations for me?" The big, open eating area had a half dozen strategically placed checkpoints that contained silverware, utensils, linen napkins, and a host of other small dining room necessities. "Fill what needs restocking and then take off when you're done. All right?"

"Thank you, ma'am. I'll do that."

Hating to pull away from this tiny woman, Zane forced himself to do it. He then took off his apron, using it to wipe down the mess he'd made, the best he could do to make up for not giving Mickey his best today. Even though Zane, with his modest height, towered over Violet, she still felt like a warm, booming, full-bosomed grandmother to Zane -- at least what he imagined one would feel like, if he'd ever had one.

After apologizing to Mickey, and getting a grumbling, "Forget about it" in return, Zane threw his apron in the bin for the wash.

Just as Zane put his hand on the swinging door to exit the kitchen, Violet asked, "How'd that cute brother and sister of yours like that spaghetti pie last night for dinner?"

Violet had brought in her special spaghetti pie from home last night, along with the order that Zane take home for his siblings what she could not possibly finish on her own. While her charity was transparent, her kindness was equally sincere, and Zane fought the urge to rest his head on her narrow shoulder as if it were the softest, most welcoming pillow.

Choked up, probably more than he should be, Zane shared, "They gobbled it all up, then burped and had smiles when they were done."

"Good, good. I tell you, I love it myself; I always have; but I can't seem to get out of the habit of making it family size even though it's only me at home at night. It's nice to know I don't have to feel guilty when I make it in the future. Hey," she perked up, "you just let me know when you want a Sunday to yourself, sweetie. I'd love to have those kids out to my property one day. They can go crazy running around with the goats and dogs, and then I can fill them up with homemade lemonade and chocolate-chip cookies before bringing them back to you. How does that sound?"

Zane put his hand against his heart, feeling the deep, tight pounding. "That's very generous." When in the restaurant, he'd often heard Violet's grandchildren talk about how much they loved Violet's property, and her odd group of animals that lived there with her.

"I would love to spoil them." As Violet got back to preparing her lunch, she winked at him. "You just let me know when."

His chest expanding with sweet pain, Zane pushed through to the body of the restaurant. The second he did, the warm tightness changed to a clammy twist in his gut. Clint sat at one of the few occupied tables, chatting with a waitress as they transacted his bill.

"Oh, there he is," Zane heard Clint say as he stood. Then he added to Delilah, the young server, "The meal was delicious, sweetheart. Thank you."

"Our pleasure." Delilah didn't cringe at the endearment; at only seventeen, she'd once told Zane she was used to pretty much every man older than twenty-five calling her words like that. Dipping her head, she said, "Please come again." As she passed by Zane, she rolled her eyes and gave his arm a little squeeze.

Holding his breath, and his anger -- and the sickness in his belly -- Zane waited until Delilah was out of earshot before striding to Clint. "I don't get paid until next week." Zane's voice went a little high and tight, but he couldn't control the sudden dryness in his throat. "I will get you more money as soon as I can."

"What? Did I say anything?" Clint looked like super glue wouldn't stick to him. "I just like this restaurant, Zane." Sliding his hands into his snug jeans pockets, he stooped down and lowered his voice. "I'm liking it more and more every time I come."

His stomach lurching, Zane dropped to a heated whisper too. "I'm not helping you rob this place. If you threaten me again, I will tell the cops what you are thinking about doing here."

"And risk me telling them how many times you had to borrow money from me?" Clint tsked and shook his head. "And have it end up getting back to your aunt?"

Oh my God. Blood fled from Zane's head, leaving him dizzy. His legs went shaky, and he grabbed hold of the booth to keep upright.

"Yeah, I didn't think so." Clint spoke as if they were chatting about going to church. "See," a flash of darkness slipped into his falsely charming stare, "I don't give people money without finding out a little bit about them first. I know you're barely holding onto that family of yours. I don't know how the courts will feel about the fact that you took money from me more than once and can't seem to stay on a reasonable schedule to pay it back."

Not at all trying to play bigger than he was anymore, Zane looked at Clint and tried to will his situation and truth into the cowboy's head. "I will give you everything I can spare next week. I promise."

"Well then I don't think we'll have a problem," Clint replied, smiling that coconspirator smile that had lulled Zane into trust the first time they'd met. "Make sure to tell the owner how much I love her place." He tipped his hat. "Bye."

Zane almost slumped, but shot straight up as Noah entered the restaurant, crossing paths with Clint on his way to the exit.

Noah locked in on Zane, and he immediately frowned and turned to look back at Clint as the man disappeared through the entry area to outside. Getting close to Zane, Noah dipped down and looked right into Zane's eyes. "Are you okay?" He only touched Zane's arm -- something completely innocent to anyone who might see -- but God, that warm big hand stroked up to Zane's shoulder, and Zane instantly felt strength feed back into his spine. Noah glanced toward the entrance again. "Who was that?"

"Nobody," Zane blurted. Noah turned that narrowed stare straight back on Zane. The piercing power in Noah's eyes penetrated Zane and pushed guilt into his gut. Wanting to spill everything, but knowing he couldn't risk it, Zane forced himself to shrug. "All right, fine. He's some guy who comes in and leaves an unpleasant taste in everyone's mouths." That was at least somewhat true. He -- and from the look he'd shared with Delilah, she too -- would both be happy if Clint never entered this restaurant again. Zane forced a smile. "But don't worry. I handled him."

"If you're sure." The only other party remaining from the late lunch crowd moved past them to leave, and Noah inched even closer to Zane to give them room. He lowered his mouth oh so close to Zane's cheek. "Just let me know if you want me to beat him up for you." His lips, so light it might have been a phantom touch and not even real, brushed against Noah's ear. "'Cause I will, you know. I like you that much."

This time Noah's teasing, his very genuine charm, pulled a real smile out of Zane. "I might enjoy that, but I don't like the idea of having to post your bail to get you back home to me afterward." Grinning, studying this incredible man, Zane couldn't fight the lightness returning to his heart. "Brief high without a good long-term reward, you see."

A twinkle lit Noah's eyes, making the brown breathtaking. "I like how you're already looking out for me." He slid his hands into his jeans pockets and jerked his shoulder toward the doors. "You ready to go?"

"Almost." Zane patted himself down until he found his order pad in his back pocket. He would use it to take notes for his final task of the day. "Give me fifteen minutes to finish up and then we're out of here."

As Zane took his first step, Noah reached out and grabbed his hand. He took a quick check of the room, and finding it empty he once again put his lips dangerously close to Zane -- against his temple this time -- and whispered, "It has never registered with me before that there's a motel at the end of this block. Those neon letters stood out to me today." Noah pulled back to make eye contact, and his nostrils flared. "We only have two quick jobs this afternoon. If we focus we can get them done incredibly fast."

Oh mother trucker. Zane's cock nudged against his khakis and his ass channel throbbed. "Sit tight." Taking his chance while he had it, Zane leaned up and pecked a fast kiss to Noah's cheek. "We'll be in your truck and leaving in less than eight minutes."

As Zane ran across the restaurant to check the first station, Noah's soft chuckle filled the empty restaurant. *Good God.* The sound went right through Zane, like a deeply intimate touch, and he shivered. He loved the sound of Noah happy.

As for the other, as long as he paid Clint next week, then everything would be fine. It had to be. Clint would not want the law scrutinizing him any more than Zane wanted Patty knowing about his financial struggles. It was to their mutual benefit that they both kept quiet.

THE SECOND THE DOOR AT Zane's back swung open, he stumbled inside the motel room, Noah still attached to him in an eating, searing kiss. Zane's skin was already on fire, and with each consecutive plundering of his mouth, his core ratcheted closer to combusting. Noah's lips were on his, the man touched over every inch of Zane's back and ass, and his fingers dug deliciously into Zane's flesh through his clothes.

The room they'd been given was on the back side of the motel; the second both men had realized not a soul seemed to have taken temporary residence in this place they'd pounced on each other, not able to wait to get to the room.

Noah kicked the door closed, the steel toe of his work boot forcing the door to slam and shake the walls. The keys, along with the blanket and wipes they'd brought in from the truck, flew across the room and landed on the bed. Zane bumped into a table to his right. With a rumbling growl, Noah wrapped his arm around Zane and hoisted him right up onto it. Instantly parting his thighs, Zane dragged Noah in, tucking them together as close as they could possibly get, and sank his tongue into Noah's mouth for another intoxicating taste of this man.

With a low moan, Noah leaned hard into Zane, tangling their tongues, but abruptly crushed his fingers into Zane's hips and broke the kiss. "Wait, wait." Noah's chest heaved in deep, unsteady waves, and his dick was so hard that its shape was clearly defined against his jeans. His focus was pinpoint sharp though, drilling into Zane in a way that made him tremble. "I feel like we should at least take a few minutes to have some element of a proper date, or at least have a conversation or something, before I tear off your clothes and fuck you raw."

"All right." Breathing just as heavily, Zane licked his lips. They felt so full already; he bet if he looked in a mirror they would appear swollen and red. He rested his forearms on Noah's shoulders, pecked a soft kiss to his lips, and said, "Hi."

"Hi, honey." Noah's entire being, his voice, his eyes, the tension in his muscles softened visibly when he spoke that one endearment. In that one sweet word, he made Zane's bones ache with consuming need. "I missed you these last two days." Noah brushed his knuckles against Zane's cheek.

With the slightest turn of his head, Zane pressed a kiss to Noah's hand. "I missed you too." Noah's gentle sincerity pushed at the brazen bravery recently awakened in Zane. Tangling his hand in Noah's shirt, Zane pulled the guy in and murmured hotly against his lips, "But right now I really want you to fuck me."

"God help me," Noah dug his fingers into Zane's hair and tilted his head back, keeping them unbearably close, "I really want that too."

Zane grinned. "Good talk then."

His lips tilted up just as much, Noah replied, "I liked it too." He then descended the rest of the way and reclaimed Zane with a clinging kiss.

Every touch and kiss Noah delivered seared a brand into Zane he instinctually knew would live on his flesh forever. The knowledge that from now on, every time he looked at his naked body in a mirror he would somehow see and feel everywhere Noah had laid hands and mouth on him, sent liquid fire straight through Zane's blood and sent him up in flames.

Noah scraped his teeth across Zane's cheek, nibbling his way to Zane's ear. As he licked around the shell and then slipped his tongue inside for a quick stab, he tore at the buttons on the front of Zane's shirt. "Christ," Noah lowered his hands to the button and zipper on Zane's khakis and pushed his hand inside, "you make me so fucking hungry." Noah ran his hand down Zane's cock through his underwear, stroking with delicious firmness, and Zane bit his lip to counter the deep pleasure. The contact was so good it already had Zane pumping early cum and dampening his gray pair of Hanes.

Gritting his teeth against the power of Noah's hands on him, Zane scrambled onto the table and stood in the center. He trembled with the desire to fall back into Noah's arms, but while he still had enough cognitive brain activity to remember what he'd been fantasizing about for so many weeks, he ordered, "Take off every stitch of clothing, Noah Maitland." Zane looked down at that black coffee stare locked in on him, and he wanted to obey anything the man told him. Zane forced himself to visualize all that stunning muscle hidden from his eyes, and he took a tiny step back on the table, out of Noah's reach. "Remember, you promised me full nakedness this time."

While moving to the bed, Noah shot Zane a sideways glance full of heat. "You too, honey." He snapped out the flannel blanket, spread it entirely across the comforter on the bed, and then took a bottle of lube out of his back pocket before taking a seat. "I'm not nearly done looking or tasting every inch of your skin yet either."

Zane waited, watching, until Noah removed his boots and socks. Only then did Zane slip his torn shirt off his shoulders. As Noah pulled his T-shirt over his head, revealing those firmly toned shoulders and arms that had sparked Zane's need to touch, right from the start, Zane kicked off his sneakers and toed out of his socks. When Noah stood and worked open the button on his jeans, Zane's hands trembled and his breathing got a little choppy. Noah then slid the zipper down, pushed his jeans and underwear to the floor, kicked out of them, and stood before Zane in all his glorious nudity.

Oh my heavens. Everywhere Zane looked made his mouth go drier than it had been the second before. Noah's body appeared hewn for efficiency and physical labor. Every hard, thick line was pure muscle; he was golden tan everywhere, save a slightly paler hue in the middle that showed the length of the swim trunks he must wear on a regular basis. And his cock -- Zane swallowed through a case of dry mouth again

-- his cock stood out straight and proud from a nest of white-blond curls. Noah's penis was thicker and longer and full of even more blood-engorged veins in this erect state than Zane remembered. Perspiration suddenly dotted the back of Zane's neck, but his dick pushed against his underwear and khakis, and his pucker squeezed repeatedly, proving his body remembered and liked everything Noah had done to it two days ago.

Noah took the three steps needed to stand in front of Zane on the table. Looking up, intensity humming through him in visible waves, he said, "Lose the pants."

Without hesitation, without breaking his gaze from Noah's, Zane nodded and dropped his khakis and underwear to his ankles. Holding eye contact, Noah lifted each of Zane's feet, one at a time, and removed the clothes completely, tossing them to the floor. Noah took his fill of Zane, openly looking him over from top to bottom, and his cock lifted even more, pressing hard against his belly.

"Fucking shit, honey." Noah inhaled shakily, and even pressed his forehead against Zane's bare hip, as if he needed a moment to collect himself. "I know I've said it before, but you make me hard."

His chest banding with too much tightness, Zane brushed his fingers through Noah's hair and lifted his face out of hiding. "I know you think you're just an ordinary guy. You've said throwaway stuff that makes me know you don't think you're anything special. But when I look at you, Noah, all I see is incredible beauty." Zane could not stop touching the fine grooves fanning from Noah's eyes or the harsh brackets around his mouth. The man's very skin made Zane's fingers feel alive. "I swear you are the sexiest man I've ever met." With his other hand, Zane stroked the full length of his rock-hard, straining shaft, hard as hell, all due to this one man. "This proves it more than anything I can say."

Releasing a hoarse noise, Noah shifted just the slightest bit, and without a word took Zane's cock deep into his mouth, sucking him from root to tip in one full drag. An immediate cry spilled from Zane. He sank his fingers into Noah's blond locks, needing something to hold on to before his legs gave out on him. Noah wrapped his arms around Zane's legs, holding him close, and with a groan he went to town bobbing up and down on Zane's shaft again and again and again.

Ohhhh shit. Zane crushed his fingertips into Noah's scalp as the warmest, wettest suction surrounded his prick. The most delicious, focused attack forced deeper pleasure through Zane's entire being, more than he'd ever experienced in his twenty-four years on this earth. Zane bit into his lip to fight the concentration of joy enveloping his cock. He bore down with his teeth so hard he drew blood, but not even the sting of breaking his skin could compete with the glorious things Noah did to his prick.

Zane could hardly remain upright under the repeated, full slides of deep suction Noah put on his dick. Not that Zane had any knowledge of these things, but he would swear Noah had a mouth made for blowjobs. The way Noah moaned every time he took Zane to the throat shot shivers of delight through Zane, adding to the joyous thrum already vibrating through his system. Most potently drugging of all was the way Noah looked up at Zane the whole time, showing the unfettered lust living in his eyes and the pleasure he received in taking a mouthful of Zane's cock. Zane's penis wept its joy with each swipe of Noah's tongue. When a moment later Noah dipped lower to lick Zane's balls, and then pulled both ultrasensitive orbs past his lips to suck on them at the same time, Zane shot to his tiptoes and bucked his hips, out of his control.

"Ohhh God, Noah…" Zane bent over Noah, clutching at him, and rutted wildly at his face. It felt as if someone had shot pure adrenaline straight into Zane's nuts and cock. "You're gonna make me come."

Noah spit Zane out fast. His face all rigid lines, he ordered, "Not yet." Noah chopped at Zane's legs and brought him down to kneel in front of him. Sparking coal burned in Noah's eyes, turning them nearly black; he leaned in and dragged his tongue across Zane's kiss-swollen mouth. "I haven't nearly had enough of you yet." He curled his hand around Zane's hip, squeezing there, then moved on and rubbed his big, rough palm across Zane's buttocks. As he touched, he never broke his gaze from Zane. "Give me your ass."

Before Zane even became consciously aware of his actions, he turned around on the table and pressed his shoulders into the cheap wood, putting his tail end on full display for Noah. A tremble rolled through Zane, but an ache deep inside him made his passage flutter too. "It's yours."

"Christ, baby." Although Zane couldn't see him, it felt as if Noah ran three fingers down Zane's crack, teasing the line of little-exposed skin, and then rubbed his bud. "You can't possibly understand what you do to me."

Zane wanted to say *"You do the same to me,"* but just then Noah spread Zane's cheeks, wide apart enough to sting his flesh, and licked right over Zane's asshole.

Oh God -- motherfucking God. With first contact Zane gasped, and his channel shivered and squeezed. Ever since that first night, when they'd been interrupted, Zane had daydreamed about how Noah had begun to kiss his bud in such an intimate way. He'd thought about it so much he'd pulled on his dick in the shower a couple of times while imagining where a kiss like that would have led if it could have gone on longer.

Behind Zane, Noah moaned against Zane's pucker. He flicked his tongue against the small muscle with the softest, most insanely arousing touches. In response Zane whimpered, and his legs slipped wider apart on the table. Noah moved with Zane and kept his ass cheeks parted, his digits digging into Zane's buttocks. Noah switched to sucking on Zane's entrance, making every nerve ending there sing with joy. Lines of electricity shot from Zane's ass to his cock and down his limbs. His hips lifted of their own volition, and he pushed his ass harder at Noah's face. Noah growled and nipped at Zane's skin. He smacked Zane's ass, and the hot shock of contact had Zane shouting and dripping precum onto the tabletop.

Noah licked his way across the flesh he'd just reddened with his hand. In a rough tone, he murmured, "Fuck it, you taste good." His teeth scraped across Zane's sensitive skin in the most shiver-inducing way. "I love the way you respond to me." Then Noah dived right back in, eating Zane's ass as if he needed to do so in order to save his life.

Each focused, suctioning pull on Zane's pucker pulled deeper, more concentrated pleasure from within, making Zane grunt and circle his ass into Noah's face even more. Noah licked harder and flicked faster at Zane's entrance, and in response Zane pumped beads of precum from his cock in a continuous stream. His muscles grew tense and his sac felt heaver than a bag of flour, swaying between his legs and repeatedly slapping against Noah's chin. The sounds and smells of sex permeated the small motel room, and everything Noah did to Zane pushed Zane farther and farther out onto a thin tightrope, where no net existed to catch him if -- when -- he fell.

As Zane's balls lifted tight to his body, he breathlessly whispered, "Noah, oh God, please." At the exact same moment, Noah stabbed his tongue against Zane's entrance and pushed right through into Zane's ass. *Oh God.* Zane tried to put a clamp on his sac, but Noah whirled his tongue inside Zane's rim, moaning as he did it, and the twin sensation catapulted Zane headfirst into free fall. Zane jolted, electricity firing through every nerve ending in his system. As Zane came, he shouted, the noise high and tight, and he dumped line after spraying line of cum onto the table. Noah kept spearing his tongue into Zane's hole, all the way through his release, and sent enough shivers of pleasure through Zane's system to make him spit more ejaculate with each tiny invasion.

After Noah wrung the final bit of seed out of Zane, he pressed a soft kiss to Zane's hole, and then rubbed his hands up Zane's back in the gentlest caress. Against the small of Zane's back, Noah whispered, "You were incredible."

Noah's voice, the contact, his choice of words, sounded like nothing so much as an end to their time together in this motel. *No.* Panic surged through Zane; his bone-deep need for this one man was still on high alert, contaminating his bloodstream.

In a flash Zane spun on the table and threw himself against Noah. Holding onto Noah, Zane felt new life explode inside him the moment Noah wrapped him up tightly too. Zane pecked kisses all over Noah's face. "I'm sorry I shot so fast. But it doesn't matter that I came. I still want you more than anything." Looking into the fire still smoldering in Noah's dark eyes, Zane rubbed his shaft against the man's belly, feeling a new ache already overtaking him. "Carry me to that bed you paid for and fuck me until I come again."

Noah tucked his arm under Zane's ass and lifted him right off the table. "Honey," as Noah turned and began to move, he released that rare, wicked grin of his, "I already planned to do that very thing." Noah tumbled Zane down on the bed and came down on top of him, hands braced on the flannel blanket. "I was just taking a minute to bask in the spectacular way you look when you come."

Zane arched his brow up at Noah in an exaggerated manner. "But I was facing away from you."

"Darlin'," Noah dipped down and licked Zane's mouth, "when you come, you look glorious from all angles."

Zane parted his lips to accept Noah's kiss, murmuring, "There you go getting me hard again."

Zane thought he heard Noah mumble, "Good," but Noah licked deep into Zane's mouth right then, and Zane melted all over the bedding with the sweetest, most acute need. For the moment he could not process anything but Noah's kiss.

Noah sipped and fed from Zane's mouth as if Zane were the most delicious, succulent fruit and he just wanted to take his time and savor every bit of flavor and nourishment. Each soft lick or little nip from Noah, and then into a deeper tasting, felt as if they went all the way inside Zane's very being. Each element of Noah's kiss stoked the wood fires burning within Zane, slowly creating a forest fire completely out of control.

Oh God. Please. Zane reveled in Noah feasting on him; he squirmed beneath Noah, glorying in the full contact with Noah's wonderful, hard body, each shift causing their flesh to rub together in the most delicious ways.

His actions spurred by his rapidly growing feelings for this man, Zane ran his hands all over Noah, desperate to get at every inch of skin he could reach. Zane dug the blunt tips of his fingers into solid hot flesh, every action giving away how eager he was to merge into one with Noah once more.

Just as Zane scratched down Noah's back to his ass, losing himself, Noah kissed his way up to Zane's temple and said, "Open that lube for me." Noah then made eye contact for the briefest moment, just long enough to give away the raw hunger inside him, and to make Zane shiver.

Automatically complying, Zane grabbed the lube and popped the top. Just as he did, Noah began kissing his way down the perimeter of Zane's body, from the edge of his chest, to down his left side, to over his hip, and even partway down Zane's thigh. As Noah grazed Zane's flesh with soft touches and light licks, he shifted Zane's lower body and left leg, sort of rolling Zane's lower quadrant almost to his side, but not quite, to then finally ease Zane's leg up across his belly and chest.

Oh fucking shit. Noah had arranged Zane in a way that parted his ass cheeks and allowed what little air that still existed in the room to breeze across his exposed asshole. And Noah, with his hold still on Zane's leg, keeping him open, moaned and slid into a position that put his cock right in line with Zane's entrance.

"Damn it, honey," Noah rubbed his middle finger over Zane's bud, making the muscle quiver and Zane's breath catch, "you have the sweetest, most perfectly pink little hole that was surely ever created." Noah took his tremble-worthy touch away and rested his wrist on Zane's hip. "Give me some lube."

Anticipation made Zane's hand shake. But God, he wanted this so much he did his best to get himself under control before Noah could misinterpret the action as hesitation or fear. Watching Noah, attuned to his greater knowledge, Zane squeezed out as much of the thick lubricant as he assumed was the right amount. When Noah nodded, and even offered a soft smile, Zane couldn't help grinning in return, almost shyly, as it was clear Zane hadn't fooled Noah for a second. All the same, Noah obviously understood Zane and wasn't frustrated or impatient with his inexperience in any way.

Noah's natural kindness and patience settled Zane inside better than the most powerful sedative. In a shot, any residual tension flowed from his body. "Take me, Noah." Zane took a thick smear of the lube, put it right onto his pucker, and then used the rest to coat Noah's cock. He stroked Noah's length, making sure to cover his erection everywhere. The man jerked and groaned under Zane's ministrations. When Noah's shaft glistened with the slick substance, Zane added, "I swear I only need you."

Noah muttered, "Shit, honey," and a shudder rocked through his frame. Then, as he held Zane's leg up across his body, against the bed, he eased into position, his thick tip kissing Zane's hole. Lifting his head to meet Zane's gaze, Noah caught it and locked in; only then did he begin to push his cock into Zane's ass.

Ohhhhh Jesus God. Noah slowly, so goddamn slowly, eased his penis into Zane's body. Each tiny increment of Zane's ass that Noah claimed stretched Zane unbearably, burning fire around his entrance and widening his passage with painful, yet somehow delicious pleasure. The deeper Noah pushed into Zane's channel, the harsher and more unforgiving the lines mapping his face appeared -- evidence of how hard he worked to control himself. Noah slid into Zane another inch, and Zane moaned at the sweet discomfort he was quickly coming to love. Above him though, Noah shook his head, and he visibly clenched his teeth, so hard it looked as if he might shatter his jaw.

Zane's heart squeezed terribly. "Noah," he rubbed the man's rock-hard forearm, "you don't have to hold back what you want with me."

"It's not that." As Noah sank his fingertips into Zane's haunch, sweat dampened his hair and ran down his temples. "You're so fucking hot and tight, Zane." With a hiss, Noah nudged deeper. He stared down at where his cock was half buried in Zane's ass. As if looking wasn't enough, Noah ran his fingers around Zane's stretched opening, right along his cock, and hissed again. "Christ, that's insane." He lifted his focus back to Zane, revealing the rich brown pooling banked heat in his eyes. "I need to go slow for a minute or I'll come too fast."

"Noah." Zane clutched Noah's arm with both hands, trying to implore through his touch. "It's okay."

"No it isn't." Noah held onto Zane's thigh with his big worker's hand, bracing himself as he gently started rocking his hips, moving his cock within Zane, sliding the shaft with deliciously slow friction along Zane's inner walls. "We don't know when we're gonna get to do this again." Noah pressed Zane's leg down at a perpendicular angle against the bedding and -- *oh God, yes* -- it made Zane feel as though his passage was even narrower for Noah's cock to fuck. Noah looked into Zane's eyes, concealed none of the raging need in his own, and uttered, "I don't want this to be over before it starts."

"If it ends fast… Ohhh shit, Noah." Zane shouted and jerked as his entire passage collapsed and Noah got in balls deep. "If it ends fast and you can't get it up in time to fuck me again," Zane tried to keep his train of thought as Noah, slowly and deeply, repeatedly, shafted Zane's ass, kissing every nerve ending clamoring inside Zane for contact with this man's scorching, hard cock. Zane sucked in air as Noah filled him again, but he managed to say, "then I'll roll you over and fuck you."

As if a switch inside Noah had flipped, his nostrils and pupils flared, making him look almost feral. He shoved Zane's leg higher up into the bedding, putting his foot near to his head, and bore down on Zane's ass with sudden rapid-fire thrusts, owning Zane's ass with a faster, rougher taking. Noah knifed his shaft into Zane with full strikes, his eyes a haze of espresso desire. He watched himself spear into Zane to the hilt and then he ground his pubes against Zane's aggrieved hole.

Shit. Shit. The rough, raw moves sliced through Zane, straight to his core. His cock shot to full staff and pushed against his stomach. "Ohhh God…" Zane sucked in deep gulps of air, desperate for oxygen. In this compromised position, he still did his best to work his needy ass off on Noah's prick. "God, Noah. You feel so good." Zane bucked clumsily into Noah's taking. "Don't slow down."

Noah tore his stare away from his cock taking ownership of Zane's ass and put that fiery, lust-controlled gaze on Zane. "You want to fuck me one day?" Pure rust, even grittier than usual, coated Noah's tone.

"Yeah." Zane nodded, and then cried out when Noah shoved in deep and ground himself against Zane's sensitized hole again. "I-I," Zane groaned low, loving Noah's slip into a feral kind of mating, "I want to be inside you too."

"You would roll me onto my stomach?" Unfettered lust storming in his eyes, Noah shoved Zane over the rest of the way, onto his belly. "Like that?" He then surged into Zane from behind, taking Zane's ass to the hilt.

A shout of need escaped Zane. He clutched the edge of the mattress, needing a way to tether the explosion of pleasure Noah was wreaking in his ass. "Yeah." Zane gritted his teeth and punched his ass up into the fierce drive of Noah's cock. "And you would push your ass in the air for me." His knees sliding wide on the bedding, Zane tilted his hips and buttocks upward, doing his best to ram himself onto Noah's cock from the submissive position. "Begging for me," Zane panted heavily, out of control, "like I'm doing for you now."

"Fuck, baby." Noah reared upright and took hold of Zane's hips, holding him in place for a half dozen complete strokes, where he pulled his cock all the way out of Zane's ass, sending Zane's rectum into a confused state of abandonment, only to pierce his way into Zane's body again. Zane cried out with each deep strike, his body both fighting and loving this different pace of mating.

Before Zane could adjust, Noah came down on top of him completely, blanketing him with his full weight. "Would you cover me until it felt like we were fused into one being everywhere?" He circled

Zane's arms with his and shifted to tuck Zane's legs between his. He burrowed his face in next to Zane's, cocooning Zane with insane, wonderful, unbearable heat. "Like this?" Noah barely moved, but he had his cock embedded deep inside Zane's ass, and Zane swore Noah had full command over the deep throbbing in his shaft, something that pushed deliciously against Zane's anal walls.

With a throaty moan, Zane squeezed his passage around Noah's thick, long penis, and sank fully into the deep-seated pleasure. Good God, having Noah so deep inside him felt insanely perfect. "Yeah. It would feel so good." Zane clenched his muscles again, and every nerve ending in his tunnel itched and clawed for friction. "Fuck me, Noah." Unable to remain still, Zane grabbed Noah's hands. He turned his head, searching for Noah, his anchor, his safety, in the blur of the closeness of their stares. Zane tried to bump up into Noah's body, suddenly frighteningly hungry and desperate for the deep, full slide of cock in ass Noah had so quickly taught him to crave. "Show me the way you want me to fuck you."

A bright fire burned in Noah's eyes. As he trapped Zane with his gaze, he began to rock within Zane and set new flames to the fire already burning in Zane's ass. "Doesn't matter how, Zane." Noah tangled their twined hands into one big knot, slid his cock deep into Zane one more time, and pressed the gentlest, most erotic kiss to Zane's cheek. "Just so long as it's you."

Oh God, Noah. You... Zane couldn't even form a complete thought, let alone speak it. He simply clung to Noah in every way -- with his lips, and hands, and his ass around Noah's cock -- as the sweetest pain he'd ever experienced exploded in his heart and then rushed through the rest of his body. Without a noise, everything in him too choked up for sound, Zane came, releasing onto the flannel blanket, Noah's blanket, the fabric infused with this man's unique scent. As Zane came, he craned his neck so he could see Noah. Making eye contact, Zane got lost in Noah's welcoming stare, and he was unable to hold back tears. Zane's passage squeezed with exquisite tightness around Noah's invasion, and without any control over the action, his body somehow sucked Noah's cock even deeper inside his ass. Behind Zane, Noah shuddered in absolute silence. He licked wetness from Zane's cheek; as he did, he spilled himself in Zane's ass, warming Zane from the inside out, giving a part of himself over to Zane, in a way Zane hadn't even known he needed until Noah offered it so freely.

For long minutes afterward, both men remained still, Noah covering Zane, still inside him. They just breathed in tandem. Although no longer fucking, their bodies still moved as one.

Luxuriating in Noah's full weight pressing him into the bed, Zane freed one of his hands and brushed his fingers over Noah's face, needing another way to memorize all the beautiful hard lines. "How did I get so lucky to have you stumble into my life, Noah?"

After taking a nip at Zane's finger, Noah gave him a lopsided grin. "I think you stumbled into mine. At my feet. Literally."

"God, that day feels like a lifetime ago." Sighing, Zane shoved his hand under his cheek. "I don't ever want to leave the ugly, tacky perfection of this room."

Still clutching Zane's other hand, Noah brought it between them and pressed a kiss to the back. "I don't want to leave you either. Good Christ, Zane." Noah looked upward, as if toward the heavens for answers. "What we just did... How I felt... Watching and absorbing everything from you... Shit, what you do to me." Exhaling, Noah looked to Zane again, still holding Zane's hand close to his lips. "I can't explain what sex with you does to me."

Zane's brow scrunched. "You didn't feel like this when you had sex with your ex-wife?"

In an instant Noah's pupils flared wildly. He reared, right off Zane and onto his knees, severing the connection of their bodies, and scrambled to the other side of the bed.

Oh crap. The words had simply flown from Zane's mouth, no thinking behind them at all. Too late Zane realized what he'd said.

CHAPTER 14

Oh God, why did I ask Noah about sex with his ex-wife?

Zane shot to his knees too, automatically wincing and clamping his teeth. His ass was sore, and at least immediately after sex -- for the time being anyway -- his practical experience said to give his body a few minutes to adjust back to normal.

Staying where he was, Zane implored Noah to understand him from the other edge of the bed. "I'm so sorry. That was so stupid and rude of me. I shouldn't have said that."

As if a mule had kicked him in the ass, Noah suddenly jerked and came back to life. His eyes cleared, and he walked on his knees back to Zane. "No, I'm the one who is sorry." He cupped Zane's neck and pressed a kiss high on his cheek. "Are you okay?" While gliding his hand down Zane's back to his ass, he cursed and added, "I pulled out of you way too fast." Sliding his fingers down Zane's crack, when he reached Zane's asshole, he gently rubbed the tender muscle. "I could have hurt you."

Between Noah's gritty but soft tone and his ministering fingers, Zane was surprised he didn't fall straight back into the man's strong arms. His entrance closed quickly, easily settling back into place. And damn, the rest of him warmed all the way through too. "Oh God, Noah. Yes." Noah only had to touch him, and Zane's passage throbbed with pleasure. "You're making it feel better already."

Before separating, Noah grazed his lips against Zane's cheek once more. "I apologize for jerking away from you the way I did." Even deeper grooves than usual hardened Noah's appearance, but his chocolate stare warmed Zane, and it was steady too. He rubbed at his face and then wiped his hand on this thigh. Cursing again, he reached across the bed and dug under the blanket. Noah came up with the box of wipes, grabbed a handful for himself, and then said, "Here, heads up," and tossed the container to Zane.

As Zane caught the box and took some of the moistened towelettes to clean himself, Noah pushed himself up against the headboard. "When you mentioned sex with my wife -- ex-wife, Janice -- my instinct was to clam up and retreat. I pulled away out of habit." Noah paused, his hand with the wipe around his cock, and put his complete attention on Zane. Some of the harsh lines around his mouth softened a bit, and his gaze lit with the sweetest kind of heat. "But with you," Noah went back to cleaning himself, but didn't look away from Zane, "pulling away and clamming up isn't right."

Zane wiped cum and lube from his ass and between his thighs, and he frowned at Noah. "I don't understand. Have other people asked you about how sex was with your ex -- with Janice, I mean?" That seemed weird to Zane.

His mouth thinning to that hard line again, Noah nodded. "While I was married, guys who used to be casual friends did. Mostly they were acquaintances -- husbands -- who lived in the same neighborhood I used to, or we had kids in classes or activities together, and so you sort of become friendly out of circumstances... Anyway," Noah shrugged, but the gesture looked tight to Zane, "some men like to tell tales. I don't know, I guess they get a little thrill or something from hearing about how you're throwing it into the wife, or how you're doing it, or how often. I was never comfortable with talk like that. And not even because of the sexual feelings I knew I had for men. For me, sex is something personal and private." Noah bent his legs then, put his elbow on his knee, and his head to rest against his palm. Shrugging again, his voice gruff, he said, "I was always taught it isn't respectful to talk about your woman like that with your friends -- with anyone, really."

Zane's heart squeezed unbearably. He might not have known this man for long, but he could translate that taut jaw and extra glisten in his eyes as if it was a photo on a Wikipedia page with facts and tells about how to read Noah Maitland.

So very drawn to this man, in every way, Zane crawled across the bed. Coming to rest on his heels between Noah's spread legs, Zane pressed his lips to the inside of Noah's knee and then moved up to kiss his strong forearm. "Your dad taught you those rules about how to treat women -- how to treat people. Right?"

Noah's nod was choppy. "Yeah."

"He taught you the value system and sense of morality you hold yourself to, yeah? The same one you've probably taught both your sons as a father too." With Noah's nod, and the brightening in his eyes, Zane added, "I can understand more clearly now why you miss your dad and why the distance between you hurts you so much."

"Thank you." Noah's Adam's apple bobbed visibly, but his hand was rock steady as he reached out to brush the backs of his fingers against Zane's cheek. "It means a lot to me that you don't think I'm an idiot or some kind of masochist to still ache for him to be in my life."

"I could never think those kinds of things about you." Groaning, Zane kicked himself internally for dredging up this kind of pain in Noah. "I want to apologize again. After what we just did, on that table, and on this bed, it was crass of me to even hint that I was trying to compare the sex we have to what you did with Janice -- which I wasn't trying to do." Grabbing Noah's legs, Zane surged to his knees, digging in with his fingers. "I promise I wasn't fishing for compliments or asking you to compare us, or asking you to tell me I was the winner or something."

In an instant Noah shot forward and pressed his mouth to Zane's. "Shh ... no, no, no, honey." He brushed his hands through Zane's hair and down his neck to his shoulders, again and again, almost petting him. And goddamn if the contact didn't calm Zane's pulse. "I understand. I know the question was different for you; I swear I do. You're not just some guy who wants to trade war stories." As Noah pulled away to lean against the headboard, he twined their fingers together, keeping them connected. "We have feelings for each other;

we're having sex. I suppose it has to be natural to be curious and want to talk about that kind of stuff." Red suddenly suffused Noah's cheeks. "I imagine Janice has shared some stuff with Tom -- that's the guy she's dating -- too."

"Can I..." Zane snapped his lips shut tight. Taking a moment to rethink, knowing he would never forgive himself if he insulted or hurt this open, gentle family man, Zane started again. "Would it be all right if I tried to explain why I asked what I did?"

"Yeah." Noah played with Zane's hand now, and the rigidness left his face. "Shoot."

"It's just, you said something like, 'I can't explain what having sex with you makes me feel,' or 'what it does to you,' or something like that. When you said that it made me wonder, did that mean it wasn't ... or you didn't ... or... Fuck." Expelling hot air, Zane fell back on the bed and covered his face with his hand. "Damn it." He spread his fingers and looked up at Noah through a narrow gap. "I don't know how to say this without it sounding terrible."

Using the fact that they were still holding hands, Noah dragged Zane back up to a seated position. "You want to know if I just went through the motions." Every muscle in Noah's body visibly contracted once more. "You want to know if it was a chore to have sex with my ex-wife, and if I was thinking about men when we did, and if I didn't know what good sex felt like until I got inside you."

"A little, maybe," Zane admitted. Scooting closer, he draped his legs over Noah's upper thighs, just because he liked being close to him. "But much more than that, I guess I want to know *how* it was different for you -- other than what I'm assuming is the obvious. When you said what you did, I didn't think you were trying to say the sex was different or more special just because you were fucking a man's ass rather than a woman's," Zane bit his lip, and his cheeks heated; God, he hated being so unsure of even the correct casual terminology people usually used for certain body parts, "vaginally, I mean; you know, in a traditional way, with a woman." Jeez, it wasn't as if Zane had ever had sex with a woman or talked to one about her sexual parts; hell, he'd never even seen porn.

Focus, man. Zane blushed even harder. Damn it, he felt like a clueless idiot sometimes. *Just make your point already.* Silently ordering himself to direct his thoughts, Zane looked into Noah's eyes, went all warm inside, and trusted in that steadiness to help him through. "It didn't feel like you were saying sex was finally glorious because you were fucking a guy the way you'd always craved doing, rather than the woman you'd been married to for such a long time. It felt as if your point was something deeper, as if it surprised you. That's why your comment surprised me, and that's when I blurted out the question. Does what I'm asking make sense?"

The edge of Noah's lip lifted in the cutest smile, and he leaned forward to brush a kiss to Zane's mouth. "You give me more and more reasons to like you every minute we're together," he shared, making Zane's belly twist in the sweetest way. "You're right; I wasn't speechless just because I got to fuck a sweet, tight male ass. That wasn't what I meant."

"So then tell me." Zane settled himself against Noah's bent leg, honored to listen. "Tell me whatever you feel is right or appropriate, for you."

A long moment of silence stretched between them, but Zane didn't panic. Resting his weight against Noah, holding his hand, studying his unyielding yet somehow expressive face, Zane could feel the struggle within the father and former husband to find words that felt okay and right to speak.

Finally Noah exhaled, only a little shakily, and began. "I never hated or dreaded having sex with Janice. She was my first girlfriend, my first lover, my first, well, my first a lot of things. I was as close to her as it is possible to be with another person, and I trusted her with everything. Because of that, I guess, it didn't feel unnatural to be intimate with her."

Noah's mouth suddenly pulled into a deep frown and a dark flint came into his eyes. "Maybe another reason I got defensive so automatically is because when I first started going out on dates with men, I had dinner with this one guy who wanted me to trash Janice. He wanted me to tell tales about how she was a shrew and awful to be around, and that while I was married to her I cringed every time I put my dick in her pussy." Noah clenched his free hand into the bedding, twisting the fabric into a tight ball, and eyed Zane with a darkness that made Zane shiver. "He used that word, at dinner, out in public, in a crowded restaurant."

Zane crinkled his nose. "What was his deal? Was he divorced too or something?"

"Yeah, he was. I guess I stupidly thought that meant we would have something in common." Noah's frame went rigid. "I don't know what he was trying to get me to say, and honestly it probably would have made me even angrier if I'd stuck around to figure it out. I didn't."

Zane covered Noah's balled-up fist and tried to massage away the tension thrumming within him. "I get that. You're not that guy. Even if it had been awful with Janice, you wouldn't have told him so -- at least not on a first date."

Noah shook his head with a fast, jerky move. "It's just not cool to me."

"I know." Zane worked Noah's hand open and then moved on to rub at the tension kinking his arm. "It's one of the reasons I like you."

Zeroing in on Zane, Noah looked as if sun flares had fired in his eyes. "I loved Janice, you know?" He spoke as if he needed to convince Zane, as if he expected not to be believed. "I can't say we fucked like bunnies or anything, but I attribute that to how busy our lives were more than the fact that I was fighting being gay. We had sex on a regular basis, and I didn't have to psych myself up for it or close my eyes and think about a man. It was nice when we had sex. Hell, it felt good. I didn't have to struggle to come." Noah finally seemed to unlock inside, and his tone slipped back to conversational. "Maybe because of that, because it was good, and because we were so close, I didn't think the actual act of sex would be all that different with a man -- other than the obvious."

Even Zane understood that. "Right."

Lifting away from the headboard, Noah became animated. "Heck, I figured sex with a guy would feel as good, physically, and I certainly anticipated there would be another layer because I was finally being intimate with the gender I'd always wanted but up till then had suppressed. I factored all that in." Noah laughed, the sound rusty. "Or at least I thought I had."

Zane held Noah's hand, and gently said, "But it isn't what you thought it would be?"

The flares in Noah's stare lit to the fire of a thousand suns. "Fuck, Zane, it's so different with you. It's more." Husky rawness filled Noah's tone and his gaze burned straight into Zane's soul. "But that sounds disrespectful to what I had with Janice. Hell, I don't know how to explain what happens to me when I'm with you. It's this craving, this rush, and when I get near you it takes me over, in a way that reaches deep inside me with a whole different level of intensity, one I never knew existed. When I'm inside you," Noah snaked his hand around Zane's neck and tugged him in until their faces touched, "and I'm trying to get deeper," he looked at Zane in a way that felt as if it reached down and physically touched Zane's heart, "it's not because I like the way it makes my dick feel -- although that is insane in itself -- it's because the deeper I get, the more of you I can touch and know intimately..." Noah's chest rose and fell in rapid waves, and his hold tightened reflexively around Zane's neck. "When I'm with you, no matter what we're doing, it's like there's this beast clawing inside me, pushing at me to touch you and fuck you, because it feeds on that connection, and it needs it for its very survival."

"Good God, Noah." Too many emotions slammed through Zane, clogging his throat, and he could do no more than hang on to Noah as hard as Noah held him.

"I loved Janice," Noah vowed, his voice ragged now, "and I'll never say a bad thing about our sex life, or even just our life together, because there isn't anything bad to tell. But what I understood of attraction and sex before doesn't even come close to the reality of what it feels like to be inside you. There's not one additional layer to being with you, there are countless more, ones I didn't even know existed until I met you." Noah exhaled then, trembled, and he looked as if he'd just come to the end of running a marathon. "That was what I meant when I said what I said to you earlier."

Fuck. Unable to hold himself back, Zane uttered Noah's name with passion and reverence, and then fused himself to the man with a desperate, clinging kiss, needing some way to convey what Noah's words had made him feel. In response, Noah automatically parted his lips, moaning into Zane's mouth the moment their tongues touched. Pulling Zane all the way against him, Noah slashed his lips across Zane's and naturally took over, staking a claim on Zane in a way that made Zane rub even harder against Noah, searching for a way to lose himself in this man again. Noah pulled Zane's hair and angled his head to steal his way even deeper into Zane's mouth. As much as Zane wanted that very thing too, he fought the force of Noah's passion and broke their kiss.

Zane didn't go far, though. He struggled to breathe, but he looked into the depths of Noah's dark eyes and easily found his voice. "You say you don't know how to express yourself," he touched his fingers over every line on Noah's face; those grooves held character he already so adored, "but that was one of the most beautiful explanations for anything I've ever heard."

Noah pulled Zane's hand to his mouth and kissed it. "It's just the truth." He licked the center of Zane's palm; as he did, his cock twitched and nudged against Zane's.

Hell yes. Zane checked Noah's watch. Taking note of the hour, he grinned, hoping his was as wickedly sinful as Noah's sometimes was. "We don't have time for a full replay of everything we just did, but I've done a heck of a lot of thinking about how I was just starting to learn your taste that morning when my schedule dragged me away." Reaching between them, Zane stroked Noah's rapidly thickening cock. He then pushed his hand lower to give Noah's softly furred sac a little squeeze. As Noah's balls rolled and swelled in Zane's palm, Zane kissed Noah's chin and then throat, adding, "I think I have the time to get back to it right now."

Noah dug into Zane's hair and forced his head back. "You don't have to," he said, his face full of taut lines that gave away his need.

"I want to." Zane untangled Noah's hand from his hair and eased him back against the headboard. "Just sit back and relax."

Noah's chuckle turned into a groan. "Not possible." Even as he said that he settled deeper into the bedding and let his legs fall open wide. "But keep going anyway."

Laughing softly, Zane pressed kisses all across Noah's chest, quickly losing himself to the desire that constantly ignited in him whenever he was allowed to touch Noah's warm, firm flesh. No longer merely teasing, Zane moaned and eagerly licked across Noah's nipple, loving the shape and feel of the bronze-colored disc pebbling against his tongue. As Zane licked again and then nibbled on the tiny tip, Noah squirmed against the bed and his breathing became shallow.

Loving Noah's quiet responses, Zane grazed his way across Noah's wide chest with soft touches and gave the same attention to his other nipple. This time, he bit a little harder into the surrounding golden skin. Noah jerked and grabbed hold of the blanket with both hands, twisting the fabric into tight bundles on either side of his hips.

The smells of Noah's growing arousal mingled with the powder scent of the wipes he'd used to clean himself; the unique mix tickled at Zane's nose and kicked his desire up another notch. Nobody smelled quite like Noah, and Zane had never responded to a person's scent as completely as he did to this man's. With a low moan, Zane licked his way down Noah's flat stomach, eager to taste him again and learn even more about what he liked and what made him hot and hard enough to come.

Pressed up rigidly, covering Noah's belly button, sat Noah's cock. The head was deep red in color and early ejaculate already pearled in the slit. *Oh my.* As Zane looked, his own cock twitched and hardened against the soft flannel blanket. Noah's penis was a temptation too great for Zane to ignore. He licked across the top, gathering the salty precum on this tongue. The flavor of Noah exploded on Zane's taste buds, and Zane eagerly swirled his way around the glans, hungry to learn every inch of Noah's cock. Zane took the thick head into his mouth for a gentle suck, and Noah bucked and tunneled his hands into Zane's hair. Words seemed to elude the man, but every muscle in his body strained and his fingers curled into the back of Zane's head. Zane interpreted the message in one way: *Fuck, that's good. Do more.*

Zane's blood raced and his nerves tingled in complete agreement with Noah's silent request. He'd never studied his own prick or thought much about its appearance, but God, Zane didn't think he'd ever seen anything as glorious, compelling, or enticing as Noah's erect penis. Every vein, thickly engorged with blood, called to him, and he ran the tip of his tongue along each, up and down from head to root, learning and loving the roadmap that was Noah's stiff cock. With every glide of Zane's tongue, the member swelled before him, and quickly another fat bead of early seed filled the slit.

Saliva pooled in Zane's mouth, as if he was staring at a meal and he hadn't filled his belly in weeks. He sipped the liquid again, savoring that small essence of Noah. Not satisfied to play around the fringes anymore, this time Zane parted his lips fully and went down on Noah's cock, stuffing as much of the thick length into his mouth as he could without gagging. Hot salty man filled Zane's mouth. *Oh God, yes.* The taste shot adrenaline straight into Zane's heart, buzzing him with renewed energy and need. Above him Noah made a rough noise and pulled at Zane's hair, and each gesture added to Zane's pleasure. Zane immediately withdrew but then quickly took Noah into his mouth again, sucking inexpertly but eagerly, desperate for more of Noah, however he could get him.

Knowing Noah was too big and he wouldn't be able to get the man down his throat, Zane wrapped his hand around half of Noah's length and began jerking him off in time with each deep bob and retreat along the upper half of his prick. Noah tensed even more and spread his legs higher and wider, as if offering every inch of his shaft and sac to Zane. Zane had never wanted a gift more. He threw his other hand into the mix and took Noah's balls in hand, rolling their hot weight in his palm and squeezing just enough, to a point where he hoped it would feel good but not hurt.

Noah writhed on the bed, and Zane looked up to see glazed passion thickening the chocolate in his eyes. Noah's open desire filled Zane too, spurring him on to do even more. Sucking hard one more time on Noah's shaft, Zane then moved down to his balls and lapped over every centimeter he could reach, almost as if he were trying to bathe the whole sac with his tongue.

Noah groaned, something feral and deep from his gut. He put his hand over Zane's and guided him to continue stroking the full length of his shaft. "Ohhh fuck..." Noah sucked in air, the sound hissing through his clenched teeth. "What you do to me. Christ... Yeah." He pumped his hips up into the drag on his shaft. "That's so good." As Zane took up a harder, whipping stroke up and down Noah's length, Noah reached across the lip of the headboard with both arms, the span making his muscles flex and pop in the most stunningly beautiful display. Noah looked down at Zane with deep smoke inking the color in his eyes. "You're gonna make me come too fast."

Zane wanted exactly that. He wanted to give Noah such pleasure he couldn't help losing himself, just as Noah had repeatedly done to him. Zane tongued Noah's weighty sac all over one last time and then licked his way back up the underside of his cock, not stopping until he reached the head. This time, not even giving himself a moment to breathe, Zane took Noah all the way into his mouth again, sucking as hard as he could, and then pushed Noah deeper, toward the back of his throat.

He didn't even need to get fully there. The second the thick tip of Noah's cock kissed the soft palate in Zane's mouth, Noah arced off the bed and roared his release through the motel room walls. Instantly thick lines of tart, salty cum poured into Zane's mouth, coating his throat and tongue and roof of his mouth -- everywhere. The taste of Noah took Zane over, seeped into his very being. Zane moaned and took it all, getting hard as hell as he swallowed the proof of Noah's pleasure.

Before Zane had a chance to lick Noah and taste him some more, Noah cuffed his hand around the back of Zane's neck and hauled him up until they were face-to-face. Still breathing heavily, his features almost savage, Noah ordered, "Work yourself off on me." He arranged Zane in a straddle against his right thigh. "I can fucking feel how much you need to come."

No thought of how he might look or if this was strange, Zane nodded and braced himself on the bed. Targeted on Noah's dark stare, Zane rocked himself against Noah's leg, rubbing his sensitized, stiff cock again and again on Noah's thigh. *Oh shit. Yes.* The coarse hairs on Noah's leg attacked Zane's shaft in the most insanely wonderful way. Quickly Zane picked up speed, pumping and grinding himself harder and harder against Noah's leg, unable to stop or slow down.

Whipping his dick against Noah repeatedly, Zane parted his lips, struggling to breathe. "Oh fuck … Noah … Noah …" Every nerve ending in Zane's prick and balls screamed for release. Zane looked to Noah, and the sight of his harshly handsome face only made Zane grind himself harder, in a frenzy. "I want to come." The coiling within Zane twisted tighter, but he couldn't reach the place to make the wire snap. "Help me come."

Noah surged and smashed his mouth against Zane's, forcing his way inside for a voracious, invasive kiss. The moment their lips came together and their tongues slid against one another in an aggressive battle, Zane's entire body went stiff as a board. Then Noah pulled back, swiped just the very tip of his tongue against Zane's upper lip, and whispered, "My Zane." On the spot, Zane shivered and came. Holding in position, with Noah doing the same, Zane pulsed from deep within, and with each sharp beat he spilled himself against Noah's thigh.

In the aftermath, as if someone had unplugged him and taken away the juice, Zane collapsed on top of Noah, fully spent.

Noah went lax under Zane too. Exhaling, he ran his hand down Zane's back, stroking him. "That was one hell of a round two."

Grinning, Zane shifted, put his chin on Noah's chest, and tried to give the man his best sexy smile. "It begs the question, what the heck are we going to think up for round three?"

Noah rubbed his thumb across Zane's lips, making Zane tingle all over again.

Just as Noah brushed his hand up Zane's cheek, Zane went from tingly to his heart plummeting into his stomach. "Oh crap." He pulled Noah's wrist closer to his face, double-checking the time on his watch. Processing the lateness of the hour, Zane groaned and banged his forehead against Noah's chest. Looking up at Noah out of one eye, he said, "If I don't get to the mechanic's to pick up the car in about ten minutes I'm going to be late to pick up Duncan and Hailey." Without many options after school had let out, Zane had parted with some of his precious paycheck to sign up his brother and sister for summer activities at the youth center.

A rumbling noise went through Noah too. "Yeah, me too." He drew little circles with his fingers against Zane's buttocks. "Seth spent the day with Matt, but he has a date tonight, so I need to get home to Matt too."

His cheek resting on his hand, Zane looked up at Noah, his heart swelling with sweeter pain with every second he stared. "I'm at the restaurant all day and part of the evening tomorrow," he shared softly. "I probably won't see you."

Noah's mouth pulled down in a harsh line. "No, probably not."

Aching to take that hardness away, Zane added, "But the day after that, we'll have all afternoon together. Even if we're only working, it's still something."

"I'm already looking forward to it." With his hand cupped on Zane's bare ass, Noah got another one of his naughty grins. "And we can always make out in the truck between jobs."

Shifting up to rest his weight on his elbows, Zane quirked both brows at the sexy man beneath him. "You have a very clever, sinful mind, Noah Maitland. Have I ever told you that?"

Noah lifted a brow right back. "What I have is a perpetually stiff dick when I'm around you, and that forces me to be creative. Now get your sweet ass up," he smacked Zane's buttocks, firmly enough to sting, "before the feel of you rubbing all close against me forces me to pull over the truck and take care of another hard-on on the ride home."

After pushing up to stand beside the bed, Zane grabbed some more wipes and then handed the box over to Noah. As he cleaned up, he watched Noah, and a longing unlike anything he'd ever experienced washed over and left him aching. An idea came to him, but he bit his lip to prevent the suggestion from escaping. Nervousness made Zane's belly flutter, but such hunger lived there too that it beat out the sliver of uncertainty and fear.

"Listen," Zane tugged on Noah's hand to get him to look up, "I know you usually like your quiet during lunch, but if you'd like to come by the restaurant tomorrow during your lunch hour, I could make something for you, and we could eat together."

Noah's stare softened to warm, rich syrup. He rubbed his hand against his chest, over his heart. "Hell, Zane." His voice gruff, he moved in and scraped a kiss to Zane's cheek. "That is the nicest offer of a meal anyone has ever made to me. Yes. We definitely have a date for lunch tomorrow."

The fluttering moved from Zane's stomach to his chest. "I like that. A date."

His voice soft as well, Noah murmured, "Me too." Then, he openly looked Zane over from top to bottom. Growling, Noah leaned down and stole another kiss. "But seriously, though, get dressed. You need to cover all that gorgeousness up or I'll toss you onto that table again and make us both late."

As much as Zane wanted to test Noah's threat, responsibility for his siblings made him quickly scramble into his clothes.

Two days, though. Less than forty-eight hours and he would be with Noah for an entire afternoon.

Zane couldn't wait.

———

"OH GOD." VIOLENCE IN NOAH'S stomach lurched him from sleep. Everything in his gut roiled, heading north fast. He covered his mouth and rushed for his bathroom in the shadows, light from a crescent moon coming through a big window to guide his way. Noah didn't even get time to kneel and aim for the toilet. He retched into the bathtub, throwing up the contents of his dinner and evening snack -- and maybe even the lunch he'd shared with Zane -- in heaving waves.

Goddamnit, Noah had taken one look at Mrs. Tannen yesterday afternoon and known the woman was ill. He'd helped his kids through enough bugs and viruses over the years to recognize sickness, and Mrs. Tannen had that telltale look about her eyes that said she was under the weather. She'd stayed right at Noah's side, though, through every single one of a half dozen little fixes she'd needed in her small home, chatting, and Noah had just prayed that whatever she had wasn't airborne.

So much for that prayer answered.

Noah slid to the floor, his legs suddenly shakier than a newborn colt. He barely sucked in one clean breath of air though, when another contraction slammed through his abdomen. Bile surged up his esophagus, and Noah shifted just enough to vomit into the tub rather than all over the floor.

The taste of rancid, bitter acid took over Noah's mouth, but once he'd spilled his guts a second time, he fell back against the wall, spent. His muscles quivered too much to move to the sink for his toothbrush. Beyond that, the mere thought of minty toothpaste in his mouth sent a violent spasm through Noah's stomach and had him over the bathtub, heaving bile again.

Oh Christ. Noah didn't even have the energy to wipe the clammy sweat off his face. *I feel like I'm gonna die.*

He fell back against the wall, out of energy. Eventually he would have to get back to his bedroom and the phone. There was no way he could leave his cabin to work today. He needed to make a call.

ZANE DROVE ALONG THE GRAVEL road toward Noah's cabin, worry filling him as he mentally reread Noah's text that had come to him an hour ago. Usually Zane got a call or a text from Noah telling him the address of the job he was working and where Zane should join him. The text usually came about fifteen minutes before Zane's shift ended at the restaurant. Today Noah's text had come in around noon, and it had read: *No work this afternoon. Caught a bug yesterday. Okay now. Just need to sleep it off. Miss you. Enjoy free afternoon. -- N*

After Zane hugged Noah and saw for himself that he was okay, he would throttle the man. Telling Zane to just go and enjoy some free time while Noah was alone and sick -- as if Noah would ever leave Zane to get better on his own -- was ridiculous.

Or -- Zane pulled to a stop beside a blue Camry -- maybe Noah had wrangled Seth to take care of him for the day. Zane had seen Seth come and go more than once in the familiar car. Zane chuckled. Seth was probably more than ready to take a break from playing nursemaid. From what Noah had shared about his oldest son, the kid spent most of his free time with his girlfriend and had more than likely been pulled away from her to take care of his father. Seth would definitely be more than happy to have Zane take over the job of caring for Noah. The man was probably not a terribly good patient.

After grabbing a couple bags of food from the passenger seat -- one filled with food from the diner and the other from the grocery store -- Zane trudged up the steps to the porch. He knocked and then called out, "Seth? It's Zane."

The door swung open, but Noah's six-foot-one, hazel-eyed son did not stand on the other side. A statuesque, stunning brunette woman did, and she looked right at home. *In Noah's cabin.*

"Hi. Seth isn't here." The woman smiled, and God, it made her even prettier. "I'm Janice. Can I help you?"

Janice. Noah's ex-wife.

Damn.

She was perfect.

CHAPTER 15

J *anice. This is Janice. Noah's ex.*

It was entirely possible that even though Noah was the guy in bed sick, Zane might throw up right where he stood.

Zane didn't know why, but for some reason he hadn't expected Noah's ex to be so … so … so … incredibly attractive, and to have such inviting, pretty green eyes. And while she only stood on the other side of the door, something in her stance conveyed complete command, as if she owned the place.

"I'm sorry." Janice touched Zane's elbow. "Are you okay?"

"What? Yes." What the hell was wrong with him? Zane snapped himself out of his trance. "Sorry. I'm Zane." While still holding the grocery bags, he tried to stick out his hand to her. "I work with Noah. We're --" Heat suddenly filled Zane's entire being, and he clamped his mouth shut. Everything he and Noah had become to one another from that early morning when they'd kissed right in this open doorway filled Zane and warmed his core. He didn't know what Noah had told anyone about them, though, so Zane only said, "I live across the lake. Noah and I know each other. We're friends. I know he's sick. I'm here to help."

Her brow crinkling, Janice squeezed Zane's arm. "That's very generous of you, but Noah is resting right now. I have everything under control. I don't want to put more people at risk of catching what he has than necessary."

The woman took a step back, her hand on the door, and white-hot fire erupted in Zane. *No way are you shutting me out, lady.*

Just in case she was thinking about slamming the door in his face, Zane put his foot over the threshold and pressed his shoulder into the thick wood. "Thank you," he forced the same steady control into his voice as he'd had to employ when proving to a judge he was capable of raising his siblings, "but I never get sick. I've taken care of my brother and sister all my life and never once caught anything they brought home from school." With a firm grip on the two paper bags in his arms, Zane didn't force himself into Janice's face, but he did claim as much ground in the entry as she'd established when answering the door. "If you don't mind, I'll take my chances and see Noah for myself."

Janice eased away from the entrance. "Oh, well, okay." As Zane passed her, she pointed toward the living area. "He's right there on the couch. I thought it best to make him comfortable down here, that way we don't have to deal with the stairs."

"That's a good idea." The moment Zane saw Noah, half covered and sleeping heavily on the couch, he dropped his bags in a chair and rushed to the man's side. Folding to his knees, Zane put the back of his hand to Noah's forehead; an above average warmth sank into his fingers, but not crazy hot, considering that Noah's normal body temperature was probably a degree or two above the average male. Breathing easier already, Zane looked over his shoulder to where Janice stood. "Give me a list of all the medicines you've given him, and what time you administered them. I'll take over from here."

"Noah is the one who called me." Janice's matter-of-fact reply pierced Zane in the gut. "I'm not comfortable leaving him with someone I don't know."

Zane's hackles rose. He wanted to snap, but he forced himself to turn back to Noah and focus on him. "Then you'll have to work around me," he murmured, while straightening Noah's blanket to cover his bare chest, "because I am not leaving him either."

"Ahhhh." Janice drew out the soft exclamation. "My apologies. I didn't realize you were him."

Zane snapped his head around and narrowed his focus on the too-lovely Janice. "Him who?"

Janice perched herself on the edge of the couch, right near Noah's feet. "You're the only 'him' Noah has ever mentioned who has made him flustered when pressed about it." Janice looked at Zane with a twinkle in her eyes that made Zane feel put on display. "You're the guy who is borrowing his car. My kids have mentioned you, but I guess I'm tired or something because I didn't put the information together when you said your name. You're *the* Zane."

"I'm not *the* anything. I'm just Zane." The fine hairs on the back of Zane's neck tickled; it felt as if this woman were sizing him up for her former husband. Compared to how put-together and surely accomplished she was, she must think Zane a step down for Noah. Zane's face burned, but he kept his head up, facing her.

Nodding, as if to herself, Janice added, "I don't think I connected the dots right away because you're much younger than I thought you'd be."

Zane held in the growl that wanted to escape. "I'm not as young as I look. I'll be twenty-five in a week. And even if I wasn't," he put his hand over Noah's, threading their fingers together, "I know how to take care of someone who is sick. I'm stronger and more capable than you would think to look at me." This woman had no idea how many years Zane had cared for his ailing stepfather, and the backbone that work had given him. "I would never let anything happen to Noah. You don't have to stay."

Eyeing Zane for another long minute, a stretch of time that somehow felt like forever, Janice suddenly slapped her hands against her thighs and pushed to her feet. "Well all right then. I'll leave him in your capable hands." She spun, looking left and right, and then walked to the open kitchen to grab a purse and keys off the table. As she put the purse over her shoulder and headed toward the door, she added, "Seth will be up in a while to spend the night with him."

Breathing easier now, Zane nodded. "Thank you."

At the door, open once again, Janice stabbed her pointer finger at the couch. "When he wakes up, I promise you he's going to try to tell you that he's fine. He'll want to go to work tomorrow. Don't let him."

Still at the couch, Zane kept Noah's hand in his. "He's not going anywhere until he gets my okay."

Janice's gaze softened, and her voice did too. "I guess you're getting to know him a bit too."

Zane's throat closed up a little as he responded, "More and more every day."

"I already had a list of everything written down for when Seth arrived. It's there on the table. Call if you need anything." Janice waved and then slipped sunglasses over her eyes. "I'm on the speed dial. Easy to find."

"Thank you. We'll be all right."

"Bye."

Once the front door closed, Zane dropped to sit on the edge of the coffee table, his heart constricting as he looked upon Noah. Tension pulled at the man's brow, and he held his stomach, showing discomfort and pain, even while unconscious. Zane brushed damp tendrils of hair from Noah's forehead and then leaned in to brush his lips against the overly warm, furrowed skin. "Why didn't you call me to help you?" Zane's voice wavered, giving away his uncertainty and fear. He didn't understand why Noah would turn to Janice instead of him.

Still deep in sleep, though, Noah didn't respond. Maybe that was for the best. Zane might not like the answer. Pressing one more kiss, this time to the sick man's lax hand, only then did Zane get up and grab his bags. He had work to do.

Less than an hour later Zane heard Noah stirring. He ran to Noah's side just in time to see Noah blink heavily, a number of times, before he focused enough to look at Zane.

Noah pushed to sit up but then stopped and grabbed his head. "Shit, I'm dizzy. I need food." His voice was even scratchier than usual, so Zane handed him the apple juice he'd brought from the kitchen. After taking a sip, Noah lost most of the cloudiness in his eyes and he set his stare on Zane again. "I thought I heard you." A wispy smile lifted his pale lips. "But I figured it was just a nice dream."

Noah's sweet words did not make Zane melt the way they would have done twenty-four hours ago. "Nope. Flesh and blood." His body still familiar with this kind of task, Zane slid in on the couch next to Noah, put his arm around the man's waist, and helped him to his feet. "I got your text, and I came as soon as I got off work." As Zane spoke, he worked Noah's arm around his shoulder. "Up we go." He hoisted Noah to his feet and took the brunt of holding up his much larger body. "You said you're feeling hungry?"

"Yeah." Noah grimaced with every shuffling step he took. After Zane got him settled in a chair at the table, Noah took hold of Zane's hand, stalling him in place. "You shouldn't have come. You'll get sick, and you have Duncan and Hailey to think about, and your job…"

This time, the growl inside Zane slipped out. "And I have a crazy immune system that can fight off pretty much anything." Grabbing a tuft of Noah's mussed hair, Zane tilted the man's head back, and muttered, "If you'd given me a call this morning when you realized you were sick I would have told you that."

Noah flushed deep red, and Zane knew it wasn't from his fever. "I didn't want to bother you."

Sighing, Zane let go of Noah's hair and moved across the kitchen to the fridge. "I want to be bothered, Noah. I know I don't have much experience," Zane retrieved the chicken soup and popped it in the microwave, "but I kind of thought helping each other out was one of the perks of this thing we're doing together."

"You're right." Softness filled the spaces within Noah's gravelly tone. He even got up and pressed a kiss to the back of Zane's neck. "I apologize for not calling you first. Now," he stayed at Zane's side, but leaned heavily on the counter for support, "I haven't eaten in nearly twenty-four hours. Can I get some real food?" With a twist to his lips, he eyed what remained of the light chicken soup.

"You're not getting anything else." Eyeing Noah with a firm glare right back, Zane put granite in his tone. "You need to test yourself with something like soup or Jell-O first."

A bearlike rumble worked its way through the unkempt big man. "I need something with calories so I can get some energy back."

Zane pushed his slighter frame into Noah's space. "The soup and Jell-O first."

After a long-drawn-out minute, Noah finally muttered, "Fine."

Shooting Zane one last scathing look, Noah shuffled his grumbling self to the fridge and took out a couple of individual-size Jell-O packs. With his size, he ate both small servings within a one-minute time frame. He was clearly gearing up to complain again when Zane retrieved the heated chicken soup from the microwave, poured it into a mug, and shut him up.

The second Zane handed him the soup, Noah took a sip. Then apparently realizing the liquid wasn't scalding hot, he forewent the spoon entirely and gulped it down like a glass of water.

"Slow down." Zane tried to tug the mug out of Noah's hand.

Noah handed the emptied mug to Zane. "Sorry, but I'm starving." As Noah grabbed a banana from a bowl in the center of the table, he asked, "Can I get some more?" then consumed half the banana in one bite.

Immediately an audible roiling from Noah's gut filled the kitchen. The man went chalk-white, and he covered his mouth as he started to gag. No time to get Noah to the bathroom, Zane grabbed a big bowl he'd intended to use for food prep and shoved it in front of Noah, just in the nick of time. Everything Noah had eaten came right back up, and he vomited into the earthenware bowl. When he had nothing more to give, dry heaves still racked his body. His stomach contracted visibly, clearly reminding Noah it wasn't ready for food.

Zane rubbed Noah's lower back, knowing that such spasms often ripped the whole way through a body's middle. Eventually the jerking reflex within Noah came to a stop and he slumped against the table, spent.

"Here," Zane eased the bowl away from Noah's head, "let me get rid of this." Putting the bowl in one of the sink's two deep basins, Zane then grabbed a cloth, wet it down, and wiped the table clean. "I'll get you your toothbrush in a sec," he shared. "You can brush your teeth here in the kitchen and then I'll help you back to the couch."

His pallor very much still on the gray side, Noah pushed himself to his feet. Just as he started to topple, Zane rushed over and took the brunt of Noah's weight.

"What do you want to do?" Zane asked.

His tone terse, Noah said, "I want to go to the bathroom, take a piss, wash my face and hands, and brush my teeth."

"Okay, let's get you there then." Clutching Noah around the waist, Zane took a small step and got the sick man moving.

When they reached the bathroom, Zane let go of Noah at the door. Noah tried to close it, but Zane put his hand out against the wood and pushed it back against the wall. "Leave it open, in case you fall."

"Christ. Fucking Christ." Noah uttered a few more expletives on his way to the toilet, and then kept going as the splash of liquid hitting liquid let Zane know Noah was urinating. "This is embarrassing. Fucking mortifying."

"Noah," rolling his eyes, Zane tapped the back of his head against the door frame, frustration filling him, "I had my face in your crotch two days ago. I licked your balls like they were frosted doughnut holes and sucked your cock like I was trying to pull the cream out of a Twinkie." Once the toilet flushed and the water from the sink started to flow, Zane rolled his head and found Noah scrubbing his face with a wet cloth. "I hardly think seeing you puke should be a big deal between us."

"That was different." Pausing with toothpaste on his brush, Noah looked straight at Zane with sudden clarity piercing his eyes. "I hope like hell you actually wanted to do what you did to my cock and balls, and that it gave you pleasure too, or else I don't want you doing it."

As Noah started to lean his weight against the sink, Zane came in and braced him upright again. "I did want to, and I did love it." With a fast dip down, Zane pressed a kiss to Noah's strong chest. "But now I want to take care of you in a different way."

In between scrubbing his teeth and spitting out paste, Noah shared in a grumble, "In a way that involves having to supervise me while I take a piss, seeing me barely able to walk fifty feet on my own, and cleaning out bowls filled with my vomit because I couldn't even get to the bathroom in time to spare you that nastiness. I reiterate," Noah tossed his rinsed toothbrush into a cup on the sink, "it's mortifying."

Helping Noah to pivot, Zane got them moving in the direction of the living area. "I guess I know not to call you when I get sick."

"You already bragged that you never get sick."

"But if I did," they reached the couch, and Zane helped ease Noah down to sit, "I know now I shouldn't call you, because you'd be thinking it's nasty and mortifying to clean up after me the entire time you were taking care of me." Crossing his arms, Zane cocked a brow down at Noah. "Right?"

Noah growled like a bear. "Point taken." He made the concession, but he didn't sound or look happy about it. "I would want to take care of you, and I wouldn't think any part of it was a chore. You don't think it is either -- with me."

Zane clasped his hands together and lifted them toward the heavens. "Finally the smart guy who uses his common sense appears." As a reward, Zane leaned down and smacked a loud kiss to Noah's stubbly cheek. "Thank you."

"Christ, you know how to dig in, in your own way. I'm never going to win a fight with you. I can feel it already." Grousing still lived in Noah's tone, but a lopsided smile appeared and ruined the effect.

"Exactly. Which means, don't argue when I tell you to lie down and rest." Normally harsh looking on a good day -- in a way that made Zane's insides fluttery -- today Noah appeared haggard and washed-out. "Don't try to tell me you aren't tired," he added, giving in to the urge to brush his fingers through the man's hair. "I can see that you are."

Without any further complaining Noah shifted to lie back on the couch. "Can I try something to drink again, or have an ice pop or something?" He rubbed his throat, and he looked as if he had a difficult time swallowing. "I feel like I need something cold."

"I can help you with that." Before walking away, Zane arranged the blanket to cover Noah's bare feet. "Be right back."

A quick check in the freezer showed that the apple juice Zane had put in trays to freeze was still too soft for Noah to suck on. Zane didn't love the amount of refined sugar in a Popsicle but if Noah needed something cold then Zane wouldn't deny him the icy treat.

After grabbing one and then filling a glass with ice so Noah's juice would stay cold, Zane headed back to the living area. He came to a stop at the foot of the couch, his heart tugging at the sight before him. In such a short time Noah had already drifted off to sleep. He still didn't look peaceful, though, and Zane imagined that he was still a bit surly over losing an argument due to logic.

"Damn it though," out of Zane's control, a pleasant twitch teased in his cock, "even sick and mad you are still way too sexy."

The front door opened right then, and all fantasies about sex with Noah flew from Zane's mind.

Seth tossed keys and a baseball cap on a slab of wood that served as an entry table, ran his fingers through his dark hair, and then glanced up. "Oh, hey. My mom said you'd be here." Once Seth reached Zane's side, he shook Zane's hand, and then looked down at his sleeping father. "How is he doing?"

Zane moved his hand in a so-so gesture. "He tried to eat too much too fast and had a little setback. I was just about to go clean the mess in the kitchen."

"Still puking, huh?" Seth followed Zane to the kitchen. When he made his way to the sink and saw the mess, he crinkled his face. "Fun."

After putting the Popsicle and ice back in the freezer, Zane said, "Here, I'll get that." He took the bowl from Seth and headed for the bathroom. At the halfway point he changed direction and walked to the sliding door that led to the back half of the wraparound porch. Noah had to have a high-powered hose somewhere, and Zane would use it to wash out the drying vomit before cleaning the bowl with dish soap. "Your father is not exactly an easy patient," Zane shared as Seth followed him outside.

"You got that right." Seth chuckled, the sound deep like his dad's, but smooth as high-quality whiskey, whereas Noah always sounded as if he had gravel in his throat. "He is not fun to be around when he's sick."

As Zane headed down the steps at the corner of the back porch, he glanced over his shoulder at Seth with a grin. "I've already smacked him down once. Just call me on over if he starts acting up again."

Grinning back, Seth shook his head and hooted softly. "Be careful what you offer, man. When it hits two in the morning and he can't sleep, and he starts dragging himself around the house looking for something to keep busy, and then makes himself puke again because he eats something he's not supposed to," eyeing the bowl in Zane's arm, Seth made a face, "you'll be getting that call for sure."

An idea lit right in front of Zane's face, and he zeroed in on Seth. "Or I could stay with Noah all night. That is, if you'd be open to sleeping over at my place to keep an eye on Duncan and Hailey."

Seth sobered in a shot. "I was just joking about my dad. I didn't mean to make you feel guilty about leaving him with me."

"But I wasn't kidding." The more the idea filled Zane, the more it settled in just the right place in his core. "I need to leave to go get my brother and sister from town soon. I'll bring them home, make them dinner, tell them what's going on, and then you could come over to spend the night with them in case they need anything. They've hung around you a couple of times now, so they know you. And they like you; they've both said so. I think they would be fine."

"Seriously?" Seth's voice rose high.

"I don't have much for you to do over there," Zane warned. "I don't have a computer or any gaming system. And the TV only gets the local channels, and sometimes Hailey wakes up in the middle of the night --"

Seth held up a hand, shutting Zane up. "Dude. Keep an eye on my dad in a bad mood, who's probably going to throw up at least once or twice more tonight, or grab Matt's PS3 and go play video games with your brother and sister all night." Seth lifted one hand, then the other, as if he held scales, like lady justice. "Yeah, I'm taking that deal before you change your mind."

"Okay, cool." Zane beamed; he couldn't help it. "Let me get this cleaned up first, and then I'll go get Duncan and Hailey, explain about Noah, and about what's going to happen tonight."

With a quick nod, Seth backed up to the open sliding door. "My mom said my dad has bedding and stuff that needs to be washed, so I'll get that going for you."

"Sounds good. And, Seth," Zane called out, waiting for Seth's hazel gaze to meet his. "Thanks for being open to switching this up. I appreciate it."

"Nope. Seriously," the young man's eyes twinkled in a way that surely made his girlfriend want to hug him all the time, "thank you." Seth then slapped his hand against the glass a few times and went inside.

As soon as Zane was alone, he thought about what he'd just committed to, and he couldn't help the little tingle that went through him. He would be spending the whole night with Noah. Sure, the guy was sick as a dog and probably wouldn't be conscious for most of the night, but those were just details. They would be together, leaning on each other, commingling their lives, the way Zane figured people who had feelings for each other and were sleeping together were supposed to do. Beyond that, Noah was sick, and he needed somebody. Zane didn't want that someone to be anybody but him.

He's mine now. It's my right to be here.

With that truth sinking into Zane, right into the area near his heart, he got back to cleaning Noah's mess.

———

BLINKING, OPENING HIS EYES, NOAH scrubbed his face, focusing on his beamed, high ceiling. A long rectangle of moonlight cut across the dark wood, indicating the curtain across the back door had not been pulled closed for the night. *That's all right.*

The reason why the fabric had stayed open came back to Noah, and a soft place inside him swelled and warmed his belly. *It's Zane first night here with me.* The sweet man surely didn't realize the natural light from the moon and stars would fill nearly the entire cabin and make it difficult to sleep.

Noah shifted to his side and started to roll his legs off the couch, when Zane's voice cut through the night. "Don't even think about sneaking into that kitchen for junk food."

Instead of getting up, Noah looked over the side of the couch. His gaze traveled the length of Zane's body, the lower half hidden under a dark blue sheet. When he reached Zane's face, the man's pinpoint stare waited for Noah.

I don't know if I have a nurse or a warden. Noah bit back a grin as his belly fluttered and his balls pulled pleasantly in his sac. *Doesn't matter. I like him here either way.*

"I wasn't going for food," Noah shared, "although my stomach does feel much better, just so you know." Since the afternoon, Noah had thrown up twice more, but had also managed to eat some more soup later in the evening and keep it down. "I was going to pull the curtain on the sliding door. The light won't let a person sleep all night." He shot Zane a pointed look. "And not for nothing, but I'm sure you are well past needing some decent sleep."

With his hands stacked behind his head, Zane stared toward the sliding glass door. "I'm not awake because of the light."

Eyeing Zane again, Noah felt guilt creep into the myriad of other things playing in his gut. "You shouldn't be sleeping on the floor. Damn it," Noah looked from Zane up to his loft bedroom, "I told you I'd be fine down here, and to take my bed. Somebody might as well use it."

Zane's eyes twinkled to compete with the stars outside. "Noah, between you on the couch and me on the floor we have every blanket, sheet, and comforter in your cabin split between us -- and I have most of them." Zane smoothed his hand over the pile of fabric beneath him. "This floor is probably more comfortably padded than any bed in the county."

"Then why aren't you asleep?" Noah asked while tugging a pillow under his head so he could rest more comfortably on his side.

The soft light in Zane's eyes grew to a wistful little grin. "I can't stop thinking about the fact that I'm here with you," he admitted, his voice all soft and sexy in the shadows. "All night." His rolled his head and met Noah's stare. "Just you and me."

Twin lines of awareness shot north and south within Noah, both heating his depleted body. "And I'm still too fucking weak to take advantage of it." He rubbed his chest to ease the pain; getting anywhere near his cock would only cause discomfort he couldn't yet assuage.

From his position, Zane lifted up and pressed a kiss against the top of Noah's bare foot. "It's okay. I just like looking to my side and being able to see you."

"I know." Noah reached down and squeezed Zane's hand. "Me too. It was a bad attempt at humor."

"You sound better." Scooting closer to Noah's upper half, Zane sat up and pressed the back of his hand to Noah's forehead and cheeks, each touch sending lines of sweet pleasure into Noah's core. "Your voice sounds stronger, your head isn't quite as hot as it was earlier, and color is coming back into your lips."

Noah snagged Zane's hand and twined their fingers together. "You're a good doctor. Once I could taste the chicken soup and keep it down, I realized how flavorful and filling it was, without it being so much that it tore up my stomach. And everything I've wanted or needed, you've had it right here for me, before I could even think to ask for it." Noah sought the connection of Zane's eyes and couldn't look away. "Thank you for taking care of me."

"We're not done yet," mirthful warmth filled Zane's gaze once more, "but you're welcome."

"You clearly know what you're doing." Snippets of some of their earliest lunch conversations in the clearing tickled in Noah's mind, spurring his next question. "How long did you take care of your stepfather before he died?" Noah knew a little bit about Burt and the difficulties with his defective heart that had subsequently led to his death. With how efficiently Zane had handled Noah today, Noah could now see how much Zane hadn't said about the time during his stepfather's illness. Every moment Noah spent with Zane made him ache to know more about the younger man's complex history. "I'd like to hear," Noah added, "if you're comfortable talking about it."

Zane only stiffened for a moment. His eyes remained clear as he said, "By the time Burt passed -- a few months after I turned nineteen -- it had been almost four years."

Noah whistled low and long. "Good Christ, honey. You never got to be a teenager. Then with Duncan and Hailey…" It didn't take a genius or a calculator to do the math. "You've had nothing but responsibility on your shoulders for ten years."

"It's all right." The sudden twist to Zane's lips was a bit wry. "But now you know how I could get to twenty-four and not have any experience or any real idea about my sexuality."

"Yeah, when you weren't taking care of someone you were too fucking exhausted to do anything but sleep."

"I don't mind," Zane said quickly. "I'm not bitter. I don't regret it. Burt might not have ever been in the best of health, but from the moment my mom brought him into our lives he took me under his wing and made me feel like I was his in every way that mattered. His heart didn't have the strength to run around a park or to coach me in a sport, but he did other things that stayed with me longer." Pausing for a moment, Zane swallowed, and his Adam's apple bobbed visibly. "Things," his voice went scratchy, "things that meant more to me."

Noah slid down the couch, closer to Zane, and tucked the man's hand against his chest. "Like what?"

Dipping his head back to rest against the sofa cushions, Zane looked toward the ceiling. His voice slipped, as if he were going to a faraway place. "Burt helped me with my homework; he cared about my grades. I easily could have been a kid on the road to being a candidate for dropping out, but from the beginning he made me care more about school. When I was little he read to me every night; then when I got bigger and he started to get sicker, I read to him. He appreciated and loved a good story; he didn't care what age group the book was meant for or if it was considered great literature; he just liked the stories." Wiping the edge of his eye, Zane turned to his side. His eyes bright, he made contact with Noah again. "I think because Burt was limited in so many ways physically the books were an escape to other kinds of life for him. He lived an exciting life in his mind, even if he was unable to execute those desires with his body."

"He sounds like an inspiring man." Noah reached out to brush a bit more moisture from the edges of Zane's eyes. "What else made him so special to you?"

"He was so slight, yet he somehow had this great belly laugh." Here, in the shadows, Zane chuckled softly, and Noah was certain he heard his stepfather's laughter in his mind. "Burt liked to laugh. He didn't go to the best university and he didn't have the most prestigious job, but he had a quick mind. He could retell a funny incident in a way that would make you laugh harder each time he told it; he wasn't one of those 'you had to be there' people. Even when he couldn't work anymore, and eventually became bedridden, he never let his brain go to sleep. He had a fascination with science; every time there was a breakthrough in something he thought was interesting he would call us kids into his bedroom to share the information, and then he would ask us what the discovery might mean for the world or our lives in the future."

A picture of an exuberant dark-haired girl filled Noah's thoughts. "Your little sister has an interest in science. I've heard her talking to both Seth and Matt about new planets and the solar system and black holes, stuff like that."

Zane nodded, stars in his eyes. "That came from Burt. He was always a dad, you know? Even when he couldn't get out of bed anymore, or help himself in any way, he remained our emotional rock and our family leader. Somehow, just in his voice or the way he looked at us, we could feel his interest and caring about anything we said. And because of that, he was always the authority in our apartment. If I had a problem, I didn't think twice about taking it to Burt; he could talk me

224 | CAMERON DANE

through it; but even if the two of us couldn't come up with an answer by the end, he would be there with the hug and the encouragement that helped me understand that everything would be okay." Zane rubbed his cheek against his and Noah's tangled fingers, and he looked into Noah's eyes with such clarity it hurt to see it. "Burt was always a parent in the ways that mattered, even though I took over most of the physical work in the last few years of his life."

Using his free hand, Noah brushed his fingers through the strands of Zane's silky dark hair, mesmerized by the young man before him. "I can tell by how you've taken care of me that you bore an incredible burden of responsibility for Burt's welfare by the end. You know what you're doing in a way that is unflappable, and you have a core of physical strength that doesn't come from lifting weights. Muscles from a gym don't have stamina behind them, but your wiry frame does. You could pick me up, put me down, walk me around, change the sheets on this couch without moving me off of it -- for weeks if you had to -- without your body cracking. I can see that now, and it's amazing."

Zane shrugged. "I did what I had to -- what I wanted to do," he clarified. "Burt made it so that I didn't care about the man out there somewhere with my DNA. He filled me up with his love and support so much that at a certain point I knew the other guy could never measure up, and so I stopped even thinking about that other faceless man. But even more than that," Zane stopped, his throat convulsing visibly again before he could continue, "Burt gave me a family. If he hadn't come into my mom's life, and been so smart and funny and great that she fell for him -- even though he was this skinny guy that most women probably wouldn't have looked at twice -- there wouldn't be any Duncan and Hailey. Burt's gone, and my mom for even longer, but I'll always have them both because I have my brother and sister."

Noah's chest tightened with new understanding. "That's why you work so hard to keep Duncan and Hailey with you, in your care. It would crush you if you didn't have your little family intact."

Nodding, Zane clearly worked hard to keep new mist from filming his eyes. "Yeah. But more important, I think it would crush them if we weren't all together. Burt defied the odds and kept us all together for longer than the doctors or even social services thought he could." Zane's voice cracked. "Now it's up to me to do the same."

Unable to suppress the swelling in his heart, Noah leaned forward and pressed his lips to Zane's hair. "I never met the guy," he whispered roughly, still holding his mouth to Zane's head, "but I know in my gut that Burt would be amazingly proud of you." He tilted Zane's face up, got lost in those expressive sapphire eyes, and put them forehead to forehead. "I know I already admire you more than it's possible for me to express. I have from the start, because of everything you do to keep your family together."

Sniffling only a little bit, Zane touched his mouth to Noah's, clinging for a moment. "Thank you."

Noah clung right back, needing this man close to him more and more with everything he learned. "You're welcome, sweetheart."

They stayed close for long minutes, sharing each other's breath, existing as one in a different, new way.

Eventually Zane pecked kisses to Noah's cheek and temple, and pulled back a bit. "I'm glad you're feeling better, but you still look tired. Do you want me to go pull the curtain closed for you?" He started to push to his feet.

"No." Noah tugged the man back down to sitting against the couch. He looked, studied, memorized, and still it wasn't enough. His throat tightening, fighting the feelings swirling through him, Noah confessed, "I want to fall back to sleep looking at you."

Zane didn't say a word in response. Shifting to look toward the ceiling, he blinked a few times, then took Noah's hand in his. After pressing a kiss to the center of the palm, Zane put Noah's hand to rest against his cheek and held it there under the cover of his own. After making eye contact with Noah once more, Zane closed his eyes, proving just how tired he was, but he didn't let Noah go. He held Noah's hand trapped against his cheek. That was okay. Noah didn't want Zane to release him. Not tonight.

More than the fact that they'd fucked twice, more than the fact that Noah's balls swelled with the need to make them one again, it was Zane, the young, vibrant, strong man himself who held Noah, rapt, in place. The last twelve hours spent together had wound Noah completely around this man's little finger. Being a witness to Zane's strength showing itself in a myriad of ways, along with the talk they'd just shared in the wee hours of the night told Noah the truth: *I don't want him to ever let me go.*

Noah didn't just want to fall asleep next to Zane tonight. He wanted to fall asleep tucked next to the younger man for the rest of his life. So quickly, Noah already wanted forever.

Shit.

CHAPTER 16

"I'm starting work again tomorrow." From his vantage point on the couch, Noah watched Zane prepare a late meal in the kitchen. "And there isn't a damn thing you can do to stop me."

Knife in hand, chopping vegetables, Zane lifted his gaze from his task, a little grin lifting one corner of his lush mouth. "Not a damn thing, huh?"

Shaking his head, Noah smiled back with ferocity. "Not a damn thing, baby."

Now that he felt better, Noah partly grumbled for the simple fact that he liked to rile Zane up a bit and then watch how he chose to handle his patient. Noah's stomach had not clenched or gone into spasms in nearly twenty-four hours; he hadn't vomited since the first night Zane had stayed with him, and Zane knew it. With all that information, though, Zane still hadn't given Noah the okay to go back to work.

As much as Noah greedily adored spending all this time in the evenings with Zane -- this would be Zane's third night staying in Noah's cabin -- the truth was that Noah did need to get back to his job. In the last three days, when Seth hadn't looked after Noah during the time Zane had shifts at the restaurant, Seth had taken on a handful of Noah's clients whose needs had required basic repair work. But Noah had work piling up, and if he didn't get back on the job soon his loyal regulars would be forced to hire someone else to take on the repairs Noah had committed to do. Such a scenario was not acceptable to Noah, and deep down Zane knew that too.

But that didn't mean Noah couldn't see that Zane had as much fun pushing Noah's buttons -- now that Noah was better anyway -- as Noah did goading Zane into saying or doing improper things.

Noah glanced up at his loft, pictured the big bed that hadn't been used in days, and smiled at the sexy man taking ownership of his kitchen. "The only way you'll keep me in this cabin tomorrow is by tying me to my bed."

Pausing with a peeled carrot in his hand, Zane raised his brows Noah's way. "You into that kind of kink, my upstanding Mr. Maitland?" Blue diamonds danced in Zane's eyes. "You got a little bondage fantasy you want to share with me?"

A pleasant twitch stirred in Noah's balls, and thoughts of all kinds of sex with this man made a purring growl deepen to something feral. "I'd be open to trying a whole hell of a lot of things with you, my adventurous Mr. Halliday. Starting right now with whatever wicked thought is on your mind."

Zane chuckled and shook his head. "Right now I only have food on my mind. So unless you think I'm having lascivious thoughts about this carrot," he waved the long orange stick in front of him, "I'm afraid I'm going to disappoint you."

An explicit image instantly flashed in Noah's mind; his rear passage began to throb, and his voice went husky. "Put it in my ass," he said, his stare locked on Zane. *Fuck.* The forbidden desire had left his lips without forethought to pull it back.

Zane's jaw dropped. "What?"

The pulsing within Noah only intensified, and his growing cock pushed the reddened head to peek out from the waistband of his sweats. "Put it inside me." Noah's throat went dry. "I want you to."

Zane stood in place, stock-still, and shame started saturating Noah's system. "I'm sorry." Disgust that perhaps a part of him had turned too perverse, or that he'd sickened Zane with his spontaneous request, rolled new nausea through Noah's gut. "I shouldn't have said anythi --"

Zane lifted his hand. "Shut up." A breathy tightness gripped his tone. "You just surprised me, Noah." He held eye contact, and heat darkened his stare. "What you said made me so hard so fast that it paralyzed me for a minute." Zane stepped away from the counter, exposing the bulge in his cargo shorts.

Fucking shit. Noah swallowed hard. "Then come over here." Without looking away, Noah tore off his T-shirt and tossed it aside. "Right now."

Still holding the carrot, Zane swiped up a bottle of cooking oil from the counter on his way to Noah. He kneeled on the floor between Noah's legs, his bare knees cushioned by the pile of blankets still serving as his bed. After placing his treasures on the couch, Zane hooked his fingers into Noah's sweatpants and underwear, eased them off his body, and left Noah completely exposed. Noah felt naked in more ways than just his bared body.

Nervous laughter skittered up Noah's throat. "I don't know why I want you to do this." He eyed Zane as the man's smaller, deft hands worked oil into the full-size carrot; the mere sight made his channel flutter once more. "It isn't something I've ever thought about before," Noah explained quickly, vomiting words now rather than the contents of his belly. "But when I saw you standing there, and you said what you did, I had a reaction. I blurted it out before the thought fully formed coherently in my mind. I guess for that reason some part of me must not have felt it was wrong to say it to you. If you're not --"

Lifting up, Zane put his oily finger against Noah's lips. "I wouldn't be so damn hard if what I thought you wanted was wrong." The carrot fell against Noah's thigh as Zane let his digit slide from Noah's mouth to trail across his chest, teasing Noah's nipples to excruciating peaks of delight. "Half of that excitement came because you trusted me enough to freely confess to wanting such a private thing."

In response, Noah's chest banded as tightly as it ever had with this man. "I think part of what made me want this is because every time I see food now, I think of you."

His pupils flaring, Zane surged upward and slashed his mouth across Noah's in a biting, hard kiss. He strained his entire front against Noah, and Noah growled when he couldn't get skin on skin contact. Grabbing a fistful of Zane's shirt in the back, Noah shoved it up and over the man's head, cursing when it forced their mouths to part. Once the fabric cleared Zane's head, Noah dived back in for another taste, but Zane put a hand between their lips before they could merge again.

Each breath visibly labored, Zane stayed connected to Noah's hungry stare. He rubbed down Noah's abdomen, tickling his belly button, on his way to Noah's throbbing length. Taking Noah in hand, Zane worked a firm grip all the way up and then down Noah's dick, giving every nerve ending in Noah's penis a reason to sing with joy. Then Zane slid his palm down the underside of Noah's shaft, caressed his sac and taint, and Noah hissed and jerked. Damn it. Zane had a goddamn natural feel for how to handle another man.

Zane eased his middle digit between Noah's ass cheeks and fingered his hidden bud. "Spread your legs wider for me, Noah. Stretch them all the way apart." As Zane gave the gentle order, he pecked kisses to the inside of each of Noah's knees. "Go on. Let me see your hole."

Trembling like hell all over, Noah parted his legs. His span spread the full length of the long couch, and he braced his feet against the arms on either end. The move slid his ass all the way to the edge of the cushion, almost to the point of hanging over, and put him on display right where Zane knelt. *Ohhh fuck.* Noah exhaled unsteadily, but his nuts pulled right there in his sac, his cock pressed itself firmly against his abdomen, and his pucker squeezed hard enough for Zane to see it. Noah could not hide that his body wanted this even if his heart raced with the uncertainty of a new discovery.

Zane rubbed his hands along the insides of Noah's thighs, tracking oil along Noah's flesh, the warmth of his touch sinking deeply into Noah's being. He looked up into Noah's eyes, and open wonderment filled the light coming from within. "God, Noah; until you came into my life, I never knew I could want someone so much, all the time, in any way we could both imagine." Sliding his gaze down to between Noah's thighs, Zane watched himself graze his oiled-up fingers over Noah's sensitive taint, then up to surround Noah's balls; contact made Noah's sac glisten. Zane finally stroked up and down the full length of Noah's vein-engorged cock once more.

Zane teased his fingertip along Noah's wide slit. Gathering early cum, he then spread it around the under-rim of Noah's cockhead, and Noah hissed through clenched teeth. "Don't give me too much foreplay." Noah's entire lower quadrant already pulsed in earnest for something -- anything -- to enter his ass. "I won't last."

Letting go of Noah's dick, Zane poured more oil over Noah's taint, where it streamed in a neat line right over Noah's clenching, taupe-colored bud. "Have you ever?" Zane asked, holding Noah's stare as he switched to teasing Noah's entrance with his blunt pointer finger.

"Just myself, with a couple of fingers. Trust me -- Oh Christ, honey..." Right then Zane eased his pointer finger into Noah's ass, and Noah moaned from low in his gut. Noah's ring burned and his passage quivered, but he fully understood there would soon be a quick switch to intense, mind-numbing pleasure. "Trust me," Noah grew somehow harder just watching Zane's one finger work oil into his body, "it wasn't anything like what you're doing to me right now."

His gaze glittery, Zane flashed a sexy grin. "It's gonna get even less so in about a second." Zane withdrew his finger and placed the narrower end of the carrot against Noah's hole; in anticipation Noah sucked in a deep breath.

Shifting his focus between eye contact and what he was doing, Zane nudged at Noah's pucker with the top of the carrot once, then twice; on the third try he pressed just a bit harder and collapsed Noah's entrance. Without hesitation Zane forced a third of the peeled vegetable straight into Noah's ass.

"Ahh ... damn it, damn it." Noah jolted and pressed the heels of his feet even harder into the arms of the couch. An immediate shivery sensation sliced through Noah's squeezing passage, making goose bumps sprout along his inner thighs. "Goddamnit." Noah locked in on Zane as Zane continued to ease the carrot into Noah's rectum. Another tremble rushed through Noah. "It feels fucking cold inside me."

Jerking his gaze up to Noah's, Zane halted, the carrot half inside and half sticking out of Noah's ass. "I'd just taken it out of the fridge to start chopping it when you said what you did. Is it okay?" As Zane asked, he rubbed his slick fingers around Noah's invaded entrance, making the nerve endings in Noah's abused ring shriek and fire with delicious life.

Zane's touch set off a deep spasm in Noah's ass, and his channel closed tightly around the icy-cold carrot in a way that made him hiss. "Feels so strange, but it's good." Zane started to ease the long carrot deeper into Noah's body, and Noah added, "Fuck, though; hold onto that thing tight." He guided Zane to clasp the full upper fourth of the carrot's length. "But don't stop."

His eyes alight with discovery, Zane began to slide the carrot slowly, so very slowly, within Noah's passage. Zane would withdraw almost to the point of making the narrow tip pop out of Noah's opening, only to press the length home again, the gradually increasing width of the carrot forcing Noah's entrance open wider with incremental degrees. The uneven ridges of the peeled vegetable danced along Noah's anal walls with unexpected licks of bumpy friction, and when Zane twisted the buried length Noah cried out and jammed his ass up into the taking.

"Zane… Oh fuck." Noah moaned low as Zane shafted him again, faster and harder this time. Noah's toes curled into the arms of the couch, grabbing for purchase. Spread wide open, Noah hung his ass over the edge of the couch and pumped himself into the repeated thrust of the carrot. Zane plunged the orange length into Noah's hole again and again, wreaking havoc in Noah's ass. The pleasure in Noah's channel spread through his entire being like a contagion. And looking at Zane, so beautiful and sexy and full of light, made Noah believe he was getting as much pleasure out of this as Noah was. That knowledge shoved Noah deep into his rawest needs. "Do more," Noah begged, his voice ragged, his skin suffused with spiraling heat. "Do everything to me."

In a shot Zane's eyes flashed blue fire. Just as fast he bowed over Noah's lap, stuffed Noah's cock halfway into his mouth, and began sucking on the shaft. Shooting pleasure had Noah bowing off the couch, each muscle tensing as pleasure rushed through to every corner of his body.

Meanwhile Zane continued to work the carrot inside Noah's ass, teasing just inside Noah's ring with shallow fast pulses, making the ultrasensitive nerve endings there go wild. At the same time Zane eased his pretty mouth around and down Noah's dick ever so slowly. He swirled his tongue along the shaft in a torturous manner, and then sucked his way back up the width with all the speed of a sloth, only to lick with erotic precision into Noah's weeping slit and then go back down on his length again. The contrast between the rapid pace Zane set in Noah's channel and the slow drag he put on almost every inch of Noah's straining penis made the blood in Noah's veins roar so loud and so fast the sound nearly deafened him.

Then, with his lips still wide around Noah's cock, Zane blinked and looked up, making eye contact. *Fucking shit, beautiful.* The bright, open depth in Zane's pure gaze pierced into Noah's soul and mainlined rocket fuel straight into his blood, faster and with more precision than any sexual act could.

Noah cuffed the back of Zane's neck and dragged him up until their mouths hovered only centimeters apart. "It's not enough." He covered Zane's hand with his, and with a clamp of his jaw, groaned as he pulled the carrot out of his ass. "I want you." Noah reached down and rubbed Zane's rigid member through his cargo shorts. "Fuck me, Zane." His heart racing much too fast, Noah bit Zane's mouth and tried to pull the sleeker man completely on top of him. "Fuck me hard. I need you."

With another show of his newly revealed strength, Zane wrapped his arm around Noah's waist and dragged Noah to the floor, on his back, onto the makeshift bed. He shoved Noah's legs open again, this time anchoring him on the edge of the couch and the coffee table, and took over the space created, nudging his oiled-up dick against Noah's fluttering hole.

Noah gasped at first contact, and Zane licked his way past those parted lips for a raw taste. As he rubbed his cockhead against Noah's bud, his eyes glittered like a starry night. "You teased me mercilessly in the shower earlier," Zane revealed, exposing that Noah's plea for assistance, and the way he'd brushed their naked bodies together while Zane had scrubbed Noah's back, hadn't fooled Zane at all. "When I wasn't getting half hard fantasizing about offering you my ass in there, I was thinking about everything I've learned from you, and how I could reverse the tables and take you right against the pretty marble stall, with both showerheads pouring water on us while I fucked you until you couldn't stand up anymore."

This new side of Zane, the confident man who knew how to take charge and care for someone in need, had unearthed a dominant streak

-- one that shockingly made Noah's cock and balls thicken with base desire. "Do it next time," Noah said, his tone rough. "I want you to fuck me, Zane, whenever and wherever you want."

Slamming his mouth down on Noah's, Zane shut him up with a hard kiss. At the same time, he jammed his hips forward and thrust his cock deep into Noah's ass, filling him to the hilt.

As Noah's rectum took its first full penetration from another man -- from anyone -- he arched off the floor. He shouted into Zane's mouth, the sound muffled by their kiss. Zane yanked out and stabbed his cock all the way into Noah again, and new sharp pain sliced through Noah's passage. But good Christ, it was Zane inside him; that long, slender cock was tucked balls deep within Noah's body, and pain or no pain, Noah didn't want anything more than the fucking of his life from this younger man.

Noah dug his fingers into Zane's hair, holding him close, and strained his lower half up to meet every scorching slice of Zane's cock. "Fuck me, fuck me..." Noah's chute started to quiver and burn in the best possible way. Noah clung to Zane and fused their foreheads together. "Oh Christ," he gritted his teeth as Zane pushed into him to the root once more, "fuck me."

"Noah..." With each pump of his hips, Zane expelled choppy breaths against Noah's lips. "So tight and good. So hot, Noah..." Zane rocked his entire frame into Noah repeatedly, his pace rough and rushed. Some kind of wildness mixed with aggression and need, and maybe even fear, shone in his stare. "Can't go slow." Zane snapped his hips again and again. Each pump forward slid his full length with insanely fast friction against Noah's rectal walls, and in doing so sent Noah's ass into a flurry of fast and deep throbbing pulses.

Noah grunted and twisted in an effort to somehow get Zane even a centimeter more inside him. "Ohhhh fuck." Scraping his fingers down Zane's back, Noah squeezed the tight globes of the man's ass and tried to pull him harder against his body. "Fast is good. Everything is good." Bone-deep pleasure rushed between Noah's cock and ass and pulled taut lines up his belly and spine. Unable to hold back with this man, Noah clawed for more. "Don't ever stop."

"Hold on to me." Zane grabbed Noah's legs and forced them around the backs of his, tangling them into an even hotter, tighter ball.

His eyes burning bright, he wrapped his arms around Noah's head and whispered roughly against his lips, "I need to feel you everywhere." Zane then crushed his mouth down on Noah's and forced his way inside for another deep kiss.

Shouting hoarsely as every sweet need inside him for this man raged, Noah parted his lips for Zane's invasion and thrust his ass up as best he could to meet every stabbing thrust of Zane's scorching cock. Clearly sinking into his basest desires, Zane clutched fistfuls of Noah's hair, holding his head in place for a scraping, biting kiss, unlike any this man had given Noah before. Faster and harder than even his kisses, Zane pounded Noah's ass with speed that slapped his balls against Noah's buttocks in a furious rhythm. Noah's lips would be bruised tomorrow, and his channel would surely be sore as hell, but he gloried in Zane finding whatever he needed, no matter how aggressively, within Noah's body. Each touch, every kiss, the repeated fast slide of Zane's hot dick owning Noah's ass, wound Noah tighter and tighter inside. His balls swelled and his dick leaked a steady stream of early cum between the smash of their bellies.

Scratching his fingers up Zane's back, Noah sank his hands into Zane's glossy hair and strained up against him, desperate to fuse himself to this man forever. He broke the kiss but could not tear his focus away from the stormy ocean living in Zane's eyes. "Zane, oh God…" Tucked inside Noah to the root, Zane circled himself against Noah, moving his shaft against Noah's ultrasensitive passage in a way that felt like it shot Red Bull straight into Noah's balls, and Noah moaned from low in his gut.

"Zane, baby…" Noah bucked and pulsated out of control. His shaft swelled with such rigid thickness it hurt, signaling his endgame. "You're gonna make me come."

Zane's lips parted, and taut lines pulled at his beautiful, sweat-glistened features. "Fucking shit." A shudder accompanied his soft utterance. He grazed his fingers over Noah's face, his stare searching as he did, and Noah swore sun-filled skies filled Zane's eyes. Breathless, Zane lowered his mouth to Noah's, and with a grazing kiss, said, "What you do to me."

Good Christ, baby. Noah clutched Zane with such strength he surely dug nicks in the man's scalp. But fucking hell. The words Noah had previously spoken, given back to him like this -- proving Zane understood exactly what Noah had meant in that motel room nearly a week ago, and that he felt it too -- flung Noah heart-first over the edge of a cliff into release.

With barely more than a second to whisper, "Zane," against the sweet man's lips, Noah whimpered as his entire body seized and he spurted his seed between their fused stomachs. Each wave of orgasm had Noah's rectum clenching Zane's cock in a steel-tight vise. The feel of Zane embedded so deeply inside Noah only spurred another strong wave of insanely powerful spasms in Noah's cock and ass.

Above him, Zane parted his lips, and it looked as if he had trouble taking a breath. "Noah..." He pushed up to his hands, straightening his arms, his eyes a combination of wild and lost. "Noah, fuck..." Zane's frame was wound so tight, he trembled all over.

Still riding the wave himself, Noah pulled Zane back down on top of him, craving his weight and heat. Hungry for everything, Noah looked up, losing himself in Zane's eyes. "Come inside me," he begged, need rusting his voice. "I want to feel you everywhere."

A ragged noise escaped Zane. Just as he closed the distance between them, latching onto Noah with a searing kiss, he jerked between Noah's thighs. Moments later, he squeezed his eyes shut, and with their mouths pressed together, Zane unloaded his release into the farthest reaches of Noah's ass. As the first jetting line of cum tagged Noah deep in his passage, Noah jolted and his channel squeezed even tighter around Zane's cock. Zane pumped himself inside Noah time and again, and with each slide of his cock he dumped more hot ejaculate into Noah's body. Noah clung to Zane the whole way through, drowning in the essence of this perfect younger man. *Fuck, yes.*

In the aftermath, Zane continued to cover Noah for long minutes, his shaft still hard and throbbing inside Noah's body. Noah stroked Zane's sleek, muscular back, treasuring every moment alone with Zane. Eventually Zane went soft, and his cock slowly slid out of Noah's entrance. They both grunted when Zane's cockhead popped from Noah's hole. When Zane rolled off Noah and fell to his side, they continued to breathe heavily in tandem.

Pressing his lips to Noah's bicep, Zane shook his head and let out a little chuckle. "Wow." His chin came to rest on Noah's shoulder.

He flung his arm across Noah's belly, his gaze competing with the light from the stars starting to emerge outside. "That was all kinds of different from what it feels like when you fuck me. Damn it if I'm not sure which one I love more, but it's at least an equal wow."

Noah attempted to shift to his side too, but hissed as his tender entrance finally contracted into place -- as if he needed anything to remind him of what had just happened. Ignoring the sensation, he slid his arm alongside Zane's and twined their fingers together. "Jesus, honey." Noah expelled another breath heavily. "You have some staying power." Noah's sore ass would remind him of that truth more than once over the next day or so.

Right there against Noah's shoulder, Zane quirked a brow. "Probably helped that I jerked off earlier when I went to the bathroom." At Noah's scowl, Zane made a face right back. "Hey, I might not have attacked you in the shower like I wanted to earlier, but I didn't say the sight of you all naked and hot, with all that water running down your skin, was something I was able to ignore." With a grin, Zane rolled onto his back, but craned his neck to look up at Noah, a cheeky grin now showing. "If I hadn't come just an hour ago I probably wouldn't have lasted more than a minute once I got my dick in your ass."

As the shadows deepened across their bodies, Noah chuckled too. "I'm not complaining, believe me." He shook his head and whistled. "With what you did to me, I'm sure I'll start having nearly as many wet dreams about you fucking me as I already have about me fucking you."

"Yeah, me too." Zane suddenly shot upright and shifted to straddle Noah. Wiggling on top of Noah in a way that made Noah groan, Zane looked down at him with a twinkling light in his eyes. "Heck, I still have to finish making our dinner. During that time who knows how many more fun things you'll think up for us to do with all that food." Zane's glance slid to the carrot that had rolled halfway under the couch, and when he came back to Noah he made a fucking motion with his hands. "I have cucumbers and celery and all kinds of other things to inspire you."

His jaw dropping, Noah surged. "You little fucker." In one shot he rolled Zane under him and attacked his ribs with gentle pokes and light tickling. "You know you got off on sticking that carrot inside me as much as I did having you do it. I could see it in your eyes." Noah's smile suddenly slipped away, and new fear tickled up his spine. "Didn't you?"

Sobering too, Zane reached up and rubbed his thumb gently across Noah's lips and jaw. "I did. I was just teasing you. Other than my brother and sister, one of the very few things I like more than food is being with you." Zane threw the information out casually, but good God, the sentiment sank right into Noah's heart and latched on with a clamping vise. "When you and food are combined together, forget about it." Zane pinched his fingers together, pressed a kiss against them, and sent it out into the universe. "I'm halfway to heaven already."

Noah's focus slid upward. A new kind of ache, something deeper, filled his being. "You know what else would be heaven for me?" he asked, his voice soft.

"What?"

"After we eat that delicious meal you prepare, I want to take you upstairs and spend one whole night in a comfortable bed with you. Even if we're both too tired and we don't do anything more than sleep," new gruffness revealed the depth of Noah's desire, "I want to hold you all night and see you in my bed the first thing when I wake up in the morning."

"I want that too. Gosh," his arms sliding above his head in a stretch, Zane rolled his entire frame under Noah, and Noah swore he purred, "I like the thought of rising early and waking you up for work in the morning with the smells of breakfast wafting up to your bedroom to tempt you away from sleep."

A deep, satisfying warmth filled Noah's belly. "Christ, I like that too." He then processed the completion of Zane's comment and narrowed his stare. "Does that mean you're finally gonna let me get back to work tomorrow?"

Zane's smile came slow and easy, starting in his gaze. "With the way you took that fucking I just gave you, I'd say you're back to one hundred percent."

His chest filling with masculine pride, Noah sat up on Zane's stomach and cocked his head to the side. "You approve of my renewed stamina, huh?"

Sweet softness filled Zane's stare. "I approve of everything about you, Noah," he said, his tone just as gentle as his stare.

Good heavens. Noah sank into a puddle right back down on top of Zane. "Before you switch food back to the top of your list tonight," he slid his hands up Zane's outstretched arms and linked their fingers into a tight hold, "I want to give you this." He dipped down into a searching, easy kiss, moaning when Zane parted his lips and with a little lick welcomed Noah inside.

Hours later Zane's fancy dinner turned into a delicious midnight snack in bed.

CHAPTER 17

Zane frantically drew little amoeba shapes on the whiteboard, putting tiny lines in each one, then jammed the tip of his marker around them and pointed between it and Duncan and Hailey.

Sharing one half of Noah's couch, Zane's brother and sister shouted out words like, "bugs," and "popcorn," and "candy." Shaking his head, Zane jammed the marker against the big board again and tried to will the proper word into Duncan's and Hailey's heads.

"I don't know what that is!" Duncan shouted, coming up from his seat. "Do something else."

Just as fast, knowing time was ticking away, Zane went back to his picture of eyeglasses. This time he made a face around the glasses, added a graduation cap, drew a giant brain, and then circled them all together, to hopefully indicate one concept. Hailey said "school," and Duncan said "smart," and Zane made gestures with his hands, encouraging them down that line.

Right then, though, Seth held up his hand and yelled, "Time!" He sat in an overstuffed chair. Noah and Matt sat on the opposite side of the couch.

"Shoot." Zane flung the marker up in the air, catching it on the way back down. Looking to his brother and sister, he shrugged. "Sorry, guys."

Still studying the board, Hailey scrunched up her face. "What was it?"

"Look." Zane went back to his work, circling his little dotted amoeba shapes. "These are peanuts, nuts ... *nuutty.*" He drew the word out. "And this guy is wearing glasses and has a big brain and so he's smart; he's wearing a graduation cap, which is supposed to make you think of college." Zane made a waving gesture with his arm, as if the conclusion was obvious. When nobody said a word, he added, "He's a professor. *The Nutty Professor* was the answer."

With a nod, Hailey widened her eyes. "Ohhhh, okay." She crinkled her face again while watching Zane wipe the whiteboard clean. "I didn't see that with what you drew."

Noah leaned across the open space in the middle of the couch and bumped shoulders with Hailey. "I'm with you." Pinching his nose, Noah waved his hand in front of his face as if a stink had filled the air. "With what Zane drew, I wasn't thinking anything like that either."

Hiding a giggle with her hand -- as if Zane couldn't still hear the soft sound -- Hailey said, "You're terrible at drawing, Zane."

"She's right," Noah added in a deadpan tone, his face totally serious. "You kinda are."

Zane flung the dry erase marker at Noah. "Shut up, you." He rounded the coffee table, flopped down between Noah and Hailey, and glared at his man gloating so distastefully -- not to mention without merit. "You didn't turn your interpretation of Alice in Wonderland into the Mona Lisa either, da Vinci."

"Burn!" Matt shot up and made flame signals with his hands. "Dang, Dad. He burned you hard." The gangly blond kid held up his hand in front of Zane. "Nice one."

Buoyant once again, Zane accepted the high five with a resounding smack of hands. "Thank you."

Noah dragged Matt down across his lap. "Where is your loyalty, boy?" He feigned spanking his son with exaggerated sweeps of his arm and then pushed him off his lap back to his place on the couch. "My own son betrays me." Grabbing the marker, Noah stabbed it against his chest like a dagger. "Right through the heart."

Hailey giggled even harder, falling onto her side, and the sight and sound lifted Zane up into the clouds with as much lightness as he'd experienced in years. Beyond her, though, Duncan had practically wedged himself into the arm of the couch. The sight of his pulled brows and tight mouth popped Zane's balloon and sent him crashing back to earth.

Crap. Whispering, "Let's switch," to Hailey, Zane lifted her over him, placed her next to Noah, and then scooted in next to Duncan. Noah immediately zeroed in on Zane from over Hailey's head. His focus flashed to Duncan for just a heartbeat and then he came back to Zane with a nearly imperceptible nod.

"Seth," Noah gestured to his eldest with a snap, "you're up to draw. Let's go one more round."

Seth clearly, quickly took in the scene. "Yeah, sure." After jumping to his feet, he reached out and grabbed Hailey's hand. "Here, Hailey. You can be on our team for this round." He set her in the seat he'd just vacated and handed her the watch as well. "You can be in control of the stopwatch. I'll set it for you." Once he'd pushed a few buttons, he handed it into her care. "When I tell you, you just press that button on the top."

Hailey only nodded, but she held the watch as if it were the Hope Diamond. With such responsibility, Zane was certain she felt very important right now. Seth thought up a movie title, scribbled it down on a piece of paper for proof if questioned, stuffed it in his pocket, and said, "Now, Hailey! Go."

Drawing and shouting from the group ensued, and Zane took the moment to tuck closer to his brother's side. "You okay, Dunc?" He kept his voice to a whisper, even though Noah had ticked the volume up on shouting out his answers. "You look kind of funny," Zane added, "and you've become very quiet."

Duncan leaned in a bit too. "You're laughing, and you're face isn't all bunched up like you're worried about something. Usually you always look worried." The boy's attention slid to Noah, who'd busted out of his seat to shout his answers. "But lately," his voice went even softer, "not as much."

A stabbing sensation pricked Zane in the chest. *Holy mother, Dunc.* "You and Hailey are more important to me than anything, but I like

Noah a lot too. Are you still okay with that?" When Noah had been sick a few weeks back, Zane had taken the time to share with Duncan and Hailey some of the basics about his evolving feelings for the older man. Nothing explicit or even sexual or romantic was said, but rather just that he liked Noah more than just about anyone except the two of them, and that even after Noah got better, Zane still wanted to spend lots of time with him, even beyond working together. Zane had explained that being around Noah made him happy.

Looking up at Noah again, Duncan shrugged. "I always thought you would have a girlfriend one day," he reminded Zane. "I always thought one day we'd have a lady with us wherever we were living."

Zane squeezed his brother's clenched hand. "I know."

"It's weird," Duncan blurted.

Another stab pierced Zane, this time in the stomach. "I prefer the word different … or unexpected."

"It's not how I always thought things would be someday." The boy shrugged again. "But Noah is nice. I like him."

Relief flooded the holes punctured in Zane's heart and belly. "Good. You know I hope you can talk to me about anything, but if you really feel like you need to talk to a woman, you know Aunt Patty would always want to listen to you." Heck, the woman had even sent Zane a birthday card a week ago. She was trying. "I know I say the cell phone is only for emergencies, but you can always use it to talk to her. You just have to ask."

"Okay." His eyes suddenly widening, Duncan grabbed Zane's arm, and whispered, "I like Noah, though; I promise I do. He's cool."

"I believe you, and I'm glad. He's a nice man, a good man."

His stare a bit bright, Duncan shared, "I like him because he makes you laugh and smile. I know I'm only twelve, but I can still look around and notice it's hard for you to keep us all together, and that you don't sleep a lot and are always thinking about money. Noah makes it less hard for you, so I like him for that."

"You let the worrying be on me, okay?" Trying like heck not to tear up, Zane pressed a fast kiss to the top of Duncan's head. "Just like Burt kept the worry on him when he was alive."

"I'll try."

Patting his brother on the hand one last time, Zane got to his feet. "I'm gonna get a soda. You want something?"

"No thanks."

"Be right back."

Zane made a beeline for the fridge. Once he got there, and he had the door open, he had to hold still for a moment and pull himself together. He didn't want Duncan to know how much the boy's words had gotten to him. Not so much the kid's feelings about Zane and Noah; Zane had expected a period of adjustment, particularly from Duncan. More than once in the last few years Duncan had wondered aloud about a girlfriend for Zane. With Zane's life scheduled to the gills, Zane had said not to worry about a girlfriend and that it would happen when it was meant to. At the time, Zane had not had a clue that his desires would have been awakened so ferociously by another man.

Good God, though. Duncan's insight into Zane's worries and fears about money and holding them together as a unit -- something Zane had believed he'd hidden pretty well from both kids -- turned the barbecue sandwich he'd eaten for lunch rancid in his stomach. The kid was twelve years old -- and on summer vacation at that -- so he shouldn't spend a minute of his time fretting over Zane's problems. One of which was that Zane owed Clint another payment very soon.

"Hey." Noah's voice softly filled Zane's ear, and his big hand stroked down Zane's spine. "Is everything okay?" With his hand on the small of Zane's back, he guided Zane around to face him. Concern darkened Noah's stare to the color of polished coffee beans. "I don't mind if you're having trouble deciding what you want, but you've been air conditioning the kitchen with the fridge for almost five minutes."

Crap. Caught. Zane swore silently again and dropped his head down, squeezing his eyes shut for a moment. "I'm sorry."

Noah tunneled his fingers in Zane's hair and forced his face out of hiding. "Don't be sorry. Tell me what's up. I saw Duncan's face." As Noah glanced back toward the living area, where all the kids were chatting now, with Duncan still a bit pulled back though, Noah bit down hard enough to make his jaw visibly tighten. "Was this get-together with all of us premature after all?"

His voice as soft as he could make it, Zane took a few minutes to rehash his conversation with Duncan, not leaving anything out, including his own fears and anger at himself about unintentionally inviting Duncan into Zane's burden to financially care for all of them.

By the end, Zane looked up at Noah, and he couldn't hide the plea in his eyes. "What do you think?"

Warmth still enriching his stare, Noah brushed his hand down Zane's arm, taking an extended heartbeat to tangle their fingers together before letting him go. "This is just my opinion, but I don't think any of that is so bad. Duncan's hesitation with me feels about right, and what we expected. I think you handled all of his worries in the very best way you could; you kept calm; you didn't let him see how much you're sweating over it. Look at him." With a glance, Noah jerked his head toward the couch. "He's starting to push his way into the conversation a bit again. He's twelve. He understands a few more things than Hailey does, and he's acting according to his age. I know I can't tell you not to worry -- that's natural -- but I wouldn't go crazy with it or anything. I don't believe it's merited in this situation." Noah curled his hand around Zane's nape, and the feel of his rough fingers brushing Zane's neck sent crazy-fast, hot tingles down Zane's spine. "Okay?"

His stomach now fluttering in the sweetest possible way, Zane lifted up on his tiptoes and whispered at Noah's ear, "Do you always know what to say to make a guy putty in your hands?"

Mixed with a chuckle, Noah said, "Not even close." He then nuzzled the side of his head against Zane's and discreetly licked into his ear. "But I hope I'm getting a whole lot better with you."

The soft lick rocked a shiver through Zane. Pulling back, he met Noah's gaze. The intensity in Noah's eyes made the tremble in Zane deepen to a pulse all the way in his core. "If you get any better with me," Zane fought the urge to lean his full weight into the bigger man, "I'll never wear clothes again."

Noah made a soft sound dangerously near a groan. "I miss you." They'd grabbed tightly to a handful of lunch breaks shared in their clearing on days Zane had worked the whole day with Noah, and one morning Zane had gotten up early enough to spend an hour with Noah before they'd each needed to begin their individual work days. Other than that, any time they'd spent together had been with either children or working. Noah linked his fingers with Zane's again, and his eyes burned hotter than coal in a fire. "We need to find a way to steal a whole night alone together again."

Zane swayed closer, his body unable to keep distance between him and this stunning man. "I know." Their lips almost met, but at the last second they each jerked away. Noah clearly remembered they were not by themselves at the exact moment Zane had too.

Noah paced to the sink, and he released another noise, this one definitely a growl.

Zane parted his lips to sympathize, but right then a commotion ensued in the living area. As Seth stood, he loudly said, "Okay, I've decided we're bored and done with this game. Matt said he feels like having a root beer float, so I'm going to take the four of us down to the arcade to play some games and have some dessert. Come on." Seth beckoned to the other kids as he threw a glance in Noah and Zane's direction. "Y'all are on your own; you can find your own ice cream."

Noah strode to Zane's side just as Seth passed by the kitchen. "Seth, you don't --"

"Seriously, Dad," Seth broke in, "we're outta here. Especially since Hailey here," Seth pulled on the girl's braid, "openly challenged me to a game of Dance Dance Revolution."

"I did not!" Hailey craned her neck all the way back to look up at Seth, and she put her hands on her waist. "I don't even know what that is."

Laughter lit Seth's eyes, lighting the chips of emerald within the hazel. "Oh, then there's a good chance I'll beat you. Come on," he stooped down and pointed at his back, "up on my shoulders." Hailey scrambled into place so quickly it was clear Seth had hauled her around in such a way before. Once she'd situated herself, and Seth had gotten back to full height, he whistled to Matt and Duncan. "Let's go, guys." Seth made his way to the door, warning Hailey to remember to duck.

Zane grabbed Duncan, lowered his voice, and asked, "Dunc, are you cool with this?" He couldn't keep the concern out of his tone.

"Yeah, sure." The boy shrugged in that way adolescents do when they can't be bothered with such a stupid question. "Matt says he likes air hockey and foosball too, so we can play some games together. And he's gonna show me the new *Star Wars* pinball game. He says it's really cool."

On his way out the door, with Duncan now in tow, Matt waved. "Bye, Dad."

"Wait!" Rushing to the open door, Zane focused in on Seth, who'd already made his way down the steps. "Let me give you some spending money for them." He dug into his front pocket.

Seth waved the money aside. "Nope. We're good. Oh," the teen's attention shifted above Zane's head, and Zane realized that Noah stood behind him, and that Seth was now addressing his father, "before I go over to Kim's place later, I'm gonna run by the house to make sure Tom hasn't brought down the wall in the den, so I'll drop Matt at home before I bring Duncan and Hailey back."

Noah pushed in to lean against the doorjamb. "What the hell is Tom doing with the den?"

Seth replied, "He's attempting to put up that wall of bookshelves Mom has been talking about lately."

Noah reared as if someone had shoved a spoiled piece of fish in his face. "She could have called me. I'd have been happy to do it."

"She mentioned she was going to do that while we were eating breakfast," Seth explained as he opened the back door to his car and let Hailey down to the ground. "As we were leaving, though, I overheard Tom saying something about her needing to start asking him to do these kinds of things for her first, and that if her first thought was always going to be to call you then they would need to talk about the future of their relationship."

"Yeah," Matt added, standing at the passenger side door. "He sounded pretty mad, and Tom doesn't usually ever yell."

Noah blanched where he stood. "Fuck." Just as fast, he said, "Sorry, Hailey," but Hailey was already in the backseat of Seth's car and clearly hadn't heard the swear word.

Behind the wheel now, Seth got the car going and backed down the gravel road, the kids waving as he pulled away.

Once the car was gone from sight, Zane gave Noah a sideways look. He couldn't help it. "I haven't met Tom, but I already like him." Zane still couldn't forget the twist of fear in his gut when he'd knocked on this very door and found Noah's ex-wife on the other side. "I completely understand what he means."

A hint of steel hardened Noah's glare. "More than twenty years of relying on one person is a hard habit to break. I'm trying, though. I said I was. I'm sure Janice is too." Noah strode into the cabin, looking like a man with a purpose, but then abruptly came to a halt. He spun, and his gaze narrowed as he rubbed his chest, over his heart. "You know you don't have to worry about anything sexual or romantic still between me and Janice." More sandpaper than usual scratched Noah's tone. In his stare was a deep plea for belief. "There's no chance we're ever getting back together; she feels that way just as much as I do. You do understand that. Right?"

Oh, baby. Zane rushed into the cabin, straight to his complex, considerate man. "I know that." Up on his toes, Zane linked his arms around Noah's wide shoulders and leaned up to peck a fast kiss to his hard lips. Holding Noah close, without looking away, Zane let out the insecurities that had attacked him a few weeks back. "I'm sure Tom understands too. I'm not demanding that you never ask Janice to help you ever again, and I'd certainly never ask you to cut her out of your life. You have two kids together, and you still clearly like each other as people; I get that. I'm just saying when a situation arises where I can help you just as well as she could, that you ask me instead -- or at least let me try to help you first, before you go to her as backup. That's probably what Tom was saying to her too. He feels it's his right to be her automatic first call on most things now, not you."

Backing away, Noah smacked his hand against a support beam. "Shit. I probably unintentionally did make the guy feel emasculated, more than once." Noah shook his head and a humorless chuckle escaped. "I fucking thought Tom was doing a piss-poor job of trying to hide that he didn't want me around because I'm gay and he didn't approve, but I goddamn bet it was really about this. I should have known Janice wouldn't be with a guy who couldn't respect the father of her children."

Zane ran his hand down Noah's arm, hoping to ease the tension within. "Maybe you could offer Tom an afternoon where you walk around your old house telling him about all its little quirks, and how to fix them. Let him know he can call you for advice, and if possible you'll talk him through a repair so he can do it himself in the future."

"Yeah," Noah pushed his fingers through his hair, tufting the shorn blond locks, but did offer Zane a small smile, "that's a good idea."

Zane took a bow. "I'm here to serve."

"Fuck it, honey." Noah dragged Zane in and nipped his mouth with a nice, stinging bite. His eyes flashed lighter shades of chocolate as he held Zane close to him. "Do you always know what to say to make a guy putty in your hands?"

Dots of red bloomed on Zane's cheeks. "Definitely not." He leaned in, though, and rubbed himself against Noah's cock. "But it seems I'm getting better with you."

Noah's pupils flared. Sliding his hand down to knead Zane's ass, he growled, "Hell yeah, you are," and lowered his head. Just as he guided Zane's mouth to his, their lips grazing with the briefest contact, Noah blanched worse than he had a few minutes ago. He tore away from Zane. "Oh motherfucking Christ." Noah covered his face with his hand.

"What?" A shot of energy plunged straight into Zane's heart; he grabbed Noah's forearm and dragged the man back to his side. "What's the matter?"

Leaning his weight against the support beam, Noah looked as if someone had just sucker punched him. His Adam's apple working overtime, he cursed and added, "I just realized my kid cleared my house of people so that we could have sex."

A shocking spark of laughter erupted out of Zane. Noah shot a fiery glare at him, and Zane instantly muffled the mirth. "I'm sorry. I'm not laughing at you, I promise. But yeah, what you're thinking did cross my mind too." Zane tangled their hands together and tugged Noah back into his arms. "If Seth wants to give us this time," Zane wrapped his arms around Noah's taut waist and looked up into his eyes, "then let's not waste it."

"I can't. Not now." Noah appeared as if Zane had asked him to perform sexually in front of an audience. "He'll know." Pulling away, Noah dropped to sit on the arm of an overstuffed chair. "Hell's bells; he'll drop the kids off in a few hours, take one look at me, and he'll be able to read on my face that I spent the entire time they were away fucking you."

"He's going to think that anyway," Zane surmised, "so we might as well do it."

Then, sensing his salt-of-the-earth man needed some enticing, Zane kicked off his leather flip-flops and pulled his T-shirt off, tossing it at Noah when it cleared his head. Without slowing down or backing off one bit, Zane then started undoing his shorts while walking backward to the sliding glass door. Noah sat up straight, and a zing of heady victory went through Zane's system.

When Zane stepped out onto the back porch, he let his shorts and underwear fall to a pool at his feet, and Noah jerked to stand.

"Zane…" Noah remained inside the cabin, but his voice croaked. "Christ, baby. What are you doing?"

Now or never. Zane couldn't go chicken on this little seduction now. "Enjoying the afternoon," he said. He strolled to a cushioned bench and climbed up on it, on his knees, facing away from Noah. His heart thumped wildly out of control, but on the inside he silently challenged himself to finish what he'd started.

"Why don't you join me?" Zane added. He then bent himself over the railing, and with a wiggle, offered Noah his bare ass.

CHAPTER 18

Oh my fucking God. Noah hung still, staring at Zane's glorious ass swaying at him, and his body temperature shot up at least ten degrees. His cock spiked to life in his jeans too. Sunlight beamed down and caressed every inch of Zane's bare skin. From where Noah stood, ridiculous envy at the sun already touching Zane reared in him, leaving him aching. Noah wanted that contact with Zane. Zane was his, and his alone to pleasure, however he saw fit. Still, Noah stood in place inside the cabin, feasting on Zane's nudity only with his eyes. *Shit.*

Zane rolled against the railing then. He came to a stop when he kneeled on the cushioned bench, facing Noah this time, his erection jutting straight out from his tamed nest of fur. "Don't make me do this alone, Noah." Staring at Noah with the most scorching flames of blue shimmering in his eyes, Zane licked his hand from the wrist to the tips of his fingers, took hold of his stiff shaft, and began slowly stroking the slender length. "Your hands and your mouth get me a hell of a lot harder than just jerking myself off does, but if I have to I could probably make myself come just with you watching me too."

"Christ." Moaning low, Noah reached down and adjusted his rapidly hardening dick. "I've awakened an insatiable sexual beast."

"One who only wants you, Noah," Zane said, his voice tightening with each full drag he put on his cock. "I need in this way only because of you." Zane tweaked his little nipples, distending each one with small tugs that made him gasp. "For you."

Fucking shit, baby. Such powerful need slammed through Noah he shook with it. No longer caring about propriety or what anyone might think, he stumbled to a tall, open bookshelf, knowing he kept a bottle of lube in a decorative box there. As he fumbled with shaky fingers for the lube, his attention slid to a small package wrapped in blue paper with a bow stuck to it. A different kind of skittering rushed through Noah's heart at the sight, a fluttering even more powerful than sexual need. Noah grabbed the gift and the lube, and rushed to Zane with new jittery excitement humming within.

When Noah reached Zane, he swooped in, stole a fast, hard kiss, and then thrust the small box against Zane's chest. "Here. This is for you." As Noah's heart started hammering even harder, he stepped back and blurted, "Happy birthday."

Zane's mouth gaped, and his brow pulled with deep furrows. "What?"

"The other day a little birdie named Hailey mentioned that you had a cake last Sunday to celebrate your birthday." Taking Zane's hand, Noah gave it a little squeeze. "Why didn't you tell me?"

"It's not a big deal." Zane shrugged.

"It's a big deal to me." Noah pecked a fast kiss to the back of Zane's hand. "You should have said something."

Zane flushed red all the way down to his chest. "Okay; I thought if I told you, it might have come across as hitting you up for a gift, and I could never want more than what I already have when I'm with you."

In immediate response, Noah's penis shoved hard against his jeans. "Shit, baby." He popped the snap and loosened the zipper, giving his growing shaft some breathing room. "Unless you're gunning to make me come before I can get inside you, you should stop saying stuff like that. You know what it does to me."

Zane's eyes twinkled in the sunlight. He leaned up and pecked a kiss to Noah's jaw. At the same time, he guided Noah's hand down to feel the spike-stiff rod pressing hard against his belly. "The same thing you giving me this present does to me."

With a groan, Noah took his hand away before every velvety-hot inch of Zane's cock stole his complete attention. Instead, he forced a chuckle and said, "You don't even know what's in the box yet." He nudged the package against Zane's chest again, butterflies working overtime in his stomach. "Open it."

"Okay." Zane bounced a bit as he agreed, and his shyly sweet enthusiasm pulled at all kinds of strings already wrapped around Noah's heart. Zane tore through the paper like a little kid, but then paused for a moment before opening the hinged box within. When he did, he whispered, "Oh, Noah," and ran his fingertips over the matte, gunmetal-colored watch within. He then lifted his gaze to meet Noah's. "It's so beautiful."

Noah shrugged, but on the inside he did happy back flips. "You're always grabbing my wrist to check the time, so I thought you could use one of your own."

Zane arched his brow so high it went halfway up his forehead. "You don't like it when I grab your wrist?"

Growling in that special way Zane pulled out of him, Noah snaked his arm around the man's waist and tugged him to the edge of the bench, right up against Noah. "I love when you look at my watch, and I hope you still will. This," Noah tapped the box, "is for when we aren't together. I don't so much like the idea of you grabbing other guys to check the times on their watches."

Once again, Zane's brows knitted together. As he rested his wrists against Noah's shoulders, gift still in hand, he said, "You know what is kind of weird? I just realized I only do that with you. I never have with anyone else, before I met you, or since."

A powerful rush of possessiveness flooded Noah. "Good." Noah could feel the corner of the box against his shoulder, and he reached back to guide it between them. "I think it's a good-looking piece, but it's also sturdy and functional. You should be able to wear it at the restaurant and not worry about anything happening to it."

"Shit, Noah." Zane swallowed visibly. "Hearing you explain the thought behind why you chose this particular one is making my heart pound even harder." Zane managed to get the pillow holding the watch out of the box, but he couldn't get the latch to click open. A trilling chuckle escaped him, and he looked up at Noah with a shy grin. "Can you put it on for me?" He handed the gift to Noah. "It's silly, but my hands are shaking."

Noah's chest tightened wildly, nearly something painful. Still, first, he brought Zane's hand to his mouth and kissed the inside of his wrist. Only then did he take the watch off the small pillow, open it, slide it over Zane's hand, and then lock down the latch. "There." His voice scratched. "It fits." Noah didn't need Zane to know he'd estimated the size by thinking about how his fingers felt closed around Zane's wrists when holding him down during sex -- and that the memory was apparently seared so completely into his brain that he'd had the jeweler remove exactly the correct amount of links.

Zane held out his arm, moving his wrist this way and that, and let the sunlight glint off the watch from every angle. "It's perfect. I love it." Suddenly Zane threw his arms around Noah and clung to him with a python-like grip. With his face buried against Noah's neck, he whispered, "Thank you."

Just as gruff, holding Zane just as hard, Noah said back, "You're very welcome."

Zane clung to Noah for long minutes, and Noah let him, sensing the younger man needed to express his thanks, and this was how he did it. Noah welcomed the closeness; he didn't want anything else; he didn't need anything else. He just wanted Zane happy and safe, all the time.

As Noah held Zane, he rubbed circles into the man's sun-heated back, slowly letting his open hand glide in a wider and wider span with each go-round. Warmth infused Zane's smooth skin and sank into Noah's palm; the renewed tingle of growing desire sparked to life in Noah's hand and worked its way up his arm. Noah tightened his grip reflexively, and he began nibbling and sucking on Zane's shoulder, ravenous for that uniquely sweet taste of Zane's body, something only Noah understood and craved. Another growl full of ownership rumbled in him; he scraped his fingers down to Zane's ass, first squeezing the firm hills of flesh and then sliding his middle digit into the crease.

Right next to Noah's ear, Zane's breath caught with an audible gasp. He pushed his buttocks into Noah's hands, openly begging for more. Gliding his fingers through Noah's hair, Zane kissed his way up Noah's nape and jaw to his mouth, holding there as he looked up at Noah with storms of blue swirling in his eyes. "I love when you touch me." He keened as Noah pushed another finger into his crack to rub the hidden star of skin. "I can't seem to ever get enough."

Breathing heavily already, Noah let go of Zane to tear off his T-shirt and throw it aside, where it caught on the porch railing. He then quickly dug his fingers into Zane's ass cheeks again. The feel of that taut, warm flesh under Noah's hands made his cock rage behind his loosened jeans. "I want to do a hundred things to you all at once," he confessed. A combination of vulnerability and raw desire he couldn't keep hidden made his tone harsher than he felt inside. "What do you want?"

Leaning in, their mouths only millimeters apart, Zane threaded his fingers through the hairs as the base of Noah's neck in a way that made Noah shiver. "Kiss me." His open gaze pleaded as much as the words spoken.

Noah smiled against Zane's mouth. "Always," he said, just before pressing his lips to Zane's in a gentle kiss. Zane made a soft noise and tugged at Noah's hair, but Noah controlled the pace and depth of this mating of their mouths -- at least for the moment. Each grazing brush of their lips or fleeting flick of their tongues worked as a matching touch on Noah's cock, and his shaft lifted hard against his stomach and wept early beads of cum, filled with his need.

With every deeper foray into Zane's lush mouth, Noah moaned and rocked himself against his young lover, letting the friction between their bodies ignite sparks all along his exposed flesh. Unable to keep this contact at a teasing level anymore, Noah slashed his lips across Zane's and deepened the kiss, stealing his way to the back of Zane's mouth with aggressive swipes from his tongue. In response Zane surged against Noah with his entire body, his cry muffled between the seal of their kiss.

Fuck yes. Noah took the brunt of Zane's passion into his own flesh, letting it fuel his desire to own every inch of this man in any way he could. Reaching between them, Noah shoved his zipper down the rest of the way, and then pushed his underwear and jeans down just enough in front to set his cock free. The warm breeze in the air barely had a chance to drift across Noah's searing length before it reared and pushed against Zane's granite-stiff shaft, lining up as if they were meant to be soldered together. Zane jolted at the contact, but almost as fast he thrust his hand down into the mix. Along with Noah, Zane started working his fist up and down their straining shafts, right behind Noah's rough pulls. The constant contact sent Noah's dick into a frenzy of nerve endings, all clamoring for the tandem handjob.

Losing his sense of finesse, Noah bit at Zane's lips and fought his way back inside to fuck Zane's mouth in the way his dick wanted to ram into the man's ass. Instead Zane tangled his tongue with Noah's and gained equal charge in the kiss, licking at Noah as deeply as Noah had tasted him. Zane's battle for dominance pulled a wicked, swelling need in Noah's nuts.

Panting, his chest lifting and falling in big waves, Noah tore his mouth from Zane's and broke the kiss. "Zane ... Oh Christ, baby." Noah's body vibrated with pure desire. "Suck me." His penis throbbed with its own frantic heartbeat, and his request was pushed out through a constricted throat. "Please. Suck my cock."

Zane put two fingers to Noah's lips. "Shh. It's okay." He ran his hand down the underside of Noah's shaft to massage his sac, to Noah's gasp of delight. "Get up on this bench," he helped Noah up to stand on the cushioned surface, where he still kneeled, "and get that sexy dick of yours right in line with my mouth."

Before Noah could adjust to standing on the bench, Zane wrapped his kiss-reddened lips around the dark head of Noah's cock and gave it a good, hard suck. Acute pleasure rocketed to every corner of Noah's being, and a rough shout erupted from his core. With the second, deeper pull Zane put on Noah's penis, Noah hissed and punched his hips forward for more. Noah's upper body bowed backward over the porch railing, but Zane didn't slow down for one second. He easily accepted more of Noah's shaft into the hot cocoon of his mouth, and Noah could barely stand to feel the mind-numbing sensations working their way through his length to torment his balls. *Oh Christ. Christ.* Noah stretched his arms all the way across the railing, searching for a way to hold himself to this earth. Gripping the stained, sealed wood with a death grip that would leave him with splinters, Noah tried to harden himself against the feel of Zane sucking his prick. He didn't want to come before he had his cock balls-deep in Zane's ass.

Gritting his teeth, Noah didn't think anything could delight his nuts and shaft more than Zane's sweet mouth wrapped around his penis, sucking and licking and even lightly grazing his teeth over every supersensitive nerve ending living on the surface of Noah's skin. Each touch pushed Noah toward snapping. And holy hell, Zane didn't neglect Noah's balls either, and even seemed to love getting his face between Noah's legs to lick as much skin as he could. All of that pushed Noah dangerously near the edge of what he could stand to feel. But then -- *motherfucking God* -- on his knees, Zane looked up at Noah, and his eyes were glazed with desire. Zane started swaying that firm, pale ass of his, swishing the taut, enticing globes in time with each full drag of his mouth up and down Noah's cock, and Noah couldn't help jamming his dick even deeper into Zane's mouth. Zane only moaned around Noah's invasion. Between the sound of Zane's pleasure, the warmth of his constant suction on Noah's prick, and the sight of his perfect ass twitching high in the air, Noah severed what little ties he had to drawing out this encounter and making it last.

Jesus mother. Noah dragged Zane up from sucking his cock and scraped a fast kiss across his swollen lips. Base desire fueling his tone, he said gutturally, "I need to fuck you." As Noah stepped off the bench, he dug the lube out of his pocket and shoved it at Zane. "Make yourself ready for me." Noah needed a minute to regroup. He feared that in this second, if he pushed even one finger into Zane's ass to prepare him for the ride, he would shoot his load onto the porch floor.

"Noah..." Zane's eyes sparkled in the sunlight and his fingers trembled as he opened the bottle of lubricant. "I'm so hard for you." Zane remained kneeling on the bench, his cock plastered against his belly. His balls sat high and tight against his body, a deep crimson in color.

When Zane reached around to his tail end, Noah shifted, and he watched as Zane worked his pointer finger into his ass.

"Oh God..." Zane moaned with the self-fingering. His buttocks tightened, and Noah knew his channel must be clenching like crazy. Zane forced a second digit past his entrance and into his body. With two fingers tucked in his rectum, twisting deep in his passage, Zane bit his lip, and his prick leaked a milky line of precum.

His stare locked on Noah, Zane beseeched Noah with desperate hunger in his eyes. "I don't need anything more than the lube. Take me." He turned around and bent himself in half, not stopping until the side of his face was planted into the bench cushion. Reaching back, he then pulled apart his cheeks to reveal his hole. "I belong to you."

The sight of Zane offering Noah that slicked-up pink ring slammed a powerful need through Noah harder than a freight train crashing into him at full speed. Unable to check himself, Noah grabbed hold of Zane's hips with every ounce of strength he possessed and rammed his cock into Zane's ass, claiming him with one shot, to the root.

The second Noah took Zane's ass so completely, with such force, Zane shot straight upright, to his knees, shouting at the top of his lungs across the quiet afternoon sky. With one deep shudder, and one full penetration into his ass, Zane lost it, shooting an arc of ejaculate between the bars of the porch railing to the ground below. The sight of Zane, so beautiful in release -- not to mention the clamp his inner walls put on Noah's buried cock -- rocked a seizing tremble through Noah that signaled his needed to shoot too. *Fuck no. Not yet.* Noah grabbed his nuts in just the nick of time. The shock of pain stopped him from spilling his seed in Zane's ass.

Just as fast as Zane had come, he reached back and dug his fingers deep into Noah's hips. "Don't stop, don't stop." His voice was stripped bare. "Keep fucking me." The aftermath of orgasm still shivered through Zane's slighter body, and he continued to drive his passage back on Noah's embedded shaft. "You can make me come again."

Zane's desperation awakened the protector in Noah and helped to pull him into focus as nothing else could. Staying tucked deep, all the way inside Zane -- movement right now would shove Noah straight into release -- Noah curled his hand around Zane's nape to his jaw and tipped Zane up to look at him. "I'm not going anywhere, honey." Noah got caught in the brightness shining in Zane's eyes, but still he slid his hand down and wrapped it around the man's cock. "Let me help you stay hard." Noah stroked the full, semirigid length of Zane's prick; instantly Zane moaned and his penis jumped with life against Noah's palm.

With another long drag over the shaft, and a teasing pinch to the very tip, Noah watched his partner closely. Almost immediately Zane released his death grip on Noah's hips. Instead, he scraped his fingers down Noah's outer thighs, surely leaving angry red lines with his cut-to-the-nub worker's nails.

"Noah … Oh God…" As Noah worked Zane's slowly reemerging erection in his hand with an increased speed, Zane sucked in a shaky breath. "You're stunningly beautiful." Zane's gaze burned with something far brighter than lust, and Noah couldn't bear to see it without spilling every thought of forever filling his soul. *No.*

Letting go of his own balls, Noah yanked Zane's head up until not even the tip of a thumbtack would fit into the space between their mouths. Zane's pupils flared; his open desire was a tangible thing between them, and Noah groaned and seared their mouths together in a hotter-than-Hades kiss. He fought his way into Zane's mouth for a full taste, to Zane's cries of delight. At the same time, Noah continued a dragging motion up and down Zane's cock and he began to pump his dick within the man's burning tight ass.

Zane gasped against Noah's mouth and his passage clenched with exquisite tightness around Noah's invading cock. In response Noah moaned and jerked his hips again, the move sliding his penis along the quivering walls in Zane's ass. Both men trembled, and Zane's shaft went rock hard in Noah's hand once more, leaking new lines of early seed.

His eyes lighting from within, with something close to ethereal brightness, Zane whispered against Noah's lips, "Fuck me, Noah. I can take it…" He covered the hand Noah had around his erection and squeezed. "I want you so much."

An awful, wonderful pain seized Noah's chest. "You already own me," he admitted, emotion turning his voice to all jagged edges. "Heart and soul." With his slip of vulnerability, Noah claimed Zane with another rough kiss. He slammed into Zane's ass with the same raw note and slipped to a place of pure, untapped need.

Ohhh fuck. Noah kept his mouth latched to Zane's, drove into the man's slick channel again and again and again, smothering his dick in the most welcoming, tightest heat he'd ever known. Zane grunted with the more aggressive taking, but he reached out to brace himself against the porch railing, and even whispered a plea for Noah to fuck him harder.

Losing himself, Noah bit Zane's lips, swelling and reddening them even more, and then shoved Zane away. Noah pressed Zane's forehead against the railing, and he then gripped the wood with one hand. With the other, Noah ran his palm up Zane's sweat-slick spine, and then right back down to the cleft of his ass, loving the hot skin under his fingers. He marveled that such a vision of masculine beauty was his to possess.

Noah watched himself as he thrust his cock into Zane's body, two, three, four times. The sight of his shaft piercing Zane's hole repeatedly, seeing a part of his body disappear into Zane's, hearing the man's prolonged moans each time the taking happened, rocketed Noah nearly all the way home. He slapped Zane's ass, pinking the skin to match the color of his stretched pucker, and then groaned from all the way in his gut when Zane's channel rippled around his dick like an endless line of wet, nimble fingers. *Ohhh shit, yes.* Yanking all the way out of Zane's body, Noah then slammed his cock back inside, in and up, all the way to the root, and rocked Zane right up off his knees.

With the cry, "Oh God!" Zane jerked his head up from against the railing and his entire frame went tauter than a drum.

Going stiff instantly too, his heart stopping, Noah jerked Zane up until his chest rode the man's back. He pulled Zane's focus up to him. "Tell me you're okay," Noah ordered, his voice a croak.

Nodding, Zane dragged Noah's hand down to his straining cock. "You feel so good…" He worked Noah's hand with hard, fast strokes up and down his shaft. "Oh fuck, Noah…" Zane's eyes widened, and he began to shake. "I'm coming again…"

Just as Zane erupted with another sharp cry, he again shot thick lines of cum over the elevated porch to the rich green grass below. This time, when Zane's rectum clamped in a series of suffocating spasms around Noah's embedded cock, the piercing stab of gut-clenching pleasure was too great for Noah to fight. *Fucking shit.* Noah jolted too, shouting his joy to the great outdoors. He lost the tenuous hold on his control, and his orgasm unleashed a wickedly powerful river of seed from his balls. He spurted line after line of ejaculate deep in the confines of Zane's amazing, burning hot ass, loving that every drop of cum leaving his cock marked a claim of ownership inside Zane's perfect body.

At the end of his orgasm, Noah collapsed against Zane's back, all strength leaving his muscles. He struggled to regain his breath, and his frame lifted and fell in great rolling waves on top of Zane. Beneath him, still attached to him in every way, Zane sucked in gulping breaths too as he worked to return his breathing to something that resembled normal. The feel of Zane's sweaty, hot body beneath Noah's awakened another level of possessiveness in Noah, a marrow-deep need to feel the younger man next to him in bed -- everywhere -- all the time. Noah was a monogamous, commitment kind of guy, and every ounce of his body and soul wanted Zane to be his life partner in every way, for always.

With that thought, with the certainty, and how he could feel the rightness of his emotions attaching inside him, all the way down to his bones, Noah stiffened. *He's not ready. It's too fast. He's too young to say yes to forever.* At the same time those doubts crept into his bloodstream, Noah screamed a silent denial inside. Primal need surged through him and he began licking and biting Zane's nape and shoulders with ferocious intensity, desperate to maintain a connection and keep Zane tied to him for as long as possible. Noah's cock stirred in Zane's ass.

The moment Noah's shaft thickened, Zane moaned and pulled his face out of hiding.

Zane looked over his shoulder, his eyes almost drowsy as he linked with the blur of Noah's stare. "I love like hell just feeling you in my ass, and you can get me hotter than I ever imagined was possible, but I don't think even your prowess can get me hard for a third time, this fast." A small grin lifted Zane's lips, and he brushed a light kiss against Noah's jaw.

Noah gently rocked his hips against Zane's ass, hungry for the slight friction, but tried to be mindful of his partner. He rubbed his hands up and down Zane's outer thighs in a slow, sure pattern. "Are you sore?" He'd been more than a little rough, and he knew it.

New blooms of pink fought their way through the ruddiness already flushing Zane's skin. "A little," he admitted. Just then Zane's rectum fluttered around Noah's cock, milking Noah with the softest contractions in the most delicious way. Moaning once more, Zane added, "But at the same time I don't want you to pull out or stop."

His mouth pressed to Zane's shoulder, Noah smiled against the warm flesh. "Like I said; insatiable."

"Like I said," with one blink, Zane's gaze went from dreamy and sleepy to heated and full of open desire, "I'm only this way because of you."

Noah trembled from top to bottom and a sweet pain pierced his chest. "Hell, Zane…" He needed to speak his heart, but the words wouldn't push out through the lump in his throat.

"I know." Zane pressed the side of his head against the top of Noah's, and the slight contact felt like nothing so much as an enveloping embrace. "What you do to me too."

Something inside the cabin beeped just then, and the sound so surprised Noah that he jerked up and back as if someone had shot at them. The move yanked his cock out of Zane's ass, and Zane winced and shoved a hand down to his offended hole.

With a soft curse, Noah added his fingers to the mix. "I'm sorry. Fucking shit." He rubbed at Zane's pucker. Grabbing a fistful of the man's hair, Noah pulled the guy's head back and pressed a kiss to his lips. "The noise made me flash on where we are and what we were doing. I had a vision of the kids walking in on us while I have you bent over the porch railing with my dick up your ass." As Noah put his underwear and jeans back to rights -- neither had gotten any farther down than his thighs -- his mouth hardened with a grimace. "For a minute there I forgot we aren't going to be alone all day and night."

Zane lifted up on his toes and pressed a kiss to Noah's cheek. "I know. Me too." After giving Noah a quick squeeze around the waist, Zane backed up to the sliding door and into the cabin. "That was my phone, though. It's probably Duncan. If he's feeling weird again and is trying to reach me I don't want to ignore it."

Noah rushed in after Zane. "Of course not. Go. Check your phone." Eyeing Zane's nudity, and still feeling the tackiness of drying cum on his own fingertips, Noah veered away from Zane and went in another direction. "I'll bring you a washcloth and a towel so you can clean up."

Already fishing through his discarded clothing, without looking up, Zane said, "Thanks."

Once Noah reached the bathroom, he took a minute to pull his cock back out, wash his shaft and balls, and then pass a fresh washcloth over his face, sweaty chest, and armpits. When he felt decently clean again he dampened two additional cloths for Zane, then grabbed a dry towel off the rack, and headed back to the living area.

"Zane," Noah called, pausing at the kitchen bar. "Do you want something to drink? I could use some ice water."

A small crash in response sent Noah running to the living area. He found Zane on the floor, clearly having knocked over a side table and sending its contents across the floor. *Fuck.* Noah didn't give a shit about the broken lamp and picture frame. The ghostlike skin and lips making Zane appear as if he was at death's door put a fisting clamp on Noah's heart. Noah barely bothered to navigate the broken glass on his flying leap to Zane's side.

"Baby?" Squatting in front of Zane, Noah rubbed freezing skin that only minutes ago had been searing hot. "What's the matter?"

Bleak, wet eyes lifted to meet Noah's gaze. "I've lost them."

"What?" Noah snapped his fingers in front of Zane's face, trying to get him back in this room, from wherever he'd gone in his mind. "Who?"

"She wins, and I let her." Zane's voice cracked, and Noah knew the young man barely held back an avalanche of tears. "Here." Zane dropped his cell phone into Noah's hand.

What the fuck? Noah looked at the screen, and his legs went out too. *Jesus Christ.* Falling to sit on the coffee table, Noah stared down at the two-inch screen that to him seemed as big as the JumboTron in Times Square. And filling that phone screen was a clear-as-day picture of a naked Zane riding Noah's cock, in their little lunchtime hideaway -- an image forever captured of the first time they'd had sex.

CHAPTER 19

M*y life is over.* The words silently repeated in Zane's head. *My life is over.*

In front of him, Noah wiped his hand across his mouth, and he lifted an icy gaze to Zane. "What the hell?" Even harder lines took over Noah's already harsh face. "Who sent this picture of us to you?"

A hysterical bubble of laughter, one Zane couldn't control, escaped him. "Just keep scrolling. There is plenty more there. There's a note at the bottom. She has found her weapon to take Duncan and Hailey away from me."

"Your Aunt Patty?" Noah cocked a brow, as if he couldn't believe the name leaving his mouth.

"Got it in one."

As Noah looked down and scrolled his way through the rest of the photos, Zane didn't have to peer over his shoulder to refresh his memory to what Noah was seeing. Patty had sent Zane a dozen pictures via text, many of them extremely graphic sexual moments captured during the first time Zane and Noah had sex. Then a handful of others featured the two of them passionately kissing and embracing as they pushed their way into that cheap motel room the second time they'd come together sexually. At the end Patty had attached a note that read: *I have dozens more just like these. I'm meeting with my lawyer about the kids.*

Noah hurled the phone at the couch. "Son of a bitch." His eyed turned as dark a pitch as Zane had ever seen them.

Zane's heart wouldn't stop squeezing, and his voice cracked as the ruination of all his hard work swamped through his system. "I'm so stupid. She started being nicer to me, and she even sent me a birthday card. I invited her into my home to eat meals with us, and she started accepting. I thought that meant she finally wanted to be a part of our family. But all the time, she was being nice because..." Zane squeaked a wretched, forlorn little noise, "...because she must have suspected something ... I don't know how. She acted on a hunch, and I ran right to you and gave her everything she needed. After that she was just biding her time until she knew she had enough to bury me."

Zane's mind raced in a thousand different directions, searching desperately for an answer to what had tipped Patty off to his feelings for Noah in the first place. "One of the kids must have mentioned something about you during a visit or a phone conversation, and she must have picked up on something they said or how they said it. She probably drew information out of them without them even realizing what she was doing." Zane raced through the many things he'd said about Noah to any number of people in the last few months, and he squeaked again. "I'm sure I mentioned you and bragged about you as an employer in a way that kept her on my scent too. At some point she obviously decided it would be a good idea to have someone follow me. Oh God," Zane's gaze slid to the pile of clothes on the floor and then to the sliding glass door, and his heart plummeted, "they probably got pictures of what we just did outside too."

Noah's eyes slid closed and his mouth thinned down to nothing. "Fuck."

"I know." At the sight of the facts hitting Noah, Zane's heart went from his stomach all the way down to his feet. Suddenly feeling as if everyone in the world could see him naked, Zane grabbed one of the damp washcloths and began to clean himself so he could hurry back into his clothes. Guilt turned Zane's voice rusty. "If Patty decides to do it, she could ruin you too."

Noah opened his eyes, and pure black fire lived within. "No, she wouldn't. Not if she knows what's good for her." He shot up from the coffee table, began striding back and forth in a furious pattern, and stabbed a finger in Zane's direction. "And she's not going to get away with doing a damn thing to you either. Don't you worry about this one bit."

"I don't see how you can make such an irresponsible statement!" Growing hysteria pushed Zane to screeching levels, but he couldn't help it. He snatched his clothes off the floor and scrambled into them while watching Noah pace a trail into his hardwood flooring. "She can do whatever she wants now. Of course I have to worry about it."

"No." That one word from Noah sounded as if it had come up through his body from the depths of hell. "Nobody fucks with me or my family and gets away with it."

Oh God. Zane wanted to grab Noah and shake him. *Why can't he see?* "I'm not like you, Noah!" Fear grabbed hold of Zane's tongue and took command. "I don't have an ex-wife who still cares about me and who supports my sexuality. I don't have any financial resources to fight Patty, let alone an endless amount, and I damn well don't have the luxury of just hoping some bigoted judge won't agree with Patty and snatch my brother and sister straight out of my life!"

Noah shot Zane a glance that made him think he'd grown another head. "Zane," Noah came over and rubbed Zane's arm, "take a breath."

"Don't tell me to breathe!" Zane raged in Noah's face. "This is not going to get better by being Zen and breathing!"

"No," Noah leaned over Zane and roared right back, "but you won't accomplish anything by losing your shit either! You need to stop and think so that together we can figure out your best course of action."

The air went out of Zane's sails, and he dropped to sit on the couch. Images of a frail, slight man, with love shining so bright in his eyes it made him seem like a giant, filled Zane's head and heart and then cracked right through his soul. "You don't understand." Zane wiped away tears before they could fully form, but he still felt broken inside. He looked up at Noah and began spilling his final conversation with his stepfather. "Before Burt died, when he was so sick and barely able to speak anymore, I promised him I would always keep Duncan and Hailey with me. I knew it was what he wanted to hear, what he *needed* to hear, so that he could die in peace. I made him that vow, and I meant it." Zane parted his lips to go on, but for a moment nothing came out. When he finally found his voice again, it cracked terribly. "If what I've started with you gives Patty the ammunition to successfully take Duncan and Hailey away from me then I've more than failed my brother and sister. I've failed Burt as a son too."

Noah immediately folded to his knees in front of Zane, and he slid his forearms along Zane's outer thighs. "No, baby. You can't think that way. Patty is doing this. She is going against her brother's wishes and she knows it. Wishes that you told me are registered with the court, by the way. You already have that in your favor. You always have."

"But fighting this?" Zane screeched. "Being a young gay man trying to keep custody of his two siblings, against a woman who has already successfully raised two sons? Who's going to pick me?" Zane could already hear Patty's arguments flinging around in his head. "Patty will say that Burt didn't know I was gay when he made his claim to want me to have Duncan and Hailey, and so that makes his statement void. You better than anyone knows that reasonable, good people get up in arms and crazy-irrational when it comes to two men being together." Zane hated thinking it, knowing it would hurt Noah, but he needed Noah to understand the facts. "I don't have to tell you to look at your dad to know I'm speaking the truth."

The color left Noah's face, and he frowned. "Yeah, look at my dad." Just as fast as those words slipped past the hard line of his lips, Noah pulled back to the edge of the coffee table. A strange glint put warm coffee back into his stare. "Yes. Wait a minute." Noah grinned wickedly, and even chuckled. "Let's take a good look at my dad."

Zane muttered, "I'd rather not."

"But you should." Noah's grin grew even bigger. "He's a lawyer. Retired, but still a damn good attorney."

When Noah's intentions became clear, Zane drew back as if he could disappear into the couch, away from this insanity. "You're crazy."

"No," Noah shook his head, deadly serious, "I'm not. He could help you keep Duncan and Hailey."

There was no way Hoyt Maitland would represent the man his son was fucking. "Noah, you're insa --" Tires crunching on gravel out front made Zane snap his mouth shut.

The sound caught Noah's attention too, and his focus shifted to the front door. A closed door, thankfully. "That'll be the kids." He tangled his fingers in Zane's and hauled Zane to his feet. "Listen," taking hold of Zane's shoulders, Noah stood him up straight and looked into his eyes with clarity, "you go home and start gathering the things you've always had to keep on file as a way to prove you're a good provider for your brother and sister. You let me deal with getting you some pro bono legal assistance."

Going up on his toes, Zane flung his arms around Noah and held on with all his might. Noah slipped his arms around Zane's waist. The solid frame and heat in the bigger man's body sank into Zane's bones and finally started to warm him inside. Zane held on tight and whispered next to Noah's ear, "Please don't force a showdown with your father because of me. I don't want to be another battle between the two of you."

Noah cuffed the back of Zane's head and drew his face out of hiding. "Hey," his eyes clear and bright, Noah brushed his lips against Zane's, "I would do anything for you."

Choked up again, Zane buried his face against Noah's chest. "Damn it, Noah…"

Noah pressed kisses to the top and side of Zane's head. "We're gonna make this okay." He sounded gruffer than usual too. A car door squeaking reached through the cabin then. "Dry your eyes now, though." Noah offered the hem of his T-shirt. "Don't let Duncan and Hailey see you upset."

"Right." As Zane wiped his face, Noah's solid, even temperament and kindness filled his chest with the sweetest pain. Zane couldn't imagine a life without this man, yet some of the insensitive things he'd spewed and shouted only minutes ago slammed back through him and knotted sickness in his belly.

Before the kids invaded -- he could hear footsteps outside -- Zane blurted as fast as he could, "You have to know, when I said what I did about starting something with you, I didn't mean I'd wished I'd never done all the things I've done with you, or regret that I ever met you. I was upset, and the words didn't come out right. I'm scared of what Patty can take away from me. But you need to know you are right up there with Burt and Duncan and Hailey as the best things in my life. You have to believe me. I-I --"

Noah put two fingers to Zane's lips. "Hey, shh. I believe you. Don't worry about stepping on my feelings right now; that's not what is important. Okay?" Noah's touch slipped away just as the front door opened. The man easily transitioned to greet Seth. "Hey, kid." His stare narrowed on the empty space behind Seth. "Where are Duncan and Hailey?"

As Seth tossed his keys on the catchall table, he said, "I dropped them off at the cabin a few minutes ago." He then slid his hazel stare to Zane. "I told them I'd send you on home to them. They're kind of wiped out."

Already turning in a circle to search for his things, Zane replied, "Gotcha." He grabbed his phone and Hailey's little play purse from the cushions of the couch. "Let me get going then."

Noah brushed his hand against the back of Zane's. "I'll call you later." His promise to speak to his father lived in his unblinking eyes.

Shit. He's too much. With Seth arriving alone -- an adult son who obviously knew the score between Zane and Noah -- Zane took a chance and lifted to press a kiss to Noah's cheek. Noah turned his head instead and captured Zane's mouth with a soft, warm kiss.

Noah pulled away, and a playful twinkle lived in his eyes. "Bye."

Stunned, Zane said, "Bye," too. He even managed to say the same to Seth on his way out, and thank him again for looking out for Hailey and Duncan.

Once outside though, Noah's kiss in front of Seth, and the photos Patty had sent, along with the very real threat of losing his brother and sister, made Zane stumble. Too much had happened today, and the sweeps of extreme emotions Zane had gone through since stepping foot inside Noah's house earlier left him reeling. He wanted to celebrate that kiss Noah had felt comfortable enough to give him in front of Seth, but he couldn't forget that Patty held a very real threat over his head. If Zane lost Duncan and Hailey, all the comfort and openness with Noah in the world wouldn't matter.

Zane would be too gutted inside to know anything but the fact that he'd failed Burt, and that he'd lost his family.

AN HOUR LATER, AFTER SETH HAD left for his date, Noah picked up the phone. His heart pounded with a ridiculous staccato beat, so hard Noah felt certain that if he looked down he would be able to see its shape through his chest. Still, even though his palms were sweating, he dialed the number that would put him in touch with his father.

After two rings, his mother answered the phone. "Hi, sweetheart," she said. *Caller ID.* Of course Noah's father would know who it was and leave his mom to answer the call.

"Hi, Mom." Although somewhat awkward, at least Cathy Maitland tried to maintain a relationship with Noah; she still told her son she loved him, and she made fumbling attempts to ask about his new life. Noah suspected that much of his mother's discomfort came from a natural newness to learning she had a gay son, but more than that, not knowing how to manage the strained relationship between the two men in her life.

Noah must have gotten into his own head and paused for too long, because suddenly Cathy said, "Noah, is everything okay?" Concern gripped her voice. "Is something wrong with the boys?"

Crap. "No, Mom. I'm sorry. Matt and Seth are fine." *Just do it. Zane needs this.* Noah bit the bullet. "I need to talk to Dad."

"Oh." The longest, most strained pause that could exist between two people hung between Noah and Cathy. Noah could close his eyes and see his mother in his childhood living room, beckoning to his father, where the big man sat in his recliner reading a magazine. "Well…"

"I know he doesn't want to," Noah ignored the knife to the gut his father's rejection still evoked in him and instead put his full focus on the end prize, "but tell him it's important. It's not about me. Tell him it has to do with a couple of kids who need some legal help." Hoyt occasionally did pro bono work in his retirement, often on behalf of the rights of children and as an advocate for them in court.

A moment passed, wherein Noah could hear furious whispering through the phone, but not loud enough to make out the actual conversation. Then his father came on the line, saying, "What's wrong?" The bullet-precise command in Hoyt's tone took Noah back to his childhood, where he'd never felt safer than when he was with his father. "Who needs help?"

"My friend Zane," Noah answered quickly. "You saw him at my cabin with his little brother and sister the day you and Matt went to the car show." Unspoken in that sentence was that Noah and Hoyt had not spoken since the words they'd exchanged that afternoon. Fear that the disgust that had lived in his father that day still festered in him, and would cloud his judgment, Noah added quickly, his heart beating frantically, "Before you say no and that you can't help Zane because you don't approve of the relationship he has with me, you have to know that he is a rock for his brother and sister. They love him and need him. And their father, Zane's stepfather, wanted Zane to keep them together after he passed. Zane has done nothing but work and work and work to keep his brother and sister with him -- all without any help. I know those kids adore him, and he is their world, and they would be devastated if some judge came in between them and put them with their Aunt Patty, just because Zane and I have feelings for each other. His aunt wants those kids, and she took a bunch of explicit pictures of Zane and me together, which is offensive as hell on its own to me," righteous fire burned the fear right out of Noah, "but what is done is done. Zane learned today Patty is going to try to use our relationship and those pictures to take the kids away from him. Zane needs help now. Patty is meeting with a lawyer, and God knows what else she's already set in motion." Running out of steam, Noah sucked in more air, his heart squeezing. "You have to do something to help Zane keep them, Dad. You have to."

"Noah," Hoyt said. "I can't --"

"Dad, please." Hearing resignation in his father's voice, Noah interrupted, pacing his cabin as he pleaded. "You don't understand. I fought my feelings for Zane. I really did. I told myself he was too young. I tried to make myself find someone I thought on paper would seem more appropriate for me. But he developed feelings for me too. They're real. And he's so special, and he's so openhearted... I finally couldn't ignore or pretend I didn't want him. If he loses those kids because of me, because my feelings were so strong I couldn't walk away from him, I'll never forgive myself. I can't imagine what my world would be like if Janice had tried to take Matt and Seth away from me. It would have killed me if she'd done that and won. Only now, because of what I started with Zane, someone is trying to do that very thing to him. Please, Dad," Noah's throat thickened unbearably, and his voice broke, "don't say no."

Hoyt's sigh carried through the phone. "You got that habit of interrupting from your mother," Hoyt said, issuing a familiar lecture. "I was going to say I can't do anything to stop whatever this woman has set in motion so far, but with time I might be able to find something to counter her claims."

"Zane doesn't have time," Noah reminded Hoyt, urgency coursing through his very being. "Patty has already fired the first shot."

"I appreciate that, but I can't pull a miracle out of thin air. You need to get me whatever information you have about this woman, and you need to give me every legal document and court statement or decision that has been made in relation to your friend and his rights to have custody of his siblings. I have to know the facts that already exist, and have a talk with her lawyer, before I can decide on a move."

Yes. Noah went light-headed, and he sank his weight against the wall. "Thank you, Dad."

"If this father was of sound mind when he appointed his stepson as guardian to his children then I don't like it when someone tries to play dirty and override his wishes after his death. Get me the information, so I have a place to start. From there I'll see what I can dig up."

"I'll have it for you tomorrow." Emotion swelling his chest to painful proportions, Noah blurted, "I love you, Dad. Bye." Noah hung up fast, just in case his father didn't say the words back. The man had agreed to help, and right now, Noah had no right to pine for more.

Pushing himself away from the wall, Noah put in a call to Zane.

WITH THE RESTAURANT ONE BUSBOY down, Zane wiped down tables after the lunch crowd had passed, hoping that the familiar work would help focus him for his impromptu meeting with Hoyt Maitland today. Almost two weeks had passed since getting that text from Aunt Patty. She had agreed to meet Zane at her home for an informal conversation tomorrow -- although Noah and Hoyt would be with him. As of now, Zane didn't have one idea how he was going to convince the woman to back down from her plans.

Even though Noah's father had agreed to help, Zane couldn't stop his imagination from wandering months ahead into a courtroom, where he envisioned a pair of bailiffs dragging Duncan and Hailey away from him after the judge had declared him unfit and given custody to his aunt. In the time since he'd received Patty's threat, Zane had barely eaten, and when he wasn't at one of his two jobs he'd taken to plastering himself to his brother and sister, to the point where they were getting sick of him and wondering what was going on. Zane hadn't told them about Aunt Patty's power move yet. The most secret part of his soul, a piece that still believed in miracles -- after all, his mother had found Burt, and Zane had Noah now -- Zane prayed he would never have to tell them anything. Zane didn't want Duncan and Hailey to know that this woman they so loved and treasured was trying to tear them all apart.

The double doors swished behind Zane. He whirled, parting his lips on the expectation that he would see Noah and Hoyt. Instead the second bane of Zane's existence -- this one in a cowboy hat -- sauntered up to him with that familiar grin that said he planned to stir up trouble.

Before Clint could spew a single threat, Zane spat in a low tone, "I made a full payment to you last week, and you'll get another one when I get paid again. But I swear to God I do not have time to deal with you today," Zane could only focus on one crisis at a time, "so get the hell out of here right now."

Clint slipped his Stetson off easy as you please, but anyone looking in his flinty eyes would see that he was anything but a friendly cowboy. "You might want to check your manners again, because I don't think it's a good idea to mouth off to the person who holds your life in his hands."

Zane laughed outright in Clint's face; panic wouldn't let him rein it in. "You don't have any idea how much I don't care about you right now." If Patty took him to court, her lawyer would certainly uncover these stupid loans; whatever balance Zane still owed then wouldn't matter. The fact that he'd been a dumbass for not only taking one loan in the first place, but two more after that, would seal the deal on his fitness as a guardian to two kids. "You will get another payment on time. Everything else is just threats."

"You should think twice about how you talk to me, boy," Clint murmured with vicious softness. "Otherwise I might not be so nice to you next time."

The door whooshed open behind Clint, and in a split second, Noah had his hand pinched in a vise around the back of Clint's neck. Noah dipped down, right in Clint's face, and nothing but pure darkness filled his stare. "I don't know who the fuck you think you are, but you have bothered this man at his job for the last time. If I don't hear that you are as polite as a goddamn nun the next time you come into this establishment, I will find you, and you will be sipping the rest of your meals out of a straw." Noah then released Clint's neck and added, "Are we clear?"

Taking a step back, Clint lifted his hands up, hat still in one. "We're all friends here."

Noah bared his teeth like a wolf. "No we're not. Leave." Black coal fires still lit his eyes. "Now."

Clint shot Zane a look that made a shiver run down Zane's spine, and then he strode out of the restaurant.

As soon as Clint disappeared, Noah rubbed his hand across Zane's shoulders. "Are you all right?" He could surely feel Zane trembling.

"Not really," Zane admitted, "but not because of him." That wasn't entirely a lie. His nerves had been shot for nearly two weeks, because of Patty, and Noah knew it. Still, more than Noah's physical strength, it was his very nearness and calm nature that soothed some of the chaos inside Zane. Zane looked up at Noah, adoration filling his being, and squeezed his hand. "Thank you."

His face still all harsh lines, Noah countered by brushing the softest touch against Zane's cheek with his knuckles. "You and the other servers should let the owner know if that jackass comes in here and harasses any one of you again. I'm sure that's not a work environment she would want for her people."

Zane forced a tight smile. "I know; you're right." Lifting his focus past Noah, Zane automatically straightened to attention at the sight of big, silver-blond Hoyt Maitland. "Sir. It's good to see you. Thank you again for agreeing to help me." Zane had expressed his appreciation to Hoyt on multiple occasions, but God, he couldn't help himself. "This means everything to me."

Hoyt's features were as rough as his son's, and right now his face was ruddy too. Without a doubt Zane knew Noah's father wasn't yet okay with witnessing his son's affection for another man, not even an innocent, quick handhold or a brush to the cheek.

Even with his obvious discomfort, Hoyt nodded and offered his hand in greeting. After Zane shook it, Hoyt said, "Why don't we sit down?" Grim lines filled his face once more. "One of my retired investigator buddies found something I think you'll want to see."

Once they'd all taken a seat, Hoyt slid a folder across the table to Zane. Before Zane could open it, Hoyt put his hand on top of the file and lifted his gaze to Zane's. "Let me share a few things before you read what is in this file."

Hoyt's piercing stare made Zane take his hands off the table and tuck them between his knees. "Okay."

"First, one of my friends who is still practicing law is very aware of the lawyer representing your aunt. The guy is young; an up-and-comer, and he is ambitious. He also has certain personal views that would make him an eager representative of your aunt. This is not speculation; this is fact based on knowledge and observation from my colleague." Hoyt's visage graver than grave, he went on, "The firm he works for is known to have an inside track to getting their cases onto the dockets of the judges they want."

Zane blanched, and Noah muttered, "Fuck."

"As your attorney," Hoyt kept his attention on Zane, "I cannot advise you to use the information in this file in any way other than through the legal system. In point of fact, I haven't even officially read it myself. I'm just passing along information from a friend. You look at it. I can't give you one word of advice. You read it, you sleep on it, and you make the decision. Tomorrow we'll all go to your meeting with your Aunt Patty. When we get there you'll let me know if I'm to listen in on your conversation with your aunt as your legal counsel." With a nod, Hoyt took his hand away. "Understood?"

Zane nodded and opened the folder. As he began reading, he started shaking.

He had a future again. If he dared make the move necessary to take it.

CHAPTER 20

Wearing his nicest jeans, dress shirt, and the only tie he owned, Zane lifted his hand and knocked on Aunt Patty's door. Zane clutched the file from yesterday in his sweaty palm, and even though he had guzzled a bottle of water just a few minutes ago, his mouth and throat felt as if he'd spent the drive sucking on a salt lick. Noah and Hoyt stood back and to Zane's right. Once Noah had seen the glider on Patty's porch he'd stated that he and his father would wait for Zane right there and be within shouting distance if Zane needed them.

Zane fully understood, however, he needed to do this on his own.

With tension thrumming through him, Zane put his knuckles to the wood with more force. "Aunt Patty, it's Zane." Pictures of Duncan and Hailey grew front and center in Zane's mind, lending strength and volume to his words. "You agreed to have this talk. Please open the door."

The door whipped open, and Zane's aunt stood on the other side, impeccably coiffed and dressed. "I am not your aunt. I never was." She looked as though she wanted to gouge out his eyes.

"Then I will simply call you ma'am." Zane countered her rancor with manners. "But no matter how you wish for me to address you, we need to talk."

"Call my lawyer to set up an appointment. I've changed my mind."

Zane slid his hand, the one still gripping the file, against his aunt's door. *Here it goes.* "Or instead of calling your lawyer, I could call the police."

Patty scrunched her perfectly penciled eyebrows. "Why on earth would you do that?"

So she doesn't know, or she's a really good actress. Zane couldn't be sure yet. Still, out of deference to his love for Burt, he glanced up and down the nice, quiet neighborhood block, and asked, "Do you really want us talking about family matters on your porch?"

"Fine. Come inside." Patty stepped out of the entryway. "But make it quick."

Before stepping over the threshold, Zane found Noah a short distance away and held his gaze. The look exchanged only lasted a few seconds, but the encouragement and support conveyed through Noah's rich, warm eyes steadied Zane's core and helped to ease the buzzing in his head and heart. Noah tilted his head toward the glider where he would wait, and Zane knew his back was covered even though he walked into the lioness's den alone.

Patty led Zane to the kitchen and indicated with a nod that he sit down. After he did, she took a seat at the head of the table and laid one of her rigid, unblinking stares on him. "You're not keeping those kids. I already have this house ready for them, each with their own bedroom. It's just a matter of time before the court gives them to me."

As Patty spoke, she fiddled with a spoon on the linen placemat in front of her, mimicking a stirring motion, as if she were thinking about serving herself tea. "Or if you don't want those pictures becoming public, you can just tell the court you want me to have the kids. You don't have a career to worry about ruining, but I understand your sugar daddy has somehow managed to keep himself a nice reputation, even after telling everyone he's a gay. That's nice in theory," she offered a little shrug, "but I bet if they see graphic pictures of him screwing a much younger man they might think twice about how they really feel about having a homosexual working in their homes."

God, how Zane wanted to shout and rail in this woman's face, but he forced himself to merely mimic her shrug. "That's true, but then again, the public isn't who is going to decide who gets custody of Duncan and Hailey. You need a court to do that." Matching the tap of his finger against his folder to the rate Patty twirled her spoon, Zane didn't blink either. He nailed Patty to her chair with his stare as he dropped his bomb. "I think the bigger story is the fact that the woman who wants to take a pair of happy kids from a hardworking young man -- who just so happens to be gay and in a monogamous relationship with a stable, older man -- has two adult sons of her own who are currently breaking the law and have been doing so for quite a while. I think that might be the bigger headline, not to mention more relevant to the courts, than the fact that I'm in a relationship with another guy."

The spoon dropped from Patty's hand with a loud clank and she went very still. "You're lying."

"No, actually I'm not." Zane worked with every fiber of his being to remain cordial -- but was also deadly serious. "You're not the only one who's allowed to hire an investigator. My guy is retired and had a lot of free time to dig for me in a short amount of time. As it turns out," Zane flipped open the file and slid it across the table to Patty, "your boys have been busy. That auto repair shop your husband used to own -- that your oldest son now runs -- is also a chop shop. Small-time right now, according to my guy, but growing at an ambitious rate. He says your husband probably wisely kept the chop shop small in order to stay under the radar, but your son doesn't seem to share that view. I don't have to tell you that your youngest works there too, and so I'm sure he's in that mess knee-deep himself. Not that he needs it," reaching across the table, Zane flipped a few pages back in the folder for her, "because he's doing a fine job as a collector for a bookie. But better than that, it's looking a whole lot like he's started himself up a cockfighting ring. Now I don't have definitive proof on that yet, but my investigator is working on that as we speak." Zane leaned back in his chair, his attention on his aunt, and settled his arms against his chest. "How much do you want to bet it won't take him long to find it?"

With unsteady fingers, Patty flipped through all the papers in the file, creating a mess. "This isn't true."

As Zane studied the woman before him, a sad sickness started mixing with the righteousness boiling inside him. "I honestly can't tell if you're trying to con me, or are being sincere right now."

Her moves openly frantic, Patty shoved the papers in front of her back to Zane. She parted her lips, opening and closing her mouth like a fish, before finally sputtering, "This could all be falsified, and how would I know? It's certainly not beneath you."

"It's all real." Zane didn't flinch; he needed her to understand he was not bluffing. "I'm willing to take it to the nearest police station to prove it."

Beneath her makeup, in a way no foundation could cover, the color fled from Patty's face. "You wouldn't."

Zane's gut kicked in fully, and pure loss and heartache flooded him. *She truly didn't know.* He looked at this woman again -- this sad, lonely widow -- and like a line of dominoes, things started falling into place and creating an obvious picture. Other memories from Zane's childhood fizzed to the surface and filled in the color to create a complete image.

Everything within him slowing down, Zane softly shared, "You know, I always used to wonder what you could possibly think was so awful about my mom. What could she have done to make you hate her so much? Up until just now I thought it was because she was so poor, and she didn't have the greatest education, and you thought your brother married beneath himself when he fell in love and offered for her."

Patty lifted her pert surgically-enhanced nose in the air. "He did."

"No," Zane settled into his seat as the wheels inside spun a new truth for him, "I see now it wouldn't have mattered who my mother was. It was really about Burt and how he felt about your late husband -- who existed before he ever met my mother." The fact that without the file from yesterday Zane wouldn't even have been able to remember the names of Patty's children resonated with so much more meaning for him now. "Burt never wanted me to get to know your boys, even though the oldest and I are almost the same age, I think. And whenever you would come to see Burt, you always came by yourself. I think Burt knew -- or at least suspected -- that your husband was a small-time criminal, and he feared by example the man would lead his sons to become the same. Burt never wanted me around that; maybe because he didn't approve, or maybe because he feared I might see that path as the easy way out and turn to breaking the law myself. I don't know. Either way, it hurt you that Burt didn't like your husband, and so when he met my mother you punished her in the same way."

"Your mother was trash."

Zane only smiled as familiar love tightened his chest. "My mother liked pretty, sparkly things, but she was the farthest thing from trash."

Patty snorted and sneered. "I don't really care what you believe."

Every gesture Patty now made screamed at Zane of a sad woman with regrets, a woman reaching to preserve her pride, someone desperate to try again with a new family. "Maybe you do, maybe you don't. But here's what is going to happen." Zane leaned forward, all business again. "You're going to give me every copy of those photos you have, that your lawyer has, and that your investigator has, along with any memory cards or USB sticks, or whatever, that contain files of them. Anything that has evidence of those photos is to either be handed over to me or wiped clean. Then we're going to go with my lawyer to your lawyer and we're going to sign a legal agreement stating that you are fully aware that I'm a gay man, and that you still support my custody of Duncan and Hailey, and that you will never attempt to take them away from me. Oh," Zane couldn't forget the two men outside who'd done so much for him, "and neither your lawyer nor mine will hear one word about this conversation between the two of us. Clear?"

Patty drummed her fingers against the arm of her chair. "And what proof do I have that you won't turn my sons over to the authorities anyway, once I've signed this statement -- if what you're even saying about them is true." Bravado Zane now recognized as false laced her words.

"You have my word, which I've never once broken to you," Zane reminded her, "even though at every turn I knew you were wishing you could take Duncan and Hailey away from me." Because Zane could see Patty more clearly now, he let up the reins and gave her the only thing she needed to survive. "I'll also let you continue to see Duncan and Hailey, because I do understand that twisted up in all this ridiculousness, you genuinely love them. More important to me, they love you. They need you. I know you share good, fond stories of your childhood with

Burt with them; they've told some of those tales to me. I want them to continue to know their father through you, just as I talk about him with them too. I have no interest in taking that away from any of you."

Patty tried to cover it with a cough, but Zane heard the little noise of need and saw the way she put her hand to her heart. "You really won't take them away from me?"

"I'll even put that in the agreement. As long as you keep your end, I'll keep mine." Zane raised his brow. "Deal?"

The woman didn't reach her hand across the table. "If I agree, I want a few things out of you first."

Without the words, Patty had already said yes. Zane understood everything from here on out was just to save face. He settled in again and said, "Then let's talk…"

Outside, Noah got up from the glider to pace the length of the porch. He'd already done it a dozen times, but if he had to he would get up and move a few dozen more times to keep himself sane. He could not hear a damn word from inside, and every bit of the warrior in him wanted to storm into the house and take care of this mess for his man.

Christ, I love him. Noah owned the truth body and soul, but right now that grip of emotion had him twisted up into a thousand tight knots inside, rather than wrapping around him with a sense of peace. *Not knowing if he is okay in there is killing me.*

Noah went for the door.

"Don't go in there." Noah's father spoke with quiet authority from his position on the glider. "It is not your right."

Noah shot his father a glare. "You don't even begin to understand how much I believe in my gut that it is my absolute right," he said in a low, clipped tone. "My place is at Zane's side."

Hoyt laid just as hard a stare back on Noah. "You do understand what he's doing in there right now, don't you?"

With a spin and one step, Noah bent down in his father's face, and hissed in a low voice, "He's fighting fire with fire. He's doing the only thing he believes he can to keep his brother and sister at his side. If you think I'm going to get up in arms or call him out or leave him for making the wrong decision in regard to using this information, then you are sorely mistaken."

Hoyt shot up into Noah's space. Height for height, build for build, the men were an even match. "But he is also breaking the law, and he clearly understands that." Hoyt spoke in as commanding a whisper-quiet tone as Noah had. "He doesn't want you in there because I suspect he doesn't want you to be a party to it or a witness in case something was to go terribly wrong today or sometime in the future." With an audible breath, Hoyt added, "Respect that," and adjusted his suit jacket before taking a seat once more.

Noah threw himself into the glider next to his father and muttered, "Since when did you become such a believer that one man could care for another so much that he would want to protect him from harm?"

"Hey." With something powerful vibrating through him -- Noah could feel the energy arcing off his father -- Hoyt spoke in a furiously soft tone. "I've never believed that gay people aren't sincere and can't love each other as much as other people. And contrary to what you seem to believe of me, I would never for one second think that young man inside is unfit to care for his siblings -- or that any other gay man or woman would not be a suitable caretaker for a child, for that matter."

Hoyt jerked his head and met Noah's stare, and the familiar hellfire of burning judgment ripped a new gash in Noah's heart. "What I don't understand is how I could have a son who loved a girl enough to choose to go to the same college she went to, just so he could remain with her, and then also love her enough to marry her, and obviously be able to make love to her, because he played a part in giving me two grandsons. What I don't understand is how that man, a man I thought I knew, a boy I thought trusted me and told me everything, could have such a loving marriage with a woman for two decades and then just up and decide he has to be gay. How could that man at some point not think to himself, not examine the possibility that, maybe there's something going on in his brain that is making him think he is gay, but it's not really true?"

Jesus. Noah rubbed his hands over his face and up into his hair. "Because it was never spontaneous like you keep saying it was. I've always felt this way." Sighing, Noah added, "I've wanted to talk to you about this, but you aren't open to listening to me."

"But you loved Janice," Hoyt insisted with passion. "I know you did. I could see your heart in your eyes when you talked about her as a young man. And I saw that you loved the life you built with her. I cannot accept that the boy I raised had it in him to be so deceptive toward such a kindhearted woman, and to his parents, and with his children, for so many years. That's not who you are." Hoyt squeezed his son's shoulder with imploring strength. "You're an honest man. I know you are, which is why I can't understand this."

"All of what you said is true," Noah promised, his voice cracking with love for his father, "but so are my feelings for men. Specifically my feelings for Zane. Christ," Noah slid down on the glider and tipped his head against the backing to stare up at the slat ceiling, "this is so hard to explain and have make sense. But I want to try; all I've ever wanted was the chance to try to help you understand. I never lied to you and Mom, and I don't feel I ever lied to Janice, and you know how much I love my boys. I would never wish away a part of my life that gave them to me. But there was this other part that was there too, always beneath the surface, but never explored. When I started having strong feelings for one specific man, feelings I could not ignore, I knew things had to change. It was only at that point that I felt I was no longer being honest in my heart and in my life, and that is why I instigated the divorce."

"I don't understand that." Hoyt had gone almost too quiet to hear. From the corner of Noah's eye, he could see his father look down to the treated floor and clasp his hands between his spread knees. "I'm not trying to be cruel. I just don't get how you could have had romantic, loving feelings for Janice for so long and then all of a sudden have those same feelings switch to a man."

Old frustration and pain welled in Noah and lifted to the surface. "Because the feelings weren't exactly the same, but nor were any of them ever false; you need to hear me when I say that. Listen," reeling himself in before he said the wrong thing, Noah forced himself to unclench his fists, "this is way too complicated for me to explain when we're sitting on someone else's porch. I'm not even asking that you ever understand me. I'm just asking for you to start listening to me again. I miss talking to you. I miss seeing you play with my kids. I miss the respect you used to have for me. I miss your ear, and your advice." Noah's voice caught, and he wiped away an errant tear. "I miss *you*, Dad."

His nod jerky, Hoyt whispered, "I know."

"Okay."

A long moment of tense silence stretched between the men. Then, still without looking at Noah, Hoyt reached across the space between them and covered Noah's hand with his. "I love you, son." He gave Noah's hand a gentle squeeze and held on. "I'm sorry I haven't said that to you in such a long time."

Shit. Noah could barely speak. "I love you too, Dad." He then turned his hand under his father's and held on for dear life as the first remnants of one of his biggest prayers was answered. *He still loves me.*

Only a few minutes passed in peaceful silence between the two men on the porch before the front door opened to the soft murmurs of Zane's voice. Noah shot up and rushed across the porch, his worry and fear and love all exploding to the surface at once. He ate up Zane with a scrutinizing, possessive stare; darkness lived under Zane's eyes -- but that had been there for days. At the same time, a bright light behind those same eyes -- something that hadn't been there this morning -- now glowed too. The new illumination, along with a looseness in Zane's frame, allowed Noah to exhale for the first time in nearly two weeks.

Needing to touch, Noah caressed Zane's cheek and temple, craving the life-beat within. "Everything went okay?"

Zane nodded, and he even offered Noah a wan smile. "Patty is gathering a few things and making a call to her lawyer. We'll meet her there." With a slight shift, Zane then put his attention on Hoyt, who now stood as well. "She would like for all of us to go speak with her attorney right now and get an agreement signed that assures me the continued custody of my brother and sister, but also promises that she maintains visiting rights and gets to keep them in her life."

Hoyt said, "We can do that," and then began to make his way down the steps. "I'll wait in the car."

Noah dipped down and scrutinized Zane for telling tics or giveaways of additional distress. "You're okay with letting Patty keep those rights?"

Zane's back remained straight and nothing in him wobbled. "I am." His sigh filled every molecule of air around them. "We've all lost family and are still hurting in different ways. I don't want to add to splitting us up even more."

Admiration Noah couldn't fathom filled his being. He slipped his arm around Zane's waist and pressed a kiss to the side of his head. "You're a gentle soul."

Zane chuckled softly. "More like a tired one." He rubbed his cheek against Noah's upper arm and then looked up at him with exhaustion etching new shadows into the corners of his eyes. "I'd like to get this done as fast as possible so I can get home to Duncan and Hailey." Seth had already planned to spend the day at the lake with Matt, so he'd agreed to make Zane's cabin home base for the day rather than Noah's and to keep an eye on Duncan and Hailey too. "Is that okay?"

Too much love made Noah's voice even raspier than usual. "We'll make that happen as fast as we can." He tucked Zane under his arm and led him to the car. "Let's go."

⸺

"WE'RE ALMOST THERE, HONEY." NOAH took a hand off the wheel for a moment to nudge Zane in the shoulder, where he lay with his eyes closed and his head resting against the window. "Start waking up."

Just as Noah pulled onto the gravel road that circled the cabins on the lake, Zane blinked heavily, rubbed his face, and then glanced at his new watch. "I think that might have been the first full hour I've slept since Patty texted me those photos."

"You have a binding agreement in place now," Noah reminded him. He couldn't wait to see that truth sink in for Zane and for him to start breathing easily again. "You don't have to worry anymore."

Zane reached across the seating and got Noah's attention with a hand on his thigh. When Noah glanced at him, Zane said, "From Patty's window earlier, before I stepped outside, I saw your father holding your hand. I hope that means what it looked like it meant."

Noah could still feel the imprint of his father's big hand against the back of his. The phantom sensation still choked him up. "I think I understand now what his issue is with me. Now that I know it isn't the fact that I'm gay itself, but rather helping him understand what was in my head and heart for so many years that feels so contradictory to him, I have hope that with time we can get back on the right track." Noah looked to Zane again, and for the first time could genuinely see his father and Zane having the same kind of loving relationship Hoyt still maintained with Janice. "I think he wants the same."

Zane squeezed Noah's leg. "I'm happy for you."

"Thank you."

Noah pulled the car to a stop at his cabin, behind Seth's. Just as both men got out of the vehicle, Seth yanked the front door open, yelling back inside, "If you're going to keep being an asshole, I won't take you and your buddy with me and Kim to the water park next weekend. Now decide if you're going to apologize, or you're gonna lose that weekend you've been begging me for. We've been away long enough, and we have to get back."

Noah raced up the steps to the porch. "Whoa, whoa." He pulled Seth back from the open doorway. "What's going on?"

In a belligerent tone, Seth explained, "Matt was being a jerk to Duncan. He was being stubborn, and he wouldn't let up --"

"No I wasn't!" Matt shrieked from inside, in his cracking fourteen-year-old voice.

"Yes you were!" Seth bellowed back at his brother. Then he turned to Noah, and more calmly added, "I had to drag his ass out of there to have a talk with him before they came to blows. He's pissed and been giving me the silent treatment for close to an hour. That 'no I wasn't' was the first thing he's said since we left."

So much for thinking we might not have to worry too much about the kids getting along. Noah opened his mouth to ask Matt to come out and give his side of the argument, when from next to the car, Zane said, "Let's not worry about this right now. Let everyone cool off, and then we'll all figure out what happened. I need to get back to the cabin anyway." Backing up, Zane jerked his thumb toward the other side of the lake. "I don't want Duncan and Hailey to be alone for too long."

"It's okay," Seth called out. "Your friend from your work stopped by, and he said he would hang with them while I talked to Matt."

Zane pulled a face. "Mickey?" He pulled his phone out of his pocket, presumably checking for messages. "A big, older guy with gray hair and beard?"

"Not Mickey," Seth answered. "The guy said his name was Clint."

Zane went ghost-white. "Oh God." In a flash, he threw everything on the ground and started flying in a sprint around the lake toward his cabin.

"Shit," Noah hissed. *That son of a bitch.*

"Dad?" Seth paled. "He talked about the owner. He knew Zane and made it sound like he'd worked at the restaurant for a while."

"Don't worry about that right now. You stay here with Matt," Noah ordered his oldest. "If you don't get a call from me within five minutes of reaching that cabin, you call the police."

Noah didn't spare a second more in giving Seth an explanation. He took off after Zane, praying everything was okay with those two precious kids.

CHAPTER 21

Oh God. Oh my fucking God. His heart pounding out of control, breathing loudly, Zane churned up dirt and fresh grass under his shoes, running as fast as his legs would carry him. How had he ever been so stupid as to think he could manage a situation with a bastard like Clint? The man had beaten Zane up and had threatened to rob the restaurant where he worked. Zane should have known a threat like this was coming and done something more to protect his brother and sister.

Maybe I'm not the best choice to take care of them after all.

Zane stumbled, but righted himself quickly and tore up the few steps to the front door. He would live with the guilt of his bad choices tomorrow; right now only saving Duncan and Hailey mattered. He turned the door handle and slammed inside, putting his shoulder to the wood. The eerily friendly sight that met him chilled him to the bone. Clint sat sprawled comfortably in the middle of the couch, with Duncan and Hailey on either side of him, his arms around the shoulders of both kids. Clint's Stetson sat perched on his left knee, and Zane's brother and sister were grinning and giggling so genuinely that they clearly had no clue of the terrible danger they were both in. *Thank God.* At least that meant Clint hadn't hurt them in any way. Yet.

The couch faced the front door, and Clint looked up the second Zane bounded into the cabin. "Hey, you're home," Clint said with frightening, amiable ease. "We were just watching some cartoons. Why don't you join us?"

Zane felt himself shaking inside, and could only hope it didn't show on the exterior and alarm his siblings. "The kids should go," he said to Clint. "Guys," Zane forced a smile, and once again prayed it looked natural, "you have people waiting for you across the lake. Why don't you go hook back up with Seth and Matt right now? Okay?"

As Duncan and Hailey both shifted to get up, Clint pressed against their shoulders and kept them on the couch. "I think they should stay."

Right then a shadow grew under Zane's feet and stretched into the cabin. "I really think you should listen to Zane and let them leave." Noah drew alongside Zane like some Nordic avenging angel, and Zane just held himself from crying and falling to his knees. "Otherwise my son is going to start worrying about why they haven't shown up and might decide to make a very specific call."

Self-preservation clearly wouldn't let Clint ignore that mile high and wide threat about getting the police involved. "Fine. Go ahead, kids." Clint tousled their hair and pushed them to their feet. "It was nice to finally meet you. Go have fun now." The scumbag winked at them, and Zane almost threw up.

Zane rushed to Duncan and Hailey, taking only a moment to give them each a fast hug and kiss. Squatting down, he brushed at their faces and hair. "Go on. Everything is okay." He made himself look each of them in the eyes and show a steadiness he did not truly feel. "Run on over to Noah's place and stay there with Seth until I come get you." Zane gave each a nudge toward the open door.

Noah put his hand on Duncan's shoulder as the kids moved past him. "Tell Seth to hold off on that call; he'll know what I mean. I also want you to tell him I'd rather you guys all play inside until I talk to him in just a little while. All right?"

With a nod, Duncan took Hailey's hand. "Okay." As soon as he agreed, he dragged his sister out of the cabin.

Zane listened for their clomping steps to move down the stairs. Waiting until he could not hear them anymore, only then did he turn and run at Clint, momentum and adrenaline allowing him to rip the cowboy up from the couch and slam him into the wall. "How dare you come into my home and put your hands on my brother and sister."

Clint jerked his body forward, at Zane, and Zane flinched and backed off. "This is what happens when you blow me off at your place of work," Clint shared as he straightened his Western shirt. "I have to bring myself into your private little cabin sanctuary."

Noah pushed in, grabbed Clint by the front of his shirt, and put brand-new wrinkles in the cotton fabric. "I don't know who the fuck you think you are," he bit off through his teeth as he walked Clint across the cabin to the door, "but if you come near this man one more time, at his work, or here -- or at the fucking crosswalk, I don't care where -- I'll beat you down so hard you'll be two feet shorter by the time I'm done with you." He finished by shoving the cowboy out onto the porch.

Once again, Clint bounced back up like one of those Weebles children's toys that don't stay down. "Now that's gonna be kind of hard to agree to, considering this man you're defending here owes me a hell of a lot of money."

Noah swung that piercing stare onto Zane, and Zane died a little bit inside. Humiliation burned a hole through him. Zane could not look at Noah right now; he could not bear to see Noah's disappointment in him or he might wither to the floor and expire.

Going for his money clip, Zane made a token gesture with the pathetic forty bucks he had left until his next payday. "Here, take this right now; it's every penny I have." He shoved the bills against Clint's hand and forced his fingers to take hold of the cash. "I will pay you back every dollar I owe you, Clint; you already know I will. I have been paying you steadily ever since I got a second job."

"But you got way, way behind before you did," Clint reminded Zane. "You're not nearly caught up, and you're not opening yourself to other avenues to speed up the process." The offer to aid him in robbing the restaurant lived in his beady eyes.

Zane clenched his teeth so that he didn't scream. "No way. It's never going to happen."

Noah stepped forward and put himself at Zane's side. Yanking a clip out of his pocket, he said, "Whatever Zane owes you on the balance of the loan, you will get in full tomorrow." Horror filled Zane. He started to protest, but Noah spoke over him, adding, "Take everything I have," he shoved another stack of bills at Clint, "and get the fuck out of here."

As Clint thumbed through the bills Noah had given him, he looked up. "This doesn't even make a noticeable dent in his bill." Zane could see at least two one-hundred-dollar bills along with the smaller denominations, and it sickened him to know Clint spoke the truth.

"I don't care how much the total is," Noah replied, ice in his tone and coldness in his eyes. "I will go to the bank as soon as it opens tomorrow; you will have every dime he owes you, as well as every dollar you extorted through what I'm sure were shady contracts and outrageous interest rates."

"It's a private loan. It's all legal." Clint sauntered back into the cabin to pick his hat up off the floor.

"Just barely," Noah replied, "I'm sure of that. All I have to do is look at you to know you're just enough of a bottom-feeder to understand the courts aren't going to go after a guy like you. You prey on the people politicians and lawmakers don't much care about, and you probably get away with murder because of it."

"Like I said," Clint repeated, "what I do is legal."

Noah grabbed Clint by the back of his neck and dragged him outside. "But threatening this man and entering his home without his permission isn't, so unless you'd prefer to debate me about details, and make me change my mind about getting the cops involved, rather than just shutting your mouth and being happy you're getting paid, I'd suggest you get the hell off this porch and don't show your face to me again until I step into your establishment tomorrow with your money."

"As long as I get paid," Clint righted his hat on his head, "then we're all friends here."

Noah leaned forward and snarled, "No, we're not." With another low rumble, Noah muttered, "Fuck you." He cocked his arm back and smashed his fist into Clint's cheek, sending the guy reeling back to the steps. Clint sputtered and grabbed his face, but Noah only jabbed his finger at the man and said, "That's for touching those children and even hinting that you would drag them into your sorry game. Come here again, and I'll do worse next time."

Clint glared, but he wisely kept his mouth shut and made his way to his truck.

Before Zane could make a move, Noah whipped out his cell phone. "I'm calling Seth and telling him to keep the kids for a while." Some of the mutiny still gripping Noah's gaze shifted to Zane. "Should I get the cops involved with this?"

"No." Even as Zane said that, though, he understood he would have to speak to Violet tomorrow about the veiled threats Clint continued to make against her restaurant. He would abide by whatever she wanted done -- that is, if she still wanted him in her employ for withholding such information. "At least not right now."

Noah made his call, and Zane listened in on his side of the conversation. Once it sounded as if Noah was near to completing his talk, Zane beckoned for the phone. He spoke to Duncan and Hailey, assuring them everything was cool and he'd be with them soon. Both sounded fine; Zane realized if he kept talking he would eventually spike curiosity and worry in Duncan, so he said his good-byes and hung up.

As soon as Zane handed the phone back to Noah, Noah exploded. "What the hell is going on? Who is that guy?" He pierced through to Zane's gut with one look. "And this time tell me the truth."

Shame burned a hot line of fire straight down to Zane's core. "I'm such an idiot." He dropped to the couch, put his elbows on his knees, and his face in his hands. *No. Nut up, man.* So terribly embarrassed, Zane forced himself to meet Noah's scrutinizing stare, even as the gaping pit in his stomach widened. *You have to do this.*

"Before I even met you," Zane began, "I needed money, and Clint was the only one who would give it to me. I thought I could pay him back -- I was paying him back -- am paying him back. But the interest that kicked in if you were just one month late, one time, is insane, and before I knew it I owed him so far beyond what I'd ever borrowed in the first place that I was drowning." Zane struggled not to drop his attention to the floor and hide. "God, Noah," he pressed his folded hands against his mouth, "I never wanted you to know."

"Why the hell not?" Shaking his head, Noah threw his hands in the air. "I could have helped you get out from under his thumb a long time ago."

"I was mortified to have you find out I'd done something so stupid. But more than that, you've helped me so much already," Zane explained, jumping to his feet. "Every time I turn around, you're there fixing my problems for me."

Noah reared as if Zane had slapped him. "You make that sound like a bad thing."

"God." Zane wanted to grab Noah and shake him. "Don't you see? It is when I'm so fucked-up that it happens repeatedly. You helped me with a place to live and made sure the rent is way lower than it should be. You let me borrow your car without an end date to that loan in sight. Then you gave me a job." Zane ticked each inadequacy off on his fingers, right in front of Noah. "And hell, you even found some way to get your estranged father to help me -- for free -- when it looked like I was going to lose my brother and sister. And now you just agreed to give some guy a bunch of money, when you don't even know how much it is first, because I got in over my head again."

Stopping, Zane breathed in an attempt to contain the streaks of fear living inside him. He studied every wonderful solid inch of the man before him; with each second he did, within himself, more uncertainty bled from his pores. Zane wondered how Noah couldn't see it. "How are you ever going to see me as an adult or your equal -- as a man, your man, someone you can rely on -- when you keep having to bail me out? Every time it feels like we might get on equal footing, I mess up, you have to fix things for me, and I'm right back to wondering how you can ever see me as anything other than a burden that it's nice to fuck."

His brow furrowing, Noah stepped up, took Zane's face in his hands, and tilted his head back. "Zane," Noah's stare did not waver, "I don't see you that way at all."

"How could you not?" Shrieking, Zane shoved Noah's hands away from him. "I do."

Noah's mouth flattened to a hard line. He took to pacing, but always kept his focus on Zane, wherever he moved. "You see the worst in yourself because you feel sick with guilt right now, but I see a guy who sacrificed a big chunk of his own life to take care of his family, and did it without bitching and moaning. I see a guy who is willing to work his fingers to the bone, no matter what the job, because he's trying his best to earn an honest living in any way he can. I see a guy who stepped up and helped me twice when I was in a jam with my work. You earned that job I offered you." Something nearly vicious slipped into Noah's tone as he promised Zane that. "It was not charity. I see a guy who not only took care of me when I was sick, but who didn't even bat an eye when I threw up in his face, more than once. I see a guy who had enough inner strength to keep me down and away from my work until you knew I was well again. I see a guy who, yes, made an error in judgment by taking money from that asshole Clint," Noah came to a stop near the front door, with Zane across the room at the hallway opening; the empathy in Noah's chocolate eyes made it feel as if they were only inches apart, "but I also understand that you probably didn't feel like you had any other choice."

"At the time I didn't see another way," Zane agreed, his voice still screechy. "But that doesn't mean you should feel like you have to automatically jump in and bail me out. It's like you're the parent and I'm a wayward child, and you're always one step above me."

Noah suddenly went very still, and the coffee in his stare darkened to onyx. "Back the fuck up a minute here." Simmering steam seemed to rise from Noah's body. "Are you pissed at me for stepping in to help you?"

"No. Yes. I don't know." Words kept spewing out of Zane's mouth. Acute desire and fear and passion and guilt swirled through every fiber of Zane's being, more than he'd ever experienced in his life, more than he'd thought himself capable of feeling for another human being, and he couldn't stop. "Which time? Because you've helped me so many times I can't keep count."

Rolling his eyes and shaking his head, Noah appeared as if he'd woken up this morning and stepped out of his cabin onto an entirely new planet. "Are you kidding me with this bullshit?"

"Is anything I'm saying factually incorrect?" Zane challenged, damning and diminishing himself with every sentence spoken, but compelled to get this truth out between them. "Because to anyone looking at us -- to me -- I'm coming across more inept every day while you're looking a whole lot like my personal bailout machine."

Red mottled Noah's harsh face, and he raged, "Well I'm fucking sorry you're being such a shortsighted jackass about something that seems pretty damn simple to me, but I guess I can't help being an overbearing bastard when it comes to protecting and taking care of the people I love. That's just who I am, and you're gonna have to fucking deal with it, because you're one of those people. I goddamn love you, Zane, and it's never gonna stop, and that means I take care of you. I love you!" Noah slammed his hand against the wall and snarled as he flashed a hard glare Zane's way. "So start getting used to it!"

Zane's whole chest seized with the tightest, most wonderful pain, and he yelled back, "That's why I need you to see me as a man, because I goddamn love you too!" Zane flung his heart on the floor for this man to see everything. "And because I do, I want us to stand on level ground so we can be together for always!"

"Well okay! I want that too!" Not a bit of give softened Noah's features or hot stare, and he remained far on the other side of the room. Too much volatile emotion still had a visible grip on every inch of him, and he looked ready to combust. "I love you, you stubborn jerk!"

"Good!" Zane shouted back, his heart slamming wildly out of control, yet happier than he'd ever been in his life. *Oh God, he loves me.* Nodding, his hand to his chest, feeling the crazy thump in his heart that existed because of this man, Zane found his throat scratchy. His voice dropped to a near whisper. "That's good."

Across the cabin, Noah breathed heavily, his chest expanding and falling in big waves. A stalemate of silence passed between them, but the intensity and new heat in Noah's eyes made Zane feel stripped naked. Finally, gruff as hell, Noah spoke. "We each just said 'I love you.'"

For some reason, Zane found himself standing very still too. "We did." He lingered with his stare, absorbing every inch of Noah, and imagined him without clothing. Zane only saw bare, hot skin covering rock-solid muscles over the man's hard frame. Yet at the same time, Zane was aware of the overt kindness and sincerity that solidness housed within the man. Zane looked up and met Noah's stare. He didn't hide a bit of the love and passion in him. With a new thickness in his throat, he added, "And I mean it. I love you, Noah."

A pained noise suddenly spilled from Noah. He rushed to Zane and dragged him in with a hand cuffed around the back of Zane's head. The brown in Noah's eyes was so deep and rich and beautiful it hurt Zane's heart to see it. "Me too." Rough edges filled Noah's tone as he closed most of the distance between their lips. "And I could never love a man I didn't respect and see as my equal, so understand there are a dozen other words behind it when I speak those three I just gave you." Noah's fingers flitted over Zane's face; he watched himself touch Zane, as if he couldn't quite believe this moment was real. But then Noah's gaze found Zane's again, and Zane saw nothing but strength and certainty in his eyes. "I love you, honey," Noah said again, and then staked a claim on Zane's mouth with an open, raw kiss.

Oh God. Yes. Losing himself to a complete, bone-deep love he'd never thought to have, Zane wrapped his arms around Noah's waist and lifted up to cling to the full passion in his kiss.

Jesus Christ. Spiraling down into the abyss of need fast, Noah dug his fingers into the back of Zane's head, holding him still for a deep, hot, plundering kiss. *I love this man. And he loves me.*

As much as their newly spoken love bloomed, residual fear that something horrific or even fatal could have befallen Zane drove Noah's actions. Biting at Zane's mouth, Noah pulled at the tie still around Zane's neck and yanked his dress shirt out of his jeans. At the same time, he started walking forward and forcing Zane to move backward toward his bedroom. "I need to be inside you right now." Noah continued to plaster kisses all over Zane's beautiful face as they moved, desperate to put a mark of ownership on every inch of this man's body. "I was so scared when you ran." His confession cut up his throat on the way out. "I was terrified something might happen to all of you before I could get here." Noah couldn't stop touching Zane all over, even through his clothes. "You're my family now too, and I protect what is mine." Holding Zane's head, Noah scraped kiss after desperate kiss across Zane's lips, and met the blur of his gaze. "That's not something I can ever stop." His voice was stripped to something of a croak.

Zane put his fingers to Noah's lips. "I know. Shh, I know." On tiptoe, Zane curled his other hand around Noah's tie and held him close. "I just want you to know I can stand up and be there when you need me too. It might not look like it, based on my record so far," a dark shadow crossed Zane's eyes for a split second, but then his gaze cleared to pure blue, "but I promise I can."

The sincere vehemence in Zane's tone created a painful band around Noah's chest. "I believe you." He brushed Zane's hair off his forehead and willingly let himself sink into the pools of chaotic emotion living in the younger man's eyes. "I see your strength more clearly than you do, and I sincerely believe the depth of it goes all the way down to your soul." Noah's own heart catching, he pressed his hand against Zane's chest and let the fast, steady beat within fuel the conviction in his words. "Your strength is one of the thousand things that all put together made me fall so deeply in love with you."

Zane made a choking noise, and wetness brimmed his eyes. "Noah…"

Brushing his thumb across Zane's smooth cheek before the first tear could fall, Noah smiled gently. "'Noah,' nothing, honey. I've spent my whole life waiting for you. I know my heart, and even though I was terrified, and I tried to pretend, my heart settled itself on you right from the start." Now that he had Zane, the memory made Noah's heart ache in the best way possible. *The true beginning of my new life.* "I think I knew I would love you the second I looked into your eyes that day on the sidewalk."

Zane looked up at Noah, pure light glinting in his gaze, and stamped a seal of ownership on Noah's very soul. "If I told anyone else this, the words would sound crazy, but the moment you touched me, the moment you looked at me so deeply, you woke me up inside and made me feel alive. I was hungry all of a sudden, when before that I hadn't really understood more than a vague, faraway desire for food. Only with you, not only did I feel the pangs, I wanted a feast. I wanted you. Once I realized what that meant, I knew I'd been asleep because I didn't need to be awake until I met you." Zane took Noah's face in his hands and lifted up until they were almost on eye level. "You're my light and my warmth, Noah." His lips came to rest against Noah's with the softest kiss. "I want to be the same kind of safe shelter for you."

Noah's fingers tightened reflexively in Zane's hair. "You are, honey," he promised, succumbing to a base need for this stunning man again. He licked at the seam of Zane's lips and vowed again, "You already are." With another flick of his tongue that wasn't nearly enough to satisfy, Noah let out a low moan and sank in for a deeper, rawer kiss.

Zane parted his lips, clinging to Noah in every way as he accepted a rough invasion of his mouth. Digging his fingers into Noah's shoulders in a way that made Noah hard as a rock, Zane slid his tongue along Noah's, then sucked on the tip. Between their bellies Noah's cock leaked and began to slicken with precum. Noah couldn't yet fully wrap his brain around wanting another person in such an aggressively physical way, but from the moment he'd let himself believe he had a chance with Zane, on some level in his psyche, his thoughts had constantly circled around getting the younger man naked and finding some way to merge their bodies into one. Noah didn't care how or what they did; he just wanted them coming together in some way, all the time.

Grasping with less than steady hands, Noah pulled at Zane's belt buckle and tried to loosen more of his clothing. He got the belt open, but when his big fingers fumbled with the button on Zane's jeans, he nipped hard at Zane's lips and then fused their foreheads together, struggling to compose himself and normalize his breathing. "Zane, fuck…" Noah's cock raged to find a home inside Zane, and his desire made him shake. His stare locked on Zane, he raggedly whispered, "I need you."

Understanding softened the haze of passion in Zane's eyes. "Sit down on the bed." He nudged Noah backward. When Noah's knees hit the edge of the mattress, he fell to sit on the edge, and Zane folded to the floor between Noah's parted legs. His gaze holding Noah's, Zane pressed a kiss to the base of Noah's rearing cock through his clothes. "Let me take care of you." He licked up the underside of Noah's shaft through the fabric. Noah bucked his hips, and in his underwear his prick spit out another bead of early ejaculate.

Instead of working Noah's pants open and freeing his straining shaft, Zane gently eased Noah's legs apart even wider and began to kiss his way down Noah's left inner thigh, pressing just hard enough for Noah to feel the warm imprint of Zane's lips through the material. When Zane reached Noah's knee he teased the underside with his fingers, and then continued to lay a line of kisses down Noah's calf to his ankle. Without a word, his attention still lifted to Noah, Zane undid the laces on Noah's dress shoe, removed it, and then the sock. He stayed in place to remove Noah's right shoe and sock too. After setting them aside, Zane started a reverse trek up Noah's right leg, trailing kiss after kiss up Noah's inner calf, knee, and thigh until he ended with another long lick up Noah's shaft through his pants, and this time pecked a kiss to the leaking tip. *Shit.*

Zane finally worked open Noah's belt and pants, and Noah was so far gone the simple move made him shudder. Zane hardly did anything especially provocative in the way he undressed Noah, but Noah had never felt so erotically seduced in his life.

Leaving Noah's pants open in a V -- with the deep red head of Noah's dick sticking out of the waistband of his underwear -- Zane reached up, loosened Noah's tie, and slid it from around his neck. Never looking away from Noah, Zane moved to Noah's dress shirt and slipped each button loose from its hole, one by one, slowly, until no more remained fastened. He lifted up to his knees to glide the shirt off Noah's shoulders and off each arm, and let the dark blue fabric pool in a half circle around Noah's backside and hips. Only then did Zane return to Noah's dress pants. He hooked his fingers at the sides of Noah's waist; without needing a command Noah lifted to let Zane slide the material down his legs and off his body. Finally Noah sat before Zane completely nude. His skin had never been so on fire, and his shaft had never thickened or strained to such rigidity as it did in front of Zane in this moment.

Zane looked openly, and his Adam's apple bobbed visibly. "God, Noah." He ran his hands up Noah's stomach to his chest, and reverence filled his voice. "You are so stunningly handsome."

A jolt of desire rushed through Noah and left him with goose bumps. "You only think so because you love me." Nervous laughter escaped. "Thank God."

Zane replied, "I only think so because I have eyes."

Before Noah could open his mouth to dispute the truth of that statement, Zane parted his lips around the tip of Noah's cock and sucked as if he'd spent his whole adult life with a dick in his mouth. Punching his hips up in automatic response, Noah moaned long and low, unable to contain his pleasure. Zane easily took the additional length and began a rhythm, bobbing his head in a semicircular motion up and down two thirds of Noah's shaft while also working the base with his hand. Each drag Zane put on Noah's penis took the cockhead to his throat; Noah could feel his tip nudge that point repeatedly. The promised hint of a deeper heaven, only to have it taken away, acted as an additional layer to the pleasure Zane pulled from Noah's body. Within a half dozen strokes from Zane's mouth to Noah's dick, Noah fell back on the bed and threw his forearm across his eyes. He needed to do something to curb the desire already winding his body to full throttle. At least if Noah couldn't see Zane's pretty mouth wrapped around his cock -- the man's cheeks sucking in deliciously with every pulling taste -- he might regain enough control to make sure he didn't jet a load of spunk into Zane's mouth the next time his cockhead kissed the man's throat.

Rather than give Noah a moment of reprieve, Zane pushed Noah farther onto the bed, up toward the headboard. Zane crawled onto the bed too, between Noah's thighs. His face still in Noah's crotch, Zane repositioned Noah's legs, bending them until Noah's feet were braced on the mattress, his thighs spread wide.

Lifting his stare until he locked his gaze to Noah's, Zane smiled against the underside of Noah's shaft -- Noah could fucking feel the turn of his lips against the sensitized flesh -- and then licked down to suck on Noah's balls.

"Ohhhh shit, Zane..." Noah moaned as Zane put gentle suction on both orbs at the same time. In reaction Noah rammed the back of his skull against the headboard once, twice, three times, frantic for pain. He needed to distract himself in some way in order to prevent himself from coming too fast. Noah understood they didn't have all day and night to play, or for him to get hard and fill with seed once more, so he didn't want to lose himself until he sank his cock all the way inside Zane's willing ass.

But good Christ and everything holy, Noah found the jarring pain to the back of his head hardly diminished the shiver-worthy talents of Zane's mouth on his nuts. Zane rolled first one ball around on his tongue, the move getting every nerve ending in Noah's body to clamor between his legs, eager for a flick or lick from Zane's heavenly tongue. Then switching to Noah's other testicle, Zane teased the orb just enough to make Noah claw the bedding, but not quite to where he felt as if he needed to tear his way out of his skin for relief. *Fucking shit, yes.* Noah threaded his fingers into Zane's silky tresses and deeply breathed in the smells of sweat and man permeating the air in the room.

Easing back, Zane began licking with deep, full forays all around Noah's balls, up to the space where the root of Noah's dick met his sac, and then into the crease of Noah's thighs -- an extrasensitive spot

Noah loved to have touched and teased. Zane then moved lower, where he flicked his tongue with tormenting gentleness against Noah's taint. At the same time, he reached up to stroke Noah's length, each glide of his hand spreading the continuous stream of early seed around the sensitive shaft. *So fucking good.* Noah groaned and punched his fist into the bedding. With so little experience -- purely on instinct -- Zane seemed to know exactly where to touch Noah and how far to play in order to push Noah right to the edge of the cliff, but not have him hurtle over into the abyss.

Right then Zane licked his way down to Noah's exposed pucker. The shot of pure pleasure one lick wreaked in Noah's ass channel and cock made Noah curse. Noah shoved at Zane's shoulder, pushing the man away, before one more flick to his bud made him shoot his load right onto his stomach.

"Zane -- motherfucking hell, baby." Noah panted heavily, struggling to regain his composure. "You're killing me." Zane still wore all of his clothing -- although most of it was now askew -- and the sight of him still dressed while Noah raged with such raw desire only made Noah more frantic. He writhed on the cool bedding, but his flesh only grew hotter the longer he looked into Zane's piercing stare. "I need your ass now."

Instead of turning around and lowering his jeans to his hips, Zane licked his way up Noah's belly and over his chest to his chin, putting them face-to-face, and fired a new trail of hungry nerve endings under Noah's skin. "I love the way you taste, Noah." Zane grazed his lips across Noah's mouth, barely letting their lips touch before breaking the contact. "You're in my system." With one more scrape of their mouths, Zane finally pulled away, tearing off his shirt and tie once he stood next to the bed. "I never knew I could crave the taste of another person until the first time you kissed me. Since that day in the shower stall," Zane yanked open an end table drawer, "I've never wanted to stop." With one hand on his jeans zipper, Zane tossed a brown paper bag in Noah's direction. "Get yourself ready. I'm starving again too."

Without looking away from Zane, Noah ripped into the paper bag and withdrew an unopened package of lube. As Zane toed out of his shoes and socks, he shared, "I bought that back before the pictures and the threats, before it felt like everything might slip away." A catch scratched Zane's voice, and he paused with his jeans halfway down his thighs. "There were nights these last few weeks where I was so scared I would lose everything, including you, and that I was foolish and impulsive for ever thinking I had enough of a future to buy such a big tube of lube in the first place."

His heart cracking, Noah let the cellophane that had protected the lube drift to the floor. "You will never lose me, honey." He held out his hand, offering himself -- everything in him, everything he was -- to Zane. "Get rid of those jeans, and let's get started on making a dent in this stuff right now."

As Zane let his jeans fall to the floor, he put his hand in Noah's. His fingers trembled. Still, he stepped out of his pants, crawled up on Noah, and settled himself on Noah's thighs.

Noah trapped Zane's gaze in the prison of his, and he never looked down as he coated his rigid shaft with the new, ultrathick lube. The cool substance did nothing to diminish Noah's erection. In fact, Zane added his hands to the mix, and the feel of his deft, smaller fingers fluttering over Noah's cock only made Noah's length lift and throb harder.

Unable to tolerate the separation of their bodies any longer, Noah held his cock up straight with one hand and eased Zane to his knees with the other. "Take me inside." The gentle plea in Noah's thoughts left his lips as a gruff order. "Make love to me like you never want to stop."

Shifting into place, Zane clutched Noah's shoulder and lowered himself until his entrance came to rest over Noah's erection. Zane gasped at first contact, and Noah felt the man's pucker squeeze and release against the tip of his shaft. "I don't want this to ever stop."

"Then show me." Noah flexed every muscle in his body in his effort not to jam his cock straight up into Zane's ass. "Please." Curling his hands into fists against Zane's thighs, Noah slipped to a place where ragged desperation ruled him. "Now."

Zane ran his fingers up into Noah's hair, gripped a handful, and tilted Noah's head against the headboard. Lowering until their lips grazed, Zane said back, "Hold onto me tighter." When Noah opened his hands and dug his fingers deep into Zane's hips, Zane muttered, "Shit," and sucked in air. "Just like that." He then curled his arm around Noah's neck, holding on, and began bearing down on Noah's cock. Zane rocked and pushed, shifted and pressed, gritting his teeth. Then, with a burst of expelled breath, Zane cried out as his entrance collapsed and the head of Noah's cock popped into his ass.

Sharp, blinding pleasure coalesced around the upper portion of Noah's dick, and he shouted too. Then, like two magnets too powerful to be held apart, Noah crushed his lips on Zane's just as Zane slammed his ass down on Noah's length. Zane took Noah all the way inside, and the two men came together in an animalistic display of coupling. Noah thrust his hips up in a fast, rough pattern, and he ate his way into Zane's mouth. He kissed and nipped and licked, desperate to taste and claim as much of Zane as he could, no matter the method. Matching Noah beat for beat, Zane pumped his body up and down with full punches, sliding his channel all along every inch of Noah's cock, again and again, smothering Noah's length in the snuggest, most scorching welcoming heat. Zane kissed Noah back with equal ferociousness. He fought his way past Noah's lips to tangle their tongues and take deep, foraying licks over Noah's teeth and the roof of his mouth. The mating was simplistic and akin to rutting in its lack of finesse, but Noah needed it like this, and he sensed Zane did too.

Noah released his death grip on Zane's hips and moved to lock his arms around the man's waist. Holding Zane down and close to his lap for the full thrust of his cock, Noah bit and licked all over Zane's face, overcome to mark more territory. He rocked up, forcing his penis into Zane's ass to the root. When Zane clutched every glorious inch of Noah's cock with his slick tunnel, Noah groaned, and his shaft jerked within the steaming hold of Zane's ass. "You feel so amazing," Noah confessed with passion. He shafted Zane's ass with another fast, piercing drive. "I adore you."

Zane held Noah's head in place and pecked kiss after kiss to Noah's lips. "I fantasized about you like this," he uttered, and then transitioned into another rough noise as Noah filled his passage to the brim again. Zane rocked into the invasion, though, time and again, so he clearly loved receiving the fast, hard taking as much as Noah thrilled in giving it. "Way before we ever kissed, one night, I held onto the headboard with one hand." Zane wrapped his fingers around the dark wood right then, adding a visual that fueled Noah's fierce desires. "I kneeled over a bunch of pillows, and I closed my eyes, and I stuck my finger in my ass and pretended it was your cock."

Holy fuck. Noah couldn't look away from the ethereal brightness in Zane's passion-drugged stare. "Let me see." Noah fell even deeper under this man's loving, innocently erotic spell, and he did not want to be saved. With supreme will, Noah stopped slamming his hips upward, and he let his hands come to rest on Zane's thighs. "Ride me right now like you did your finger that night."

Zane homed in on Noah, and didn't look away. Grabbing the headboard with his other hand too, he locked on tight, and started an oh-so-fucking-slow rocking motion on Noah's lap, and rhythmically worked himself off on Noah's straining cock. His eyes dropped closed, and his features softened to the sweetest, dreamiest expression, making him appear as if he'd slipped to a faraway place. Yet always, Zane kept up the back and forth glide, a churn of his hips, and maintained a delicious, steady friction between the tight squeeze of his rectum and Noah's sensitized cock. The gentle, easy slides to full penetration and then withdrawal made Noah's toes curl, and the exquisite sensation wound the coil in his belly to ever tightening degrees.

So completely mesmerized, Noah didn't notice at first when Zane slowly began increasing the pace of his ride. Then Zane gasped and opened his eyes, and the new sheen coating the blue showed a man inching dangerously close to the edge. "I rode my finger hard." Zane drove his ass down on Noah's cock, changing the speed in a way that sent Noah's heated blood rushing into a tailspin. "I was so sure it was your cock deep inside me, knowing me in a way nobody else ever had." Zane's hands slipped off the headboard, but he didn't slow down. He sank his fingertips into Noah's shoulders instead, creating new bruises Noah would cherish, and pierced his ass down on Noah's shaft with rough jabs. "I wanted you, Noah. I wanted to kiss you and touch you and be with you," he licked Noah's lips and nose and then plastered their foreheads together, still riding Noah's dick hard, and breathlessly added, "even if I didn't exactly know what to do."

With a ragged groan, Noah buried his fingers in Zane's hair and held him close for another scrape of their lips. "You're a goddamn natural." Noah's balls tugged with the most dangerous tightening, and his heart slammed against his chest, out of control. "Don't stop now."

Zane nodded, the move brushing his mouth and nose against Noah's. "I tried to stifle my moans that night, but oh God..." Zane

panted short, sharp breaths, warming Noah's lips, "Noah … Noah…"
His channel put a fisting clamp on the entire length of Noah's cock.
"You were so completely in my head that I convinced myself you were
inside my body…" Reaching behind himself, Zane rubbed his parted
fingers along his stretched entrance, where Noah's cock now truly
did live in his ass, and the touch made them both tremble. His eyes
unbearably wide, Zane gripped Noah's shoulder with such strength he
dented the skin, and he confessed, "From that very first time touching
myself, I cried your name when I came."

Fucking shit, baby. Noah jerked in response. Pure unfiltered passion
and love from this man knocked him full throttle into his endgame.
"Zane…" Powerless to pull the needs of his body back in check, Noah
pumped his hips, and a cry with no sound left his throat as he came.

The moment the first burst of seed left Noah's body, Zane jolted on
top of him. "Noah … fuck…" Zane whipped his hand from his asshole
and grabbed his cock. His body went rigid and his features pulled taut
-- a man fighting the relentless need to fall into release.

Locked on Zane, the sight of him filled with such masculine beauty,
tore through Noah like an electric shock. With a second voiceless
shout, Noah let loose another wave of orgasm. He latched onto Zane's
mouth with a kiss full of possession, clinging with exploding love,
while cum poured out of his cock in spurting waves. He pumped his
hips repeatedly and drenched Zane's ass channel with his seed, leaving
every drop of his essence deep in the body of the man he loved.

Still riding high, the first wave of afterglow not yet ebbing, Noah
regained his senses enough to notice the tension still thrumming in
Zane. The burn of fiery need still darkened Zane's eyes, and Noah
processed that his abdomen wasn't yet covered in Zane's warm, sticky
ejaculate. *Christ.* Zane's cock was still hard as a steel spike, and a wash
of shame crashed Noah back to earth. "I lost it too fast." He pressed
kisses of apology to Zane's cheek as he pushed his hand between their
bellies. "Let me help you with -- "

His pupils flaring, Zane knocked Noah's hand away. "No, don't
make me come." Zane rose all the way up on his knees, and Noah's
length slipped out of his ass. With his long cock plastered with full
rigidity against his lower stomach, Zane flashed a fierce, hungry grin.
He snaked his arm around Noah's neck and dragged Noah up to

his knees. "I want you on your stomach," he stole a fast, hard kiss, something full of that hidden, incalculable strength, "with pillows under you, lifting your ass in the air for me." With that, Zane gently tumbled Noah face-first onto the bed.

"Shit, honey." Flooding fast with renewed need, his face buried in the twist of bedding, Noah pulled his knees under himself and pushed his buttocks into the air. Zane caressed Noah's ass, and the fleeting touch made Noah moan and his balls twitch.

"Remember the motel room," Zane slid three pillows under Noah, positioning them against his lower belly and crotch, "when you fucked me from behind, but you got so hard and hot describing that it was how I would one day take you?" Without waiting for Noah to respond, Zane moved in behind Noah and ran his capable, warm hands along Noah's outer thighs. "I've thought about that a lot since that afternoon. A minute ago something inside forced me to hold back from coming. I don't want to let go until I'm deep inside you, giving you a little bit of that raw, hot screwing you give me whenever we come together."

Noah shuddered. He recalled that day, remembered the desire boiling in him to take Zane. But more, his body still had sensory memory of the one time Zane had so masterfully put his cock in Noah's ass and fucked him until they'd both came. *Holy Christ.*

From the moment Noah had come out of the closet, he'd accepted that a part of his sexual desire lay in another person occasionally dominating and taking command of his body. Until he'd met Zane, he'd not known if he could ever trust someone else enough to let that person assume full control. "Do it," Noah said, a mix of a plea and order in his tone. "Fucking do it." Noah's ass hung out open in the air, perched in offering, and he'd never hungered to be claimed by another person as he did right now. "Take me." A spasm full of anticipation awakened the nerve endings in Noah's rectum. "Make me yours."

In a rapid flash of response, Zane slapped Noah's buttocks hard, making Noah yelp, then pulled the cheeks apart, and finally -- *oh God, fucking good God, yes* -- Zane latched his mouth onto Noah's quivering pucker. Noah grunted and clutched at the bedding, but sweet merciful mother, Zane rimmed Noah's hole with the enthusiasm of a starving man being given an empty plate and put in front of a buffet. In Noah's whole life, nobody had ever eaten at his bud; the concentrated, marrow-deep pleasure in such an act had him moaning into the comforter and pushing his buttocks higher in the air for more. A soft, gruff moan of, "Please," escaped his lips.

Zane smacked Noah's ass a few more times; each playful tanning of Noah's hide was a shock that wreaked more fluttering in his chute. Zane stung and warmed the taut hills of flesh with his touch, then went from sucking at Noah's ring to laving and licking all along the globes of Noah's ass, soothing flesh he'd just burned with his spanking, and added another layer of shiver-inducing sensations to the mix. Noah rolled his hips shamelessly, and his cock started to swell between his stomach and the pillows. When Zane dived back in and returned to nibbling on Noah's supersensitized entrance, relaxing the muscle more and more with each suck and flick, Noah pulled his face out of hiding, unable to merely feel this glorious rimming anymore. *Holy fuck.* He had to see everything too.

Planning to look over his shoulder, Noah instead zeroed in on a cracked mirror attached to the wall to the left of the bed. In the coated glass, he could clearly see everything Zane did to him. *Jesus motherfucking Christ.* Noah looked, and somehow his penis thickened with life even more. The sight of Zane's face buried between Noah's split cheeks, his dark hair disheveled, combined itself in Noah's head with the insane feel of Zane's tongue and lips on his hole; everything together ratcheted Noah back to complete, painful arousal. Staring at Zane's smaller, yet capable hands, the fingers holding Noah's buttocks parted for voracious licks, soft bites, and sucking against Noah's pucker, elicited powerful throbbing in Noah's cock, balls, and ass and catapulted him nearly to the point of coming again.

Goddamn fucking hell. A whimper of need unlike any Noah had ever made escaped him, and in an instant Zane pulled away and back upright. Just as fast, Zane found Noah's gaze in the mirror. Holding steady to it, Zane rubbed his thumb against Noah's entrance, applying gentle pressure. "It's all right." He ran his other hand up Noah's spine, and Noah arched his back, a soft cry leaving his lips as he reached for Zane's touch. "Let me finish getting you ready. You know I've been where you are right now too." Before Noah could moan that he didn't need anything other than Zane's cock, Zane breached Noah's hole and eased his thumb into Noah's ass.

A deep milking spasm snaked itself all the way down Noah's chute; Noah groaned from low in his gut and dropped his forehead back to the bed as his passage grabbed hold of Zane's thumb and tugged it all the way inside. He circled his ass into the invasion, loving the light sting around his rim as his entrance stretched to accept the penetration. Zane gave Noah a gentle fucking motion with his digit, and the hint of friction, something that didn't go nearly deep enough to soothe the savage beast living inside Noah, had Noah again whimpering like a dog begging for his owner to pet him.

"It's okay, sweetheart." Zane took his finger away, and Noah shouted hoarsely. He bucked backward, trying to steal Zane's thumb again. Instead, Zane moved in closer behind Noah, so close his legs pressed against Noah's inner thighs. Once more he applied a light pressure to widen Noah's stance; this time something measurably thicker and hotter than a thumb or finger pressed against Noah's asshole. Somehow, surely in a way this man himself didn't understand he could, Zane naturally took complete charge. "I'm going to give you what you need." Zane flexed his hips, and with such goddamn ease and control, he pushed his cock all the way into Noah's ass.

Shit, baby. Shit. Noah twisted the bedding in his hand and bit down on the fabric, desperate not to scream his pleasure yet again. But God damn it, Zane might not have the thickest cock in the world, but it was so blessedly long Noah felt certain the tip of his dick reached right up into Noah's guts. The sensation of this man getting so fucking deep inside him, creating the sweetest goddamn friction along every inch of Noah's passage, made Noah want to claw his way out of his skin. Zane pulled all the way out, leaving Noah bereft for a handful of heartbeats -- long enough for Noah's entrance to close and his channel to squeeze for a hot cock to take it over again -- only to then force his way in again, all the way to the root, and Noah couldn't contain a rough, guttural cry anymore.

Noah rolled his head. With the side of his face planted in the comforter, he looked to the mirror and sought Zane's gaze. "Please … Zane … Zane, please…" He found a blue stare as desperate as his brown one reflecting back in the glass, and confessed, "I feel like I'm going to rip apart from the inside out. Fuck me." Noah gritted his teeth as Zane pulled out and left his ass empty again, but still full of need.

Noah's asshole squeezed with unbearable wanting, and the contraction jerked the entire way through his body. He begged, "Fuck me fast and hard now."

Equal need darkened Zane's eyes. With a rough shout of his own, he punched through Noah's shrinking entrance and tore into his ass again. This time, though, Zane grabbed hold of Noah's hips and yanked him back for each fast, driving thrust of his cock, forcing Noah to meet the ramming force in each of Zane's repeated penetrations. *Fuck yes.* No longer caring how he sounded, Noah grunted and moaned and shouted with every deep taking of his ass, reveling in the fierce pounding his man gave him.

More than merely glorying in the bone-shattering pleasure coursing through every inch of his body, Noah watched Zane in the mirror and got lost in the sheer lust consuming the younger man. Zane owned Noah right now, and he wore the command visibly in dozens of ways. He curled his fingers into Noah's flesh, hard enough to break skin, and pulled Noah back with force, onto his cock, again and again. Zane slammed his hips at Noah's backside with complete authority. Sweat from the passionate encounter plastered his dark brown hair in a skullcap against his head. In addition, his face held new taut lines that conveyed the incredible hold he maintained over his own needs. Every small and big element in this moment coalesced in Noah's head, heart, and core, and a fiery pleasure ripped up and down his spine with such intensity it made him shake.

"Ohhh fuck, baby…" Locked on Zane in the mirror, feeling the man's cock foraging so deeply into his flaming ass, Noah spiraled down into a place where nothing but need and passion for Zane existed. The depth of Noah's feelings cut through him with more devastation than a six-inch jagged skinning blade. "You're fucking me so goddamn good…" Noah humped the pile of pillows under him as frantically as he jammed his ass back onto Zane's long, hot cock. "I can't … So close again…" His balls pulled with delicious tightness in his sac.

Zane swooped down on top of Noah, snaked his arms under Noah's torso, and yanked Noah up to his hands and knees. Breathing heavily, right against Noah's ear, Zane licked the outer rim. On top of Noah, smothering Noah with his body heat, Zane trembled. "Let go for me, Noah." Zane rocked his weight against Noah's tail end, his shaft fully embedded in Noah's ass. One hand remained on Noah's chest, right over his heart, but Zane slid the other down and took Noah's stiff dick in his hand. "I need to feel you come." Zane stroked Noah from root to tip once, twice, using the firmest fucking hold. Then he pressed his lips to Noah's neck, held there, and added, "Pull my cum out of me." He pumped his hips, offering the hottest goddamn friction to Noah's tender, ultrasensitized passage, and ran his hand down the underside of Noah's shaft to massage his balls. "Make me lose myself in your ass."

So depleted, Noah only had one thing left to give. He reached down to where Zane held his sac and tangled his fingers with the other man's. Looking to the mirror, he succumbed once again to the beauty of the other man reflected back at him, with eyes so gentle and kind the sight twisted deep in Noah's soul. "I love you, Zane." Noah had never sounded raspier or more unforgiving, but the pure light in Zane's open stare ripped the raw emotion out of him without tenderness or finesse. "I love you so goddamn much it hurts to feel it." He choked as Zane squeezed his nuts and rubbed his shaft. An all-consuming pleasure gutted its way through Noah, hurling him with breakneck speed toward his end. "But with you," the first shudder of release tore through Noah, and in response Zane jerked on top of him, inside him, "I don't want the pain to ever stop. Ohhhhh fucckkk…"

Right then orgasm hit Noah with the force of a hurricane. Everything turned guttural, and Noah slipped to a low, harsh cry. His cock still in Zane's hand, Noah jerked his hips, and the first spray of semen spilled from his body and rained down on the trio of pillows. At the same time, behind him, Zane made a strangled noise and bit into Noah's neck, just as Noah's channel began to squeeze with fist-tight spasms around Zane's buried penis. Within seconds, Zane's shaft thickened inside Noah, pushing against his clenching walls. A heartbeat later Zane spilled himself in Noah's ass. Hot cum spurted within Noah, warming his passage, and Noah moaned with the pleasure of the marking. His rectal muscles flared; the delicious sensation shimmered all the way through him, resonating so deeply he clutched Zane's hand around his dick and spit another line of ejaculate onto the bedding.

Both men held in place for long minutes in the aftermath, panting heavily, their bodies still one. Two such powerful orgasms for

Noah, one coming so quickly on top of the other, sapped Noah of his strength. Zane felt like a puddle of lax muscles strung together on top of him too. On any other day Noah might believe himself fit enough to try to remain on his hands and knees endlessly, living in his fantasy of having another man -- this man -- inside him for hours on end, not moving until they needed food to sustain themselves. But so much had happened today, beyond the physical aspect of the mating they'd just put their bodies through, and as all of those things flooded back into Noah, his legs and arms loosened to jelly.

Shit. We're in love. And we said it out loud. Noah lost the power in his limbs a little bit more. Before Noah could give a warning, before he dropped face-first onto the mattress, Zane lifted his weight off Noah. With a groan he pulled his cock from Noah's ass.

Zane fell to the bed beside Noah, on his back, and looked up at Noah with flecks of brilliant sapphires still burning in his eyes. He reached up and flitted his fingertips over Noah's lips and cheeks. "There aren't words good enough for me to explain how much I love you, and for how blessed I feel that you stopped on the sidewalk that day and let me into your life." He continued to graze his fingers over Noah's shoulder and arm, almost absently, as if it were as normal and natural a part of his day as breathing. "I was going to tell you something like that a minute ago," Zane chuckled, and new pink bloomed under the afterglow still making his skin glisten, "but when you started coming so powerfully, I lost myself, and all I could do was fall into the pleasure you were feeling and willfully let it suck me into the abyss too."

Noah's chest expanded with perfect, wonderful pain. "Believe me," he dipped down and brushed a kiss to Zane's lush lips, "I'm familiar with the sensation." His arms and legs finally gave out and he fell onto his side. "You won't pull many back-to-back orgasms out of me like you just did, though." Noah stretched the full length of his body and groaned happily as each muscle flexed and pulled. "You wiped me out, honey."

Zane wrinkled his nose. "Oh, I don't think so. If we had the time," he grabbed Noah's wrist to look at his watch, even though he wore his own, "I think I could entice you into the shower, suds you up, and have you hard and ready to go again by the time I rinsed you off. As it stands right now," Zane rolled out of bed, "you'll have to settle for a warm washcloth and the promise of next time." Shades of deep midnight clouded Zane's eyes. "I want to get back to Duncan and Hailey so they can see that I'm really all right."

Reluctant as hell to move from this cocoon, Noah pushed to sit upright at the foot of the bed anyway. "Seth would have called if they were upset," he pointed out, following Zane to the bathroom with his stare, admiring his nakedness, "but I understand your need to get back to them."

Zane paused at the bathroom, his hand on the door frame. "Thank you." His gaze slid to the open bedroom door and the hallway beyond. His features hardened, and Noah knew he replayed the ugly scene with Clint in his mind. Zane came back to eye contact with Noah, and a mixture Noah could read as embarrassment and gratitude lived in his stare. "For everything."

Zane disappeared into the bathroom then. Noah rushed across the room and right in behind him, determined to eradicate the tumultuous emotions still visibly living inside Zane over the situation with Clint.

Noah found Zane already wetting down a couple of washcloths. "You don't have to thank me." Noah accepted one of the damp washcloths with a murmur of appreciation. "Don't even try to tell me you wouldn't do the same if our circumstances were reversed." His focus remained pinpoint on Zane as he wiped down his dick, sac, and inner thighs.

As Zane washed his front down too, he glared at Noah. "But that isn't the situation we're in; the reality we live in has you turning over a substantial amount of money to someone on my behalf." Wet cloth in hand, Zane jabbed a finger full of promise at Noah's chest. "I'm going to pay you back every cent you give to Clint. Instead of paying him on a schedule, I'll pay you."

A sigh escaped Noah. "Baby, you make my life richer than any amount of money ever could." He held up a hand before Zane could protest. "But again, I understand why you want to pay me back and keep things square between us. I'll take the money on whatever schedule you need us to make."

Openly studying Zane from top to bottom, awed by his sexiness, Noah growled and tugged the man in close. "But just so you know, you could probably do a few things to negotiate a lower monthly payment with me -- things you couldn't do with that bastard Clint." Noah swiped up the other damp towel, but rather than finish cleaning himself, he reached around Zane and rubbed the nubby fabric between the smooth hills of Zane's pert ass, down to his hole. "You could probably do a whole hell of a lot of things and get whatever rate you want." Noah dipped down, barely letting their lips touch, as he worked just the tip of his cloth-covered digit into Zane's ass to both tease and clean his body.

Zane leaned into Noah, holding onto his biceps, and a little trilling moan played in his throat. "Yeah?"

Noah licked just inside Zane's lips. "Yeah."

His fingers flexing into Noah's muscles, Zane pressed himself against Noah harder and began a slow grind between their cocks. "God, I'd like to try one or two of those things right now." He started to sway even more, but abruptly pulled away. "Shoot." Shaking his head, he tunneled his fingers through his hair. With another curse, he set his big, soulful stare onto Noah. "I can't."

Noah groaned, but the grumbling held a mountain's worth of understanding. "I know. Go." He slapped Zane on the ass and nudged him back into the bedroom. "It's a crime to cover that body, but go ahead and get dressed."

Moving back into the bedroom, already out of Noah's sight, Zane called out, "I know how you feel. But we'll be together again soon."

Soon. The word sat like a lead balloon in Noah's gut. As he quickly finished cleaning himself and drying off, the terrible weight of more separations and sporadic stolen moments dug a hole inside him, one that clandestine meetings in motel rooms and lunches where they didn't eat a bit of food couldn't fill. "Soon" wasn't a word that satisfied everything Noah wanted and craved with this man. "Always" was the only one that made Noah's heart feel full and healthy with every nourishing thing it needed to survive.

Shit. Noah stumbled on his way out of the bathroom. Already dressed, Zane sat on the edge of the bed, one foot pulled up to the mattress, sock in hand. The sight of him doing something so simple, such as putting on his shoes and socks, grabbed at the very heart of everything Noah wanted with Zane. A normal life. Every single day. Together. *But is Zane there already too?*

Rushing across the room to where his pants and underwear had landed, Noah hastened to get dressed. But still, his attention slid repeatedly to Zane, and the ache in his soul for permanence grew. Drawn to Zane, needing to get close enough to feel his life force, Noah moved to sit at Zane's feet, where his own shoes and socks still lay. "Listen…" His heart pounding and his hands shaking, Noah looked up at Zane, into the warmth burning in his blue stare, and waded into the waters of the only future he wanted. "Our relationship changed today," he said, while putting on his socks and shoes. "In a big way."

The sight of Zane's lopsided smile turned somersaults in Noah's stomach. "Yeah." Leaning forward, Zane brushed his fingers through Noah's hair and then grazed the softest touch across Noah's cheek, making Noah shiver. "I thought I'd be terrified to tell you how much I love you, but in the heat of that moment the truth just flew out of me. Once it did, I wasn't scared anymore. You'd said it too, and I knew you meant it, and it was exhilarating and liberating and insane. And like you always have a way of doing," with a gentle hand around Noah's neck, Zane drew Noah to his knees and pressed the sweetest kiss against his cheek, "the way you said it, the passion and conviction in you, made me feel so safe."

An invisible rope between their bodies tugged Noah hard in his core, with such power that not even fear would let him ignore it. "I've had strong feelings for you from almost the beginning. Even when I told myself they were inappropriate and I held back, I couldn't stop what I felt. But then, when I was sick, and you spent those nights with me…" Everything inside him seizing with welcoming pain, Noah kneeled before Zane, his heart and soul flayed open for Zane to see. "Baby, when I got to see your face as I fell asleep, and hear you moving around in the morning, I understood it would be a hundred times harder to say good-bye every day afterward, knowing we couldn't be together all night. And it was hard. It is still. At night, I lie awake with the thought of sharing a bed with you all the time." Bracing his hands on the bed on either side of Zane, Noah spoke his heart, no matter the lump in his throat or the catch that had latched onto the swell of love filling him inside. "I want to make a home with you, Zane. If you're on the same page, I want us to make a plan toward us living together one day in the near future. All of us. That obviously includes your brother and sister too."

"I don't…" A sob wrenched out of Zane. His hand flew to his mouth, and he reared back and shook his head.

"Just hear me out," Noah pleaded, a rasp coating his voice. "Soon enough Rita is going to want this cabin back so she can sell it. But that's okay. My cabin is larger anyway, and there is plenty of land to redesign the layout of the house and add more rooms. I'm pretty competent with additions, and the elements I don't have proficiency in I know the right people to call who will be honest and deal straight with me. But I also know you pretty well too, so I know your immediate thought is that I will take over and it will become about me supporting you and taking care of you financially, but it won't be that way." With a clutching hold, Noah implored Zane to believe him. "I would never want to make you feel small; it would crush me if I ever thought I had. I want us to do this together, with your input all the way, and we'll work out the finances so we're both taking care of the expenses together.

"Before we get there, though," everything rushed out of Noah in an avalanche of words, but the need to get everything said, before he forgot, without leaving an argument unspoken, drove Noah with a relentless single-minded focus, "I want to figure out the stages that make sense to show all of the kids the depth of our relationship, what we mean to each other, and how we go about introducing levels of affection between us in front of them."

Noah explained further, knowing he needed to. "When Janice started seeing Tom more seriously, she and I had a talk about how that would affect Seth and Matt. We knew we needed to agree to guidelines, and we understood from the start we would present a united front for them so they were never confused, and so that they never would be successful in trying to pit us against one another. Janice and I also talked in general about how I would keep her in the loop about my relationships, and we would have the same conversation and talk about being united for the kids when I fell in love with someone too. I still believe in that, and I think it's vitally important. But being with you, listening to your insights," Noah tangled his hands in Zane's, holding on with every ounce of love in him, "you've made me see that you need to be included in that talk as well. This conversation about the kids is not just for Janice and me. It's for all of us. And even on top of that, when I was sick, you made me open my eyes enough to know now that Tom should be a part of everything too.

"I love you, Zane," dipping down, Noah pressed kisses to the backs of Zane's hands, "and I don't want to spend one more night away from you than is necessary. What do you think?" Stripped emotionally naked, Noah sat before Zane on bended knee. "Will you say yes to eventually living with me? Will you let me call Janice and set up a time for all of us to talk soon? Make a plan? Together?"

"Noah… Shit…" Making an ugly sobbing noise, Zane wiped his eyes as tears streamed down his cheeks. "I was never going to say no; I was just so overwhelmed I didn't know what to say." He tucked Noah's hand, twined in his, against his chest. "I'm so honored you want me in all of these personal parts of your life."

Noah's heart cracked open somehow more. "Honey, you are my life. Everywhere I am, you are too." He freed his hand to wipe away his man's tears. "There's no negotiating that."

Exhaling unsteadily, Zane cupped Noah's cheek and pulled him in close. "I love you," he whispered, his lips pressed to Noah's.

Noah couldn't tamp down the leap in his heart. "Is that a yes?"

"Yes." Their faces touching, their gazes connected, Zane nodded. "Yes."

"To everything?" Christ, Noah felt it, but his soul needed the words.

"To everything," Zane agreed.

An animalistic noise escaped Noah. With his heart exploding, he crushed his mouth to Zane's, needing to taste and to seal the deal on their future. Zane licked his way into Noah's mouth, clearly staking a claim on his man too. But he quickly softened the rough tangle of tongues to something more gentle and loving, taking control, and soothed the beast in Noah who needed to feast.

Brushing one more loving kiss to Noah's lips, Zane then broke the kiss, but kept Noah close to him. "I reach for you in my bed every night too. I know how I feel about you," all the light glittering in Zane's gaze backed up his vow, "and it's past time to start being more open, and to help everyone in our lives get comfortable with us being together too. Starting right now." Zane snagged Noah's shirt from the mussed bedding and thrust it at his chest. "Finish getting dressed."

"Yes, sir." Noah saluted smartly. With a grin, he worked his shirt to the right way out and slipped it on. As he did, his mind raced. Noah knew that for Zane, getting *"everyone"* comfortable with their relationship chiefly meant helping his brother and sister get to a place where they loved and trusted Noah as much as Zane already did. Matt more than Seth would need some time to adjust too. Noah's youngest hadn't exactly loved it when Tom had taken such an important role in Janice's life, but the kid had eventually come around and now loved and accepted Tom as an adult with authority and importance in his life. Children were the one area where Noah accepted he would have to exhibit some patience, and because of that he didn't growl with frustration at the knowledge that he would not be able to fall into bed with Zane tonight. Rather, Noah put himself to a plan of action that would get him on the road to what both he and Zane wanted. *A full life together.*

"Let's go make an early dinner with the kids," Noah suggested. "Afterward we can all find something to watch together on TV. This can be the first of them seeing us together in some familial way, every day."

Zane perked up as if Noah had just offered him the keys to a castle. "I like that." Up on tiptoes, he settled his arms around Noah's shoulders and looked up with adoration in his eyes. "I even know what we can all cook together."

"Oh yeah?" His arm around Zane's waist, Noah lifted the smaller man for a fast kiss. "Are you going to be the king of the kitchen in our household?" he asked, wearing a mock scowl and glare.

Zane smirked right back. "I've seen what passes as an acceptable meal to you, and I've seen what you keep in your fridge when I'm not there to stock it. You're damn straight I'm in charge of the kitchen." Stepping back, moving toward the hallway, Zane waggled his brows and openly leered at Noah. "Your only job is to sit at my table every night and look pretty for me."

Following his man, Noah barked with laughter. "I love it. Nobody has ever called me pretty before."

All the teasing slid out of Zane's eyes. "You're more than pretty, Noah. You're downright beautiful." A sudden huskiness filled Zane's voice, and his stare burned with desire and love. "Both inside and out."

Noah shuddered. Christ, until he'd met this man, Noah had never trembled so much under someone's gaze and touch. "Fucking hell, honey." An extra layer of rust coated Noah's tone, but he couldn't control that either. With a soft curse, he swooped past Zane, grabbing his hand as he did, and started dragging him toward the porch. "Let's go home before you achieve a miracle and make me hard enough to drag you down to this floor and have my way with you again."

"Home." Catching up to walk alongside Noah, Zane tugged against Noah for long enough to close and lock the door. "I like the sound of that."

Noah damn well did too. "Let's go."

Hands linked together in a gripping hold, they walked around the lake toward their family and future.

Epilogue

So excited he could barely hold still long enough to put the car in park and turn off the engine, Zane popped out of the driver side door like a kernel of corn finally bursting into a piece of popcorn.

Zane ran toward the cabin, itching to tell Noah his good news. As his foot hit the first step the gruffest, sexiest voice he'd ever known halted his ascent. "I'm in the water, honey!" With a spin toward the lake, Zane homed in on Noah treading water a dozen feet out from the dock. "It's gorgeous today. Come join me."

Holy God. Zane's breath caught, and his heart immediately began to hammer with a different kind of desire. Water hid most of Noah's body from Zane's view, but sunlight beamed directly down on him, as if it couldn't stay away from his perfection, and highlighted his broad tan shoulders and chest. The natural light showed every hard line of Noah's handsome face in a way that made him even sexier, although Zane did not know how such a feat was possible. Zane's cock throbbed in response, as it always did when he got in sight of Noah.

They'd been together for just over a year -- living together now for four months -- and in that time Zane's passion and ardor for this man had only grown. The depth of love that consumed Zane whenever he merely thought about Noah, let alone got close to him, sank somehow deeper into his bones -- his very marrow -- with every day they added to their relationship.

Patience had definitely been needed in regard to the kids, but they were all in a good place now, most of the time anyway. Duncan and Hailey now accepted Noah as an extension of Zane and gave him the same love and respect they did to Zane. And at Zane's side -- reluctantly at first -- Matt had discovered an interest in food that had allowed him to bond with Zane in a way the boy hadn't anticipated. Seth spent most of his time at school in Raleigh, but he'd been cool with Noah and Zane as a couple from the start. Even Noah's mother and father accepted and cared for Zane and his siblings now too. And best of all, Noah had his father back in his life, with all the love and respect he'd missed for such a long period of time after coming out of the closet. Zane could not be happier for his man -- or for himself.

A year and a half ago Zane never would have believed a future like this was meant for him, but these days he couldn't wait to wake up every morning. Of course back then he never could have dreamed he would have met a man like Noah, let alone fallen in love with him or have the privilege of sharing a life with such a beautiful person.

A life. My life. Our life. In a shot, Zane's news came rushing back to him and snapped him out of his stupor. *I can't wait to tell him!*

"Noah!" Like a giddy kid, Zane kicked off his shoes and began running toward the lake at breakneck speed. He tore out of his shirt and left that on the grass, but didn't get a single other stitch of clothing off as he shouted, "I got it!" and flung himself off the edge of the dock, straight into Noah's open arms.

Noah caught Zane to him, holding onto the slighter man tightly as they whooshed backward with momentum and dipped under the water. Instinct made Noah close his eyes and hold his breath, but as they broke the surface Zane sputtered and coughed in Noah's face. Water ran in rivulets from Zane's soaked hair down his cheeks.

"Are you okay?" Concern filled Noah's core. He pushed Zane's hair back, wiped at his face, and kept him above water with an arm anchored around his waist. "You came at me with a ton more speed than you ever have before."

Zane coughed again, but said, "I'm fine. It's okay." He finally took a clean breath, and when he did, his eyes lit like the moon reflecting off clear water; he squeezed Noah's shoulders while bouncing up and down against Noah's waist. "I got it, Noah." He squealed like a little kid getting a rare, coveted, full-size candy bar while trick or treating. "I got it."

Puzzled, Noah started using his legs to push them toward the dock. "Got what?"

Zane laughed and rolled his eyes. "I know, right? Duh. Sorry. It's just I wasn't expecting it so fast either. That's why I'm so excited." He bounced against Noah in the most delicious way once more. "Right before I left the restaurant today, Violet pulled me into her office and offered me a full-time job, officially training under Mickey." Giving Noah a fast hug, Zane added, "She told me Mickey says he needs me there full time if she expects me to be ready to take over his job in a few years. Mickey wants to retire in two years, Noah," Zane practically vibrated in Noah's arms as he shared his news, "and he and Violet both want me to have his job when he does."

Zane's excitement made Noah's heart melt right into the water. "That's fantastic, baby." He brushed his knuckles against Zane's cheek, and his voice cracked. "I'm so proud of you."

"There's even more," Zane went on, animated as all get out. "I not only get full time at the restaurant now, but I get a raise in my hourly wage to go along with those hours. And when I take over for Mickey I get even more because I get a salary with holiday bonuses and benefits." Zane wrapped his arms and legs around Noah and shook him wildly. "Can you believe it?"

Noah nodded, and another lump filled his throat. "Christ, look at me," he said, chuckling. He goddamn had tears in his eyes. "I'm so fucking happy for you, Zane." His feet hitting rocks under the water, right beside the dock, Noah crushed Zane to him in a suffocating hug. Pressing a kiss to Zane's ear, he said roughly, "I know you didn't talk about this possibility of one day taking over Mickey's job much. I know you didn't want to jinx it, but I know how much you wanted this." Noah grazed kisses down Zane's cheek to his lips and gave him another soft peck. Noah could not look away from the pure joy glittering in Zane's stare. "It's your dream coming true, honey. Nobody deserves this more than you."

"When Violet told me, the first thing I wanted to do was come home and tell you." Resting his elbows on Noah's shoulders, Zane absently played his fingertips around the shells of Noah's ears and into his hair. "Seeing you happy for me makes me even happier."

"I'm thrilled for you," Noah promised, the vow resonating in his core. "I don't even have the words."

"Violet wants me to start as soon as I can, but I told her I wouldn't leave you high and dry without an assistant." Zane's features turned sober. "That means you need to start looking for another employee. I'm going to stay with you until you find someone you like and trust." Zane suddenly changed from playing to pulling Noah's hair, putting their faces close enough to make their noses touch. "Don't feel like you have to rush for me."

Zane's earnest and faithful nature flooded Noah's heart with warmth. "Don't worry about me. Seth will be home next week. He'll be with us for a while, so he can take over the part-time work you've been doing until I find someone else." Noah licked the tip of Zane's nose, catching a droplet of water on his tongue. "You let Violet know you can go full time right away."

A huge grin lit Zane's entire face, but then a softness suddenly misted his eyes. "I'll miss our lunches together in the clearing." In his gaze lived dozens of memories of make-out sessions, including dozens more consummations when they hadn't been able to put the brakes on their passion.

"Yeah," Noah lifted a brow, proposing a little fun in that one move, as his prick began to stir in his swim trunks, "but now that we're open and together, we have all kinds of time to make out." Already slipping into the sweetest desire he'd ever known, Noah hoisted Zane out of the water and laid him out on a towel on the dock. He came down on top of his partner -- the man who owned his heart; there wasn't really an adequate word for what Zane meant to Noah -- and brushed a soft kiss across his warm lips. "The kids won't be home all night," Noah reminded Zane as he settled into the V of his parted thighs. Christ, how he loved lying tangled with his man.

"Mmm…" Zane drew Noah down until their lips met. He licked with delicious intent against the parted seam. "Remind me to thank your mom and dad for taking all of them for the weekend."

Noah groaned and bit playfully at Zane's mouth. "Unless you want to kill my growing hard-on," he rocked evidence of his thickening erection against the bulge pushing in Zane's wet pants, "let's not talk about them right now."

With a murmured, "I definitely wouldn't want to do that," Zane wound his arms around Noah's waist and rocked up against him. He parted his lips and invited Noah inside for a deep kiss.

Noah took Zane's mouth slow and easy, knowing he had a world of time to warm the man up to a point where he was clawing and scratching Noah's back to shreds in between pleas to make their bodies one. They often still fucked with frenetic speed and force and aggression; the power and passion behind those bouts of mating made it feel as if each of those times they came together was the first time all over again, as if they feared they might never get the opportunity to enter the other person's body again. But every once in a while now, they would understand and remember they had forever together. On those occasions, if they had the cabin to themselves, they could now maintain enough control to drag out their lovemaking for hours on end. Today Noah wanted to keep Zane on the dock, under him, writhing and pleading for Noah to make him come, for as long as he could. Noah didn't want to stop pleasuring his man until the sun went down, crickets began to sing around them, and the mosquitoes and lightning bugs drove them inside. Then Noah wanted to carry Zane to their bed and start all over again.

With every gentle bite Noah put on Zane's lips, he flicked his tongue into the man's mouth for a quick taste of his unique honey. He braced an elbow on the dock and lifted up a bit to push his hand between their bodies. "I need you naked under me."

As Noah began to fumble with undoing Zane's wet pants, Zane murmured, "Noah, you feel so good." He started a rhythm of lifting his hips to rub their cocks together. "I need all of you too." He scratched his fingers down the small of Noah's naked back and pushed them under Noah's shorts. The trunks hung low on Noah's hips anyway, and Zane easily eased them down past Noah's thighs. Sunlight immediately warmed Noah's bared buttocks, but Zane quickly cupped the hills of flesh and squeezed. He slipped his thumbs into the crease, and a little bit of Noah's control flew away.

"Christ." Noah hummed, and he lifted his ass into Zane's kneading massage. "I love when you do that." His passage squeezed, needy already, and his dick lifted higher against his belly.

Beneath him, Zane looked up, a twinkle full of lustful cheekiness in his eyes. "I know."

Noah dipped down to nip Zane in retaliation when a piercing whistle broke through the afternoon air.

"Nice ass, Maitland!" followed in an annoyingly familiar voice.

Noah jerked his head up, glanced to the side, and growled. Yep, he knew that voice and wolf whistle. Grey stood on the pebbled path to his and Sirus's cabin, a grocery bag in one hand, openly giving Noah a thumbs-up with the other.

Son of a bitch. Noah shot the asshole, who was actually now one of his dearest friends, the finger. "Fuck you, Cole! Go away!" Noah and Zane had discussed how quiet it was this weekend with the other three cabins on the lake empty, but apparently they weren't as alone as Noah had thought. Sirus appeared too. He moved off the path, away from a car, a bag in his arm too, and waved at Noah and Zane.

Jesus fucking shit. Noah dropped his forehead to rest against Zane's and shook his head.

Zane pecked a kiss to Noah's lips and chuckled. "Don't worry about Grey." His gaze slipped from humorous to downright sinful. He began rocking up into Noah once more and teasing his thumbs along the crack of Noah's ass. "We're all right where we are. Sirus has enough manners to drag Grey away."

Slipping under the enticing spell of this man once more, Noah groaned as he stole another kiss. "Good point. I don't care what they're doing right now anyway." Even as Noah said that, from his peripheral vision, he was grateful to see Sirus hauling Grey toward their cabin. "I only want to focus on celebrating you." With that, Noah went back to working open Zane's pants.

The moment Noah slipped his hand inside Zane's underwear and stroked his shaft, Zane moaned. He arched under Noah and stretched his arms above his head against the dock. "Do whatever you want with me." Zane looked up at Noah, and in his gaze Noah could see pure love emanating from his soul. "I'm all yours."

Noah's heart lurched up into his throat. "And I'm forever thankful you are." He released Zane's cock to run his hands up the man's arms and link their fingers together in two intricate knots. "I love you, honey." Good Christ, Noah would never tire of looking into this man's warm blue eyes. "Congratulations on your promotion."

"Thank you." Zane lifted his legs, locked them around Noah's waist, and tied them together even more. "Now kiss me again, and get this celebration started."

"My pleasure." Noah dipped his head, brushed their lips together with exquisite tenderness, and did just that.

THE END

About the Author

I am an air force brat and spent most of my growing up years living overseas in Italy and England, as well as Florida, Georgia, Ohio, and Virginia while we were stateside. I now live in Florida once again with my big, wonderfully pushy family and my three-legged cat, Harry. I have been reading romance novels since I was twelve years old, and twenty-five years later I still adore them. Currently, I have an unexplainable obsession with hockey goaltenders, zombies, and an unabashed affection for *The Daily Show* with Jon Stewart.

Find me on the web at
WWW.CAMERONDANE.COM

CPSIA information can be obtained at www.ICGtesting.com
Printed in the USA
LVOW05s1954191113

361960LV00001B/330/P